P

LAST CH

"LAST CHANCE TO RUN cleverly builds suspe...
the nerve-racking conclusion...Satisfaction is guaranteed when
Dianna Love writes a story."
~~Amelia Richard, SingleTitles.com

"LAST CHANCE TO RUN...reminded me of Cinderella.
Well, if Cinderella was on the run from a maniac killer and
Prince Charming wielded a gun and flew a plane. Great read.
Check it out!"
~~Bryonna Nobles, The Paperback Cafe

"...Love can do what few writers can--give that HEA with
the heart-twisting love story, interwoven with the big backbone
of a thriller. Last Chance To Run is all of that. This is a
fantastic, satisfying, fast-paced read."
~~ Katy A, Amazon

"Brilliant!! Now THIS BOOK is what I LOVE about
Romantic Suspense; a gritty suspenseful story AND enough
steam to make me squirm (in a GOOD way :))."
~~ Sheryl, Goodreads

"Dianna never disappoints! ... would have give it a 10 if
they would let!!! Very enjoyable read, can't wait for the next
one :-)."
~~ Amy, Goodreads

THE BOOK HOUSE
Over 100, 000 books instock!
480 Veterans Memorial Hwy SW
Mableton, GA 30126
770-944-3275

LAST CHANCE
TO RUN

DIANNA
NEW YORK TIMES BESTSELLING AUTHOR
LOVE

Copyright © 2012 by Dianna Love Snell
All Rights Reserved.
First Edition – December 2012

Publisher is Silver Hawk Press, LLC

*This story is a significantly revised version of the much shorter original story titled Worth Every Risk

No part of this work may be reproduced in any fashion without the express, written consent of the copyright holder.

This book is a work of fiction. All characters and events portrayed herein are fictitious and are not based on any real persons living or dead.

Dedication

This book is dedicated to all the readers who have supported me along the way. Thank YOU!

Acknowledgment

A note of appreciation to Cassondra Murray, my talented first read and wonderful assistant. Thanks also to Steve Doyle for expert advice on Special Force operations and weapons, plus feedback from reading early versions of the story. I appreciate Debbie and Bill Kaufman's generosity in answering questions on airports and the FAA. Thanks to Kim Killion for a cover I love and to Jennifer Jakes for formatting the pages, to Judy Carney and Mimi Munk for copy editing and to Hope Williams for being one of my early readers. Also, a hug to Sherrilyn Kenyon for her support and rockin' cover quote. And, of course, thank you to my husband who is the best and my hero – you make every day a day to remember. Any mistakes or adjustments in detail for the purpose of fiction are entirely my own doing.

Author Note

I love to hear from readers at dianna@authordiannalove.com, on FACEBOOK at Dianna Love Fan Page (visit the READER LOUNGE) or by mail at Dianna Love, 1029 N. Peachtree Pkwy, Suite 335, Peachtree City, GA 30269.

If you'd like a FREE glossy cover card of *Last Chance To Run*, signed by me, please stop by www.KeeperKase.com where you'll find more free cards.

Chapter 1

Lightning crackled nearby. Close, but not close enough.

Escape tonight or ... there was no second option.

"Come on, God, *please*." Angel whispered the desperate prayer for the hundredth time since midnight. But lights still burned through Mason Lorde's opulent compound where she'd been imprisoned for the last ten days.

She had to get over this compulsion about being honest. The last time she'd done the right thing, she'd landed in a real prison with a warden and crazy female inmates threatening her life. That had been thanks to her father.

One more thing she had to get over. Trusting any man.

Wind howled across the beveled panes, rattling the French doors and sounding cold when August weather was anything but.

"I should have asked for a hurricane instead of a thunderstorm," she muttered under her breath. But hurricanes weren't as prevalent along the North Carolina coast as lightning storms. All she needed was a brief power outage. Not that she had any reason to believe in divine intervention at this point in her life.

A short life if she didn't get out of this place now.

She rolled a golf-ball-shaped compass in her hand, a dangerous stress reliever. She'd stolen it from his office, and to hell with any guilt she felt.

It would get her fingers snapped like twigs if Mason caught her with his solid gold desk toy.

No chance he'd let her off easy.

She'd learned that the hard way. Just like everything else in her life.

Mason Lorde, her dream employer. The bastard had turned into her worst nightmare. But with a conviction in her past, who could blame her for jumping at a chance for a job with a highly reputed firm? Assisting the manager in one of the warehouses for Lorde's revered import enterprise beat cleaning toilets or scavenging aluminum cans any day.

She'd thought.

Brilliant light flashed across the heavens, illuminating the edges of the brass bed at her shoulder. She glanced at the burgundy silk duvet covering the lump she'd built with pillows. Would that gain her an extra minute?

Maybe. She hated maybe. Reminded her how often her worthless court-appointed attorney had spouted that word.

Maybe you'll receive leniency for a first offense.

Maybe you'll get out early on good behavior.

Neither happened.

Maybe men would stop screwing her over at some point, but she wasn't counting on that, either.

Angel consulted her black plastic sports watch.

In sixteen minutes Kenner would begin his two a.m. round.

On the dot.

Unlike the rest of the security, the knuckle-dragging commander now in charge of Mason's thirty-room mansion lacked any tolerance. Kenner had been brought in from another of Mason's locations to replace Jeff, who'd overseen the property for the past ten years, according to his last screaming words.

He'd pleaded for his life.

Then Mason had ... nausea rolled through her stomach.

Another glance at her timepiece. Fifteen minutes, forty-eight seconds left.

She reached for the doorknob, desperate to flee, but paused short of touching it. She had no allies beyond patience. It wasn't as if Kenner would repeat Jeff's mistake. Poor Jeff, too slow on the uptake to be hanging with a bunch of killers. He'd smoked one too many cigarettes a week ago while she'd scurried down the Italian marble hallways in a fevered attempt to escape.

One of the other guards had caught her.

Mason didn't tolerate mistakes. He'd ordered everyone to witness Jeff's punishment. Angel, in particular. She still had bruises from where she'd been dragged outside and shoved up front for the show being performed for her benefit.

The citizens of nearby Raleigh would never believe what went on inside this private compound belonging to one of their most prominent city businessmen.

Just over six feet tall, with thick golden hair and a champion's physique, Mason, the Nordic antichrist, had calmly raised his .357 magnum revolver to Jeff's head and squeezed the trigger.

A deafening explosion. Then blood. *So much blood.*

She clenched her fists. The horror lived on, burned on the insides of her eyelids.

And the smell. Who could forget the god-awful coppery stench of fresh blood? Her stomach roiled again.

Hard to believe a week had passed. Seemed like just minutes ago. She squeezed her eyes shut and saw it all again. The hole in Jeff's forehead. His eyes locked open in horror. The back of his head ... she swallowed and took a breath. She'd carry that brutal image for as long as she lived.

Along with the responsibility for his death.

And all because of a job she'd thought was a godsend. What had she done so wrong in her life to have ended up involved with a criminal *again*?

The first time, she'd been eighteen. And naïve to the point of being clueless about drugs. *That* had cost her.

She'd had no reason to think her own father would take advantage of her job as a city courier and use her to mule drugs without her knowledge.

Then throw her under the judge's gavel to save his own hide.

This time, she was not going down without a fight.

If she got out of here tonight, she had the hammer that would bring down Mason. And prove her own innocence. She patted the heavy band wrapped around her waist like a money belt. The strip of plastic held a fortune in gold coins that would bring her salvation.

Or the end of her life.

Twelve minutes, forty-two seconds until room check.

Jagged sparks flashed across the eerie sky, nearer, but still too far away. Her heart pounded against her breastbone.

Come on, God. Don't I deserve one break?

Thunder rumbled through the black heavens, longer than it had during the two power outages earlier in the week. They were common occurrences at the estate, cured each time temporarily by generators. She'd timed the last two blackouts. Should the Almighty-in-charge-of-weather deign to knock out the main electrical feed once more, she'd have nine minutes until three thousand volts surged through the chain link fence again.

Three thousand volts or face Mason when he returned tomorrow morning – not much of a choice.

The goal was simple. Escape or die trying.

She still nursed wounds from her penance for that first attempt. Her hand unconsciously went to her sore ribs and she licked her cut lip. The guards hadn't harmed her beyond bruising, but Mason enjoyed doling out his personal brand of punishment.

The psycho had actually gotten aroused as he'd beaten her.

In the dignified tone of a pompous professor, Mason had explained his actions. "Consider this step one in teaching you compliance and submission, Angelina."

He'd wasted his time.

There would be no step two.

Thunder barreled across the sky, directly overhead this time, rattling the delicate glass panels between her and the storm.

Ten minutes, eighteen seconds left.

Her restless fingers worried the cold silver band Mason had locked on her wrist. He'd smiled when he assured her the tracking device was for her own protection. That had been right before he promised to return by the time she'd healed.

Cracked bones and bruises weren't major concerns, but

living to see her twenty-sixth birthday had become questionable.

The guards had breathed a collective sigh of relief after her beating, sure that she would stay put.

Only a crazy person would try to escape again.

"We'll see who's crazy," she whispered. "You son-of-a – "

Lightning exploded in a clap of thunder, so close her arm hairs stood on end.

The entire compound fell dark.

Angel hit the self-timer on her watch and dropped the compass down the front of her Lycra running top beneath a butter-yellow T-shirt. Mason's choice of color. Not hers. Combined with matching shorts, she'd stand out like a beacon when the first lights popped back on.

She pushed the French doors open and rushed into a cool rain that battered the second floor private balcony. She nudged the doors shut behind her. A worn navy blue ball cap shielded her eyes from the downpour and hid shoulder-length auburn hair she'd fastened into a ponytail.

No going back now. Guards would enter the empty bedroom by the time lights flicked on.

Feeling blindly in the dark for the rail that enclosed the balcony, she gripped the ledge, climbed over then locked her legs around the ten-inch thick center column. Her arms strained to hold her body's dead weight. Tremors shook her at the fear of falling twenty feet. Wet polished marble offered no traction to slow her descent.

She slid down the soaked surface. Friction burned both her hands and exposed legs in seconds. Tears, mixed with rain, poured down her face from the searing pain.

She lost her grip ... and clenched her muscles, waiting for the impact. She plummeted through a black vortex. Sharp points stabbed into her shoulders and hips when she landed, but no excruciating pain from a broken bone.

She'd been spared by a boxwood hedge.

Like a turtle on its back in a bed of nails, she lay still, panting hard against the pain in her ribs. The insides of her legs throbbed and wet bullets of rain pelted her face. Drawing a deep breath, she kicked both feet and rolled to her side, dropping into a crouch to listen.

No thud of heavy footsteps – yet.

Time to get moving. Through the darkness, she counted memorized steps across the lawn. Lightning crackled and fingered through the dark sky. When grass changed to concrete, she sidestepped around the Olympic-size pool. Raindrops slapped the chlorinated water.

Her feet met grass again exactly on count. She picked up the pace. Her shoulder bumped against a stone arbor strangled by jasmine vines. She tripped on a thick stem and went down hard, scraping her palms.

She gulped a deep breath. Listened for shouts, boots splashing across wet ground, any sound of being hunted.

Still clear.

Jumping up, she lunged into the blackness, running hard, fighting the panic exploding in her chest.

Heel to toe, heel to toe. Don't smack the ground.

Finally, the big elm came into view during a quick flash of lightning. She stepped around the tree, sucking in short gasps of air. Running a marathon was easier than racing a hundred feet through the dark, expecting to get shot. Her heart hammered with terrified beats. She had to calm down and stick to her plan. Her hand shook violently as she made two stabs to press the button that illuminated her watch face.

Four minutes and twelve seconds.

Plenty of time if everything stayed status quo.

For the past ten days she'd pretended to be afraid of her shadow. Maybe the ruse had paid off. As long as no one rushed to be Mr. Efficient and cranked the generators ahead of schedule.

She sprinted eight big steps forward and stopped. Drenched to the bone, trembling from fear, she reached out in the darkness to grasp the ten-foot-tall security fence. Survival instincts stayed her hand at the last second, but there was only one way to know if the electricity was activated.

She stuck a finger on it.

No tingle.

She glanced up at the angry heavens. *Thank you.*

The current normally surging through the steel mesh could toss a grown man like a discarded rag doll. She grabbed a handhold on the fence.

Kenner's roar of anger from the balcony reached her.

He'd found her empty bed.

Clenching one handhold then another as fast as she could, she struggled up the fence.

Freedom was only a foot away. She hauled herself over the top. Her hand slipped. Soft flesh tore on the twisted ends of the chain link. She bit down hard to swallow a cry of pain. No sense giving Kenner a tip on which direction she'd run. He'd find out soon enough anyway. She slipped, kicking frantically for any foothold. Falling from this height could mean a snapped ankle, and speed was her best weapon right now. She caught a toehold, scrambled down the other side, and leaped away from the fence.

Lights blazed on across the compound. Two minutes early.

She froze. Wet chain link sizzled with renewed power.

Every survival instinct she had screamed at her to tear through the woods like a madwoman. But hitting a tree might knock her out or daze her. Instant capture. Instead, she backed away from the fence, her feet on autopilot when she turned and plowed forward. Every time lightning streaked across the sky and lit up the woods, she raced ahead, dodging trees. Thick underbrush clawed at her arms. Pain from the cuts burning her skin demanded attention.

She pushed harder.

Sheets of rain blasted through breaks in the trees. Thunder boomed overhead.

How far could Mason's men track her?

Would the storm interfere with the bracelet's signal? She hoped for that miracle since God had been accommodating so far.

A jagged branch snagged the edge of her thin shorts and ripped a searing gash across her thigh. An adrenaline spike masked the pain, but her lungs begged for oxygen.

She was an endurance runner, not a sprinter.

At an unexpected opening in the brush, she stumbled to a stop, sucking air. Snatching the gold paperweight from between her breasts, she flipped it to the compass embedded in the top. She got her bearings during the next brilliant lightning display.

The small airfield she'd seen on a map in Mason's office should be dead ahead.

Tucking away the compass, she started to move then jerked around at a noise.

Distant barking and howls broke through the deluge. Mason's dogs trained by expert trackers. Between the animals and the stupid bracelet, they were on her trail. She pushed on with one thought — surely someone at the airfield would help her.

What if they knew Mason? *What if someone at the airport worked for Mason?* At the very least, he flew in there and might be a client who paid for hangar space.

"What ifs" would get her killed if she slowed down.

She ran her fingers compulsively over the band of coins strapped around her waist. Those eight rare coins were as important as her next breath.

She'd sworn once that she would *never* go to jail again. Her one and only conviction had not been her fault. The police hadn't believed her story then.

They'd laugh in her face this time — right before they handcuffed her.

Taking Mason's *Saint-Gauden's Double Eagle* coins had stamped her death warrant. But they didn't belong to Mason either. He'd stolen the rare pieces from a museum to trade for what he called a once-in-a-lifetime find. Some panel made out of amber from back in the fifteenth century.

She smiled in spite of her pain.

Mason would be empty handed when it came time to deliver the coins on Sunday.

One more way to pay that bastard back. If she didn't get caught by Mason or the FBI first.

The FBI should be thrilled to have the stolen coins returned, and her testimony on Mason's international crime ring. But no one would listen to her until she could prove she had no part in the original theft.

Mason claimed he had evidence that would implicate *her* in the theft. And who would the authorities believe? A local dignitary or a nobody ex-con?

As if someone had thrown a switch, the downpour fizzled into a steady shower. She burst through a break in the trees and slowed while her eyes adjusted, but moved forward steadily.

The ground fell away. She stumbled down a short drop into a ditch, landing on her knees. No pain because adrenaline still rushed through her, but she'd have bruises on bruises after this. She climbed up and touched pavement.

The runway.

The good news? No fence around this airport. She scrambled to stand and drew a quaking breath. Freedom got closer by the minute.

The bays of pursuit dogs pierced the night. They were closing in.

A fence at this point might've had merits.

Searching past the runway, she spotted the bright glow of an open hangar a quarter of a mile away. With no time to waste, she sprinted toward the illuminated area.

Running felt good in spite of how her thigh throbbed. Blood trickled from the deep gash. Forcing her heart to pump harder only made her bleed more, but she'd survived worse.

She softened her steps as she neared the hangar then crept to the edge of the building. A tall, lanky man in mechanic's coveralls loaded boxes into a sleek twin-prop cargo plane.

When the worker finished, he walked across the spotless floor toward a brightly lit office.

She could just make out two men on the other side of a glass door. The mechanic pushed the door open and announced the airplane was ready to go.

Angel hesitated. She'd always obeyed the law before. Now, the "slightly illegal things" she never would have done in the past just kept stacking up. Clenching her jaw against the unavoidable twinge of guilt, she made her decision.

That was the old Angel.

The new one wanted to survive and accepted that she'd never outrun those dogs on the ground.

One way or another, she was leaving on that plane.

Chapter 2

Zane peered through the dull glass office door into the pristine hangar where Hack's man loaded the last box into Zane's Cessna 404 Titan. He moved over to the pot of strong coffee always ready for pilots and filled his thermos.

"You ain't listenin', son."

"I have to make this run," Zane answered Hack absently, then shifted around to face the terminal manager.

"You cain't be serious 'bout flyin' in this mess." Hack laid a dog-eared queen of spades down, completing another game of solitaire.

Oh, yeah, dead serious. He had five days left to prove he deserved the charter contract High Vision Enterprises had up for grabs. The other two charter groups had enough equipment and personnel to cover deliveries *anywhere* in the continental US. Zane was already at a disadvantage in that he only wanted the southeastern region, but he'd impressed High Vision last week by delivering a shipment the other two carriers had turned down. This was another opportunity Zane wouldn't pass up.

Couldn't pass up.

Zane's skills as a pilot had given him a reputation across the business for doing what couldn't be done. His roster of clients had grown steadily since he'd opened for his first cargo flight. But he had other reasons for going after High Vision's business. He had a deal on the side nobody knew about. That deal hinged on getting contracts with companies like High Vision – companies of interest to the DEA.

The money he made on the side as an undercover

informant would save his baby sister's life. He'd almost lost her to her demons once.

He'd unintentionally abandoned her when he went into the military. Not again.

"I'll be fine," Zane said. Genetically engineered white mice, packed in the six cases being loaded on his plane, had to arrive alive and on time. He didn't give a rat's ass about the mice. No pun intended. But he also didn't plan to blow the best chance he had at cinching the deal with High Vision.

"H-o-o-wee!" Hack raised one gray eyebrow at the weather radar on the huge, outdated CRT computer monitor to his left. The dial-up connection was deadly slow, and the animated radar loop crept across the screen. "Nobody oughta fly in a front like this. Don't be fooled none by that little break out there. It's a comin' in hard."

Zane grunted just to give the old guy a response.

Hack shifted his bulk to lean forward, and the vinyl office chair squeaked in protest. "You hear 'bout that fella down in Montgomery? Told his wife he *had* ta fly in that bad squall come off the Gulf. Said he'd lose his contract with Shoreline Delivery if he didn't. They used a bag to pick up parts of that man. He was scattered plumb across Alabama."

Zane shrugged. Life was a gamble.

Odds were no worse now than when he'd put everything on the line for his brothers in arms, which he'd do again in a minute.

It would take more than lousy weather to make him pass up a chance to get one step closer to security for him and his sister.

Everyone vied for High Vision's business. If he didn't meet the delivery deadline, somebody else would the next time.

"Don't you git it?" Hack continued. "That pilot didn't keep the contract noways. He shoulda just stayed home. If he had, he'd be alive an' flyin' today."

Sure, bad weather upped the potential for a problem, but compared to Zane's combat flight experience, making Jacksonville tonight would warrant only a little more attention than usual. Of course, his military record, training, and background appeared nowhere on the credentials for Black Jack Charters.

And neither did his real last name, Jackson.

As Zane Black, he kept his personal life separate from work, and from the sometimes-rough characters he encountered. People who wanted him to fly cargo that was illegal at best, a danger to American citizens at worst. His alter-identity had been part of the deal he'd cut with the DEA when they'd become his partner in the charter business.

They bought the plane and set him up. He busted ass to get contracts of his own – and contracts that interested them.

Damned lucrative work that was filling up a bank account for his sister's business scary fast.

Beyond that, doing this for his country was work he believed in. Something that made hauling around smelly vermin a little easier.

He'd flown more than his share of dangerous missions in his career as a pilot. On the last one, he'd barely walked away. In the Air Force, he'd been a respected fighter pilot instead of humping commercial cargo for a living.

But that was three years ago and this was today.

Hack's police scanner crackled with a short conversation in law enforcement code.

"Slow night for the boys in blue," Hack declared.

"What happened now?" Zane asked with feigned confusion over the cryptic announcements. He'd spoken 10-codes like a native language in his former life. Police agency codes were different than military, but since he'd been doing the side work for his friends in the DEA, he'd learned the police agency usage. He knew exactly what the codes squawking on that radio meant, and what had transpired.

"Got a couple hotheads havin' at it in a beer joint parkin' lot down the road."

Hack's man loading the Titan shoved the office door open and announced, "All fueled and loaded. Ready to go. You got to feed those critters if you're late?"

Zane lifted a shoulder. "Beats me. Vision doesn't make allowances for late. Thanks, Tyler. I'll close it up." He preferred to shut the cargo hatch himself and know for sure everything was buttoned up tight.

With a nod, Tyler pulled the door closed, strolled across the hangar, and disappeared into the maintenance shop.

Rain drummed against the metal roof.

"H-o-o-wee. Listen to it come down out there. You hang around and we'll have us a couple hands o' poker."

Zane ignored Hack. A blur of yellow in the hangar caught his attention.

He couldn't believe his eyes.

Had a woman just slipped into his airplane?

Was she nuts?

And where in the hell had she come from?

Zane snatched up the thermos. "Thanks for the coffee." He left before Hack could offer one more warning about aeronautic suicide. The last thing he needed tonight was trouble, even if it came in a long-legged package.

When he stepped outside, an odd sound carried on the swirling wind. Misting rain drifted through the haze of light beyond the hangar.

He stopped to listen.

Dogs bayed in the distance. Bobbing lights flashed near the woods at the far side of the runway. It didn't take a detective to figure out they were hunting something – or someone.

His stowaway was sadly mistaken if she thought he'd help a fugitive.

Zane paused.

A fugitive on the run from the law would be all over Hack's police scanner, but the only alert sent out in the last thirty minutes had been the parking lot bar brawl.

Concern tapped along his spine.

He stuck his head inside the cargo door of the Titan and scanned the secured load. The tie-down straps were cinched tight, as they should be. Hundreds of tiny toenails scratched frantically against the aerated crates. A faint putrid smell accompanied the chattering racket.

In the shadows at the rear, he spotted a bruised leg. Blood trickled from deep scratches. His vision adjusted. Two enormous, terrified, whiskey-dark eyes came into focus between a break in the crates.

Who was she and why were they after her?

And if the police weren't the ones chasing her, who had turned dogs loose to track her?

Amplified barks and howls echoed louder across the airfield. The bleeding leg disappeared and the two eyes ducked away. A memory crashed into him of his younger sister, battered and bleeding, in the wrong place at the wrong time.

No one had lifted a finger to help her.

Three years of buried guilt roared to the surface. He'd cursed the spineless men who'd turned deaf ears to his sister's screams.

He'd cursed himself worse for not being there to save her.

Zane climbed inside, slammed the cargo door behind him, then tossed the thermos into a bag on the floor. He moved forward into the left seat, cranked the engines, and jerked on his headset.

As he pulled out to taxi, he passed two black Land Rovers screaming into the airport, sliding to a stop on the taxiway to his left. Out jumped five men in dark suits with bodies the size of refrigerators.

Static crackled in his ear. He keyed the radio to activate the automatic runway lights then spoke into his headset microphone. "November Zero Niner Niner Five Papa preparing for takeoff."

Two trackers with dogs appeared in his headlights, further down the runway. The ensemble raced toward him. Both men struggled to keep up with hounds charging against their leashes, amped up on the scent of the hunt.

Zane gunned the engine, taxied straight ahead.

Hack's excited voice burst inside his headset. "Zane, come on back. Got some men here want to see you."

What if the brutes were with law enforcement? He'd have to hand her over. No woman was worth getting arrested and having people digging around into his background.

A hundred yards ahead, men dove away from the churning props, dragging the bloodhounds with them.

He clicked on his mike. "Are they Feds?"

"No. Private security, but they really want to talk. Says there's big money in it for you."

Big money had a suspicious ring to it. Zane continued to flip levers. "What type of security?"

He swung around the far end of the taxiway, barely slowing. A squeak sounded in the rear, but he couldn't decide if it had four legs or two.

Two sets of high beams shot around the opposite end of the runway thirty-five hundred feet away to face him. What was the chance those headlights belonged to the two sport utilities full of muscle? Pretty fucking good.

He eased the throttles forward.

What kind of trouble was this woman in?

To keep an eye on his cargo, he'd installed a rear view mirror. He shot a quick look at the cargo hold. A pair of wide eyes stared back, more panicked than before.

He understood that look.

She was running for her life.

After a long silence, Hack finally answered his question. "Private security, uh, like ... Big Joe Levetti."

Hair stood up across Zane's neck.

Hack had always joked that Big Joe had D-E-A-T-H tattooed across his knuckles. No way would Zane turn that haunted, frightened woman over to a bunch of hired guns.

He barked one last message into the radio. "You're breaking up. I've got IFR clearance from center. I'm gone." As the aircraft picked up speed, the four headlights racing toward him grew larger. Zane gripped the controls tighter. His pilot's manual didn't cover playing chicken in a loaded Titan on a rainy night. But his military experience made this an easy call.

Besides, he'd never been one to play by the rules.

Buffeted by the wind, the plane rocked and careened closer to the Land Rovers, the distance between them shortening with every second. He mentally calculated the added weight of the stowaway in the back.

He'd never get this aircraft up before reaching the vehicles if they held their ground.

He'd never be able to stop in time either.

Chapter 3

Two Range Rovers bore down the runway, seconds from colliding with Zane's Titan.

He clenched the yoke, shoving harder, demanding all his twin turbocharged engines could give him. His aircraft plowed into the force of the wind, fighting to lift off the runway. He counted seconds.

Five ... four ... three...

Headlights peeled off in opposite directions at the last second.

He shot the space between them and felt the lumbering craft catch air.

"*Yes!*" Zane laughed out loud and exhaled a deep breath at the same time. He hadn't felt an adrenaline kick this strong since running his last missions.

On the radar, a gap in the weather had opened up to the west. Not a trouble-free route, but a safer one for the moment. He radioed for permission to alter his flight plan.

When he got approval, he maneuvered his plane up to the new altitude where the skies were friendlier and free of traffic. Hack would tell him that's because no other fool would be flying in this. After placing the Titan on autopilot, Zane whipped off his headset and unbuckled.

With a small window of time before things got dicey, he wanted answers from his stowaway.

He hit the dome light switch and twisted around to look over his shoulder, calling back, "Welcome to Black Jack Airlines, now known as Fleeing Felons Express. Sure you're on the right flight?"

Between the Titan's motor rumble, rain slapping the

metal skin, and mice digging to China, he didn't think his stowaway had heard him. A small voice in his brain needled him. *Did you stop to consider if she was a mental escapee – with a gun or a knife?*

No. Gut instinct had saved him too many times to question it now. Besides, that would still have been all over law enforcement radio. This woman needed help.

"Want some coffee?" he asked a little louder and swung his legs around to the side of his seat. He didn't want to go get her, but neither did he intend to fly with her unrestrained if she didn't convince him she was no danger.

No answer.

"Coffee's all that's offered on this flight." He watched as large curious eyes appeared. Then her lips moved, but he couldn't hear her. He cupped his ear to let her know and to hopefully draw her closer.

"Coffee's good," she called out in a cautious voice barely discernable over the noisy cargo.

"I've got it on autopilot. Can't leave the cockpit. Come on up here."

A dirty yellow running shoe appeared first, followed by an endless leg from behind the crates. When the second shoe and sleek limb slid out, he took in every inch of her smoking legs flawed only by cuts and bruises.

His temper flared at whatever had caused her to end up in this shape. His fist curled with the need to pound someone, but who? *Lock down your temper and keep things calm.*

She slowly unfolded a body that had to be stiff from cramming into a tight spot. The painful grimace that followed confirmed her discomfort.

Man, she had to be at least five-eight. Thin, athletic women had never appealed to him. His taste ran along the lines of lush curves with an accommodating disposition.

How long since he'd had either? Too long.

Passenger seats had been removed for maximum capacity in the Titan. Stooped over, his stowaway traversed the narrow passage along the twelve feet of cargo space, reaching out to the crates and the cabin's low ceiling for support along the way.

Her muted yellow T-shirt, still soaked from the rain,

clung suggestively to her chest.

Okay, she had curves after all, and in the right places, but he wasn't at home in a Ft. Lauderdale bar about to exchange addresses, and this woman had a bad-ass bunch of men chasing her. Now that he'd plunged into the fray and swept their prize out of reach, they'd probably come after him.

That bothered him even less than the weather.

But who was she? Some rich guy's toy of the month?

Women couldn't stay out of trouble. He knew first hand.

She raised her head until the bill of her ball cap no longer hid her face. Two of the prettiest doe-shaped amber eyes adorned with thick cinnamon lashes gazed at him tentatively. She chewed on her lip. Hesitant. Fingers trembling.

Seeing that hit him in the gut.

No matter what her story was, no woman deserved to be run to ground like an animal by a bunch of hired goons.

He'd give her a moment to settle her nerves before strapping her into the co-pilot's seat where he could keep an eye on her. Reaching over, he swatted several rags off a metal box that was tied down behind the right seat.

Splitting his attention between the controls and her, he turned to tell her she was welcome to sit down. That's when he got a close look at the cuts and bruises on her legs. Some spots were yellowed from being a day or two old.

The temper he'd buckled down broke loose. "What the hell happened to you?"

She backed up a step.

Damn. *Way to go, dickhead.* As if she wasn't a step from diving out of the plane as it was. He had solid control of his flash temper, except for a few things, and nothing snapped his control faster than a man harming a woman. Now he regretted leaving Hack's airport before having a heart to heart, or fist to nose, with those goons.

Scrubbing a hand over his face did little to wipe away his anger. Zane took a long breath and tried again. This time in a human voice. "Sorry, didn't mean to yell. Please, have a seat."

Either she believed him or was too spent to stand bent over any longer and moved toward the metal box. She cupped her arm protectively around her waist as she leaned over and his first thought was she had internal injuries.

But the movement pulled her T-shirt tight enough to outline a bulge around her middle that didn't belong to that slender build.

What could she be wearing like a belt?

A money belt? Had she stolen something after all?

Before he could say another word, a call over the radio beckoned him.

~*~

Angel caught the pilot's pointed look at her arm that shielded the coins hidden beneath her shirt. He'd noticed, been curious, but, thank God, he hadn't said anything. That would open a line of dialogue she'd just as soon avoid. When he twisted around to face the cockpit, he slid his headset back over his ears and spoke into his mike.

She eased down onto the makeshift seat.

Her hand shook when she brushed a loose hair behind her ear.

Get a grip. She'd accomplished the impossible and gotten away from Mason Lorde. *For now.*

Not exactly a textbook escape, but she had no complaints – now that they were airborne. Of course, she'd had her doubts about that back on the runway.

Who was this guy?

Why hadn't he handed her over to Mason's men?

She glanced toward heaven for a moment. *Not complaining, mind you. Just sayin' it's strange.*

He'd *known* she was hiding on his plane when he taxied out of the hangar, but still lifted off with men chasing them. That departure had been anything but standard. And he'd actually *laughed* after barely missing those two sport utilities.

Her stomach muscles hadn't unclenched yet.

Had she stowed away with *Indiana Jones* or a lunatic?

And now that he'd helped her, what would he want from her? Nobody did anything for free. *Especially not men.* Every man she'd ever known had used her to get something he wanted.

"What's your name?" The pilot's deep voice interrupted her thoughts.

She gazed up into the cocoa eyes of her savior. Big guy, at least three or four inches over six feet. His leather flight jacket hugged impressive shoulders and he had the thick chest of a jock, maybe a linebacker.

Those warm eyes patiently waiting for an answer didn't *look* crazy.

Short black hair had been cut and styled with careless abandon that pulled off sexy without trying. His face was carved of sharp lines from the narrow nose to his square jaw. Not a soft place anywhere except those thick black eyelashes that would be too pretty on a less rugged male.

Words flew around her mind when she looked at him.

Daring. Powerful. *Rogue.*

Maybe Indy Jones did exist.

Constantly monitoring all those gauges and lights in the cockpit, he reached past his seat and snatched up a second pair of headphones that he handed her.

As she slipped them on, she heard him say, "Now we can talk without yelling and I can monitor the radio. What's your name?"

"Angel." That's all anyone needed to know. Angelina Farentino had been many things – a star athlete, a courier, a convict. But Angel was the woman inside who wanted a new life with new dreams and no prison record.

"Zane Black, at your service." His firm lips widened in a devilish grin.

That smile could melt an iceberg.

She finally remembered her manners. "Thank you for ... what you did." For that she got a dismissive nod as if he rescued women every day. Maybe he did.

He seemed to be waiting for her to volunteer information.

Not going to happen. She searched for something to keep the topic about him. "Impressive take off."

Waving a hand in dismissal, he said, "That was nothing. Piece o' cake."

This one almost certainly turned female heads regularly with those beautiful eyes and that devil-may-care smile, but she'd always found one thing more attractive in a man than all that – confidence – and Zane Black had it in spades.

But what did she know?

She'd found Mason attractive at first, too.

Zane's eyes twinkled with amusement. "Impressive escape on your part. How far did you have to run?"

"Not far."

The silence stretched between them, urging her to say more, but she knew better. She'd volunteered information once that had convicted her of a crime she never committed. She'd volunteered information a second time and was running for her life because of it.

Time to stop being so blasted helpful.

Zane's curious gaze traveled down her damp T-shirt to her waist.

She wrapped her arms across her middle. Poor attempt to hide the obvious bulge the coins created. She held her breath, expecting the inevitable questions.

Why were those men chasing you?

What did they want?

And, of course, *what did you do wrong?*

But, surprisingly, none of those came out of his mouth.

Instead, he pulled a towel from a duffel bag behind his seat. "Here, why don't you dry off? If you're cold, I have a blanket in the back."

On the heels of being imprisoned and abused at the hands of Mason, this stranger's consideration left her speechless until she remembered her brain needed to shake loose a response.

"Thanks. I'm not cold, just a little tired." Her adrenaline rush had bled out, leaving aches, pains, and exhaustion in its wake. Only frayed nerves kept her from keeling over. "I'd love that coffee now."

He poured some in a thick paper cup and handed it to her. His fingers brushed hers when she took the offering, catching her off guard at the sensation that wicked under her skin. She shifted on the metal box, angling her legs to get more comfortable, which might have been easier if every move didn't send pain shafting through her body.

The sexy pilot lost his smile when he took in her legs once more and studied them with grim assessment. "We need to clean you up."

"I'm fine, really," she protested mildly, not wanting to be touched. "Just a few scratches." Minor injuries from her run compared to Mason's abuse.

"You *are* a badass if that's just a few scratches." He grinned, underscoring that he found her harrowing getaway impressive.

She couldn't recall the last time she'd impressed anyone with anything except her running speed, and warmed at his teasing compliment.

Ignoring her claim that she was okay, he made a quick check on things in his cockpit then unhooked a first-aid kit mounted on the wall near his seat. Removing assorted medical supplies, he reached for her leg then hesitated, his hand in mid-air obviously waiting for her permission.

Long seconds passed as they locked stares.

Just give him a nod. How could she not after all he'd done? Her stomach clenched. Lowering her guard and trusting a man had put her in this position.

Zane continued to hold his hand out with endless patience written in his face. No man was that patient.

She wouldn't bleed to death. Mason hadn't raped her, yet, but he'd left her reluctant to allow any man to touch her. The reasons to say no just kept piling up in her head until Zane withdrew his hand and eased back.

Understanding filled his eyes.

How could *he* understand?

She didn't know, but he did. And the fact that he did was the tipping point that caused her to reconsider his offer. This man was not the enemy and she had no one to turn to. He was offering help. All she had to do was give a tiny bit of trust.

Hadn't he earned that by risking his life to save her?

Offering him an apologetic smile, she lifted one leg for him to clean. His long fingers wrapped around her ankle and her pulse jumped.

He tenderly cleaned the cuts with an antiseptic cloth. It stung, but she could handle that better than the embarrassment of a stranger seeing what Mason had done.

No man would ever lay a hand on her again and walk away unscathed.

Zane lingered over a particularly nasty bruise.

She knew the minute he noticed the difference between fresh injuries she'd gained during her escape and those she'd had longer. He drew a slow breath as if trying to get past the fading yellow and blue splotches.

But he said nothing and she silently thanked him.

The airplane skimmed along through inky darkness punctuated by flashes of light from storm clouds a little ways off. She closed her eyes, fantasizing that she could stay up here forever where she was safe. An unfamiliar feeling.

Warm fingers grazed her legs with more care than she'd known since her mother had died.

After Mason's brutality, this man's consideration was a balm to her ragged emotions. She hadn't felt the sting of tears in years because she'd simply refused to cry, but Zane's kindness drew on emotions she'd buried to survive.

He'd lulled her into a semi-comatose state until he replaced the cloth with fingers that glided across her skin, applying a salve.

Her eyes flew open to see the top of his head where he bent over her leg. Close enough to smell his fresh aftershave. Her skin tingled and came alive. She clamped her lips shut to keep from sucking in air at the way her body was reacting. Heat sizzled along her legs, racing up to where they met and...

He leaned forward, his hands moving higher along her leg.

She bit hard on her back teeth, determined not to tremble and give him the wrong idea. He was only smoothing antibiotic cream over her skin, not trying to tantalize her.

Tell that to your body.

Her next breath drew in a scent of male, lots of male. The sexy combination overrode her shaky nerves to ignite a burst of feminine response – the last thing she'd expected.

Sure as heck hadn't seen that coming. What could be wrong with her to be turned on *now* of all times?

One look at the attractive pilot answered her question.

She liked large men. And sexy men.

Zane Black fit the bill on both counts. He was gorgeous and had the kind of touch a woman craved.

Her breathing hitched.

He glanced up. His warm eyes darkened with a gleam of

interest.

She gave him a that-wasn't-what-you-thought-you-heard shrug and waited to see if her bluff worked or if he was going to make a crack about how she could join the mile-high club.

But he didn't. With a quick look at his instruments, he went back to his ministrations.

Life had been strange to this point, but not this strange. She'd escaped a maniac who would unleash all his extensive resources to find her. Mason would be out of his mind over losing the fortune in rare coins, but he also had a deadline for delivering them.

Regardless, if she handed those over to him now, he wouldn't let her walk away.

No one embarrassed Mason and survived.

She had a chance. Slim, but still a chance if tonight was any sign.

Being saved by a dark warrior who could turn a nun's head topped everything she'd faced before.

At Zane's gentle pull, her leg moved up and across his lap as he sat straighter.

She didn't resist, didn't want to. After six days of pure torture, Angel struggled to muster the cool disinterest she normally offered men. But Zane applied salve over her legs as earnestly as a sculptor working on his masterpiece.

A warm tremor stirred in the pit of her stomach again. Her breathing quickened at the intimate contact.

Dammit, there couldn't be a worse time for her to be attracted to a man, but clearly her body lived in the moment with no concern for the future. After all the misery men had put her through, she could come up with only one explanation for this strange attraction. As part of her training for a triathlon she'd hoped to compete in, she'd taken a survival course. The instructor had explained how complete strangers would bond almost immediately when thrown into life and death situations.

Made sense.

Mix fear of dying and adrenaline overload with one mouth-watering, white-knight hunk for instant attraction.

And that would explain her lack of a love life since she hadn't run into anyone like Zane before.

"Let me see your arms," he said.

She jerked at his voice.

His chest moved with a sigh she couldn't hear. "Sorry, didn't mean to startle you."

"No." She lifted her hand in apology. "I'm jumpy."

"With reason." He smiled and her silly heart felt special.

Without thinking, she extended her free arm for him to see the scratched skin. Stupid move. That was the arm with the plain silver band locked on her wrist.

When he said nothing about it, she relaxed. He probably ignored the bracelet as a piece of junk jewelry.

One she had to remove soon.

Asking for a hacksaw right now might throw a kink into how well things were going. If Zane knew that bracelet was a tracking device, he'd jump to the conclusion that she was a criminal and bring in the police. That would be major FUBAR.

Never again would she blatantly trust anyone, especially the law.

Locked away for ten days with Mason and his death squad had reminded her just how vulnerable a woman could be, no matter what kind of physical condition she maintained.

Zane's deep voice boomed in her headphones. "Speaking of being jumpy and given the send off we just got – want to tell me what's going on? I can radio ahead to have someone in law enforcement meet us at the next stop." His concerned voice flowed over her like a hot shower on a winter morning, but the question snapped her back to cold reality.

He'd waited longer to ask those questions than she'd expected, and he deserved an answer. But telling this guy anything significant would be foolhardy.

Still, she despised lying.

Her mother had lied constantly about drinking even when her breath reeked of cheap whiskey. She'd lied her way straight into a casket, abandoning Angel.

Her father had lied for years about how he lost a job and where he went at night. Then, to convince the District Attorney he was giving up everyone, her father had told the all-time whopper about her toting drugs. He'd never been much of a parent, but that had shriveled up what was left of her heart.

The wimpy attorney she'd been assigned had lied about trying to win her case, and made the bare minimum of court-required visits while she lingered in jail.

No one took responsibility for the truth.

She'd tell the truth or say nothing.

Lies had cost her a future she'd trained years to earn. Her life had changed irrevocably seven years ago, but then, as always, she'd adapted. Now, however, she might spend the rest of her days in a federal prison for getting involved with Mason Lorde.

Men and lies went hand in hand.

Even if this pilot were different, she'd never see him again. The less he knew, the better off they'd both be.

"Angel, maybe—"

"Have you ever had a relationship go bad?" she asked.

"A few that were difficult, but not quite *that* bad." Zane raised an eyebrow loaded with skepticism.

"It's complicated. I won't burden you." *You wouldn't believe me anyhow.*

"Burden me. I have nowhere to go for a while."

Just my luck to be rescued by Dr. Phil. Damn. "I wanted out of an arrangement. He didn't see it my way." Angel lifted her shoulders to sell her escape as no big deal.

Rain pattered against the outer covering of the fuselage and the cargo chattered during the empty pause.

Zane's eyes hardened.

He probably assumed she meant a personal relationship. She should be so lucky to have a normal woman's problems. To clear up his confusion would involve details she could never share.

After several seconds, he held out his hand to her. "Let's check your other arm."

She hesitated to uncover her middle and couldn't take another moment of his hands on her skin. Not if she wanted to keep her ridiculous hormones under control. "I'm okay, really. Thank you."

Don't ask me about what's bulging under my shirt.

His eyes flickered with a moment of indecision that raised hairs on her skin in warning, but he didn't press her further.

In an effort to change the subject, she asked, "Where're we headed?"

"Jacksonville."

Her quota of divine help had just run out.

Mason had a division in Jacksonville.

Chapter 4

"You're landing at the Jacksonville International Airport?" A frisson of worry slipped into Angel's voice in spite of her effort to sound casual. Could Mason's men have gotten Zane's flight plan?

Zane eyed her as though he could see right through to the secrets she harbored, but he shook his head. "No. I'm making a delivery to a client at a private airfield."

"How, uh, soon?"

"Little over an hour if the storm doesn't force me to circle too far out." He turned toward the control panel, searching for something amid the mass of lights and gauges, then faced her again, apparently satisfied for the moment. "Where you headed?"

"South." That was as good a directional choice as any. To avoid focusing on herself any longer, she pushed the subject off course. "Is this your plane?"

"Yep. I have a charter company."

"What kind of charters?" Seemed like a cargo pilot wouldn't have to work in the middle of the night, flying through storms. Not that she was complaining since she'd benefited by whatever had forced him to fly in this mess.

"I handle special cargo that normally can't be transported by most commercial carriers. We're based in Ft. Lauderdale at Sunshine Airfield. Those ventilated boxes contain lab mice my client needs right away. I'm headed home as soon as I deliver them."

She gulped coffee to cover a shudder. Ugh, she hated rats. The slight smell and frantic scratching emanating from the boxes suddenly made sense.

"Sounds like an expensive way to ship rodents."

"These are *special* rodents."

"They do tricks?" She couldn't resist teasing him if for no other reason than to get another dose of that hot smile of his.

She got her wish.

He answered her with a grin that made her want to preen under his attention. She barely stopped herself from sighing before a slap of common sense tamped down her burgeoning attraction.

Hadn't Mason turned her head just as easily?

All charm and teasing when she'd worked in his warehouse. Too late, she'd found out what kind of animal hid behind the million-dollar smile and impeccable manners. This pilot might behave like a perfect gentleman, but only a fool flirted with a man who'd helped her escape without even knowing who she was or why she'd been running.

Would she ever learn?

Confusion crossed Zane's face. "What's wrong?"

She flushed the irritation from her face and gave him a polite smile. "Nothing. I just wondered how long the airplane would fly by itself." *Yeah, right.* Well, she *had* thought about that a few minutes ago. To support her claim, she glanced at the controls.

"We're good until I take it off of autopilot in just a minute." He put away the first-aid kit and shifted to face forward in the left seat. "We'll be hitting a rough patch of weather soon. You should come up here and buckle in."

Having never flown, and definitely not in a small plane, she hesitated at the idea of being buckled in so close to the windshield.

Limitless black heavens changed from a constant patter of rain to a loud drumming over the entire craft.

Zane issued a quick order. "Jump in the co-pilot's seat now before it gets worse."

Wrong time to have a distracted pilot.

She bent her legs to stand, gritting her teeth at the ache in her stiff muscles. She managed to get into the seat and not hang herself on the headphone cord.

He reached over without waiting for her okay this time

and secured her harness, then took control of the airplane. She didn't move a muscle while the plane dipped and bucked against the turbulent atmosphere.

Zane calmly discussed weather and exchanged flight information with an air traffic controller. Vicious wind and rain pummeled the outer shell. When the fuselage shuddered hard several times, she questioned her choice of nights to run.

But without the storm there would have been no escape.

Temperature outside the plane had cooled. Her damp clothes chilled her to the bone, but she refused to complain while Zane had his hands full flying in this mess.

Warm air began to migrate through her space. When another dry towel fell in her lap, she wrapped it around her shoulders and cut her eyes left. He maneuvered the buffeted aircraft with amazing dexterity.

In the middle of fighting a storm, he'd actually noticed the goose bumps on her arm? And he'd cared enough to pause what he was doing and try to make it better. Could this man be just as decent as he seemed? Where had Zane Black been when she'd been in the market for a nice guy?

The airplane dropped hard in a downdraft.

Her stomach lurched. Just when she thought her heart might climb into her throat from sheer terror, Zane glanced over long enough to wink and smile.

That little reassurance was all she needed.

Air Traffic Control finally cleared them to enter the Jacksonville air space. The aircraft began to drop steadily. Nothing in the darkness below resembled an airport.

He pressed his mike, but didn't talk. Down below, out of nowhere, two straight lines of white lights beamed up from a tiny spot on the ground. Would the landing be as wild as the take off?

The aircraft lights danced across the wet runway ahead of them. She wrapped her arms around the harness and held her breath, but the touch down was surprisingly smooth.

A light mist drizzled against the windshield as he slowed the plane.

Halogen lights glowed over the flat terrain surrounding the airport.

This facility appeared larger than the one they'd departed near Raleigh. Three imposing hangars and a single-story brick terminal stood along one side of the airport.

As he finished his radio confirmation, Zane taxied to a parking spot near the center hangar. With the engines silent, chattering noise from the aerated crates echoed through the cabin. He flipped off his headset.

"Why don't you stay put until I locate my client then we'll get something to eat?" he suggested.

"Sure thing." Not a chance. What if this pilot called in the police? He might even think he was doing her a favor. She hadn't seen any vehicles pulling into the airport as they taxied to the hangars, which might mean the men chasing her hadn't gotten Zane's flight plan.

Settling back into the seat to convince him she was content to wait, she hoped he'd be gone long enough for her to disable or remove the armband. There had to be tools on board. Surely Mason's men couldn't track her this far away, but no point in taking that chance.

Zane opened the cargo hatch and left the steps in place when he exited the airplane.

Angel waited until he'd walked around to the opposite side and headed toward the terminal where soft lights glowed inside. She'd been eyeing a pair of yellow work gloves on the floor behind his seat and reached over to snag them. They swallowed her hands, but she could make them work. Unbuckling her harness, she hurried to the rear of the cargo hold to search through the darkness for a bag or storage bin.

She ran her hands across a rectangular box mounted against the wall. The latch popped open. With a shaft of ambient light drifting in from the open hatch, she could identify a screwdriver, pliers, and a file kind of thing, but smiled when her gloved fingers caught on two sharp points – tin snips.

Maybe her luck hadn't run out after all.

She caught the sound of someone calling out a greeting and started forward in the cabin. Through the rain-streaked window next to the pilot's seat, she spied Zane speaking with a man wearing khaki pants and a windbreaker. His client. That meant Zane would be back soon. She dropped down and quickly cut through the bracelet, then crimped the metal pieces several times, hoping to destroy the tracking components.

Another peek outside the cockpit and her moment of relief came to a screeching halt.

A black Land Rover bearing the signature gold triangle of Lorde Industries crept into the airport and parked next to the far hangar. Dread fingered across her skin. Mason's men *had* tracked her after all, which meant they must have gotten access to Zane's flight plan. She checked Zane to see if he'd noticed the Land Rover, but he stood talking with his back to the vehicle.

Life never got any easier.

Her pulse throbbed in her throat. If Mason's men caught her with the coins she had no bargaining power and no way out of this mess. And Zane Black would be a mere inconvenience in their way.

She searched through the bag he'd pulled the thermos from earlier. She'd never been one to pilfer through someone else's personal belongings, but this wasn't a normal circumstance. Her hand closed around a flashlight. *Bingo.*

Most of the containers in the cargo hold were consigned to High Vision Laboratories. Shielding the light from the windows, she ran the beam close over the labels on miscellaneous packages and boxes in the rear.

She had to find one not slated for Jacksonville.

Giving up the coins could mean her death, but the last thing she wanted to do was get caught by Mason's men with the coins on her. She'd have zero bargaining power. She'd hide them in a package in here, then once she had them back, she'd stick to her plan and find someone to corroborate her alibi for the day they were stolen.

None of this would've happened if she hadn't recognized a stolen painting hidden in Mason's warehouse. The priceless work of art had been plastered all over the news for the better part a week. Shocked by the discovery, her first thought had been that she had a chance to prove she was an employee worthy of trust. She'd innocently brought the painting to the attention of her sainted employer and put her life in jeopardy.

Now all she wanted from the FBI was freedom and a slot in the WITSEC program where Mason couldn't get to her.

Why not? She had no family and no life at this point.

A soft package three-foot square, a foot thick and covered in brown paper lay in the very back of the cabin. The company label on the upper left corner stated, "Best custom boat enclosures east of the Mississippi." She made a mental note that it was addressed to the Security Office for the Gulf Winds Marina in Ft. Lauderdale, Florida, Attention: Slip 18.

Not as close geographically as she'd like, but a safe distance from Mason's home turf – and a long way from here. She just hoped she could reach Gulf Winds Marina by the time the coins arrived and that the boat owner was in no rush to install the boat curtains.

First she had to live long enough to reach the marina.

Removing the gloves, she carefully pried the wrapping tape away from the paper covering the package and ran her hand deep into the heavy canvas material, feeling seams and pockets. Groping blindly along the edge of the material, she snagged a hemmed pocket wide enough to slip three fingers inside.

With a quick jerk of the plastic sleeve of coins under her T-shirt, the clear tape holding the ends together broke.

Feeding the narrow sleeve of coins into the canvas pocket was tedious as pushing a rope. Once she'd pressed the tape on the large package back in place, Angel scurried forward and wiped down everything she'd touched without the gloves, including the tin snips she put back into the tool box.

She'd been convicted of a crime she didn't commit based on a single fingerprint. Never again.

Her cellmate had laughed at her over the fastidious habit that bordered on OCD, but Angel ignored the jibes. After a year in jail, wiping anything she touched was now as ingrained as taking her next breath.

Rushing to the window, she made one more quick check of Zane's position.

He was headed back to the airplane.

She searched the area beyond him. The man in khakis he'd spoken to was nowhere in sight.

Neither was the black sport utility with the triangle logo. Good sign or bad sign?

She had to make a run for it. Now.

Angel tiptoed down the steps, cringing when one creaked. Her legs were pumping before her feet touched pavement. She scurried through the shadows, down to the front of several private airplanes secured with ropes to the tarmac.

The rain had ceased and every sound seemed amplified.

Her heart raced at the tiny noise her sneakers made even though she moved softly between the planes. She stooped next to a yellow aircraft with a double black stripe along its fuselage that glowed like a midnight sun.

Through the stillness, she caught the sound of Zane's shoes scrunching against the steps to his airplane, no more than seventy-five feet away.

Something scraped the pavement near Angel.

Her hair stood on end. She froze and listened for another sound to tell which way someone was moving. Two seconds passed and fear overran all caution.

She made a half pivot away, foot lifted to take off.

A thick arm clamped around her chest and jerked her back against a hard-as-concrete wall of body.

"No!" She choked the word out before his hairy-knuckled hand cut off her next breath. Kicking frantically, she fought to break loose. The stench of nicotine on his fingers gave Vic away. He ran Mason's Jacksonville division.

He dragged her backwards.

Angel dug in her heels to slow him down. Muscles contracted in her chest. She couldn't breathe. He got her to the nose of the yellow airplane, but no farther.

Vic made a gurgling sound, then his hands jerked away.

She spun out of his grasp.

He struggled in a headlock of Zane's powerful arms.

"You know this guy?" Zane barked, clearly in control of the situation.

"He jumped me."

A strangled noise wheezed out of Vic. Zane wrenched a little tighter. "Go call the police."

"No!"

"*No?*"

Angel silently pleaded for him to understand, glad that Zane had the upper hand and Vic had come alone. "Thanks for the ride. I'm sorry."

She turned and ran.

Chapter 5

"Who are you?" Zane loosened his grip enough to let the mugger speak. He had a Keltec .32 stuffed in his boot, but hadn't taken the time to pull it out when he'd had the opening to grab this guy in a chokehold. His captive reeked of cigarette stench and heavy aftershave.

How did this goon know Angel?

The stocky bruiser, a head shorter than Zane, appeared neither threatened nor concerned. "Take your hands off of me, you fool."

Shouldn't he be concerned since I have the clear advantage? Of course, back in his special ops day, Zane had known guys on the team who were much shorter than him that he never wanted as an enemy. Silent and deadly.

But this guy was nothing more than a thug.

Zane ground his teeth at the absurdity of all this. Angel might have done him a favor by not calling the police. High Vision had made it clear they did not tolerate unnecessary media attention, regardless of the reason. They had enough bad media with PETA groups.

And the DEA wouldn't be any happier to see Zane's face in the news either.

No problem. He preferred a low profile for his own reasons.

His chin-high captive warned, "You've got maybe ten seconds to let me go." He sounded annoyed and impatient, not the least intimidated.

The idea of turning this scumbag loose was a piss poor option. Amused by the guy's show of bravado, Zane started to ask, "Or what, Shorty?" when he heard the distinctive "click" of a gun hammer cocked next to his ear.

"Turn him loose," a baritone voice ordered.

Zane dropped his arms and backed away, hands in the air.

Smoothing back his slick black hair, the cocky mugger jerked away from Zane's grasp. He spun around and straightened his Indigo silk suit with a look of pure hatred on his dark, Mediterranean face. He threw a short chin jerk as some signal to his gun-toting partner.

"Turn around," the partner demanded. The tap of cool metal on Zane's cheek accompanied the terse order.

Zane shifted slowly with deliberate movements to face the owner of the suppressed 9mm Smith and Wesson pointed at his head. A faint light cast by the distant halogens outlined the mahogany-skinned gunman's stern features. He stood inch for inch as tall as Zane and outweighed him by twenty pounds that looked put on by steroids. The mountainous body filled out a dark, tailored suit no CEO would refuse to hang in his closet.

That suppressor was an expensive toy. These two were high-priced hired guns. What had Angel gotten mixed up in? Was she some mob leader's babe?

"Where'd she go?" Shorty asked, evidently the one in charge.

Zane thanked his Air Force Special Ops training for being able to read people and adapt at lightning speed. He affected his best rendition of a confused look accompanied by good old boy repertoire.

"Hey, man, I don't even know the broad. I take off with some maniac driving down the fuckin' runway, get up to ten thousand feet and she climbs out of the cargo hold. Says some guy doesn't want to let her go. Must be a hell of a lover's quarrel. She belong to one of you?"

The two best-dressed henchmen in Jacksonville exchanged unreadable looks.

But Zane had picked up just enough hesitation on their parts – combined with the suppressor on the weapon – to figure out these guys were expected to operate below the radar, draw no attention. Or he'd be dead right now.

He continued, "I don't fly passenger charter. She said she'd pay me to drop her off here for a little vacation, but she didn't flash any cash. You got an address where I can send a bill? I've got to make this month's lease payment."

Shorty stepped up close. An ugly smirk on his face matched the evil coffee-bean eyes. He flipped a switchblade open, the sharp tip nicking the underside of Zane's chin.

Several possible reactions came to Zane. Snatching away that knife and shoving it into Shorty's throat while disarming his sidekick topped the list. But that would leave a body to explain and blow his good old boy routine.

"Listen closely," Shorty warned. "You mention this little event to anyone and we'll be back to see you. And if you *ever* touch me again, I'll cut off your hands." He snapped the knife shut, threw a "let's go" head jerk at his towering sidekick and stalked off toward a black sport utility thirty yards away.

Walking sideways, the big guy kept his gun leveled on Zane until he reached the driver's door.

Zane squinted to see the emblem on the door. He saw a flash of gold as the door opened, but in the low light the markings were impossible to make out. Gravel crunched as the driver backed up fast, spun around, and tore out of the terminal.

Too far to get a tag number.

He let out a pent up breath. Lethal encounters still played through his nightmares, years after he'd been rescued from enemy territory in a country where US forces were not welcome – the longest fifty-four hours of his life as a prisoner.

He never gave up a lick of intel.

When he left the military, his best friend, Ben Trenton, and another buddy from his military days, Vance Dern, were already working with the DEA. Ben and Vance had convinced Zane to consider an offer from the agency as a paid informant with Vance as Zane's handler.

His answer? *No, no, and by the way, no.* Zane had a business to build and no time to play spy games.

Then Vance laid out a cherry deal that included the DEA paying for Zane's Titan, even signing it over to him, and saying they *wanted* him to build his charter business.

All he had to do was fly the runs they needed and feed them info when he got it. Go after charter accounts "of interest to them." He kept everything he made in bona fide charters and got paid for his undercover work.

Money from both ends, without being on the DEA's official payroll.

Sweet.

He needed the unofficial side work to pad a special account he'd set up to help his sister's new business get off the ground.

Any real criminal involvement would put his charter business – and his DEA gig – at risk. Bottom line?

He shouldn't get involved in someone else's troubles.

Okay, that might be logical, but it didn't do a damn thing to shut up his conscience that hadn't stopped yammering about Angel's fate. He'd put his life on the line for people he didn't even know almost daily in his former life.

More than his duty, protecting the innocent was in his DNA. He could not turn his back on someone in need, especially a woman.

Just who in the hell *was* Angel, and where had she gone?

Black night wrapped the airport. He scanned the direction she'd run as if he expected her to be waiting within sight. Had she made it to the road and flagged a vehicle?

She could be a stone's throw from him or traveling seventy miles an hour in an over-the-road transport truck right now.

One look at those legs would bring any eighteen-wheeler to a screeching halt.

An hour later, Zane checked the Titan, disappointed to find it empty. His analytical mind flipped through what little he knew. Those goons had found her quickly, suggesting they were local. They couldn't have made the trip by car.

Hack didn't have Zane's flight plan.

That meant one of two things. Either those guys had a contact where the flight plan was filed or Angel was tagged with a tracking device.

If she still had the tracker on her, they'd find her again. This time she might not have someone willing to save her.

He mentally kicked himself for worrying when he had no idea how to find her.

The woman had shared only her first name and she was tangled up in something that smelled suspicious.

Forget about her and deal with your already loaded plate.

If only it were that easy.

Terrified eyes and a battered body kept flashing through his mind. Something more tugged at him, but he was too tired to figure it out and unwilling to analyze anything else right now.

A hint of dawn lightened the skies enough to see clouds moving off to the east. Zane checked his watch. It had been a hell of a start to Wednesday morning. Most people were on their way to work as his day wound down.

Climbing into the cockpit to prepare a flight plan for home, he glanced over at the cup holder and grinned.

Maybe he *could* find out who Angel was after all.

He dug out a small plastic bag from a pocket next to his seat. He put the bag over his hand like a glove and used it to pick up the cup, then turned it inside out so the cup was inside.

It paid to have friends in the right places.

Ben was a forensic science specialist for the Miami DEA division. The man could process fingerprints and track the DNA of a gnat. He was the only person Zane would trust with Angel's prints right now. Ben and Vance would be very interested in the high-priced thugs after Angel, no doubt, but they didn't need to know that yet.

Zane froze. What the hell was he doing, holding out on his two best friends – men he'd trust with his life – because of a woman he barely knew?

Should he tell them? If he did, Vance would have to follow procedure and report everything to the proper authorities, which might end with Angel surrounded by law enforcement.

His mind clicked through that scenario. She'd escaped someplace dangerous and stowed away on an airplane without a clue where she was going or if she could trust the pilot.

That was desperate.

Zane couldn't do it. He wouldn't add to her problems by sticking law enforcement on her when he had no evidence she'd committed a crime, and neither would he put Vance or Ben in the middle of this.

Was he being a fool?

Probably, but he couldn't forget the way she'd looked at him as if he could protect her from the world. Then he'd touched her and forgotten there was a world beyond the two of them.

She'd gotten to him.

Did she belong in jail?

Maybe or maybe not. But until he found out for sure, he couldn't stand the thought of anyone hurting her any more than she'd already been abused.

His gaze landed on that coffee cup in the plastic bag. First he had to find out the identity of the woman who had his insides tied in a knot.

He sure as hell hoped Angel wasn't running for the wrong reasons because if she was, Ben was sworn to act on what he found and Zane couldn't ask him not to.

And damn, he'd hate to see the doe-eyed girl go to jail.

Chapter 6

Food. Water. Now. Or Angel wouldn't make another mile.

Not after making a twelve-mile run from the private airport where Zane had landed to reach downtown Jacksonville by daylight.

What had Zane done with Vic?

She hoped he'd turned Vic loose and hadn't called the police, but right now she needed to worry about getting her hands on some cash. Then water, and food, if her stomach could take it.

As hiding places went, this one stank. Really.

But this narrow cut between a high-rise building and a dumpster had been her best option at daybreak. Based on the smell of rotten food, the dumpster probably belonged to a restaurant in the brick building she leaned against. Tuesday morning workers would be showing up soon and she didn't want to be standing here when someone came out to empty the trash.

Mason had an office somewhere in this city. Could be here in downtown Jacksonville.

Every black Range Rover that passed by sent her diving out of sight.

As if that didn't look suspicious? But the last black sport utility she'd seen half an hour ago had the Lorde Industries logo on the side.

A wave of dizziness assailed her. She breathed through her mouth. If she passed out, she'd put herself in a vulnerable position that could bring in the police.

Late August heat rose with the morning sun. She licked

her dry lips and swallowed against a debilitating thirst. Her stomach rumbled in spite of the nauseating stench from the dumpster. She hadn't eaten since yesterday afternoon.

Sweat trickled from under her ball cap, stinging her eyes. She flipped it around backwards to peek beyond the corner of the building and check the sidewalk.

A steady flow of cars tried to beat the red lights, the drivers trying to slide into work before nine. Dehydrated or not, Angel still wanted one of those coffees cruising by in the hands of pedestrians just a few feet away. Smelled heavenly. She lifted the damp tail of her T-shirt and used it to wipe perspiration burning her eyes.

Keep procrastinating about stepping out in the open, and dehydration would get her before Mason did.

She lifted her foot to take a step.

A loud *boom* shocked her.

Angel jerked backwards against the wall and scratched her shoulder in the process.

Grinding gears echoed loudly in the canyon of tall structures. She glanced at the dilapidated pickup truck that rolled by. The boom had been a backfire.

Calm down. She'd be hallucinating giant rabbits soon if she didn't get food and water. She took a couple of deep breaths.

Where was her white knight now?

Home safe in Ft. Lauderdale, she hoped.

Ebony hair, eyes the color of dark tea, and as imposing as a house, Zane Black might have championed her, but he was not some fairytale knight. He was someone far more deadly. There'd been a dangerous glint in his eyes when he'd had Mason's man in a headlock. Zane handled himself like he'd been in a tight spot with an enemy before.

Guilt still punched her over abandoning him.

For a minute, just a brief flash in time, he'd sent her heart tripping. Had made her feel warm and protected, cared about. She rolled her eyes. Timing was everything and hers had pretty much stunk since the day she fell from the womb.

But her rogue pilot had all the makings of Mr. Perfect. Too bad she'd never have the chance to enjoy him beyond a fantasy. And even if she had that chance, no decent and honest man would want a woman with her past.

She swallowed and inhaled a fortifying breath, determined to get moving.

With a quick glance each way to check pedestrian traffic, Angel veered from the alley and merged into a mixed group of business people and teens moving at a steady pace. She slowed her steps until she ended up near several young people wearing stylish grunge. Hanging with one wave of humans after another, she kept walking when she wanted to lie down and sleep.

Toying unconsciously with the ruby heirloom ring on her right hand, she lifted her finger and gave the ring a hard look. Her dying mother had passed the cherished possession to Angel at twelve. She had no siblings to squabble over the gift.

And she had nothing left as a memory of her mother, except this ring. Her mother hadn't been perfect, but who was?

At least she *had* loved Angel. Now no one did.

Her ring probably had little value beyond the sentimental, but the idea of giving up her only connection to her mother twisted a knife in Angel's stomach. How much would she have to sacrifice just to live a normal life? Her mother had been a survivor and would expect Angel to do whatever it took, even if that meant trading this ring for food.

But she also needed to change clothes and find transportation.

Her throat tightened at forfeiting the ring. She clenched her eyes shut to stem any ridiculous tears.

Life had taught her not to covet anything more than survival. And she'd learned her lessons well.

She had to find a way to that marina in Ft. Lauderdale where the coins were headed. Mason's gold compass would have brought more than this ring at a pawnshop.

If she hadn't lost the shiny little ball.

Even if she still had the coins and was willing to sell them, she couldn't take that risk. Any dealer would know they were stolen. Losing even one coin would jeopardize her chance at staying out of prison.

The ring was her only hope and not much of one.

If someone would give her money for it.

Suck it up and deal with the situation.

She'd heard that mantra enough to last a lifetime.

The foot traffic thinned outside the central business district. She went on alert as the area went downhill. Small independent stores with expanded metal doors and steel bars over the windows filled the lower levels of shabby buildings.

She held her breath as she passed a longhaired man in baggy clothes who hadn't seen a bar of soap in a while. On the opposite side of the street, a woman pushing a banged-up grocery cart full of junk.

Would that be me some day?

A faded banner in the lower corner of a discount shoe store caught Angel's attention, forcing her feet to stop.

She recognized the event's insignia.

In two months, the Tamarind International Triathlon would be held in Colorado. Elite competitors would travel from all corners of the world.

Last year, the event had been in Greece.

She'd trained for the last sixteen months straight for that race – to prove to the world and herself that she was still a competitive athlete, not a criminal. Every waking minute not spent working to feed herself, she'd pushed her body to the limit. Her running times in particular had improved, making her a contender. Or she *would* have been one, if she hadn't been so set on proving she was a conscientious employee.

When she'd informed Mason about finding the stolen painting, he'd just chuckled and said, "Welcome to the *family*, Angel. I chose well in hiring you. Just the person I wanted on my personal *acquisition* team. You'll need some training, but I'll handle that myself."

Refusing to join his band of merry thieves hadn't gone over well, to say the least.

"Be a better person" had been her motto after her release from prison.

She'd always believed she could overcome the problems dealt her, but right now, being a better person had her running for her life and trying to avoid being locked away.

When a shop front with burglar bars on the door and windows came into view, she knew what she had to do. Twisting off her mother's ring, Angel stepped through the door of Quick Deal Pawnshop.

But would she walk out with enough money to reach Ft. Lauderdale?

Chapter 7

"What do you *mean* there's no print on the coffee cup? Even *I* touched that cup at one point," Zane barked into his cell phone while he wove his truck through Ft. Lauderdale's Wednesday afternoon traffic. That news pretty much ruined what was turning into the longest day he'd ever endured.

He eyed the dregs left in his coffee cup.

That sludge wouldn't fix his level of sleep deprivation. Crawling into his own bed last night should have been the ticket to a solid eight to ten hours sleep, but he'd tossed and turned during the few hours he'd managed to stay horizontal.

Long bruised and bleeding legs had haunted his dreams.

He'd given up and spent the rest of the night searching the Internet for anything he could use as a lead. Nada.

That he understood, but *no* fingerprint on the cup?

"Sorry, Zane, I've been all over this thing. It's clean as my mother's kitchen floor," Ben said.

"Damn." Zane raked his hand across his head. Where else would Angel have left a print? She'd been on her own for over twenty-four hours. Was she still alive? "I'm going back to check the Titan again. I'll swing by as soon as I get something."

"Sooner the better or I might not be here."

"Haven't you had that baby yet?" Zane teased. "Thought Kerry was gonna pop while I was gone to Raleigh."

A wife, and now a baby. Ben had chosen well.

Zane had never envied another person and wasn't ready to settle down, but there were days he'd trade his empty life for one like his buddy's. He'd met Ben in grade school and they'd grown up together in Texas. Always had each other's backs. Even when Zane flew fighter planes halfway around the world, they'd never gone a full week without a phone call.

"She's overdue." Ben's weary voice attested to the strain of waiting to be a father for the first time. "We're now scheduled to induce on Tuesday, if she doesn't go into labor before that. Her doctor assured me we'd be able to reach him over Labor Day weekend. Hey, man, if I'm not here I might be able to get a friend to run the prints for you."

"If you aren't there, I'll wait. I don't want anybody else in on this. Not even Vance."

Ben's pause stretched too long. "Zane ... Buddy, what're you up to?"

"I'll tell you about it when I stop by." Zane wasn't ready to discuss this yet, not even with Ben. And definitely not over an unsecured cell phone.

"Don't mess up your gig with the agency."

"I don't plan to."

"Wheels turn slow in the dot gov," Ben sympathized, using current computer-based slang for government agency. "But investigating on your own is bad juju. If you get into deep water, they won't blow a big investigation to pull you out."

Too late for that advice. "I hear you."

Ben made a grumbling noise but didn't push his point. "Get me a print as soon as you can and I'll try to turn it around quick."

"Thanks, man. See you later." Zane swung into the terminal of Sunshine Airfield and parked next to the Titan. He yawned as he opened the cargo door then jerked his head back. Good God. Mouse stink left over from the critters woke him up like no caffeine could.

A slash of light from the late afternoon sun reflected off of something small just beneath the copilot seat.

Standing on the ground, he moved his shoulders down to eye level with the corner of the seat. He leaned close to confirm what he saw.

A silver band.

Sometimes the best tool was his small pocketknife. He used the blade tip to move the band out from under the seat. It had been cut in half and crimped in several spots.

His stowaway had made good use of the time when he'd left her in the Titan while he met with his High Vision representative. This had to be a tracking device. And he'd bet she'd used his tools to cut it off of her arm.

He'd lift a print off of *this*.

Zane could do that, thanks to Ben.

When Vance had offered Zane serious cash for keeping his ears open and passing on any tips that would help the DEA, Ben had spent a day teaching him how to pull fingerprints *just in case*. He'd given Zane the small box that contained aluminum dusting powder and a zephyr brush. Wearing latex gloves and safety glasses, he brushed everything that Angel could have come in contact with, including the silver band and the tools in his toolbox.

A half hour later, he hadn't found a single fingerprint, meaning she'd intentionally wiped the areas clean.

Not an encouraging sign for a person with nothing to hide.

And now he had to clean the damn powder off of everything in the cabin.

Who was she hiding from? He'd searched online for any police activity in the Raleigh area from the night before. Nothing significant had shown up, leading him to believe someone chased her for personal reasons.

Hack said the guys who'd come barreling into his airport had left just as quickly. And that the vehicles had some sort of triangle logo on the car doors. Whoever chased Angel had deep pockets.

The lack of fingerprints stumped Zane.

Why would she go to the trouble of hiding her identity from a pilot? Did she think he'd call in the police?

Probably. That's what *he* would think, if he were in her grubby yellow running shoes. In fact, he'd offered to call ahead to have the police meet them in Jacksonville.

Damn. That had to be why she ran.

But what did she have to hide?

Someone wanted her back badly enough to band her with a tracking device and send men who played rough.

Zane clenched his fists. Spineless bastard. He'd seen the brutal marks on Angel's body. He couldn't blame her for covering her tracks so well, but he should have pushed for more information, a last name at least.

Even as he considered it, he knew it wouldn't have happened. Pushing a terrified woman ranked right up there with booting a puppy.

He wiped the powder off the toolbox then picked it up to reposition it, and something gold rolled out from behind it.

He snapped on his latex gloves again and lifted the small ball up to view.

On a flat side of the golf-ball-shaped object, an embedded compass gave him a northeast heading from where he stood. And the compass was dead-on. That meant the thing was non-magnetic. Probably made of solid gold.

Damned expensive paperweight.

What was this thing doing in his aircraft?

There was only one reason for a compass to end up lost in his airplane last night. A passenger had lost it.

And he'd carried only one passenger in months.

Angel.

Zane grinned at this break. Lifting a print from the pebbled surface was beyond his skill level, but if he could convince Ben to do a little overtime, the genius print matcher would have an identity for him by Thursday morning.

Chapter 8

Mason assessed each of the six men standing in a line on the back lawn of his property. Long shadows stretched from the trees behind them as if the setting sun wanted to point out each one responsible for the fury burning his scalp.

Someone needed killing.

It was beyond the pale that these men had lost Angelina. He hired the best when it came to security for a reason. Jeff had been the exception and he'd been around for a long time. He'd been loyal, certainly.

But he'd outlived his usefulness.

Jeff *should* have been able to keep Angelina contained.

And yet in hindsight, Mason could understand Jeff's screwing up.

But these men?

Ten armed and dangerous guards, including these six, had allowed one woman to escape.

He couldn't tolerate ineptness and every one of these men knew it. But now was not the time to vent his frustration. Now was the time for results. The best way to get what he wanted was to offer an incentive. "Kenner will go over the plan when we're through here. I want Angelina back. I'll award a half million dollars to the man who brings her in alive and with the eight coins she stole from me."

A pittance compared to what those coins – and vengeance – were worth.

Six sets of eyes stared back with cold confidence.

Kenner ordered the men to meet him in the guard quarters. Once they dispersed, Kenner told Mason, "We need a tracker."

"Agreed." Mason had men in Jacksonville checking every way out of the city by public or mass transportation. "Get a list of the best who can be discreet. I'll be in my office."

When he walked into the office in his private estate outside of Raleigh, he eyed the glass case where he'd placed the coins. He'd been certain that Angelina believed him when he told her he had eye witnesses willing to testify that she was seen leaving the museum at the time of the coin theft.

That should have brought her to heel.

But the bitch had stolen the coins instead.

He still couldn't believe it.

His cell phone played a piece of music with dire notes, meaning the caller was unknown. The only person he'd given this number to who didn't already have a ringtone was Angelina. Had she come to her senses?

Grinning, he answered, "Lorde."

"Listen very carefully as I do not repeat myself," a decidedly male voice ordered.

Mason cut in, "Who the hell is this?"

"You can call me Czarion. Have you found the coins yet?"

Shock didn't begin to describe Mason's first reaction. His second one was to yank the phone away and check ... no caller ID. His next move was to pull it back and say, "What coins?"

A lofty sigh came across the lines then Czarion said, "I don't have time for this. You stole eight *St. Gaulden's Double Eagle* coins, one of which is a 1933. You intended to trade them to a German for a panel from the Amber Room."

Mason sat down in his chair. Hard. It couldn't be the FBI. They didn't call up and discuss a felony when they could just raid the compound.

"Since we both know that you *had* the coins, let's move this along. For someone as adept at art theft as you are, Mr. Lorde, I would have thought you'd do a better job of protecting those coins."

Criticizing Mason generally ended with bloodshed. The insult pissed him off enough that he regained his footing. "What's your interest in the coins?"

"Better. Now we can deal with the business part of this

call. You will locate those coins within five days and be prepared to deliver them to me when you do."

"Why would I do that?"

"Because if you don't, you'll pay a hefty price starting with your operation."

Mason wouldn't be paying the price. This idiot would. Just as soon as Mason located him. "Threatening my operation could be bad for your health. Interfering with it would be *painful* and deadly."

"You should realize by now that you're dealing with someone far out of your league."

The ego of some men amazed Mason. He leaned back in his chair, amused by someone stupid enough to threaten him. This guy obviously had no idea of the depth of Mason's resources and how quickly he'd stomp a pest. "Maybe you should enlighten me on just how far out of my league you are so I can show proper respect."

When the line remained silent for a moment, Mason gloated.

Czarion spoke again. "You own forty-three locations, which include distinctive properties in New York, Atlanta, Raleigh, Dallas, and Los Angeles. Twelve are warehouses where you store both legal and illegal inventory..." Czarion spouted a list of items that no person should have access to besides Mason. "During your trip to Palm Beach eight days ago, you completed a trade with the Russian broker Valkimir. I was surprised to learn of the Degas and Ming vase in your New York vault as both had belonged to a sheik I'd believed had better security. That should remove any doubt on your part as to the vulnerability of your operation."

Son of a bitch! Mason stood, clutching the phone so hard his hand shook. Who was this guy and how could he know that much?

He calmed himself. Losing control lost battles and he intended to win this one. He wanted this asshole's head in jar to put in his office. "What do you want?"

"At the risk of repeating myself, the coins."

"Are you after the Amber Room panel?" Mason had acquired the gold coins specifically to trade for an eighteenth century artifact from the room sculpted of amber, considered by many to be the eighth wonder of the world. King Fredrich Wilhelm I had gifted it to Tsar Peter the Great who had once admired the room. The Tsar had moved it to Königsberg Castle, the one the damned Russians had destroyed during World War II.

They'd torched the castle *after* the room had been looted.

Czarion said, "I've already told you what I want. I'll contact you in five days, on Monday, unless you retrieve the coins sooner, which I'll know. If you fail to meet my deadline, I'll destroy one of your properties, regardless of who or what is nearby. And there will be clear evidence pointing the finger at you for the body count. I'll continue to destroy one property each day until you fulfill your part of this agreement ... that is until you run out of possessions. And then I will kill you."

After years of dealing with liars, Mason knew when he heard the truth. Muscles in his neck tightened with the rage pulsing through him. "You can have the coins."

"That was never in question."

Ignoring him, Mason considered one way to solve all his problems right now. He tested Czarion one more time. "Since you know so much, I'm surprised you don't know who has the coins."

"Oh, but I do. Angelina Farentino took them when she escaped your compound. Can't say that I blame the girl, considering your perverted sex habits."

You'll die in slow agony, because I'll keep you alive and awake for a very long time once I find you. "Why are you calling me if you know who has the coins?"

"You interfered with my plans when your men captured the thief who'd originally targeted the coins. You tortured him to find out the name of the German buyer and how the thief had planned to get past security. Had you not done so, I would be talking to him. You took the coins. You lost them. You get them back. And do it in a way that does not draw the attention of law enforcement."

The line went dead.

Mason fought the urge to scramble a team to find this Czarion. He didn't give two shits for the people around his properties who would die. He had insurance to cover the loss of his investments. But not his exceptional art inventory.

Because no one had known he had it. Not until now.

A knock rapped at the door. When Mason called his man in, Kenner entered. "I've got the list."

Standing, Mason shook his head. "Not necessary. I realize who I have to send, but I want you to review everyone in charge of our warehouses, and start with the ones that hold my private art." He called the stolen pieces *private art* to all of his staff, to prevent a verbal slip up by someone who didn't possess his level of discipline.

"Sure. Anything in particular?"

"I want to know if you suspect anyone of giving out information on our operation."

"Yes, sir." Kenner left.

Mason raised his phone into view and hit a speed dial number to the one person absolutely capable of finding and capturing Angelina. A top-level operator. Mason seldom used him because he was expensive, unpredictable, and hard to control, but this situation called for bringing in a true predator.

When the call connected, Mason said, "I have a job for you, CK."

Chapter 9

If the coins have been discovered in the package of boat curtains, the FBI will be waiting for me.

Angel gripped her knee to keep it from bouncing up and down, glad not to have someone in the seat next to her. How could it be Thursday? Over a full day had passed since she'd abandoned the coins and Zane. Her gaze strayed to Ft. Lauderdale's palm trees, concrete-block houses and the occasional plastic pink flamingo flying past her window on the Broward County Transit bus.

Maybe Zane hadn't delivered the boat curtains yet or maybe the boat owner was waiting to install them over the holiday weekend.

She clutched the edge of her seat. Maybe, maybe, maybe.

There was the word again.

With her rotten luck, the boat owner was installing the curtains right now, to have his boat ready *for* the holiday weekend.

Worry had rolled around in her stomach until it felt like a lead ball with spikes. Sleep had been sporadic at best on the bus ride down the length of Florida.

She pressed her face to the window where one souvenir shop after another, each decorated with giant seashells and water floats, dotted the beach scene.

Nothing like New York where she'd been a courier.

A job she wouldn't take again even if cleaning toilets was her only other option.

That wasn't exactly true. She'd enjoyed courier service, especially given the added bonus of constantly training.

But one delivery had ended everything.

To be fair, it hadn't been the delivery so much as blind trust in a man. Her father.

When the bus turned away from the beach and the street signs Angel had been watching for came into view, she straightened in her seat. Rolling up the cuffs of her long-sleeved white blouse, she leaned forward and tucked her shirttail into the faded jeans she'd found in a salvage store near the pawnshop. Her running shorts and T-shirt were stuffed inside a linen shoulder bag along with the ball cap.

She'd twisted her hair up and stuffed it under a floppy hat. Sunglasses finished her disguise, covering half of her face. She could pass for an incognito celebrity on a tight budget.

The bus rolled to a stop just past the cross street she'd been anticipating.

Angel descended the metal steps quickly and jogged away at a subtle pace, feeling better than she had a day ago even if she wasn't fully rested. Using directions given to her at the downtown bus terminal, she located the marina with no trouble. Her shirt had stuck to her back, soaked with moisture from the thick humidity, by the time she passed through the Gulf Winds Marina entrance.

No one paid her any attention.

Floridians definitely had an easygoing attitude.

Small white signs above each dock listed the slip numbers. The second one read "11-20."

To avoid being caught by Mason's men watching the bus stations, she'd thumbed rides with truckers who'd been kind enough to call from one to the next after the first one gave her a ride outside of Jacksonville. She'd arrived before dawn in Ft. Lauderdale where she'd found a place to grab a catnap, then scouted out the local city bus system and schedules only to get lost switching buses.

After all that, she deserved a moment of pride at standing in front of the dock for slip eighteen.

Now tell me the package with my coins has not been opened yet.

For the benefit of anyone watching, she strolled casually down the weathered planks when she wanted to run. Most of the slips held twenty-to-thirty-foot-long boats backed up under the covered docks.

A copper-tanned young man dressed only in a pair of cutoffs scrubbed a boat named *Wet Dream* moored in slip seventeen.

A snow-white, center-console fishing boat, outfitted with impressive tackle, floated silently in slip nineteen.

Two seagulls paddled through the middle of slip eighteen.

No boat. Really?

Now what? Turning to the guy still laboring on *Wet Dream* she called over, "Excuse me."

He dropped the scrub brush and ambled to the rear of the boat. "Yes, ma'am?"

"Do you know who owns the boat that stays in slip eighteen?"

"No, ma'am."

She waited for him to offer more than a charming smile, but he didn't seem inclined to elaborate. This was a little too laid back.

"Do you know the *name* of the boat that belongs here?" she asked.

"Can't say. That slip's been empty for three months. Heard someone just rented it, but the boat hasn't shown up yet."

The package had been addressed to the Security Office for the marina, which now made sense. The boat hadn't arrived.

"I noticed the Security Office was closed when I passed it on the way in. Have any idea when it will be open?"

"Yes, ma'am. Soon as I finish cleaning this boat, I'll be back up there."

Going through the tiny office shouldn't take long.

She smiled.

He grinned with apparent satisfaction over having given her the right answer.

Angel saw the advantage in being female for a change. "Well, you'll save me some time. My company sent a package of boat curtains marked for Slip 18 in error. I'm supposed to make sure it arrives at the correct boat. Would you mind if I checked to see if you have that package?" She held her breath, waiting on him to ask the obvious questions starting with identification, what boat it was intended for, and on and on. She had no idea what she'd say next, but somehow she'd gain access to that office.

The guy didn't ask her the first question, just shook his head and said, "I'll save you a lot of time. We haven't had a delivery like that all week."

Damn. Where was that package?

A possibility popped into her mind.

"Do you know where Sunshine Airfield is?" she asked.

He smiled. "Yes, ma'am."

Chapter 10

By late afternoon Thursday, Zane had to accept the obvious no matter how much he tried to avoid it.

Angel had to be tangled up in something criminal.

He'd spent another night on the Internet, looking for anything on a missing woman from Raleigh who matched Angel's description. That meant the men tracking her didn't need, or want, law enforcement involved.

And she'd sure as hell avoided the law. Why?

He wheeled his truck into Sunshine Airfield ready to unleash his frustration on someone. On top of what should have been two hours of errands turning into four, Ben had called just after daylight with the first bad news to kick off Zane's day. The partial prints Ben had been able to pull from the gold compass had not been enough for a database search, and Zane owed him a bottle of Jack Daniels for the wasted night of work.

As Zane drew near the whitewashed, single-story office building that served as the terminal, he slowed to speak with a leather-faced elderly man who stepped from the office door.

Rolling down the window on his truck, Zane forced civility back into his tone. He liked the old guy and managed to smile when he called out, "*Hola, Salvador.*"

Salvador's sole purpose in life these days was to make coffee in the airfield office and offer a game of checkers to anyone willing to be beaten by the wily opponent. Long since retired from managing the terminal, he was unwilling to abandon the airport entirely.

"*Buenos dias, Señor Jackson.*"

Zane chatted amiably in Spanish with Salvador about the airport activities of the past few weeks. Zane kept his language skills sharp though he used them sparingly. It was amazing what someone would say when they thought you couldn't understand their language. Vance and Ben had made good use of a few tidbits Zane had gotten in just that way.

Talking to Salvador reminded him he would be in hot water with Suarez, a client waiting on two packages. In a hurry to get the cup with Angel's print back to Ben, Zane had stayed in Jacksonville only long enough to pick up Suarez's first package when he learned the second one had been delayed in customs.

Suarez had been more trouble than the money was worth and every shipment turned into a pain in the ass, but he was a client and Zane tried his best to make the man happy.

With a nod goodbye, Zane moved on to the last building. The overhead door to his hangar stood wide-open, allowing access to anyone, but he had no worries. His mechanic was bent over the Titan, working neck-deep on the scheduled service required before Zane could fly again.

As he strolled by, the mechanic had his head down looking for something and talking ... to himself? No, he had a Bluetooth receiver hooked on his ear. He lifted a finger off his flashlight in acknowledgement and turned as though to stop what he was doing. Zane waved him off and headed through the hangar and down a short hall to the storage room. He needed a stack of rags to replace the ones he'd used cleaning up the damn fingerprint powder yesterday.

Just as he reached for the door, a crinkling sound on the other side stayed his hand. Had a cat or raccoon gotten in there? A cat wasn't a problem, but he wanted no part of a cornered raccoon.

Rotating the handle slowly, he eased the door ajar and peered inside.

No wild animal. At least he didn't think so.

A fine-looking derriere, covered by a pair of faded jeans, was stuck up in the air in full view.

Bent over at the waist, the denim-clad owner inspected a large package on the floor.

Zane's gaze skimmed down to the yellow running shoes. It couldn't be.

Chapter 11

Where is that blasted package?

Angel leaned down to read the label on another odd-shaped box. Assorted shipping containers and mechanical parts covered every inch of the disorganized storage room from cluttered floor space to packed shelves.

None were addressed to the Gulf Winds Marina.

She lifted her hands to her hips as she straightened up.

Iron fingers locked around her wrists, snatching her hands behind her.

"Oh, oh ... no." She wrenched around to see who held her prisoner and came face-to-face with the pilot who'd saved her. Staring up into his narrowed gaze, every coherent thought fled her mind.

"Nice to see you again, Angel." Rich brown eyes walked up and down her. He'd said her name with just enough edge to sound mocking as if he'd just figured out she was anything but. "The Annie Hall look's different. Incognito?"

His warm demeanor from the day before was gone. His eyes now flashed stormy-dark. Just as angry looking as he sounded.

She dropped her head down and her shoulders slumped from relief. He didn't appear happy to see her again, but at least he didn't sound as though he wanted to kill her.

Twisting around for a second glance, Angel realized she might need to revise her first impression. She was neck deep in trouble with him. They hadn't parted in the best of circumstances. Getting back into his good graces as quickly as possible was her first mission.

"Hi. How are you?" She lifted her eyebrows up, reaching

for hopeful in her voice.

"How *am* I? As in, was the flight back smooth? Or as in, how did I get away from your buddy?"

"I'm sorry about that," she whispered. What had Vic done after she'd left? It dawned on her later that Mason's men never traveled alone. Had they ganged up on Zane and hurt him? "Did you have a problem with that guy?"

"Problem?" Heavy sarcasm laced his voice. "Nooo, not unless you consider having his sidekick shove a gun in my face a problem."

"Oh, God. What happened?"

Zane shrugged. "I told them I didn't know who you were and thought you'd had a falling-out with your boyfriend. Once you were gone, they lost interest and let me go."

Her luck had never been on the upswing, but right now it spiraled from bad to worse. She'd spent a large portion of her funds on clothes and bus fare. In the past twenty-eight hours, she'd had one meal and a few hours of sleep. Now she couldn't find the blasted package hiding the coins.

If the sole person who knew where the package of boat curtains had gone handed her over to the police, she was sunk.

This would be a great time to turn on her feminine wiles, if she had any.

"I didn't mean to leave you stuck," she started.

"Having a hard time buying that since you *did* leave me stuck."

Wrong tactic. *Just give him the truth and hope he'll understand.* "What I mean is I didn't mean to involve you in my problems. I had no idea where I was going when we left Raleigh. I didn't know that would happen or I would have told you to let me out as soon as you landed."

He didn't say a word.

She was making no headway with flyboy. "You may not believe me, but I do appreciate you getting me out of Raleigh. I thought you had that guy handled. If I'd known someone else was around, I'd have stayed to help you even if it meant getting caught. That's the truth."

She took a breath and turned to see if she'd made a dent in that stern expression.

His face softened. The muscle in his jaw no longer

twitched. He wouldn't harm her, but he still might call the authorities. Between smoothing things over with this guy and figuring out what had happened to the package – without specifically asking where it was – she had her work cut out.

How had a simple plan to hide the coins gotten so screwed up?

Wrenching against his steel grasp was a waste of energy. She dug around for a sweet tone, something she hadn't used in a long time, and implored, "Would you let go, please? You're hurting my wrists."

His fingers loosened immediately.

She pulled one hand free and swung around to face him.

He held onto her other wrist, giving her no chance to escape. If he knew how desperate she was to find those coins, he'd realize she had no plans to take off yet. He massaged her wrist with his thumb then looked down and scowled.

What did that mean with this man?

Were they okay or did he still want to strangle her?

He muttered, "I didn't realize how tight I held you. That's going to make a damn bruise." He didn't stop working the sting out of her skin until both wrists had been given equal attention.

No man had ever confused her so much or so often.

Zane Black went from annoyed to caring within a heartbeat. Like the heartbeats rapidly thumping in her chest from his soothing touch. He'd touched her more in two days than any male had in the past seven years. With the exception of her one failed relationship as a teen, contact with a man had not been by her choice. Her limited experience with men amounted to being handcuffed by the police and physically abused by Mason.

No man had been gentle with her until now, or protective as Zane had been during the flight, and none had ever elicited the physical response that standing close to Zane caused.

She'd *never* been turned on by a man merely rubbing her wrists.

Chocolate cake had raised her pulse more than male interest in the past.

Cake lost hands down right now.

"Angel, why don't you tell me what's going on before someone gets hurt, mainly you?"

Her heart did a small trip at his genuine concern. His intense stare roamed over her face as if searching for a way to slip past her defenses.

When he didn't release her wrist, she took a step back, needing space to think, and bumped up against the wall. What could she say that he'd believe? Even if he accepted her story as true, he'd want to call in the police. That would hammer the final nail in her coffin. Once the authorities pulled up her record, they'd put her away forever. Against a prominent businessman like Mason, her word had less value than dirt without undeniable evidence.

She had one shot at beating this problem and remaining free, and it didn't include local law enforcement.

Besides, with her luck, Mason would bail her out so that she'd land right back where she'd been up until two days ago.

Telling Zane anything would put him at risk, as well.

She gave him the only truth she could. "I can take care of myself. You're better off not being involved."

His black brows furrowed. "Why?"

"Even if you knew, you couldn't help me."

He frowned, gears grinding behind those dark eyes. "Look, if this guy chasing you is an obsessive – and abusive – male, there are laws that will protect you."

"The police won't take my side."

That made him pause. His expression shuttered.

She'd made a mistake just then.

"Why?" he pressed. "If you've broken the law, turning yourself in would be better than being caught."

She bristled. Had he found the coins?

No, she didn't think so. If he had, he'd probably be calling the police right now. Still, he was beginning to remind her of the DA who'd railroaded her into jail seven years ago.

When she didn't reply, Zane kept prodding. "How much trouble are you in?"

Wasn't it just like an arrogant man to make assumptions with no possibility for an "in between"?

Either she was a hunted girlfriend or a criminal.

Lack of rest and little food fueled her already testy mood and punched her frustration level to its top limit. A wise woman would calm down and sweet talk Zane, but she was sick to death of men either lying to her or assuming she'd committed a crime.

Snatching her hands away, she shoved them defiantly on her hips and leaned toward him. "If you don't know my story, that makes me a criminal?"

"I didn't say that."

"What *are* you saying? I admit I broke the law, but only when I stowed away on your airplane. I'm tired and out of patience. Just tell me. Are you going to have me arrested or not?"

"Hold it, Angel." He lifted his hands in surrender. "I'm just trying to help you. Don't blow up at me."

"Blow up? This is not blowing up. This is me trying to keep you out of harm's way." She crossed her arms and leaned back against the wall, muttering, "Raleigh's my problem, not yours. Can't you leave it at that?"

Zane stepped forward and slapped his hands on the wall at each side of her head. He leaned down, eyes sparking with anger simmering just beneath the surface. "No."

She lost her ability to think the minute his heat surrounded her. "Why ... not?" came out murmured on a soft exhale.

He didn't answer at first, as though struggling to decide something. "Because I'm afraid something will happen to you."

"You don't even know me." She hadn't said that with any conviction.

"I know enough." He lowered a hand to her neck. His fingers gently brushed the sensitive skin.

She shivered. Licked her lips. And felt her nipples harden.

He stilled. All sign of anger was gone, shoved aside by something far more dangerous. Desire. His nostrils flared.

He leaned a little closer, his gaze holding hers as if some invisible power had locked their eyes together. His lips were a breath away, close enough to kiss her.

Her next breath came out fast and raspy. She must be losing her mind, because she wanted that kiss.

"Excuse me, Señor."

At hearing someone else in the room, she and Zane bumped as they jumped apart to face the open door. One step inside the room stood a handsome Latin man of average height, wearing a smart fawn-colored suit with an eggshell silk shirt open at the collar.

His eyes twinkled when he smiled at her then he spoke to Zane. "I am here for my shipment."

Zane's dark mood flipped to jovial. "Mr. Suarez, nice to see you. We were just going over the inventory log."

Angel lifted an eyebrow at that blatant lie, but held her peace. She'd stowed away on the man's plane, left him dealing with Vic, and broken into his storage room. The least she owed him was to play along.

Lifting his shoulders in a quick shrug, Zane continued in an apologetic tone. "Only one box came through customs before I left Jacksonville."

Mr. Suarez's smile fell. "But why? We discussed this before you left." His language switched into a rapid litany of angry Spanish.

She stood silently while Mr. Suarez ranted that this was the third time Zane had failed to deliver, that Zane was inept and Suarez was ready to sever ties with Black Jack Charters altogether.

She glanced up at Zane's placid face.

God love him, he didn't understand a word.

But a person didn't have to be fluent in Spanish to realize Suarez was very angry. She elbowed Zane who flashed her an innocent look of *what?*

Mr. Suarez fell silent, evidently waiting for an explanation. She nudged Zane again. This time he must have taken the hint.

"What can I say? I didn't get the box." Zane shrugged again.

That was it? He might be a crack pilot, but Zane was sorely lacking in people skills. Since he'd helped her, the least she could do was return the favor.

Angel offered his client a smile then responded in Spanish, telling him, "*Mr. Suarez, please forgive my friend.*

He is an exceptional pilot, but a little rough around the edges. Unfortunately basic business skills were not required to get a pilot's license."

Had Zane just kicked her? She narrowed her eyes at him.

He lifted both eyebrows like *hmm?*

Suarez's lips lifted a tiny bit, but he gave no indication his temper had completely cooled, so she continued appeasing him in his language.

"You are very understanding with Mr. Black's shortcomings and we really appreciate your patience. If you'll give us a chance to correct the problem, he'll check into this matter and get back with you once he has answers on your missing package."

She finished with, *"Please accept our sincere apology. You and your business mean a great deal to Black Jack Airlines."*

Suarez returned her smile with a sensational one. The man oozed European aristocratic elegance. He stepped forward when she offered a hand to shake, but lifted it to his lips and kissed the back of her fingers.

Had that been a sigh escaping her lips? Who could blame her? No woman was immune to that kind of flattery.

"Senorita, you are as wonderful to do business with as you are to gaze upon," Suarez said in his language. Then he cut his eyes hard at Zane and added in English, "I suggest you keep this woman if you wish to continue delivering for my company."

Zane lifted a small box off the floor that he handed to Suarez then hooked an arm around Angel's shoulders. He shifted her back to the point of forcing Suarez to release her hand.

"I was just telling Angel what a great team we make," Zane said. "She generally pops in and out when she wants, but we're hammering out a plan that will work for both of us. Umph."

She elbowed him one more time in the ribs for outright lying.

Grinning, Suarez said goodbye as he left with the package under his arm.

She jerked away from Zane. "Don't you care about

keeping that client?"

"He's not going anywhere," he dismissed casually. "Only a few groups operate the way we do and none of them fly out of South Florida."

"I wouldn't be so sure. He said he was thinking about dropping your service." She waited to see how Mr. Arrogant liked hearing that little tidbit.

He didn't say anything at first. Crossing his arms, Zane shifted his feet apart and cocked his head to the left, studying her. His stance didn't intimidate her, but she worried what was going on under that short black hair.

He asked, "Where'd you learn to speak Spanish?"

"I took two years of it in high school and tutored English to the Puerto Rican children in my neighborhood." She cocked her chin up at him. "You should consider a few classes."

"You're right, but not about classes. I need to make a better effort to appease Suarez since he's a significant customer. I think you should stick around and translate for me."

Bad idea. "No." Angel shook her head. "I can't do that."

"Why? Where're you going?" he prodded.

Nowhere until she found the coins.

Before she could answer, he asked, "Where're you staying?"

"I don't have a place yet, but I'm not planning on hanging around long."

He leaned toward her and asked, "By the way, just what were you looking for in here?"

Oops.

Not the time to ask about a missing package of boat canvas. The truth would only open a bottomless pit of questions. Sometimes gray worked better than black as long as it was close to the truth. "When I came in the mechanic said I could wait for you."

Well done, not really a lie.

"You thought he meant *here* instead of the office?"

Right now Angel wished she were as skilled at acting as she was at physical training. She tried for a surprised look. "Ohhh, you have an office. That would have been a better choice."

He rolled his eyes and shook his head, letting her know her attempt at playing innocent had been a wasted effort.

Zane put his hands on her shoulders and she held very still. "I'll tell you what. This contract with Suarez is only for a short time. I'll give you a place to live in exchange for translating."

The last thing she could agree to do was hang around and help with his business. On the other hand, figuring out how to eat, sleep, and find transportation on less than a hundred dollars would be a challenge. Even with the transmitter bracelet gone, hiding from Mason for any length of time without a chunk of money would be unrealistic.

More like impossible. His resources were practically unlimited.

And, Zane was the only common denominator for locating the coins.

Rocking back on his heels, like he had all day to wait for her answer, he pulled his hands back and slid them into the pockets of faded jeans that fit him like a glove. The snug powder gray T-shirt hugged his broad chest. Her eyes traveled lower to a worn brown leather belt just above...

Embarrassed, her eyes shot up to his face in time to catch the mirth in his gaze confirming he'd caught her roaming vision.

Like she needed to encourage this strange attraction between them? Spending time in close proximity to this man might not be advisable.

"You still owe me for the flight out of Raleigh," he pointed out.

She rolled her eyes this time. He *would* play his ace. Besides, she had no other option.

"*O*-kay," she huffed. "But I'm not promising how long I'll stay."

"Fair enough." Zane checked his watch. "It's close to four. Let's go."

"Go where?"

"Home."

She hadn't even considered where he'd offered for a place to stay. "You mean *your* home?" she clarified.

"Don't worry. I have a foldout and you should know by

now you're safe with me."

True. He wouldn't harm her and he'd try to stop someone else from hurting her. He wasn't the problem.

She was. Just standing near him short-circuited the common sense area of her brain. Her body had none when it came to Zane.

Crazy hormones were throwing a party just for him and didn't give a fig about coins or Mason.

Strain of the last two days settled in all at once, causing her to feel a bit lightheaded. She blinked her eyes to clear her vision and admitted she couldn't be picky when she desperately needed at least one solid night's sleep.

Zane lifted a hand toward the exit. "Ready?"

With a final nod of acceptance, Angel picked up the linen shoulder bag she'd dropped near the door and stepped out ahead of Zane, then he led the way to a massive Dodge pickup.

That figured. The man wouldn't fit in anything smaller.

Flashy mag wheels gripped raised-letter tires. The four-wheel-drive machine had been painted Saturday-night-lipstick-red and accessorized with chrome jewelry.

No wonder men referred to their vehicles as feminine counterparts.

Zane opened the passenger door. The new leather scent engulfed her as she stepped up to the high captain seat. A wide console separated them, suiting her just fine. Calm dove-gray covered the interior, contradicting the screaming exterior.

She checked all around the inside of the truck for a brown paper package with Gulf Winds Marina labeled as the destination.

No such luck.

Several ropes were piled across the narrow back seat of the extended cab. A large bundle of half-inch thick rope lay in the rear floorboard. What in the world did he use that for?

She switched mental gears to more important concerns.

How soon would Zane fly out again? She needed another shot at hunting for the package in his hangar. If it didn't turn up there, she'd head back to the marina in case the boat curtains had been floating around in transit and finally arrived.

Either way, once she had a solid night of sleep, she'd be on the run again.

Chapter 12

Watching Angel climb into his truck, Zane was amazed she could still stand upright.

Had she even slept since he'd last seen her? He wouldn't bet on it based on the exhaustion in her eyes. What had she gone through to reach Ft. Lauderdale? She must have had *some* funds for the secondhand clothes and transportation, but he had a feeling she didn't have much or she wouldn't have agreed to stay with him.

His suspicions flared at everything she'd done from wiping her fingerprints to showing up in his hangar. He should turn her over to the police to let them determine if she needed protection or incarceration.

But her fear was palpable.

Every protective instinct had roared to the surface the minute he'd found her again. He'd be damned if he'd let her slip away this time.

Life had taught him that not everyone who avoided the law was a criminal. Judging this situation without all the facts could get someone seriously injured, or killed.

Bringing in the authorities might shove her into more danger. He couldn't do that. Not until he had answers. He'd never forgive himself if something happened to her because of nothing more than suspicious activity.

With enough money and connections, whoever chased her could get to her anywhere. He'd heard some of Ben's stories. Protective custody sometimes amounted to caging the prey for a fenced hunt by the bad guys.

Zane walked around and climbed in the driver's side, cranking the engine. One look at Angel's long legs now covered in jeans reminded him of the old bruises on her thighs.

He'd like to pay a personal visit to the person who had inflicted those wounds.

With the kind of men she had on her tail, how had Angel made it all the way here alive? And why did she fight him so hard when she knew he was trying to help her?

Sure, he was a stranger, but if she had anyone else to turn to, she'd have gone to that person.

Frustration welled inside him.

His gut just did not want to believe that she was a criminal.

What about wiping her fingerprints off every surface she touched? Okay, so his gut failed the Sherlock test.

Pulling out on the highway, he mulled over yet another suspicious action – finding her in his storage room.

Had she been looking for the gold compass?

Possibly.

In the few minutes he'd been driving, his misgivings climbed until he began questioning the logic of bringing her into his home. He never brought business home, and purposely kept his two lives separate for his sister's benefit.

This could be a stupendous mistake.

But then he caught a small movement in his peripheral vision and glanced at her.

Angel rode quietly, staring straight ahead. Her squared shoulders boasted of confidence, but the death grip she had on that linen bag belied her stiff carriage.

He made yet another hundred-and-eighty-degree spin from guarded to protective.

She chewed on her lower lip. One hand relaxed, slipped from the bag in her lap. The ring he'd noticed on the flight was now missing from her finger.

Had she traded the ring for clothes or a few bucks?

Her fingers trembled against the material. Fear? Exhaustion? Hunger? Or all three?

Dammit. He had one thing straight in his mind. No one was getting their hands on her until he had his answers.

No one.

He had more than a few questions, but the best way to draw information from a reluctant individual was with slow, calculated conversation.

Right now, this angel was too spent and jumpy.

Guess he should be glad that Suarez had stopped by. Oh, his libido hadn't been a bit happy about the interruption, but the dressed up, pain-in-the-butt, Latin pretty boy's visit had been opportune. Given Zane a way to gain Angel's cooperation.

Having her close tonight would work in his favor. Now that he had her staying with him, it would be easy to get her print by the end of tonight. He had the perfect plan. Once he got her prints tonight, he'd drop them at Ben's lab first thing in the morning.

Then he'd know if he had to call in the authorities.

His chest squeezed at the idea of making that call.

He'd broken rules to save a life, but never to protect a criminal.

Chapter 13

Parking in front of the sandstone apartment building he'd lived in for a year, Zane mentally patted himself on the back for picking up the place earlier and restocking the refrigerator. He hadn't cleaned with a guest in mind, just made it habitable after being gone for most of two weeks.

Angel didn't let him reach her side of the truck before she jumped out, looking dead on her feet. She'd be able to crash out for a hard night's rest tonight if he had to stand guard over her the whole time.

He unlocked his navy-blue front door, stepping aside to allow Angel to enter first. Chilly air smelling of lemon furniture polish greeted them.

Hazy sunlight filtered through the patio doors into the expansive living room he didn't spend enough time in. She ambled to the middle of the room and stopped in front of the sliding glass doors. The linen bag slipped from her fingers to land next to her sneakers.

She stared with quiet assessment at the spectacular ocean vista beyond his patio. That had sold him on this location.

Stone walkways separated tiered layers of immaculate flowering gardens along a boardwalk to the pristine sandy beach. Curling emerald waves from the Atlantic crashed against the shore.

The sparkling serenity was lost on Zane.

He couldn't focus past the foreground. Loose strands of auburn hair dangled below her floppy hat. The white cotton shirt disappeared at the waistband of jeans that covered a sweet pair of cheeks.

"What a beautiful view," she sighed.

Honey, you have no idea. "One of the best I've ever seen," he muttered. He'd love to pull the hat off and finish the vision.

She looked over her shoulder at him. "What?"

Bright sunlight in the background haloed around her. Highlights danced across the curves of her body, tantalizing the image his mind was determined to create.

Oh yeah, he'd take that hat off.

In his fantasy, it would land on top of a pair of jeans and white cotton shirt already tossed on the bedroom floor.

"What'd you say?" she asked, exhaustion running her words together.

"Nothing," he answered. "Make yourself at home."

She didn't move a muscle. "Have you lived here long?"

"You mean in this apartment or Ft. Lauderdale?" He walked into the kitchen. "How about something to drink?"

"Water, please," she called out. "How long have you lived in Ft. Lauderdale?"

He handed her a chilled bottle on his way to open the glass doors to the patio.

"Three years." Heat blanketed him as he stepped onto the green and white ceramic tile. With the crook of his finger, Zane motioned Angel to follow then pulled out a black wrought-iron chair with a plush outdoor cushion on the seat.

"Take a load off."

Just as Angel set her water on the mosaic table surface, the doorbell chimed.

Damn. *Don't be Trish.* "Sit tight. I'll be right back." Zane strolled away, intent on handling this quickly.

Angel popped up, ready to leave if she recognized his guest. She had a clear view of Zane, but not the other person.

At the door, he stepped back to allow a tall young woman to enter. Thick black hair covered her head, falling in dainty curls around her face. She was striking with her dark hair and creamy complexion.

She wrapped two delicate arms around Zane's neck and planted a kiss on his cheek. They spoke quietly for a moment, Zane sounding serious about something he was saying.

Seeing those two together pricked her temper. She couldn't be jealous. She hardly knew this man.

Or the woman Zane was so cozy with. Black curls bounced every time she moved. Reminded Angel of a pixie, all delicate and pretty.

Angel had never been considered delicate.

She'd had to be in shape as an athlete and tough in prison. Delicate equaled dead in there. Eyeing Zane's visitor, Angel doubted that graceful, curvaceous body hugging all over him had ever spent forty-eight hours living through a torturous survival weekend or running a marathon.

Or living on catnaps for a year for fear of getting her throat slit.

She had every reason to be proud of what she'd accomplished. So why was she suffering a moment of feeling inadequate just because she stood so close to feminine perfection?

Zane's smile flattened out into a straight-line frown.

Now *that* improved Angel's mood.

A bit uncharitable on my part isn't it? Too bad. She could live with the guilt.

She moved a little closer to catch what was being said.

The twenty-something woman prancing around Zane in an ankle-length bright peach dress and straw sandals laced up her calf could be a professional model. She had a southern accent when she spoke. "Sugar, I'm fine, really. I told you. Heidi came to get me as soon as I called. You missed me, didn't you?"

"I always miss you," Zane answered, with a smile that bordered on tolerant.

Beginning to seriously dislike the beautiful visitor, Angel stepped all the way around the table and leaned forward to hear better.

The dark-eyed woman wrapped an arm around Zane's waist, hugging herself to him. "I came by three times this week looking for you. You're harder to catch than a shadow. Thanks for my surprise. I found the birdhouses when I came in this morning." Her sultry voice carried just enough sincerity to validate Angel's suspicions.

This woman was more to Zane than just a friend.

Did he intend to entertain another female while Angel slept on the couch? Not going to happen.

He gathered the dark-haired beauty close in an affectionate embrace.

Angel suffered a moment of longing. She wanted those strong arms wrapped around *her* body.

Hold it. What was wrong with her? This guy had a life and at least one girlfriend. What he did should not matter to her.

Besides, she'd be long gone once the coins surfaced. Hopefully tomorrow.

So watching those two shouldn't grate on her nerves.

"Who's that?"

Angel snapped to attention at the woman's question.

Zane strolled back to the patio with an arm around his guest's waist and said, "Trish, meet Angel, a friend of mine. Angel, this is my sister, Trish."

His sister? Ohhh. Immediate mood improvement. "Nice to meet you." Angel stuck her hand out.

Trish gave her an up and down once over then leaned forward, a little unsteady, to take her hand. "Angel, huh? Interesting name. Nice to meet you, too."

The tart smell of alcohol brushed over Angel. She forced herself not to wrinkle her nose in reaction and held her smile in place.

Trish turned to Zane. "I didn't realize you had company, but I'm glad you've given up celibacy. At least that rules out your being a priest." She chuckled at some personal joke.

"Trish." His single word came out full of warning.

"Okay, okay. No games today." She turned back to Angel, "Be nice to him. He's all I have." Trish pecked her brother's cheek. "Gotta go. Heidi's waiting. See you later, Sugar." With that she pranced out the door, reminiscent of a child on her way to play.

Angel started to call her back to correct Trish's misconception of the situation, but that familiar smell of alcohol had hijacked her thoughts. An odor that brought back sad memories of Angel watching as her mother died of the disease. She couldn't help thinking that Trish might be past the point of comprehending anything Angel tried to explain.

She moved backward until she could prop against the railing and watch as Zane closed the front door and returned to the patio. His impressive shoulders seemed to droop as though he carried an invisible yoke made of cast iron. He obviously cared about his sister.

Angel shrugged it off, turning her attention to the afternoon wind fanning nearby palm trees. Stiff-leaved branches rattled with each brief gust, giving background music to the serenity.

Zane stepped outside and took up a relaxed position, leaning against the outer wall across from her. He shoved his hands into the front pockets of his jeans in what was becoming a standard look for him. "Sorry. Wasn't expecting her."

Guess they were going to talk about his sister after all. "I enjoyed meeting her. She looks like you around the eyes and mouth. How close are you in age?"

"Trish is twenty-three. I'm nine years older."

"Why the big gap?"

"She was a mistake."

Hell of a way to describe his sister. What could she say to that? "I see."

"Whoa." Zane threw a hand up as a stop sign. "You don't understand. I love my baby sister like my next breath. *I* don't think she's a mistake, but my parents never planned on a second child."

Had Trish felt unwanted and turned to alcohol to numb the pain? Angel had lived around alcoholism. Drinking during the middle of the afternoon and middle of the week weren't good signs. "Does she work?"

"Trish has a small gift shop not far from here."

"How long has she had the shop?"

"About three months. I want to get her moved to Las Olas Boulevard, an older area of Ft. Lauderdale that's been revitalized."

"Why move if she's only been open three months?"

"Because she..." He paused as if he'd almost said too much and mentally edited as he spoke. "The gift shop's okay, but her heart's in working with antiquities. She could

make a go of it on Las Olas, but that takes a lot of capital.
We'll get there."

We? Was Zane in partnership with his sister? Sounded
like he had a financial investment as well as a personal one.
Why was Trish drinking during the day and stopping by
here when she had a business to run?

As though talking to himself, he murmured, "I won't lose
her."

Angel jerked her eyes to his face. She understood that
look, the desperate drive to keep someone alive. Had Trish's
new business happened as a result of her drinking?
Something Zane encouraged to keep his sister busy and
away from a bottle?

Angel understood wanting to fix someone, thinking that
if you tried hard enough and came up with all the right
ideas, it would stop the person you loved from destroying
her life.

But alcoholism had to be cured from the inside out and
that took the person with the problem wanting to make the
change.

Zane wouldn't want to hear that, especially from a
stranger so Angel offered, "Trish has the personality for a
people business."

He paused and answered slowly, a bit cranky. "She's
definitely a social butterfly."

Where was that edge in his voice coming from? "Lucky
for her that you travel and can find things for her store like
the birdhouse."

"Yeah, but that's not anything of value. Everyone carries
that kind of crap in home decorating shops. Trish should be
an estate appraiser. That's what she studied to do. Loves all
that old stuff." He seemed to have wandered off in thought,
brooding about something.

"It must be nice to for her to be self-employed and close
enough to pop in." Angel smiled, trying for something
positive to lift his spirits.

A longer pause, then Zane said, "But what you're really
saying is that you're surprised to see her here in the middle
of the day when she has a business to run."

Well, that was stupid. Now she'd ticked him off. She
remembered the days of being on edge whenever someone

mentioned her mother. Always expecting to be criticized because her mother was a drunk. Zane could be just as hypersensitive about his sister. "I didn't mean it to sound that way. I like Trish. She seems very sweet."

One thing she'd say about Zane was that his anger flared and dissipated with the same speed.

He lifted a hand and rubbed his chin. "You didn't do anything wrong. I get a little uptight when it comes to Trish. Her life hasn't been easy." He stared off into the distance. "My parents gave me every opportunity, but by the time Trish *accidentally* came along, they were tired of child rearing – what little they'd been interested in to begin with. I took off and she got the leftovers."

Angel couldn't stop the next words from falling out of her mouth because she'd drilled one mantra into her own head daily for years.

"Hard knocks make you a stronger person. From the sound of it, your sister is probably pretty tough." Seeing a family side of Zane piqued her interest to know more about the man who'd opened his home to her. "What do you mean by leftovers? You said you took off. Where'd you go?"

Even as he sheathed his face in a calm expression, pain trickled into his eyes. "I went into the Air Force when she turned nine. My parents pawned her off on friends and relatives so they could..." He paused to make air quotes. "'Enjoy their life.' Almost like they knew they'd die in a car crash before they reached fifty."

"I'm sorry, Zane."

He lifted his head as if hearing his name drew him. Standing away from the wall, he moved forward, slowly consuming her personal space.

She should back away and make her boundaries clear.

But she didn't. The only reason to withdraw would be out of fear and she wasn't afraid of him.

She'd lived her life in tiny moments for a long time and didn't want this one to end. Not yet. Probably exhaustion talking, but she wasn't up for arguing.

When he stood in front of her, Zane bent his head forward, focusing all that intense scrutiny on her. A formidable power swirled around him. He was rugged and confident and sexy as hell. Mere inches separated his face from hers. That urge was back. The one that had her holding her breath, wishing he'd follow through on the offer in his eyes. Just a kiss.

Where would be the harm?

But she couldn't instigate it.

She had so little experience with men she'd make a fool of herself.

He asked in low voice, "Now that we've cleared up Trish's history, what's yours ... *Angel?*"

When he said her name like that, as if it were a pet name, his voice reached inside her and stroked her heart.

She couldn't breathe for fighting this wild craving he brought on. A tornado churned behind the dark eyes drilling straight into her soul. Balmy ocean air ruffled his T-shirt and lifted fine hairs across her face.

He used a finger to brush the hairs away from her cheek. "Talk to me, Angel."

The softer he spoke the more he hypnotized her, but she didn't want to talk. Clouds diffused the late afternoon sun sweeping her along in the moment.

His aftershave teased her senses, blended with the salt air to draw her towards him. She wanted to erase the stern line of his wonderful mouth.

Angel raised her hand then lost the nerve to touch his lips.

He caught her hand, wrapping it in his long fingers. "You said I couldn't help. What can someone else do that I can't?"

His deep voice kept reeling her in closer and closer.

"Nothing," she whispered, not thinking about her answer beyond mumbling a response born of fatigue. If she curled up in the safety of his arms, would she finally sleep through the night? She couldn't think clearly. His large, warm hands had moved to her arms where he stroked slowly up and down, waking up her skin.

One kiss. She'd never wanted to kiss a man more than right now.

He leaned forward a tiny bit, their faces only a whisper apart. She softened her lips, anticipating.

"The truth, Angel, just tell me the truth so I can help you. Why are you avoiding the law?"

That broke the spell.

She flinched and backed away, cursing herself for letting her guard down when she should be vigilant. He still thought she'd committed a crime and had tried to seduce her into saying something she shouldn't. She managed to keep her temper in check. Only it wasn't just temper this time. It hurt.

So much for trusting men.

He asked, "What's wrong?"

Did he really expect her to believe he hadn't been trying to pull something? "Nothing."

"*Nothing* is female talk for something. I don't understand what I did wrong."

He was kidding, right? "Other than making me feel like a fool?"

"How'd I do that?" His surprise was too sincere to be faked.

Now she'd talked herself into a corner. "Never mind."

He lifted his hands. "Never mind is like nothing. Loaded with hidden meaning. Why're you angry?"

She'd wanted someone to ask her that for years so she could rant about all the injustices she'd suffered in silence. Maybe it was time to speak her mind. "You were trying to trick me."

"How?"

"By acting like you wanted to kiss me when that wasn't what you wanted at all."

"Like hell. I do want to kiss you."

She'd have enjoyed a moment of thrill over that admission if he hadn't shouted it. "Really? Does the idea of kissing a woman always make you this angry?"

"No, just you."

She couldn't think what to say to that. Well, the hell with him. She would not let him see how that had stuck a splinter in her heart. "Glad we got that straight."

He lifted his fist and thunked his head. "That didn't come out right."

Taking a breath, she composed herself to answer calmly. "I think it was perfectly clear." Before he could say another word, she changed the subject. "I hope a shower comes with my room-and-board deal, because I'd love one right now."

A muscle in his cheek jumped. He didn't make a sound.

To his credit, he wasn't shouting at her.

Not that he intimidated her. Far from it.

She hadn't realized until meeting Zane just how *much* she liked large men. Or maybe she just liked this one.

When he finally spoke, it came out with resignation and acceptance. "You still have the yellow shorts and T-shirt?"

"Yes, but I need to wash them."

"Tell you what. Give me those, then take off what you have on and drop your clothes outside of the bathroom over there." He pointed down the hall before continuing. "Take your time. Soak in the Jacuzzi if you want while I toss everything in the washer. There's a dispenser with soap and shampoo. Linens are in the tall cabinet. The bottom drawer of the middle cabinet has new toothbrushes, disposable things and female stuff you're welcome to use."

Oh? She made a sound of surprise before she caught herself. *Celibate, my ass.* His sister clearly wasn't up on just how much female traffic ran through this apartment.

"Don't give me that look, Angel."

"What look?" She could do innocent.

"Like I'm a man ho. My sister hates to be alone and, as you witnessed, she shows up whenever. She put that drawer together for when she spends the night here. There's a hairdryer and whatever in there, too."

She experienced a moment of relief for no reason, at least none that would make a lick of sense if she dissected it.

Digging out her clothes from the linen bag, she felt a little strange about handing the bundle to him. When was the last time anyone had washed *her* clothes? She'd done the laundry for everyone at home from the time she'd reached ten years old.

When Zane took the handful and disappeared into the kitchen, Angel headed for the bathroom where she peeled off the clothes she wore and deposited them outside the door. Every conceivable luxury installed in the luscious bath had been decorated in black marble with copper flecks and adorned with copper hardware. Very masculine.

Zane must do well in spite of his poor customer service attitude.

When she had a steaming hot tub of water and bubbles – *thank you, Trish* – Angel sank into what was certainly one step from heaven. Her muscles moaned at the welcome feel of hot water. She bathed slowly, enjoying more luxuries such as a razor and girlie soap. Soaked to the point of wrinkling, Angel finally forced herself to step over to the beveled glass shower so she could rinse off and wash her hair.

At the wall-to-wall mirror above the vanity, she tried to avoid her reflection until feminine vanity forced her to see how well she was healing. She'd lost some body weight from lack of eating and sleeping over the past week. Just a few yellowish fist-sized bruises remained across her back and thighs, but one ugly one still shined on her side. The last of her cuts were starting to heal.

Look at the positive. All those battle scars still belonged to a living body.

She brushed the tangles from her hair, and the parts that had dried began to curl half-heartedly. Couldn't she have curly *or* straight hair? No, it fell in half-assed curls. After seeing Trish's cute bobbed cut, Angel would love to cut hers, but couldn't. Not yet.

Shorten it now and she'd have few options if she had to change her appearance even more. For the time being she'd stuff the wimpy mass under her hat.

No disguise would keep Mason at bay for long.

Every hour that went by decreased her chances of remaining free.

Had Mason had incriminating evidence against her delivered anonymously to the FBI?

The coins had been stolen from Bolen Gallery in Boston. They were beyond rare. The news still carried sound bites. She needed to find someone who remembered a lone female runner on the trails outside Raleigh during the time of the theft – a person above reproach who would swear under oath that Angel had an ironclad alibi.

But how? Run an ad for witnesses?

She'd been a loner since getting out of prison and had lived in a two-room house out in the woods. The theft had happened over a weekend, or someone would have seen her working around Mason's warehouse. He swore he had evidence that placed her at the scene of the crime. Truth or lie?

Deal with one problem at a time.

The plan was coins first, alibi next, then cut a deal with the FBI. Until then, she had to stay on her toes to *avoid* the FBI. And, if she pulled all this off, *she'd* have the evidence to hang Mason.

He'd handled the clear sleeves that protected the coins.

This time, the fingerprint that put someone in prison would be his.

After wiping down everything she'd touched in the bathroom, Angel stuck her head out the door. Country music played in the living room. She called out softly, "Hello. I'm done. Are my clothes dry?"

Silence.She wrapped a thick towel around her that only reached a few inches above her knees and barely covered her breasts, but she wanted her clothes. Now. Holding the front of the towel with both hands, she tiptoed out to search for the laundry room and saw the washer and dryer through an open door on the other side of the kitchen.

Her clean clothes sat folded on top of the dryer.

But that meant walking across the kitchen half naked.

Where was Zane? Had he stepped out?

The bath had refreshed her more than she realized and now she was rethinking the idea of staying here tonight. That meant the risk of bringing trouble to Zane's door. All she had to do was check at the marina each day until the package arrived. She could find shelter until then, somewhere far from Zane and his sister.

He'd done more than enough by helping her escape Raleigh.

If she worked out a WITSEC deal with the FBI, she'd have them send a letter to Zane explaining everything.

Her chest hurt at the idea of leaving. It would be so easy to stay, but Zane couldn't solve her problems and didn't deserve to be caught in the crossfire if Mason caught up with her.

She'd have to dress right here for any hope at getting out the door fast enough.

Chapter 14

Zane heard Angel call out the second time as he finished his conversation with the High Vision representative.

No definitive time as yet for picking up their overseas shipment expected to arrive in Jacksonville any day now. He'd fly out the minute he was notified. Zane had three days left to prove to High Vision he was the perfect choice to handle their southeastern cargo shipping.

It might be easier to hand the entire contract to one of the other two groups contending for their business, but Zane had outperformed both of them every time they went head to head in the southeast. This was his territory.

By the time he ended his call and checked on Angel, the bathroom was vacant. His stomach fell.

Was she gone again?

He rushed toward the kitchen, halting one step from plowing through the knee-to-shoulder café doors that hung between the kitchen and living room.

The curvaceous body that had raced through his dreams came into view, barely covered with a towel.

Good thing he'd stopped here. The swinging doors hid just how much he appreciated what the terrycloth didn't cover of Angel's body. His mouth turned to cotton just looking at those legs. *Don't even think about looking at her chest.*

She turned around and caught him staring. Guilty.

Now handcuff me and make me pay.

He should turn around and walk away. But if it were that easy, he'd have done it already.

She cleared her throat and asked, "Did you want

something?"

Loaded question. Hell, yes, he wanted something. Her.

Admitting that wouldn't earn him any points. Not after he'd screwed up on the patio. Had he really said wanting to kiss her made him angry? *Idiot.* She'd thought he was trying to trick her.

He scrubbed a hand over his face. "Find everything okay?"

"Yes."

Damp strands of cinnamon hair licked her shoulders. One wisp clung to her cheek. She tucked the end of the towel in tighter at the top of her toga wrap, sending his damned gaze there. Drops of water trickled down her slender neck to the slight crevice created by two soft mounds of ivory breast.

Following that trickle with his tongue would be heaven.

Spending a night in the same apartment with her and only *thinking* about chasing that water droplet might kill him.

"Give me a minute and I'll get dressed." She lifted the wad of clothes to her chest.

He wanted to kick himself. She didn't need some guy leering at her after all she'd been through. And he didn't even know everything she'd been through.

"I heard you call, but I was on the phone," he mumbled, backing away. "I'll wait in the front room." He turned and walked away, hearing the sounds of her footsteps hurrying behind him from the kitchen to the bathroom. By the time the door closed, he still stood at rock hard attention. If she dressed slowly enough, he might be at ease by the time she got back.

Think about ... flying.

What the hell was wrong with him? He had better control than that, but dammit he'd never been turned on so fast around a woman who wasn't trying to raise his interest.

Angel sure as hell wasn't trying to encourage him. She wouldn't even be here now if he hadn't coerced her into staying with him. He'd have done worse than manipulate her if it kept her off the streets and somewhere he could protect her.

No, he couldn't blame Angel for his lack of control.

He'd dated some hot women and had no trouble finding someone to spend a night burning off energy with, so this clawing need to keep her close and to touch her made no sense. He was overdue for some serious downtime. This proved it, because Angel was pretty, but nothing like the women he normally chose.

He'd never gone for thin and muscular.

Liar. That body was trim and well toned.

And her eyes were too big for her face.

Soft eyes that carried too much living for someone her age and more emotion than she liked revealing. When her guard dropped an inch, her lashes would lower to half-mast.

Then she'd smile.

Yeah, she had a heart-stopping smile and legs ... good Lord, what a set ... that went on forever and...

Hell. He started getting hard again and she wasn't even in the room.

He had the discipline of a goat.

Shaking his head, he wandered into the kitchen. Maybe another bottle of ice-cold water would help – poured over his crotch.

If that didn't do the trick, then how about remembering that he had yet to figure out whether she was a criminal. That should douse any spark of desire that flamed up.

Angel walked into the kitchen just as Zane managed to stuff his reaction to her under a veil of polite indifference.

She eyed him warily and hooked a thumb on the waist of her jeans.

For some reason, it dawned on him right then that she hadn't given him any panties to wash.

Don't go there.

He'd understand his reaction if she dressed in some skimpy outfit, had her hair styled and makeup exaggerating her finer qualities, but she didn't have a speck of makeup and only wore the cotton shirt and jeans again.

Damn if it wasn't fresh and attractive. He particularly liked the soft, barely-there curls showing up as her hair air-dried. What would it feel like to run his hands through those fine strands or feel them brush against his chest?

He gritted his teeth. Polite indifference, remember?

Got it.

She turned her shirtsleeves up at her wrists, eyes not really settling on any one spot. "Thanks for letting me use your bath. I feel much better." A loud growl erupted from her stomach.

"Sounds like you're ready for dinner." When was the last time she'd eaten? "Give me a minute to clean up and we'll grab a bite." He wanted to check the bathroom before they went anywhere. Before walking away, he pinned her with a serious stare. "You *will* be here when I come back, won't you?"

That she took a moment to answer told him she'd been contemplating leaving, but he'd noticed that she tended to dance around the truth rather than rattle off a lie. After a long sigh, she nodded. "I'll wait."

Zane accepted her word, but also had a security monitor in his bathroom with lights that would indicate if anyone opened a door or a window. He shut himself inside the bathroom then squatted down to view the counter and faucets. Every inch had been wiped clean. He lifted the water bottle she'd tossed into the trash basket next, but knew he'd find no fingerprints there either.

Impressive, in an extremely suspicious way.

No problem.

He had the perfect place to eat. The owner would supply him with her entire set of tableware if Zane asked for it.

Making quick work of his shower while keeping an eye on the security monitor, Zane strolled back into his living room. He found Angel planted in the middle of the floor gazing out the glass doors. Was she so uncomfortable around the strange environment that she wouldn't sit down on the leather furniture?

Or was she so careful to not leave a print?

"Ready?" he asked.

Turning to answer him, concern shadowed her face. "Can't we

just order a pizza?"

"I know a great little Italian restaurant, really a hole in the wall. Only locals go there. They make the best pizza, but you should try their lasagna."

She slumped in defeat, obviously tired. Once he fed her a decent meal, she'd probably sleep like the dead.

Cutting her eyes back over to the glass doors to where purple twilight closed in on the beach, she must have seen something that made her decision. "If it's not too expensive," she mumbled.

"I'll buy dinner. Consider it a bonus for pacifying Suarez today." He doubted money mattered as much in her agreement to go as the fact that the sun was setting. Dark offered protection from being easily seen.

"Just a minute." She retrieved her hat and bag, twisted her hair up and shoved the hat on. "Okay, I'm ready."

Hat or not, he'd recognize that body. Who did she hope to outfox? He herded her to the truck, ready to finally nail down her identity. But would he be just as pleased with himself once he had fingerprint results tomorrow?

In the four miles to the restaurant, the scenery deteriorated from snazzy to worn out. While he described how the area had changed in a mere three years, Angel looked where he pointed but rode in silence, hands in her lap, touching nothing. Her discipline was remarkable, and at the same time disconcerting.

He pulled into a rundown strip mall with one significant store in the center surrounded by small eclectic retail shops. Once a high-end grocery, the cavernous anchor of the center now housed a sprawling flea market he'd spent a couple of outings wandering through with Trish when he couldn't get out of it.

Parking in front of *De Nikki's*, he strolled around to open Angel's door. She stepped down, eyes cautiously flicking about, which put him on alert.

Inside the restaurant, a rotund Nikki, with a salt-and-pepper handlebar mustache, greeted Zane like a lost cousin. Nikki had a heavy crowd for this early on a Thursday night. Must have something to do with the upcoming holiday weekend when locals dined out the night before the tourists descended.

As Nikki directed them to a small table in the back, Zane almost ran over Angel when she abruptly stopped in front of him.

He caught her shoulders to keep from knocking her

down.

"What's wrong?" he asked, quickly scanning the room, taking in the people and assessing everything for threats in a matter of seconds. Nothing appeared out of place. What had pricked her attention?

The smile she offered him was countermanded by vivid apprehension in her eyes.

"Clumsy. I stumbled."

Nikki had noticed them not following and walked back. "Problem?"

She smiled the way women do to make men think everything is fine. "Where's your ladies room?"

Nikki pointed to the far side of the entrance. "To the left of the front door, next to the hostess stand."

Zane didn't want to let her out of his sight, but what could he do? He'd sound ridiculous telling her not to go, especially while Nikki listened. He caught her by the arm as she stepped away. "Are you okay?"

"I'm fine."

She didn't look fine. Something had rattled her.

"Please, Zane, people are staring." Angel slipped from his hold and walked quickly back the way they'd come then scooted into the ladies room.

He gave the dining room another once over before going to wait for her at the hostess stand. Nothing unusual stood out. He might be reading more into this than he should.

Nikki stepped around Zane and asked, "Is there a problem, Mr. Zane?"

Before he answered, Zane waited until a slender, middle-aged man in a gunmetal gray suit stepped past them on his way to the front door. Zane gave the man a second look, then grimaced at the direction of his thoughts. Here he was, acting suspicious of Nikki's clientele when in truth Angel was the dubious one.

He answered Nikki. "No. My friend hasn't felt well and I'm a little concerned. I'll wait to see how she's doing before we sit down."

"Oh, poor thing. Not a problem. You just tell me if you want me to fix something to go."

"Thanks, Nikki. Oh, one more thing. Is that the only door in and out of the bathroom?"

Nikki gave him a quizzical look. "Yes. That is it."

Ten minutes later, patience spent, Zane asked Nikki to send a waitress in to check on Angel.

The girl returned immediately, wide-eyed and confused. "The bathroom is empty."

Chapter 15

Zane pounded his steering wheel.

What could have spooked Angel?

He'd been confident she couldn't get past him. He knew the *men's* room had no other way out than the door used to enter. Unfortunately, an exterior wall on one side of the ladies room held two old-fashioned crank-out windows, which she'd managed to slip through.

His chest tightened at the thought of her alone again on the streets. The change of clothes helped to camouflage her, but she'd been worried about spending money on food. How far could she travel on limited funds?

Another aggravating thought hit him.

He still didn't have a fingerprint. Damn.

Zane kept methodically cruising streets around the area near the restaurant. Maybe she'd run a sufficient distance to feel safe and stop. If she saw his truck, he wanted to believe she'd trust him enough to come out of hiding.

Trust him? She didn't trust him at all or she'd tell him who was chasing her.

He drove slowly through the residential sections near the restaurant, up and down back streets. Solitary streetlights illuminated crossroads, but not much else. She could be hidden anywhere within the unlit maze of thirty-year-old homes surrounded by enormous tropical vegetation.

No lost female flagged him down.

An hour later, he quit the hunt, frustrated at losing her a second time. His own stomach growling, he picked up a pizza on his way home. A mild wind blew through the silent parking lot of his complex as he locked the truck. He carried the pizza into his apartment, dropped it in the kitchen then walked through the living room to slide the door open to his patio.

And froze.

Angel was curled up in a corner, asleep and hidden from view by a thick bush on the other side of the patio railing.

She was alive. He kept telling himself that so his chest would relax.

For the second time that day, relief flooded through him.

He should shake her until her teeth rattled for the anxiety she'd put him through. But lying there with that floppy hat half on her head, she looked so vulnerable that all he wanted to do was wrap her in his arms, tuck her close, and keep her safe.

Another day of this and he'd lose his mind.

He opened the door slowly and stepped into the warm night breeze. She stirred. Her eyes blinked open then she jerked, looking around, clearly trying to orient herself. Two exhausted amber eyes peered up at him, looking as relieved as he felt.

He gave her a moment then walked over and squatted down. "Hey there."

She murmured something that echoed his words.

He ran the back of his finger lightly along her baby soft cheek, inhaling the fresh smell of shampoo, no mousse, no spray, just plain shampoo. How could soap and shampoo smell sexy? He didn't know, but it did.

The urge to kiss her hit him square in the chest.

Kissing her might make him feel better, but he wouldn't risk anything that would send her running again. He spoke softly to not startle her. "I was worried about you. Where'd you go?"

She rubbed her eyes and mumbled something that sounded like, "A guy stared. Didn't know, um, had to go. Sorry, don't worry."

Her eyes fluttered a couple of times.

This little Energizer Bunny was out of energy. No run left in her. Damp hair stuck to her face from a light sheen of sweat. She must have traveled the four miles back on foot.

"Come on, Angel, you need to sleep." He snaked his arm around her waist to lift her to a standing position.

She let him lead her forward, but once inside the apartment she stopped, shook her head, and said, "Not until I get another shower."

The back of her blouse was damp from her exertions. He'd seen no clothes other than the running outfit she'd worn when he first met her.

"Sure. I'll give you one of my T-shirts to sleep in and we'll throw your clothes back in the washer," he said.

"Thanks. Really sorry to be so much trouble."

"Honey, it's no trouble, but I wish you'd tell me what's going on."

She smiled, the shy expression too sweet to be criminal. "I don't want you to get mixed up in this mess. You've been so nice to me. I owe you that."

He sighed. One tap and she'd fall over. He hadn't slept much during the last two weeks himself. Any questions would keep until tomorrow. "I'll get you the T-shirt."

By the time Angel walked into the kitchen fresh from her shower, Zane sat at the counter sifting through mail. She wore his pale blue cotton T-shirt with a redfish busting a wave on the front. It hung halfway down her thighs.

Nothing else, just her and the T-shirt. He knew it.

Warning signals screamed from the side of his brain that had been trained to take note of suspicious activity. No one wiped her fingerprints clean everywhere she went. She'd been held captive – he was certain – and then chased down by a deadly group. He'd caught her digging through his storage room looking for something he'd bet played a major role in her tenuous situation. Hard not to think that when his instincts said she'd followed him from Jacksonville looking for whatever she'd lost.

His mission should be clear – determine her identity and find out if she was tangled up in anything illegal that could cause him big trouble.

With complete lack of regard for all that logic, his body was still interested in all that creamy skin not covered by his T-shirt.

She's probably cold, the brain in his pants suggested. Yeah. She might be chilled, need him to run his hands over that exposed skin and warm her up.

Or he might just be a goat after all.

Zane beat his randy side back into submission and tried to see her with the objective threat assessment skills expected of someone with his background.

He'd studied the enemy. He should pay more attention to the criminal behavior.

But she didn't fit the profile of a threat of any kind. Damp hair framed her face. A soapy clean fragrance filled the air between them. She couldn't seem to *lie* to him without acting as though she felt guilty. His eyes trailed down the two enticing legs that spanned the break between shirttail and floor.

There were dozens of reasons he should keep an emotional wall between the two of them.

But right now he didn't want a wall between them.

Hell, he didn't want that T-shirt between the two of them and couldn't ignore the inappropriate thought pounding through his mind.

The only thought firing every cell in his brain.

He wanted her. Bad.

"Pizza smells good." She raised her eyebrows, waiting to be invited.

Don't make her ask for food, moron. "Sure. Here." He opened the box. "Want it heated?"

"Nuh uh. It's perfect." She picked up a slice and proceeded to devour it like he'd served her Beluga caviar. She licked her rosy lips after each bite, the pink tongue destroying his state of mind.

He broke loose a slice and lifted it to his mouth. Kept his eyes averted, anything to shut down the crazy fantasies over how much he wanted to feel that mouth on his body. She'd wiped out three slices by the time he'd finished one.

But then he'd lost his appetite – for food.

Pausing, she caught her breath, seeming at peace after eating pizza. "I'm ready for bed."

Dangerous visual.

He should be able to sleep around the clock at this point, but had serious doubts he'd get any rest. Not with her lying on a bed within the same walls – wearing next to nothing. Before he could dislodge that image, she interrupted his thoughts.

"If the foldout has sheets ... I'm set."

No way. If she slept that close to the front door she'd turn into smoke and float out through the keyhole.

He cleared his throat. "You sleep in the bedroom. I've got buddies who come by unannounced sometimes. You don't want to be out here if one of them shows up." He could tell she didn't believe him, but what argument could she offer?

It was true anyway. Ben was liable to show up at any hour, too ramped up on his weird geek adrenaline to go home after working a bust or a crime scene. Or he *would* be liable to show up, if his wife wasn't about to spit out a Ben Mini-Me.

Angel finished a last bite of pizza, then grabbed a sponge and scrubbed her area with the efficiency of a compulsive cleaner. Could that explain the neatnik personality?

Maybe she had a germ phobia.

Yeah, sure. If he believed that, he'd be buying swampland in the Mojave Desert next.

At the door to his bedroom, he watched her climb between the sheets. Silky hair trailed across the pillow. She rolled onto her side with a whispered, "Good night."

That pumped another painful throb through his groin. Zane pulled the door almost shut then headed for a shower.

Cold water would only do so much.

He was up and down during the night to confirm she still slept in his bed. With each check on her, she'd shifted to a different position, slowly leaving less and less sheet covering her.

The last time he peered through the small opening between the door and the doorframe, a band of moonlight beamed over her backside from the break in the drapes. She lay face down on her stomach. The T-shirt had ridden up to her waist from tossing about.

Yep, he'd been right. No underwear.

Shit.

He'd never been a damned voyeur. Forcing himself back to the foldout, he battled through the few hours left until daylight. The bad thing about going so long without rest was the danger of sleeping too deeply, which wouldn't be a problem if not for needing to hear Angel if she tried to sneak out.

No *if* to it.

When she *did* sneak out, he'd be ready for her.

Chapter 16

Mason answered his cell phone. "Lorde."

"ML, got news," CK reported.

"Good news, I hope." Mason was in neither a patient nor a forgiving mood. But one man had never failed him. If anyone could find his treasure and the bitch who'd stolen it, CK was that man.

"It's all in how you look at it. Your hot little number has gone south."

"How far south?" Mason sat forward in his leather chair, hand automatically reaching for the gold compass that had also gone missing. Angelina wouldn't get far now that his bounty hunter had caught her trail.

"Way down. She thumbed rides with truckers. Last one dropped her in Ft. Lauderdale."

Florida. Why would she go there? Her background checks had been thorough. Angelina's parents were dead. She had no siblings, didn't even list a next of kin when he'd hired her. Had listed a charity sponsoring Olympic hopefuls as her beneficiary for her retirement fund.

When he'd hired her, her prison record had played in her favor. She hadn't known it at the time, just thrilled that he'd offered her a position in his warehouse.

And she'd been his best employee, busting her butt above and beyond in every aspect of her job.

How could he have misjudged her so badly? He'd been certain she'd play ball once he brought her into the secret side of his international organization. Who'd have expected an ex-con to possess an honest streak?

Mason asked, "What's next?"

"Just got the background on that pilot who picked her up."

"Vic said the guy didn't know anything about her."

"Could be, but he flies out of a Ft. Lauderdale airfield."

Mason considered everything. "You think they're working together?"

"Hard to imagine, based on her info in the file you gave me. The pilot checks out like Mr. Clean, nothing to indicate any connection between those two or between him and you. But she probably found out where he lives or at least where he keeps his plane."

"And the little bitch went running down there looking for a shoulder to cry on and a place to hide," Mason thought out loud.

"Want the pilot picked up?"

"Not yet." Mason hadn't reached this point in his life by allowing anyone to intimidate him, but that fucking Czarion had warned him against drawing the attention of law enforcement. "Find her and put a tail on the pilot. Grab her the minute you can, but catch her alone. I want her by Saturday and without drawing attention. Call me as soon as you have her. Do whatever it takes, but make sure she's alive."

"Will do." The connection ended.

When the time came to end Angelina's life, Mason wanted that privilege. He just hoped he hadn't given CK too much leeway with capturing her. CK could stretch the meaning of "do whatever it takes." The downside of dealing with this bounty hunter was his rumored sex binges.

Mason had wanted Angelina from the minute she'd walked into his warehouse and would have enjoyed her at his compound the first time he'd visited her here if not for her ill-advised attempt to flee. He'd been forced to teach her humility, then wait on her recovery.

Silly twit. She'd been useless for days after that, unconscious most of the time. When he found her this time, he'd bring her to heel, but with restraint. He wanted her fully aware and pleading for mercy when he took her.

Just as soon as he had the coins in hand and Czarion off his back. She'd pay for that, too.

No one humiliated Mason and lived.

Chapter 17

Angel struggled, her feet wouldn't move. Couldn't run.

She came awake with a start and pushed up on her elbows.

No men with guns. No dogs. No Mason.

Her feet were tangled in a sheet. She fell back against the gigantic bed, smelling Zane as if he slept next to her.

She missed him. No reason to miss someone she shouldn't even be hanging around, but she did and had awakened an hour ago searching the room for him before crashing back to sleep.

Shouldn't have fallen back asleep and opened the door to nightmares.

Mason's ice-blue eyes had seemed so real her skin still crawled at the thought of him touching her. She shook it off and climbed out of the gigantic bed, stretching her stiff muscles. The room felt big and protective, like Zane. A framed photo on a teak chest across the room caught her eye. Using the tail of her T-shirt as a barrier against touching the frame, she carried the photo to the window.

She angled the picture under the light. A much younger Zane hugged a teenage Trish who was dressed in a graduation gown. Pride burst through his wide grin. The man was seriously hot without the smile, but add that and his desirability stock went up triple.

Trish had been blessed with the devotion of an older brother.

What would it have been like to grow up with a strong, protective male watching over her?

All Angel could credit her father with was feeding and clothing her and her mother. He'd been more a stranger than a parent. She'd never questioned his late night security work. Not until a detective had snapped handcuffs on her wrists, then charged her with delivering drugs for her father.

She'd received a crash course in the world behind bars.

Honesty had always been her policy – a trait learned at her mother's knee long before alcohol had changed that – but the detective had taught Angel the fallacy in being forthright. She'd spilled everything, answering every inquiry he put to her in the interrogation room. She'd been sure she'd walk out a free woman.

Then he'd turned the tape recording over to the District Attorney who'd used her as another notch in his political belt.

Her first hard lesson in life had been simple.

Don't trust a man, particularly if he had anything to do with law enforcement.

Angel replaced the photo and slipped through the door connecting Zane's bedroom to his master bathroom. A haggard face stared back at her from the mirror. She twisted her hair into a knot on top of her head while she waited for the air-conditioning to kick on again. The pleasant hum of the cooling system would cover any noise she'd make attending to her personal needs and dressing.

Trish's large vanity drawer was filled with a stash of hair clips, makeup, lotions, and other feminine needs. When Angel found a bottle of plum colored nail polish, she had the sudden urge to primp.

The last time she'd dolled up had been in high school. As a lanky teen, taller than the majority of the girls and many boys, she'd been more at home on the track than on a date. Her one serious relationship had lasted two weeks. Just long enough to lose her virginity to a boy who'd sworn his love then revoked that decree by sleeping with Angel's only girlfriend.

Her nails needed help, but plum polish wouldn't save them. She hadn't worn makeup since getting out of jail, preferring to project a clear "not interested" message to men in general.

Most men heeded her unspoken message, allowing her a wide berth – until Zane.

Tall, sexy, imposing Zane.

If she hung around any longer she'd be tempted to give in to the desire she'd seen burn through his gaze more than once. Talk about a heady feeling for someone like her. He kept his emotions hidden beneath a "just want to help" façade most of the time, but some reactions were too strong for anyone to shield.

Other women might be put off by a man his size walking his eyes up and down their bodies, but for the first time in many years Angel had welcomed the flattery. Her dormant feminine side had come alive, curious to find out what those suggestive gazes offered. She *so* wanted to meet him halfway.

To know that kind of happiness just once in her life.

Timing had never been in her favor.

Reality trampled her fantasies. She rolled her eyes. In what universe would she have a relationship with someone like Zane? Her attraction to the sexy pilot could not cause her to lose sight of goals one and two – survival and vindication.

A man had gotten her into this mess. Getting involved with another one wouldn't solve her problems.

Enough daydreaming.

If she'd had any other option last night, she'd have avoided coming back here, but she had no excuse to stay now when Mason would retaliate against Zane with deadly force. Her debt to Zane just kept growing.

Putting him and Trish at risk was no way to pay it back.

She peeked out the door to the living room.

Zane still slept, snoring softly. She smiled at knowing that little detail.

Padding to the laundry room, she changed to her too-bright running shorts, jog top, and T-shirt. No choice when she needed the freedom to run if need be. After he'd helped her, the last thing she'd do was take anything from him, even though he'd probably hand over every t-shirt he owned if he thought she needed them. That was just the kind of man he was. She jammed her other clothes into the shoulder bag before pulling on the limp baseball cap.

Her Annie Hall look, as Zane had tagged it, had failed to fool a middle-aged man in a gray suit at the restaurant. She'd barely caught his expression of surprise when they'd entered. His face had shuttered back to bored so quickly she'd have missed the tiny change had she not been intentionally searching the room for a note of recognition.

There was always the possibility that she'd imagined the brief facial alteration, but she didn't think so. He might be one of Mason's men or someone he'd hired from down here.

Mason's subordinates showed no mercy to anyone who got in their way. She'd prayed that the man in the restaurant would follow her instead of Zane, but he'd have to have been fleet of foot to keep up with her.

Even tired, she ran world-class times.

Add in adrenaline and no one would catch her.

Maybe she'd been wrong to run to Zane, but she'd been out of options and ... damn him, he'd made her want him.

Want to run to him.

Opening her eyes to find Zane looking at her when he'd found her curled up on his patio had been better than the day she'd walked out of prison and her body trembled at the deep breath of freedom she'd inhaled. Zane was unlike any other man she'd ever met. He went from roaring annoyance to gentle and kind at warp speed.

A complete gentleman.

Yeah, until he stripped you with his eyes in the kitchen.

That didn't actually make him any less of a gentleman in her eyes, just a man enjoying what he saw.

She'd forgotten what it was like to crave a man's touch. But she craved Zane's.

Angel pinched the bridge of her nose.

Get out of here. She had to, before she did something stupid like give Mason a reason to kill the most decent man she'd ever known.

She tiptoed to the front door, running shoes in hand.

Zane slept with a white undershirt covering his broad chest, a mat of black hair curled at the scoop neck. One rope-muscled thigh poked out from under the thin sheet covering his lower half.

The man was pure sex wrapped up in a steel casing.

She smiled sadly then mouthed the words, "You're sweet.

Bye," and blew a kiss.

~*~

Zane flicked one eyelid open just wide enough to catch Angel's air kiss as the door closed. Hot damn, he'd been right to deactivate his alarm system last night on the gamble that she'd run this morning. Now he had a shot at gathering some intel. Anything that would give him a clue to who she was and who or what she was running from.

He grabbed the shoes he'd stashed under the end table. The shirt and shorts he'd worn to bed for her benefit saved the time he'd spend having to dress. That would keep her from gaining much of a head start. He laced his running shoes and ran out the door.

Intentionally letting her go was a calculated risk that would blow up in his face if he lost track of her.

He saw her turn south down the main highway just as he hit the sidewalk, but she was still close enough that he could keep her in sight. Brilliant rays of sun pierced the ruby horizon above the ocean on his left, highlighting her perfectly in the distance.

Angel's stride lengthened to a loping jog.

Where could she be headed?

In spite of the early morning cool air, sweat trickled down his back from the rising humidity. He maintained a steady pace over the first mile. As he kept a safe space between them, his mind worked through the possibilities.

Could she be meeting someone?

He kept track of her with his peripheral vision. A person could feel someone watching them. Based on what he'd seen, Angel should be looking for thugs in huge SUVs and shouldn't notice just another runner among several others taking advantage of the early morning low temps.

Her repeated, quick head checks answered his main question.

She wasn't meeting anyone, but avoiding someone.

She cut across the street then took a sharp corner. Twice she made a complete loop to end up somewhere she'd already passed. He didn't understand at first, but finally grasped that she was backtracking to circle behind anyone who might be following.

It was a good tactic, and she was smart. But he'd been following her for half an hour and she hadn't realized he was on her tail. He'd had training. He'd bet his truck that she'd had none and was running on pure street-hardened instinct. He admired her evasive maneuvers.

As he neared a heavy business district, the street traffic picked up on the divided four-lane highway alongside where they ran.

How long could she hold this pace?

The screech of tires against asphalt disrupted the morning peace.

One look at the black sport utility and Angel took off as if she'd been shot from a cannon.

Chapter 18

At the skidding sound of a vehicle braking hard, Angel stumbled and spun around.

A black Land Rover. No identifying logo on the side, but she didn't need a gold triangle to confirm she was in trouble.

She spun away. Pedestrians impeded her progress as she cut in and out of small groups ambling along the sidewalks. She dashed through the middle of an intersection, running against the traffic then shifted easterly, towards the beach.

Rounding a corner, she slid to a stop, stymied.

Either the buildings were too tight, with one fence connected to the next, or the land so sparse it offered nowhere to hide. She stood out bright as a caution flag in a car race.

Keep moving or die.

She spotted an opening to the beach between two towering condominiums further down and plowed through the soft dunes toward the surf. The hot breath of fear clogged her lungs. Would he kill her and walk away from the coins?

No. Not Mason.

Wading through the deep sand conjured the image of sinking into a quicksand pit. She whipped her head around, expecting a black sport utility to fly airborne over the dunes, ala Hollywood.

On the other side of the dunes, the sand firmed under her feet.

Miles of shimmering beach stretched in both directions bordered by the rolling ocean on one side and an endless row of skyscraping structures on the other.

She turned south into a salty breeze.

With solid ground underfoot, she sped down the packed surface trying to outdistance Mason's men, even if she hadn't outwitted them. They might be incapable of hanging with her on foot, but their radios could always outrun her.

She passed a group of shirtless old men surf fishing. A loose shoelace slapped one ankle. Way down the beach, tiny people speckled the wide shoreline. None were running towards her with guns drawn so she stopped and squatted down to retie the shoelace.

Her fingers deftly performed the task while her eyes swept over the beach. She started to rise when a *ping* sounded.

Sand blasted up next to her foot.

She charged away from the surf with the speed of a missile seeking a target and sped toward the protection of the buildings and highway. She hadn't moved this fast since the last time she'd been in a dead heat finish at a road race. Her heart beat painfully against her breastbone.

Maybe Mason *would* kill her.

Otherwise, why would his men take a shot at her – unless they assumed she carried the coins on her body?

At the ocean side of a high-rise condominium, she slowed enough to work her way around the fence circling the pool area. A driveway bordered the side. She scampered down the paved path to a connecting parking lot.

Finding the only obvious hiding spot between a tour van and a late model Cadillac, Angel ducked down to get her bearings.

She forced herself to take deep, slow breaths to quiet her panting.

A car passed slowly.

She raised her head above the sedan hood to see a two-lane road with vacant structures and local retail businesses scattered among souvenir shops.

None were open for business, yet. Damn.

She had to keep moving until she found a place to hide. An abandoned building was her best bet for cover until nightfall.

Three well-done senior citizens picked their way down the sidewalk, a block south from where she hid. From the north, a cocoa-skinned teenage girl in tights pumped weights, speed walking towards Angel on the same side of the street.

As the girl passed her, Angel jumped out to the sidewalk and dashed across the thoroughfare at the nearest intersection.

She turned down an alley next to a long, derelict brick building and grabbed the first door.

It was locked tight. *Damn!* She ran further down and tried two more. No good. The last one opened. With a quick look behind her, she stepped inside the dark space.

She squeezed her eyes shut and opened them slowly. With her eyes adjusted, she stumbled through debris on the floor, breathing the mildew-tinged air. Shafts of light pierced through cracks in the disintegrating roof.

This had potential.

Noises echoed through the hollow structure. She stopped. Scurrying sounds wafted to her from different directions. The place was probably a breeding ground for every imaginable critter. Domestic animals weren't a concern, but after her time in jail she had a deep-seated fear of rats.

Flashes of light beaconed from a door swinging half off the hinges on the far side of the narrow building. She picked her way to the opening then waited for several minutes, making sure the coast was clear, before forcing herself to move again.

At the rear of the building, a narrow street ran along like a back door access road. A large produce truck was being unloaded at a grocery a block away to her right. She eased to her left, moving away from the activity until encountering a wooden barricade that connected the next two buildings, blocking any exit.

The longer she remained exposed, the higher her pulse jacked. It would take a helicopter to keep up with her twisting route, but right now she had a deep appreciation for a duck flying around on opening day of hunting season.

The nearby crunch of footsteps on gravel froze her.

She started to go, then stopped.

Which way? Her heartbeats spiked the longer she stood paralyzed in indecision.

What had she learned in survival training?

Indecision got you killed. Instincts took over.

She ran in short bursts, casting hasty looks over her shoulder, and paused behind a stack of tires at the rear of an abandoned gas station. Her heart raced, every breath coming in painful bursts.

She fought to keep the panic at bay, but couldn't ignore the truth.

Mason would eventually kill her.

She didn't want it to be today.

Her options were disintegrating into thin air. She had no clue where she was or how to find transportation out of this city. Her hands shook as she swiped perspiration away from her eyes. The hat had flown off, somewhere. She could feel her hair hanging loose on one side.

It didn't matter.

The gunman had recognized her, hat or no hat.

Hands shaking, she picked her way around the garbage-strewn rear of the gas station and peered down a wall shrouded in thick green ivy vines. Next door, clumps of thorny sandspur plants covered the vacant lot, offering no protection.

The derelict station offered the only possible hideout she could find. There were several doorway openings not completely overtaken by vines on the whitewashed concrete block structure. With trembling fingers, she felt her way along the wall as she eased toward the street, sticking tight as a shadow to the building.

Yellow shoes and a bright yellow shirt – some shadow.

As she passed the first two openings, dilapidated exterior bathrooms, she gave each an obligatory glance then held her breath against the stench and moved on.

She considered ducking into the next open doorway to what at one time must have been the waiting area of the service station. Tall half broken glass windows stretched from the other side of the doorway to wrap around the front.

Damn. She couldn't hide there. Had to keep moving.

She headed toward the street. Just as she cleared the doorway of the station, a massive hand covered her mouth and a powerful arm encircled her chest, jerking her inside.

He had her.

Chapter 19

"Shhh. It's me, Zane."

Angel slumped, her back against his chest and her relief so vivid it was a living thing. When he moved the hand that covered her mouth, she muttered, "I don't deserve your help, but I'm glad to have it."

With her no longer resisting, he switched his hold from one of capture and restraint to support and comfort. He cupped the side of her face, lowering a finger to stroke along her neck.

Her heart hammered under his arm. Her breathing rushed out in gasps.

She'd had the hell scared out of her.

He'd had the hell scared out of him, too.

Following her had been challenge enough. His heart had lurched up into his throat when the bullet barely missed her. It had taken everything he could muster to try to catch her when she'd torn away at one hell of a quick pace.

Why hadn't the shooter gone for her body? The shot hit too far in front of her to have been aimed for the bulk of the target.

Had the shooter meant to kill or only wound?

Or run her into an ambush?

Who in the hell was after her? The bullet could have just as easily hit her head as the ground next to her shoe.

Her body quaked against his chest. Trying to calm her, he rubbed her arm, still glistening with moisture from her exertion. He couldn't resist brushing his lips over her hair, so damned glad he'd found her and caught her before she ran back out into danger.

Zane expelled a breath of pent up anxiety.

An eternity had passed after seeing her head toward the gas station. He'd stood in the doorway worried he'd guessed wrong and she was gone, permanently. His usual calm control had almost deserted him. He'd been seconds from bolting out of the building to search for her when she walked up.

Zane folded her closer, enjoying the feel of her body next to his. She was safe and alive, for the moment.

Just as soon as he got her somewhere safe, she'd get an earful from him. Expecting patience at this point was too much. She'd tell him who was chasing her and why. No more cat and mouse games.

The thought of anyone harming Angel brought out a deadly side of him unlike anything since his time in the second Gulf War. He'd left his share of casualties over the years, but he'd never intentionally hurt anyone who hadn't deserved it. The next person to put a mark on Angel would land on top of his physical retribution list.

First he had to get her out of here – alive. "Are you okay, Angel?"

She drew a deep breath and pushed against his hold.

When he loosened his grip, she turned around.

Don't yell at her. But dammit, he needed to yell at someone. Fear for her life had him ready to unleash his frustration.

Then she raised an ashen face and tear-rimmed eyes to him. Her body shook from head to toe. One side of her hair drooped to her shoulders, while the other remained in a badly twisted knot. Sweat trickled down the side of her neck from the effort she'd expended to escape capture.

Her eyes searched his. She obviously waited for judgment, a naked plea for understanding written across her face.

His heart twisted. He'd always believed the world was made up of good guys and bad guys and knowing who wore the white or black hats had been a simple process. Until Angel.

Every logical neuron in his being placed her on the wrong side of the law. His heart begged to differ and defend her honor.

Therein lay the problem. His heart had a lousy track record.

Her bottom lip quivered.

To hell with the debate raging between his brain and his heart. Zane pulled her to his chest, wrapping her in his arms. Her sleek body fit perfectly next to his.

An old man, leaning on a cane, strolled past the front of their hideout, tapping the ground as he went.

Zane shifted her deeper into the shadows. He scanned the surroundings beyond the dingy glass windows for any sign of threat. When nothing ominous moved along the silent street he returned his attention to Angel.

She tilted her head back, looking as though she was going to speak, but chewed on her bottom lip instead. Firm breasts slowly rubbed against his chest as her breathing eased. The slight movement sent wild cravings through him.

He swallowed.

The pink tip of her tongue appeared and left a wet trail across her cinnamon lips. Time slowed as he stared into the depths of eyes the color of fine bourbon.

At that moment, nothing could have stopped him from what he wanted to do. Had to do.

He gently kissed her, tasting the salty sweetness of her lips. He'd meant it to be gentle, full of comfort, but her response kicked him in the chest. She'd hesitated at first then moved into his arms, molding to him. Her hands pushed up his back to hook around each shoulder, anchoring him tighter.

Hunger and need balled into a flash fire of heat.

She kissed him back, bold and urgent. His tongue slid in to caress her mouth along the smooth inside. Her delicate tongue tormented his. Muscles along his shoulders rippled with each grip of her fingers.

He slipped his hands under the back of her damp shirt to caress every creamy inch of smooth skin then press her closer to him. She clutched his neck as if afraid he'd break the contact.

Not a chance.

He tore his mouth from hers to explore the smooth skin along her neck, tasting the salty dampness from her run.

She purred against his chest, flexing up for more like a kitten in need of cuddles.

Slipping one hand under the front strap of her tight running top, he grazed her nipple with his thumb.

She gasped and arched forward against him. Heat seared him from his chest down through his groin.

His arousal pulsed through his nylon shorts, leaving no doubt that he wanted her.

He did. To the point he hurt with the need to do so much more than kiss her. To see her amber eyes flash wildly when he brought her to climax. When she pushed her hips up against him, he grazed her nipple once more and heard her suck in her breath. As if drawn to the very core of her heat, his fingers slipped away from her breast to trail down her abdomen.

She moaned in protest at the change.

Until he lifted the edge of her shorts to where panties had been built into the design. He scraped his finger against the thin barrier of material shielding her heat.

"Zane ... uh..." She started panting.

He hadn't thought he could get any harder, but he did the minute she rubbed against his hand.

A car horn blew outside, startling him.

He might as well have had cold water thrown on him. Zane froze with his hands in every inappropriate place he could possibly have them and gritted his teeth. Damn it all. What the hell was wrong with him? Some maniac stalked her and he'd dropped his guard.

Another minute and he'd have ripped those shorts off her and dropped his pants.

He had a disgusting *lack* of self-control around this woman.

Withdrawing both roaming hands, he held Angel by the shoulders when she swayed. Passion glazed her eyes. He wanted to kiss her soft lips all over again.

She blinked, then seemed to come back to this world in the next instant and pushed away. Confusion and surprise flashed in her eyes. He could handle that, but the embarrassment he saw before she lowered her lashes cut him deep. He'd done that.

When her lips parted to speak, he shook his head.

Her delicate brows knitted together in irritation. She opened her mouth again, determined to have her say.

He put two fingers on her lips and let his gaze roam past her until she understood they had to be quiet.

Based on activity outside the abandoned gas station and the amount of daylight, he guessed the time to be nearing seven in the morning. A young boy rode past on a tangerine bicycle oblivious to any danger lurking nearby.

Zane leaned close to Angel's ear. "We're moving out. Stay close to me."

"No."

Wrong answer.

He whispered, "The last time you said that I had a gun shoved in my face. Do as I say. We'll discuss this later."

He pinned her tight against his chest in an unspoken order to cooperate. The scowl he gave her didn't seem to deter her at all.

She yanked hard on the back of his shirt then pushed up on her toes. He lowered his ear close to her mouth, fully expecting the berating he deserved for behaving like a hormonal teen.

"Let me go ahead," she whispered. "I had an ... incident on the beach. Someone is following me. It's risky for you to be with me. I'll meet you somewhere."

Zane couldn't believe his ears. Unarmed, wearing clothes bright enough to be a bull's target, she was trying to shield him. His words were terse to cut through any more argument. "Incident, my ass. Someone shot at you."

She stared with shock and murmured, "You saw that?"

He nodded. Leaning close again, he said, "I know all the back ways out of here. If someone's following you, they won't see us. Trust me."

Her face displayed a myriad of emotions, then something he wanted to call trust entered her eyes. What had she been through to be so cautious about trusting a man who'd come to her aid twice and expected nothing in return?

Liar. He'd been seriously close to undressing her three minutes ago. But that hadn't been due to expecting anything in return. Just the raw need to have her.

Zane rubbed her back lightly and gave her shoulders a reassuring squeeze. He took her hand, leading her outside before she could resist his help.

She never stumbled as he scuttled them through a maze of narrow passageways, taking several detours in and out of vacant buildings. Though he'd followed her for miles, she'd circled so much they weren't far from his apartment. In less than an hour, they trotted into the parking lot at his apartment.

In his rush to leave, Zane had left the apartment unlocked. Any other time he wouldn't be concerned, but that was before someone had taken a shot at Angel.

He punched the code to open his truck door, then pulled his .40-caliber Sig from the leather holster tucked in the console. He hesitated in indecision over what to do with Angel for several seconds. The last thing he wanted to do was expose her to a hidden danger within, but he'd learned better than to let her out of his sight.

Pushing the door open slowly, he glanced inside, first to the right, then around the corner at his unmade foldout bed. Frigid air welcomed him. When Zane stepped inside, Angel tried to move next to him, but he swung her close to his back and kept a tight grip on her wrist, careful not to bruise her. Room-by-room, he cleared his house, something he hadn't had to do since he was shot down and searching for shelter in enemy territory. Ten minutes later he was convinced no one waited inside for them.

In the living room, he rounded on Angel. Arms crossed, feet apart, he was ready for answers. "Okay, enough of these charades. What's going on?"

"I told you."

"You said you had an arrangement that went sour," he pressed. "This doesn't look like a pissed off boyfriend. Who is this guy and what does he want?"

Angel wrapped her arms around her chest and moved away from him to stand in front of the terrace doors. "I can't tell you." She sounded as disappointed as he felt.

"Then explain why you can't."

She spun around to answer, hair swatting her face. "Don't you understand? He *is* dangerous. Worse than that. I *have* to go. If he finds me with you he'll – "

"He'll what?" Zane interrupted.

"He'll hurt us both. He'll kill me, and anyone who helps

me is in just as much danger. I couldn't live with it if
something happened to you because of me."

No one was going to kill her.

Her distress was sincere. This hunted woman put his
safety ahead of her own.

It happened again. The lines between black and white
blurred a little more.

He'd always been the toughest kid in his class, never
bested by an adversary from football to martial arts. He'd
been his sister's protector, his squadron's leader and the
first to race toward the enemy.

No one had ever stood between him and a threat.

He'd learned to defend himself at a young age both
physically and emotionally with no one to rise to his
defense. The depth of Angel's concern pushed him into
turbulent emotional territory, with no navigational charts.

In the same breath she had refused to answer his
questions, aggravating him beyond reason, then confused
him with her selfless consideration for his safety.

His world to this point had been simple.

Everyone was primarily either good or bad. Guilty or
innocent. Black or white with not a whole lot of gray.

How was he going to figure out where Angel fit in that
world?

Not knowing was giving him hell.

He had resources to call on who could help her, but he
had to know she wasn't in some kind of serious trouble with
the law.

Somehow, he doubted that would change her mind. "I
need you to trust me."

She didn't hurry to answer, a sign that she gave
consideration to what she intended to say. "The funny thing
is that I do trust you, but that doesn't mean I'm willing to
put you in the middle of something you aren't responsible
for. The less you know, the better. I made a bad choice. Now
I need to fix my mistake and I can't guarantee this isn't
going to turn out badly."

Zane sighed. Convincing her to go to the police might be
his best recourse after all. The longer he delayed, the higher
her risk was of injury or capture by the wrong people.
"Since this guy is so dangerous, why don't you go to the

police?"

Her face turned guarded. "No. He, uh, has contacts everywhere. I can't risk talking to the police."

"Even if I vouched for someone in law enforcement? There are laws to protect women from men who stalk and brutalize them, regardless of the circumstances. Especially when the guy tries to shoot you."

She shook her head. "It's more complicated than being stalked."

There it was again. That bad feeling that she hid something not quite kosher. By the end of the day, he would have a fingerprint if he had to tie her down.

She squinted her eyes at him then. "Why do you carry a gun in your truck, Zane?"

"I have a permit to carry concealed. Not everybody you meet in the cargo business is nice." Especially when the DEA asked him to take contracts with less than savory characters at times. A frown furrowed her brow. *Please don't press that point.* Zane's cell phone rang in the distance. Saved by the jingle. "Don't move." He retrieved the phone. His pulse jumped when he recognized the High Vision dispatch number.

This was the call he'd been waiting on.

What was he going to do with Angel if he had to fly out?

Zane stood where he could watch her from the doorway while he answered out of her hearing.

"Black here," Zane said.

Samuel Ritter's familiar voice started issuing instructions, as usual. "You've got a pickup at Bentley Field near St. Simons Island in south Georgia for High Vision this afternoon. Has to arrive in Ft. Lauderdale in time for a transfer to Miami by 1900. A High Vision representative will meet you at Sunshine Airfield when you return."

That wasn't the location or shipment Zane expected. "I didn't think your company had a branch there." Plus Zane had never brought any of their cargo shipments back to Sunshine Field.

"We don't. The chief financial officer has a home on St. Simon's Island," Sammy clarified. "This shipment is specifically for him."

Damn. Flying something for the CFO was a positive sign.

And a test, he'd bet. He didn't care as long as they gave him the cargo contract. Zane checked the clock on the microwave. Making the run was no problem, but he couldn't leave Angel alone.

"I can be there by one o'clock. What can you tell me about the load?"

"All I've been told is it's a high-priority shipment from the CFO's wife, something personal. They'll let you inspect the package before loading. Supposedly it's approximately three-by-three and they don't want the contents discussed for security reasons. Based on the insurance value noted, I'd handle it with kid gloves."

"I always do." Zane could see his goal within reach. The High Vision cargo contract for this region would guarantee his ability to fund a great nest egg for his sister's antiquities business. He'd put her in a place on Las Olas Boulevard where she and her business would be respected.

He could sub out additional charter contracts that weren't specifically for the DEA. Build his business and get a more stable flight schedule for himself at the same time.

More than all of that, he could get Trish the help she needed, starting with that uber-expensive rehab. Without Zane even asking, Ben had researched them all and handed Zane a file on the best place. Ben always came through.

Zane would not lose his baby sister. But for that to work, she needed his support. He had to be around and couldn't do that making every run himself at all hours of the day and night to maintain his reputation as a hotshot. That wasn't a name he would've used for himself in the military, but if his competition thought of him that way, and it earned him business, so be it. They could call him Fred Flintstone for all he cared.

He checked his watch and told Sammy, "I'll confirm delivery by 1730."

"Ten-four."

Zane snapped the phone shut and turned to Angel. "I've got to make a run up to Georgia, just south of Savannah, and back."

She cheered up at that. "Have a good flight."

In a hurry to get rid of him, was she? "You're going with me."

"Why?" Not smiling now.

"You did agree to translate, didn't you?" Zane gave himself a mental pat on the back for quick thinking.

Her mouth dropped open then she snapped it shut. "You need me to translate in *Georgia?*"

"There's a possibility." A rare possibility, but one never knew what to expect, he reasoned.

A thought hit him. Maybe she was uncomfortable being stuck in close quarters with him after the incident in the gas station. She'd clearly been embarrassed. Had what little gain he'd made toward earning her trust been negated by his lust and lack of control?

"Angel, another thing. Sorry about what happened in that building earlier. Won't happen again." He hoped. No promises if she walked out of the bathroom in a towel again.

She said nothing, but her jaw set and she gave him a curt nod.

Now he felt lower than a snake's belly. What had he thought she'd say? That she'd loved kissing him and feeling his hands all over her, and wanted him to touch her again?

Yes.

So much for his moment of fantasy. At least there was one thing he could get right. He knew what she'd probably like about now. "Why don't you grab a shower?"

From her exaggerated sigh he concluded she was obviously not happy with him or his plan for her day. Then her face brightened. "Tell you what. I'll go with you if you'll agree to spend some time cleaning up your storage room."

"Why? There's nothing wrong with it."

"That place is a wreck. How do you even find stuff and know for sure if anyone has picked up their cargo?"

"I have a system," he muttered.

"Not an efficient one by the looks of that place." She shifted her pose and lifted her chin with a stubborn look he was starting to recognize. "If you want me to stay here and accept your generosity, then I want to help you get organized."

I am organized, dammit. But for once she was talking about accepting his help. Not wanting to discourage that, he conceded, "We'll look at the room when we get back."

"Great." She carried her bag of clothes to his master bathroom and snapped the door shut.

While she cleaned up, Zane jumped through his own shower in the hall bathroom and threw on a collared golf shirt and khaki pants. He slid his loaded Keltec .32 down the inside of his boot. The Sig, just like the ones the DEA issued, he stashed in the false center of a hardback novel, which he tucked into his flight bag. It was similar to the weapon he'd trained with in the Air Force and carried in his survival vest when he'd flown combat missions, so it hadn't taken any adjustment.

He walked into the kitchen to find Angel wearing her jeans and white shirt.

At this rate, after a week of washing, that outfit would disintegrate. She leaned forward on the counter with a slice of cold pizza in one hand. Her downcast eyes drifted back and forth across the front page of yesterday's paper. An almost empty glass of milk rested near the edge of the paper.

"You can have anything you want," Zane pointed out to her. "You don't have to eat day-old pizza."

"This is great. You have no idea how badly you miss pizza until you can't get it for a year." She'd mumbled her answer without looking up from the newspaper.

Where had she lived that she couldn't get pizza? He'd file that away for now.

Zane checked his watch. They had to get moving. "You ready to go?"

She didn't even hesitate as she cleaned up after herself, wiped down the counter and washed the glass. She hefted the linen bag to her shoulder. "Lead the way."

After scooting her out to the truck, Zane made three switchbacks on his way to the airfield. He detected no one following them, but someone had spotted Angel while she was running down the beach. *If* her pursuers had figured out that she was with him, logically they should have come after her by now.

Nice if he could relax and take that as a good sign, but unfortunately, logic and criminals didn't always go hand in hand, which meant he'd have to be on guard for anything at this point.

Where would her pursuers show up next?

Chapter 20

Zane was sorry about the kiss.

Sorry about *that* kiss?

Angel stewed in the co-pilot seat as Zane reached cruising altitude. Granted, they hadn't picked the best time to do a sexy cha-cha, standing in that abandoned station, but he clearly regretted it. What had happened?

She'd been sure he was enjoying himself as much as she had. Well, maybe not as much as *she* had – not when he'd slipped his fingers inside her bra top. And started to do the same with her shorts.

Her nipples perked up at the reminder. The pair of traitors hardened just thinking about his touch. If he'd kept his hands on her another couple of minutes in that old gas station, the heat coming off her skin would have torched her clothes.

But something had changed by the time they'd returned to his apartment. For him anyway. Maybe he'd come to his senses and realized he could do so much better.

With his looks, he probably had a string of beautiful, sophisticated women vying for his attention. Bet he never tossed out a penalty flag after kissing one of *them*.

She certainly wasn't beautiful or sophisticated.

But that didn't stop her from thinking of how much she'd like to have a man like Zane.

Impossible dream.

Okay, so who cared? If he wanted to act like nothing had happened between them, so would she.

Zane's voice buzzed in her headphones. "While we have a little time, how about telling me something about yourself?"

"Like what?"

"What type of work do you do?"

She'd been pedaling a bike as a courier when she'd been arrested for unknowingly delivering drugs for her father. After jail she'd taken a job as a maid in a filthy motel where rooms were rented by the hour, she'd shoveled refuse at the dump, and waited tables in a strip club because a respectable restaurant didn't want an ex-con.

Getting hired by one of the largest import-export companies in the country should have been a red flag for her, but no. She'd been too eager to make good.

Two months into her employment, she'd earned a raise and moved up to the position of inventory clerk. And *that* job had come with opportunities for advancement – from small time jailbird to fulltime felon.

Give him the short version. "You could say I'm between jobs right now."

"What *have* you done?"

She couldn't see behind those aviator glasses he wore, but she'd bet he rolled his eyes at her evasive answer. "I was a bike courier once. How'd you find me this morning?"

"I normally jog in the mornings. When I heard you leave, I slipped on my shoes to run with you, but you were way ahead of me by the time you reached the beach. Next thing I knew, I saw a bullet strike the sand and you took off like a rocket."

Okay, bringing up this morning was a bad idea.

Zane turned his dark sunglasses on her. "You're pretty fast, even to be running on adrenaline. Did you run track in school?"

"Yes." She pushed that out through clenched teeth. She could deal with the subtle interrogation, but reminding her of what she'd lost punctured an emotional artery.

No one she'd graduated with had spoken to her again after her conviction. Thankfully, the people she'd been training around since she walked out of prison knew nothing of her record, only that her marathon race times were exceptional.

Oh, crap. All the medals she'd earned before being arrested were still on the wall of her two-room house in Raleigh. No going back there.

Just like always, she'd busted her butt to earn something only to lose it.

Zane's simple question opened a wound she'd thought had healed years ago. Six years spent struggling to survive after getting released had given her little time to think about lost dreams.

Over the past year, though, she'd committed the sin of dreaming again. Running the Tamarind triathlon in Colorado in two months was to be her big chance at returning to the athletic community and regaining a margin of respect.

Thanks, Mason, for destroying that dream.

She felt Zane's eyes on her again. Knew he wanted more than a one-word answer. "I ran in high school." She made a show of checking her watch. "How long's our flight?"

"Bentley Field is a little over two hours away. Where'd you go to high school?"

Her throat tightened. "A podunk place. How long have you flown?"

"Fourteen years. I mentioned being in the Air Force. That was until a few years ago."

"How long were you in?" Angel asked.

He shook his head and smiled. "Not fair. It's my turn to ask. If we're going to play question volleyball how about answering mine since I'm answering yours?"

"Fair enough." She'd share what she could.

"Have you run competitively?" Zane started again.

Two national titles plus a room full of regional trophies by the time she'd reached sixteen. Yeah, that qualified as competitive running.

Her father had hocked her brass trophies for pocket cash.

Tears stung her eyes. Fidgeting, she glanced around and saw a pair of Ray-Ban sunglasses in a side pocket. She yanked them out and slid the dark sunglasses over her eyes, careful to touch only the wire frames, which were too narrow to hold a fingerprint. "I ran track in school and a few local races. Why'd you leave the Air Force?"

His smile faltered. What? Mr. Got-to-know-everything didn't like question volleyball all of a sudden?

She smiled, feeling a little smug.

"After our parents were killed, Trish started having problems. I was no help to her flying jets on the other side of the ocean. By the time I got back to Texas she was in the hospital."

Fingers on his right hand flexed out and back in, gripping the yoke. Angel didn't think he was going to continue until she heard his low voice in her headset.

"Her best friend, Heidi, found her after Trish had gone to a hotel with some guy and he'd beaten her half to death. Trish told Heidi she'd screamed until she'd passed out, but no one helped. The place was full of crack-heads. The one thing I can't tolerate is drugs."

Angel's shoulders sagged. Okay, they were even. Neither had intentionally forced painful memories on the other. Guilt layered his deep sadness.

She understood how it felt to carry guilt. But his was misplaced. "You're there for Trish now. You can't change the past, but you can influence the future. And you're doing that."

He didn't acknowledge her comment, but the harsh lines in his face relaxed.

"It's your serve," she teased, hoping to lighten the mood, rewarded when his mouth quirked up with a half-smile.

"What's your best time in a race?"

Angel hesitated, fiddled with her seatbelt then lifted her chin with pride she couldn't hide. She'd been good at one thing in her life and all she had left to show for it were memories. "I've run close to five-minute pace."

"No kidding? Did you get a track scholarship?"

She nodded, throat thick with emotion then realized he hadn't seen her head move. "Yes."

"Where'd you go?"

"I didn't."

Zane cut his head around to face her. "Why not? With professional training, you might have made the Olympics."

What should she tell him? That one of the most prestigious universities in the country rescinded their offer when they found out she'd be delayed a year while serving her time in prison? *No way.*

"It wasn't my choice. They withdrew the offer," she said.

"You should have submitted to another college. For

someone with your speed, there had to be plenty of universities who would have taken you ... as long as your grades were up to par."

"I had a three-point-eight." She'd have carried a better grade average than that if training and working a job hadn't drained her time. "They just decided they didn't want me."

"Did you try to get into another college?"

The steady drone of the engines filled several seconds before she rubbed her neck then answered. "No. Can we call it a tie game and quit here?"

~*~

Zane wanted to push for more, but knew when to quit. Better to chisel away than try to get it all in one chunk. "Sure."

She gave him a polite smile then turned to look out the window.

"*They didn't want me,*" she'd said. It wasn't the words so much as the cold pain behind them that struck him. How could a university not want a talented athlete who had the grades? She'd said it hadn't been her choice.

Only one reason came to mind. She'd done something to warrant revocation of the scholarship.

Five minute pace.

After watching her this morning, he believed it. She'd been some school's star runner. Her name had to show up in a database with cross-referencing race results and high school track stars.

Ben could narrow the possibilities down by searching the top ten percent of women finalists across the country in the last ten years.

What would cause a school to reject a talented athlete? That was the meat of the question. Ben had a practically limitless network of information at his fingertips. There probably weren't a lot of prominent female athletes named Angel, if that *was* her real name.

Definitely world-class level. He'd love to watch her fly through the end of a race and cheer her on as she led the pack. Those gazelle-like legs gracefully tearing across the ground. He'd be there to hug her when she won.

Whoa. Where had that ridiculous thought come from?

The devil's advocate in Zane forced him to put this all back into perspective, starting with the facts he now had. She'd lost a scholarship due to some infraction, getting information out of her was harder than pulling a Kardashian away from a television camera, and Angel was a suspiciously compulsive cleaner. Plus he'd met her under damned crazy circumstances.

So what's the conclusion?

Ben would say she's a person of interest to law enforcement.

But for what?

But if nothing panned out in Ben's search, Zane would be forced to involve the police or turn her loose to fend for herself.

Neither option would give him peace.

Besides, bringing in the police would mean explaining how he'd met Angel. Nobody would be happy about that, starting with the DEA. No-win situation, no matter which way he went.

If he were older, he'd have a healthy inheritance waiting for him that he could use to help Trish. But he couldn't touch it until he reached the age of forty. That left him to make the best of the skills he had for both him and Trish in the meantime.

And there was the small matter of needing to believe in what he did for a living. Running cargo wouldn't provide that. But this DEA gig gave him a way to still make a difference to the country he loved.

Nothing would wholly compensate for the loss of his military career, but he was making it.

And Trish had lost much more.

A lot of jet jockeys couldn't make the switch to slower aircraft, but everyone made sacrifices in life. He'd given up the adrenaline rush of Mach 2, and gained one beautiful, *alive* sister. He could live happily with that trade.

And damn whatever he had to do to make all of this work out.

He confirmed clearance to land.

Angel sat up straight in her seat, watching him as he went through a check of his systems. She seemed ... impressed?

Ego stroke moment.

Then she slipped her headset off and switched it out for her hat as someone radioed him from Bentley Field. "You must be getting big bucks working on the Friday before Labor Day, flyboy."

"How goes it, Jason?" Zane had met the young mechanic on a recent stopover when the Titan needed a minor adjustment.

"The same. Underpaid and overworked. You expecting company?"

"You mean the High Vision people?" Zane asked.

"Naw, they're here, too, but you got a welcoming committee out here and you're the only bird we're expecting right now."

Ah hell.

Keying up the mike, Zane asked Jason, "Would you know if this has anything to do with the High Vision shipment? Dispatcher didn't have much information."

"Oh, yeah, it does. You'd think it was the crown prince of Europe with all the security that showed up."

That didn't sound right. "Supposed to be cargo, not a passenger."

"Depends on how you look at it. You're the limo ride for a little white mutt headed to Miami for a weekend of R&R with his four-legged lady."

Zane flipped through his memory bank on the corporate management of High Vision. Their CFO and his wife raised champion Bichon Frise dogs, including a stud worth more than a lot of people earned in a year. He understood the lack of information when Sammy had called Zane about this load. The CFO was worried about the animal being stolen during transport.

Now he put it all together. "Don't tell me TAF's waiting for me."

"Okay, I won't. I hate being the bearer of bad news."

Damn, it was TAF, the moniker for Treat Animals Fairly. A bunch of PETA wannabes that caused more trouble than good. "Just my luck. See you in a few."

"Not me, flyboy. I just bought a new bass rig with a hot Mercury outboard. I'll be on the water by sunset. Catch you next time."

No wonder the High Vision CFO had kept the identity of the cargo secret. In addition to assuring his wife's prize show dog was safe, the CFO wanted to avoid any media when it came to TAF, which was always negative.

Obviously, TAF had better intel than anyone realized.

This bunch did not want to cross him, not with Zane so close to signing a contract with High Vision.

He always went for a smooth landing, but he outdid himself on this one. Angel didn't say a word, but her eyebrow lifted just enough to tell him she'd noticed. At the terminal side of the runway, Zane swung off and parked on the ramp then took in the waiting congregation.

Two elderly women, linked arm-in-arm, were dressed in matching flowered, short-sleeve dresses that fell midway of their chunky calves. Black ankle-high boots complemented their military-style buzz cuts.

A wiry little man held down his dirt-brown hat against the wind swiftly kicking up dust. Standing next to him was a middle-aged, flame-haired woman and a short man almost as wide as he was tall. Sunshine glinted off of the thin brown hair covering his basketball-shaped head.

Zane unbuckled his seatbelt and slipped out of the cockpit. When he opened the cargo door to step down, loose sand blasted his face in a rush of burning air. A hand pushed against his back and he turned to find Angel climbing out.

"What are you doing out here?" he asked.

"I'm your translator, remember?" She didn't even try to hide the smile that came along with the sarcasm. "If you handle this group anything like you did Mr. Suarez, you'll be lucky to stay in business through next week."

Feisty thing. Keeping her within reach might not be a bad idea. "Stay close to me. This bunch can be a roaring pain."

Zane stepped past the nose of the plane and the odd group advanced several feet. The skinny guy fighting to keep a crinkled hat on his head cleared his throat and spoke.

"I'm Earnest Earwood. We represent TAF, which stands for Treat Animals Fairly." Each word tumbled from his mouth like a telegraph operator reading a message. "We're here to protest your part in the mistreatment of animals."

One of the two gray-haired women standing with their arms linked spoke up. "I'm Berta Nielson and this is my sister, Valerie."

Valerie jumped in. "We don't think these poor animals should be put through pain and suffering."

Berta pointed at Zane. "How would you like to be faced with the same future?"

The dog was headed for a weekend of rousing sex with a ready and able partner.

Zane would love it. He smiled. "I could tolerate it."

Valerie's faced screwed into the shape of a dishrag after heavy use. "That's appalling. What kind of man are you?"

One that hasn't been with a woman in way too damn long, Zane thought remorsefully. "You don't think my cargo deserves to be used in an experiment?" He was trying hard not to chuckle.

Angel arched an eyebrow at him.

"No animal should be put through that kind of suffering." The redhead had a high-pitched voice, painful to hear. "We're the Thorntons and we've spent our lives protecting animals."

Most of the critical laboratory shipments for High Vision were handled in the middle of the night, just to avoid TAF groups showing up to protest. This disorganized association was composed of radical protesters who rarely had their facts straight – as evidence, they thought Zane was here for a High Vision *business* shipment – and generally caused headaches for the bona fide animal rights organizations.

Zane had to get rid of them without stirring up the media. How deep a hole would they dig for themselves if he handed them a shovel? "Maybe the animal being transported would enjoy this particular experiment."

Eyes bulged and mouths popped open like hungry guppies.

Zane smiled at their reactions.

The main four spouted off at the same time.

"You're a monster."

"How can you say that?"

"We shall call in reinforcements."

"How do you sleep at night?"

Mr. Thornton still hadn't commented.

Angel gaped at Zane like he'd lost his mind. "You can't even keep people calm in English," she whispered tersely. "How *do* you stay in business?"

He narrowed his eyes at her.

Angel pushed past Zane to address the crowd. "Excuse me. *Excuse me!*"

The shouting died down to a rumble. Angry eyes surveyed her.

She turned to Zane. "Your charter company would never do anything to harm an animal. Right?"

When he didn't say anything, she bumped her heel into his shin. "Umph."

Angel must have taken his grunt as an affirmative. She smiled at the crowd and asked, "What specifically is your complaint?"

Berta's caterpillar eyebrows ran together in a straight line across her forehead. "TAF opposes unnecessary and cruel testing on animals. We have a report that Black Jack Charters is transporting a test animal today."

Angel twisted sideways to Zane. "Is that true?"

He smiled and nodded "yes" then almost busted up laughing at Angel's incredulous face.

"Just as we thought." Earnest choked out the words through a raspy throat. "He even admits to his dastardly ways."

When Earnest succumbed to coughing, Valerie took a shot at Zane. "You wouldn't be so happy if you were put in the same position as that poor animal."

Zane grinned. "Au contraire. If I had a willing mate waiting for a romantic weekend with me, you'd probably have to remove my smile surgically."

The crowd stilled. Not a sound was heard over the whirring of the wind. Everyone stared at him in shocked silence until Angel squinted in concentration and pushed for an explanation.

"Zane, what are you talking about?"

So much for having fun.

His sigh vanished in the breeze. "Our cargo is a pedigreed show dog being sent for a weekend of recreational sex. The evil testing he'll be put through is to determine if he can make little champion puppies. If it does kill him, that doesn't sound like a bad way to go, if you ask me."

Wild threads of hair that escaped from Angel's hair clip blew across her face. The corners of her mouth curled up. "You have a wicked streak."

"Honey, you don't know the half of it." He winked at her for good measure. For the first time since leaving the apartment, he was in her good graces again. Warmth spread over him at her pixie smile.

"Earnest, you said there was a monkey being shipped today. Where's the monkey?" Berta wasted no time assaulting a new target. Poor Earnest was no match.

"Hold on, Berta. This isn't my fault. The Thorntons said Valerie told them the same thing."

"Blast it all, Earnest. You're an idiot. Valerie heard you tell me. That's why she told them."

Zane had enjoyed all he could stand. "If you'll excuse us, we have a deadline."

No one so much as turned to acknowledge him as they formed a circle of finger pointers.

A pair of men wearing green High Vision security suits walked up with a dog crate.

It took less than ten minutes to make the transfer, load the cargo, and call for clearance to take off, a polite formality at the uncontrolled field.

Back in the air, Zane ignored the whining going on behind him.

Angel twisted around. "I think he's scared."

"He'll settle down in a little while."

"What's his name?"

Zane had no idea. "It was like Sir something-something Chutney."

Another mournful whine sounded from the cage.

"Poor Chut."

She twisted around again, like a wolf mama worried about her pup.

"He's a show dog, Angel. They're high strung so don't touch him."

Ignoring his warning, she yanked off the headset and unbuckled her harness then climbed out of her seat and dropped down on her hands and knees in the cargo area.

He couldn't engage the autopilot yet. Keeping an eye on her in his rearview mirror, he raised his voice so she'd hear him. "Be careful. He might bite."

"He won't hurt me. Please don't yell. You're frightening him even more."

She sat down on the floor of the plane, turned so that she had the dog cage on her left and Zane on her right. When she opened the wire door, Chut made a couple of tentative steps through the opening. In the next heartbeat, he straddled her lap.

She beamed a triumphant smile up at the mirror and carried the dog back to her co-pilot seat. Once she was settled with her headphones back in place, she sat back, running her fingers across the mutt's white-as-fresh-snow coat. "He smells nice. Powdery."

Zane said, "You're going to be sorry if he gets excited and makes a mess."

"No, I'm not. Everyone needs to be held sometimes." She smiled at the dog. "Isn't that right, Sir Chut?" She turned to Zane. "I think Chut's thirsty. Got any water?"

Zane started to tell her he was sure the dog had been well hydrated before being handed off, but stopped himself in time. He'd never seen Angel this invested. Or this distracted. He'd be stupid to shut it down. "Sure, just hang on a minute until I get the autopilot set."

He made sure the instruments were doing their jobs, then found a plastic cup, used his pocketknife to cut the height down to half, filled the temporary dog bowl with water from a bottle he had in his bag, and held it out to her on the palm of his hand.

"Thanks. Here, Chut, have a drink."

Chut lapped up water, dripping it all over his coat and Angel's lap.

When the dog finally lost interest in the water, Zane lifted the cup from her fingers and said, "I've got a cup holder on this side. I'll put it over here in case he wants more later."

Angel let him take the cup and laughed when Chut licked her chin.

Zane smiled, too. Finally, he had Angel's fingerprint.

Chapter 21

Mason ceased his useless pacing across his New York office, and stared out at the fifteenth-floor view of Manhattan.

He wouldn't be here, but he had to appear as though he were doing business as usual. CK wasn't producing results fast enough. Granted, Mason had given the bounty hunter stringent guidelines on capturing Angelina, because of that prick Czarion, but he'd thought CK would have cornered her by now, even with the need to be discreet.

Had she found a hole to tuck into and hide?

Perhaps Mason should give her reason to get mobile again.

He studied the traffic below, tossing around idea after idea until it dawned on him that he had the perfect solution sitting on ice. Literally.

Snatching his phone, he made a call to his favorite reporter, the one who owed him a favor.

Chapter 22

"When are we going to organize your storage room?" Angel drummed her fingers on her crossed arms and watched the sun sink closer to the ocean. The traffic ahead of Zane's truck moved at a slug's pace along A1A.

"It'll wait until tomorrow."

Tomorrow was another whole day. She couldn't wait that long, but her only other option was to ask about the package of boat curtains. How was she going to do that without raising his suspicions?

He added, "It's too late to start on that at this time of day."

She stewed quietly. Once he'd landed at Sunshine Airfield and handled the transfer to the man in a green suit waiting to pick up Chut, Zane rushed her to the truck, claiming he had to run an errand before dark.

He turned off the beach highway and she unfolded her arms.

She recognized the area.

The Gulf Winds Marina sign came into view.

She couldn't have been more surprised if he'd driven up to the Taj Mahal. Keeping her excitement hidden took real effort.

Had Zane loaded the package into the truck without her noticing? She calmly stretched and looked behind her, pretending to take in the scenery.

The truck bed was empty.

Her palms dampened at the possibility of finding the package of boat curtains.

Nibbling on her lip, she asked with as much indifference

as she could muster, "What are we doing here?"

"Quick stop," Zane answered, explaining nothing. "Won't take more than ten minutes." He parked his big truck in front of the dock for slip 18 and opened his door, saying, "Just keep your head down and I'll be right back."

"No." She hadn't meant to snap at him.

He stood there, hand clenched on his open door. "That's becoming my least favorite word. No, what?"

"I want to come with you, please." She smiled to sweeten her request.

Zane's eyes took in the marina lot. Two empty late model pickups and a rusty Jeep sat in the desolate parking area.

She could see his line of thought, but there were no massive black sport utilities hovering nearby. Not much more activity in the marina than the last time she'd been here. "I'll be fine. Don't you think someone would have shown their face by now if they knew I was with you?"

"Yeah, but..." He scratched his chin, and appeared to reconsider. "Now that I think about it, I'd rather not leave you alone here anyhow."

Sold! She hopped out and hurried around the front of the truck. "Don't worry. I'll stay close."

It took all her discipline not to run down the dock.

The young man from the day before had obviously finished washing "Wet Dream" because slip seventeen was empty.

Next to it, in slip eighteen floated a wooden cabin cruiser Noah had probably passed over before he built his own ark. The ancient teak deck was sun bleached gray. What little varnish that still covered the mahogany trim along the sides of the cabin had sprung loose in peeled tufts.

Now she'd find out what had happened to the boat curtains.

Zane stepped down onto the deck of the archaic vessel appropriately named "Hard Luck."

"Should you be walking around on that boat?" Angel asked.

Zane grinned up at her. "Sure. I own it."

Chapter 23

Angel couldn't believe her ears.

Zane owned that floating wreck in Slip 18?

The custom curtains were for *his* boat?

"Don't look so shocked." Zane stood with hands on hips, grinning at her. "Pilots like the water, too. I plan to restore it. Bought it in Miami and hired a captain to bring it up here for me."

Still, she was speechless.

Casting an admiring glance at his ark, he said, "I won't be able to work on it for another couple of months, but she'll be ship shape by next spring."

Angel caught half of what he'd said. *Where* was that package of new canvas enclosures? This boat wasn't anywhere near ready for side curtains.

Zane stared up at her expectantly.

She realized he was waiting for her to say something about the boat. "It's, uh, nice. Lot of potential, roomy."

Right answer. He grinned even wider. Like a man who'd won the lottery.

He'd need a big jackpot to make this thing into a usable watercraft.

Zane opened the cabin and stepped down into what appeared to be a living area. "Stuffy in this cabin." He opened small windows, pushed them out from the inside and lifted the hatch. She'd squatted down on the dock to watch him, hoping to see a brown paper package miraculously lying around in the open.

No such luck.

She stepped around on the walkway extension from the

main dock that had been built between the slips. Putting her fisted hand against the sidewall of the hard top that covered the cockpit, she used it for support and jumped down onto the deck. At the cabin door, she found Zane digging through a small cabinet above a compact kitchen area. He pulled out two key rings, each with an orange plastic float attached.

She moved out of the way when he climbed out to the deck.

He stuck the keys into the dual ignitions then dropped down on one knee in the rear center of the deck to raise a hinged section. With a flip of his wrist, he switched a silver toggle.

After standing up he explained. "Have to switch the battery on."

Sounded reasonable. She had no clue what he was talking about, having never been on a pleasure boat, but he said it with such authority she assumed he was correct.

Zane stepped over to the wheel, gripped the control handles mounted against the wall on his right and shoved them forward a couple times then returned them to the middle position. After several attempts, the right motor cranked with a throaty rumble. The left one started up on the first try, eliciting a triumphant grin from Zane.

Men and their toys.

He tinkered with the controls for a few minutes, then tapped one of the gauges and frowned.

She leaned in to see what concerned him. "Something not working?"

He shook his head, more to himself than to her. "No, the problem is that it does work."

"I don't understand."

Zane studied the dash. "These are the gas gauges. Both tanks are too low on fuel. I had a message from the captain that he ran into weather and arrived later than he'd planned, so he couldn't fill it before docking. I can't blame him, but I have to get it fueled soon."

"Why? Are you taking it for a ride?" If he went for a ride in this thing, low fuel should be the least of his worries.

A life jacket, flare gun, inflatable raft – those were items to be concerned about.

"No, it's for safety," he continued. "An empty tank is more dangerous than a full one. Gas fumes combust quicker than solid fuel." When he'd finished running the engines, Zane returned the keys to their hiding spot.

Leaving the ignition keys *onboard* the boat amazed her. Attitudes in Florida appeared a lot more trusting than in New York or Raleigh.

"I forgot to grab the new bow lines from the truck and I need to see the manager. You ready?" He stood next to the side offering his hand to help her back onto the dock.

She caught herself before "no" popped out of her mouth. "I'd like to wait here, if it's okay with you. I've never spent any time around boats, especially like this one." That was basically true since the closest she'd ever come to boating was riding a ferry.

Zane eyed up and down the dock, but few crafts remained in port on the beautiful day. "Promise me you'll stay right here."

"Of course."

He appeared doubtful, but glanced around then left. Even she realized it would be hard for her to get away without him seeing her.

As soon as Zane stepped off the end of the dock onto the parking lot, Angel scrambled below to dig through cabinets and drawers. The air in the cabin smelled of mildew. Thank goodness he'd opened the windows and hatches.

The coins had to still be hidden in the boat curtains or the curtains would be installed and Zane would have figured out that she was the one who'd hidden them.

She searched through shelves above four flat cushions put together like a puzzle to create a bed that ran wall to wall. The nautical pattern on the tattered covers had faded severely in the center area where sun had burned through the hatch when it was open.

When she heard Zane moving around up top, she quickly shifted her search to the drawers where she could claim curiosity if caught. He could see through the open hatch. She dug through odd lures, matches in a watertight capsule and several sets of sunshades in two drawers.

A cabinet below the tiny sink held rags, a rusty battery-operated light that didn't appear operable, rolls of clear line and a green plastic divided container full of assorted hooks.

The boat rocked slightly toward the narrow walkway that extended off the main dock and ran between boats. Zane must have stepped off to tie ropes.

She spun back to the bed to find out if anything was beneath those cushions.

She'd just discovered individual compartments when she heard, "Make yourself at home."

Angel swung around to face Zane standing at the top of the steps to the cabin. Her heart took a hit on that one. How had he gotten back on the boat so quietly and without rocking it?

"Sorry, I was just curious." She sucked in a deep breath. Nope, that didn't calm her one bit. "There's so much stuff in here. Did the boat come with all this...?"

"Tackle?"

Junk had been her next word, but she nodded.

"The last owner left some of it there. Normal with a cabin cruiser this old. The rest I stocked the other day when I got back from Jacksonville."

That had to mean he'd brought the boat curtains here, but asking him about that package would be all he'd need to start asking her questions.

He was still watching her. She glanced around the cabin, nodding. "Boy, is there a lot of storage in here. Amazing. You really picked a good one."

Zane's narrowed eyes had her thinking he didn't quite buy the act, but he didn't challenge her. "I'll change out the bow lines and we'll go."

Now? What the heck had he been doing before?

Light showered back through the door once his massive body shifted out of the way. She could hear him shuffling around, and decided she'd be better served to wipe off anything she touched and come back alone later to dig through the boat.

Leaving with the knowledge the coins might be within reach strained the limits of her patience. As a child she'd been impatient, but twelve months in a jail cell had taught her diligence. Waiting for the perfect opportunity to escape Mason had paid off and, so far, his men hadn't captured her.

She'd wait for her chance, but she *would* get those coins back.

Her life depended on it.

Would they be safe here?

You didn't find them. Good point.

Out on the deck, Angel found Zane waiting for her on the walkway that ran alongside the boat. He reached down to give her a hand up. Their gazes locked when he caught her upper arms and lifted. His strength amazed her when she practically flew up into his arms.

Tall, with a thin athletic body, Angel had never thought of herself as even remotely petite, but sometimes Zane made her feel as though she were delicate.

Like now.

Her feet barely touched the dock. She wrapped her fingers around his waist.

His hands moved to rest on her shoulders, softly rubbing her tight muscles. Dark eyes turned black with desire the longer he stared at her.

Standing so close to him, her body ignored all input from her mind. His arms slid down around her back. She leaned into the embrace, unable to resist the comfort offered. With a little pressure, he raised her up until she stood on her toes.

She held her breath anticipating another sensual kiss.

He had that look that said he was going to do it then ... at the last second, he dropped a quick peck on her forehead and loosened his grip to go.

Damn him. She refused to be dismissed so easily and held on. She lifted up and nipped his lower lip. Her fingers crawled up his back until she pulled them together.

He growled, teetering on the edge of a decision, then kissed her.

And no question that he meant it. No teasing. He went in for the kill. Her heart beat hard enough to explode. His tongue tangled with hers in a fevered volley.

He held her close and cupped his palm against her face, holding her exactly where he could destroy any resistance with his mouth.

One notion chased through her mind.

If he apologized for this, she'd push him overboard.

She was vaguely aware he'd moved from her mouth to her ear, but she knew exactly where his hand was when his palm skittered over her breast. Her knees threatened to buckle.

She moaned.

He cursed.

Something splashed the water in the empty slip behind Zane. The world came back into focus too soon.

His hand disappeared from where he'd touched her. His lips had stilled and all the wonderful sensations shooting through her ended abruptly.

Glaring up into his mahogany eyes, she warned, "Don't you dare apologize if you value your life."

He said nothing, just let out a long sigh.

She braced herself for whatever annoying response he'd have this time.

A feral smile spread across his face. "What am I going to do with you?"

She had a few suggestions if he couldn't come up with any. Angel lifted her chin in a silent challenge.

He shook his head. "You have no idea how close you are to real danger. Let's go before you find out."

She released an exaggerated breath for his benefit.

He kissed her quickly then grabbed her hand, led her up the dock and loaded her in the truck. As Zane cranked the truck, she noticed the large rope still piled in the back.

"You forgot to get one of your ropes," she mentioned.

"That's for the anchor. I'm not changing it today. That takes a while."

They left the marina heading in the direction of his apartment. This time she wasn't traveling by a bus on an indirect route, which allowed her to make note of the quickest way back to the marina. Thanks to her marathon and triathlon training, she had the ability to quickly pick up directions and landmarks.

Warm air off the blistering pavement blew through her open window as Zane weaved through thick Labor Day weekend traffic.

With her arm outside the window, she waved her hand against the force of the air, enjoying a childhood practice. Her eyes roamed over the passenger side mirror. A beer truck followed Zane's pickup then she saw a dark sport utility swing a little wide behind a van four cars back.

Hair stood up along her neck. A gut feeling triggered her antennae for danger. Traffic slowed to a stop. She got a better view of the suspicious vehicle when Zane moved his pickup over to the left lane.

The make was a Yukon, not a Land Rover.

Paranoia must have her imagining that every dark sport utility followed her. But when she noticed the vehicle sliding over into Zane's lane in what appeared to be a late decision, her heart began to pound against her chest.

No other cars moved in the two lanes to her right. Heavy traffic chugged forward moving a few feet at a time, clogging the flow of vehicles through the massive intersection.

What would be the point of jockeying across lanes?

The driver could just be antsy, but what if she was right? Would someone dare to walk right up to the truck while she sat caught in the traffic jam?

Zane moved into the left turn lane.

She watched the side mirror.

The navy blue Yukon was now two cars back – just entering the turn lane, too.

Don't panic. Could be nothing.

Zane shifted to turn the radio on. Late seventies rock and roll poured out at low volume.

"I hate traffic the Friday before a holiday," he mumbled.

Breathing was difficult. She couldn't answer him. They inched forward as the gap between cars tightened. Their truck sat in a virtual parking lot with nowhere to maneuver if they had to get away.

She chewed on her bottom lip. If whoever it was took a shot at her, Zane might be in the line of fire this time.

Zane asked, "Are you okay?"

Turning around and shrugging, she said, "Yes, fine. It's the traffic. I hate it, too."

The longer he studied her, the more nervous she became. She had a strange feeling he anticipated her movements.

Zane had found her too easily this morning. And he handled a gun like he knew what he was doing. He must have learned about more than flying in the Air Force. That still wouldn't convince her to stay around him if Mason's men showed up. But for now, she was going nowhere since she knew Zane had the coins.

Should she mention the Yukon? Nothing had happened other than her bout of paranoia.

The minute she gave him reason to worry he'd want to keep her locked up in his apartment. She had to get back to the marina. Maybe she'd change her tactic from offering to rearrange the storage room, which had annoyed Zane, to helping him clean up his boat, which ought to thrill him.

Especially if she cleaned the kitchen and bathroom, the least favorite areas for most men.

That plan had potential.

Feeling relaxed for the first time in days, she threw another casual glance at her side view mirror and did a double take. The passenger door swung away from the Yukon. Someone stepped out, all but his gray pants hidden by the door.

Her lungs backed up in full panic mode.

She cut her eyes at Zane who was looking intently at something in his rearview mirror. Were men coming up on his left? She quietly unclipped her seatbelt and dove out of the truck, running flat out.

At the sound of Angel's door opening, Zane wrenched around to find himself alone in the cab. He slammed the truck into park, hit the release on his seatbelt and jumped out, running around the front of the truck.

Horns started blowing with the traffic light change.

She was already through the traffic jam and disappeared around a corner.

People were yelling. The beer truck laid on his horn.

Zane took one look back at the vehicles behind him to see if anyone was pursuing her.

No. So why had she run?

He stomped back to the driver's side and dove in, throwing it in gear and driving through the intersection as the light turned yellow.

Damn! She was gone again. He wanted to bang his head against a wall.

Slapping the wheel, he blew out a breath. At least this time, he'd gotten a break. She'd been too involved with the dog on their way back from Jacksonville to notice he'd taken the cup she'd used to serve Chut water.

With one good fingerprint he'd finally know who she was—whether he found her again or not.

The minute he had her identification, he was turning it over to the police and requesting they put out an APB for her safety.

~*~

Zane drove straight to his apartment. The last time Angel vanished she'd gone back there, but the route had been shorter and easy to remember. Ten miles of turns and bridges separated his home and the marina.

He swung into the first parking spot and wished with every breath he took she'd be waiting at his door.

Negative.

Regardless, he dashed into the house just to make sure she wasn't magically sitting at the kitchen counter eating cold pizza. The further he went on his irrational search, the deeper his disappointment.

His immaculate apartment appeared undisturbed. And there *should* be no trace of her. He paced the floor, opened the microwave and shut it, and decided he was losing his mind.

His perfectly tidy apartment had suddenly become a problem. Now it was as strong a reminder of his compulsive-cleaner houseguest as her yellow running shoes would be if they'd sat in the middle of the floor.

Shit.

Grabbing his keys on the way out, he punched in Ben's number and jogged to the truck. The fingerprint specialist might give him grief, but he'd always come through when Zane had to have a name.

And he *had* to have a name. Now.

He had to find her or report her as missing.

Chapter 24

Angel watched from a fast food restaurant as Zane pulled away from his apartment complex. She'd been lucky to arrive ahead of him, but it had taken accepting a ride from a kid with a motorcycle who'd dropped her a few blocks away.

No one had followed Zane in or out of his apartment parking lot. At least *he* was still safe. She waited another half hour until clouds covered the sliver of moon to give her plenty of darkness before she started hunting a way into the complex without attracting undue attention.

It took her even longer to zigzag a convoluted half-mile route that sometimes meant crawling between bushes and buildings, but she finally managed to sneak around to the rear of the apartment. Hunched over most of the time, she worked through the thick foliage, hesitating when tenants strolled by on the paths.

When she found the patio belonging to Zane's apartment, she rolled over the wrought-iron railing onto the tiled floor. The cool surface offered a better hiding place than sitting in his comfortable deck chairs. With no idea where Zane had gone, she probably had a long wait until she could get inside the apartment.

If he let her back in.

He had to be pissed and she couldn't even justify her panic. When she'd gotten through the traffic and found a place to stop, she'd looked back to see all the vehicles turning left. Even the dark blue Yukon.

Had she imagined the threat?

Her gut said no, that she was right to run, but her gut

didn't have to face Zane's anger.

She'd just eased down in the corner of the patio into a semi-comfortable position when she heard the muffled two-tone chime from Zane's front door. A tap-tap-tap against the door sounded, but no voice called out to see if anyone was home.

Could that be one of Mason's men at the front door?

Why would he knock? To pretend he was a visitor or making a delivery?

If that was Mason's men, would they be watching the rear to intercept her if she ran?

Damn. Sit here like an easy target? Or run and make herself visible?

She crawled around behind the chairs to hide, as far out of sight as possible. Trapped.

A shiver raced down her spine when she saw the front door handle turn and the deep blue barrier inch open.

The piercing security alarm screeched with the broken connection.

Angel scrunched down so low in the corner of the patio that her knees and chin met. She needed an escape route if the intruder proved to be a threat, but where would she go at this point?

A narrow hand slipped inside the front door and punched several numbers on the flashing panel, quieting the hideous noise. Zane's sister peeked around the edge of the door into his apartment.

Trish leaned in further and called, "Sugar, are you home? If you are, get your drawers on 'cause I'm coming in." She calmly entered, then closed the door, turned, and walked to look down the hallway toward Zane's bedroom.

"*Za-ane.*" She shrugged and strolled into the kitchen.

Angel expelled the breath she'd been holding and her heartbeat slowed to halfway reasonable.

How long would his sister stay or, worse, what if she wanted to sit outside? She mentally ticked through a selection of possible scenarios, all of which ended with being found hiding on the patio.

Another rule from her survival training popped into her mind.

The best defense is a good offense.

And truth be known, Trish had no idea what type of relationship she and Zane shared so finding Angel here without him might not look unusual.

Even better, maybe Trish knew where he'd stored the canvas boat curtains.

Angel stood up, straightened her clothes, and twisted all of her hair back up into the clasp she'd borrowed earlier from Trish's drawer. She tapped on the glass door, waited a minute and then rapped harder the second time.

When Trish stuck her head out of the kitchen she immediately cocked it to one side in that confused-dog look before her eyebrows shot up in recognition. A cheery smile popped into place as she hurried across the room to unlock the glass doors, chattering the whole time.

"Oh, Sugar, I'm so sorry. I didn't see you sitting out there. Did you lock yourself out?"

That worked. "Yeah, I was locked out. Good timing for you to show up."

Seriously good timing.

She hadn't paid attention to Trish's soft southern accent the first time they'd met, but caught it now.

"Come on in, Sug, it's too hot to sit out there. I don't know how you and Zane stand the heat. The man loves his fresh air. Let's close the door and enjoy the AC."

Trish's ankle-length fuchsia dress dotted with yellow squiggles blared in stark contrast to Zane's coffee brown and forest green décor. The dark-haired beauty circled the sofa carrying a glass full of cola-looking liquid, before sinking into the soft green leather.

"Want something to drink, Sugar?"

"No, I'm fine. Thanks for letting me in."

"No problem." Trish eyed her curiously. "I hadn't even heard of you before yesterday. So, where'd you meet my brother?"

A reasonable question under any other circumstance, but not one Angel had anticipated. Telling Zane's sister he'd helped her escape armed men didn't strike her as a wise idea.

"We met in North Carolina. I was in a hurry to leave, so he gave me a ride to Jacksonville." Basically true.

"You live here or just visiting?"

Though Angel knew his sister's intent was not to put her on the spot, it didn't alleviate her discomfort. The fact that they'd never meet again didn't change the way Angel felt about blatantly lying to her.

Her father had lied as part of his plea bargain. Basically, he'd sacrificed her to save his own skin. Mason had lied when he hired her. Angel would stay as close to the truth as possible.

That didn't mean she couldn't be a little creative.

"Actually, I'm visiting. I plan to relocate in the future, but haven't made up my mind where yet. How long have you been here?"

"I moved here three years ago when Zane did. Before that I lived in Houston. We grew up just outside the city limits. Our parents died while Zane was in the Air Force so he opted out early. He didn't feel any real tie to Houston, and I'd missed him terribly. When he picked Ft. Lauderdale, so did I."

Trish's deep brown eyes softened every time she mentioned her brother.

Angel envied the close sibling relationship. Zane's love for his sister had been written all over his face when he'd hugged her the day before.

Before Trish could ask her another question she'd have to dodge, Angel said, "Zane said you're really good at appraising antiques."

Trish looked away, looking decidedly uncomfortable and mumbled, "He's biased."

Sore topic. Angel changed direction to fix her mistake. "He also tells me you have a gift shop. Sounds like a fun business. Tell me about it."

That brought a smile to Trish's face, but not her voice. "It's an eclectic mix of doodads. Been open three months."

Zane was right. His sister's heart wasn't in the gift shop. But would moving her shop to this other Las Olas area make any difference? Angel wanted to do anything to help Zane and she liked Trish, but the best she could offer was encouragement. "Takes time to build a business, but Zane says you're great with people."

Trish leaned back, kicking her crossed leg with a nervous bounce. "I told him things would pick up this winter when the snowbirds show up."

"That makes sense. So you're partners?"

"I couldn't have done it without Zane's help. I had no idea where to start with opening a business, but..." Trish shrugged, a version of Zane's. "I'm getting the hang of it. He takes care of all the real business and I work with the customers."

Angel wondered where the tough breaks Zane had mentioned came in. His parents may not have doted on Trish, but she was bright and pleasant, obviously loved her brother and operated her own shop. *Sometimes.* His sister was sitting here again during business hours. Maybe Trish had someone covering for her when she showed up unannounced like this.

Trish waved her hand from side to side. "Yo, Angel, back to earth."

"Sorry, what were you saying?"

"I asked you where Zane is?"

Oops. "He didn't tell me where he was going, but he'll probably be back before you know it." Fair answer.

"He doesn't even have an answering machine. Can you believe that? I called earlier here to see what his plans were, but didn't get him," Trish said, jiggling her glass.

Angel started to ask why Trish didn't call Zane's cell phone, but changed her mind. The more she let Trish talk, the less *she* had to say.

"So anyhow, I jumped the bus and took a chance he was here. But it's just as well. I'm getting to know you instead. Can't say that I've met any female friends of Zane's since he moved here."

Interesting. "Why not?" Angel asked.

Trish's thick black lashes met when she smiled. She shoved her shoulders up in another shrug. "He's never had a problem meeting women. They fall all over him. But a twit in Texas burned him years ago. They were pretty intense for two months, until he found out she was *engaged* to somebody else."

What a bitch.

Trish continued swishing the cubes around in her glass and rambled on. "I don't think he ever got over it. These days he sees everything in a hard line, right or wrong. If there's one thing my brother hates, it's being deceived. Personally, I was glad to see the gold digger gone. My brother's generous to a fault and I can't stand anyone taking advantage of him."

Trish glanced at Angel and her eyes narrowed for just a second, then lit with a smile again.

In spite of all Trish's flighty mannerisms, she had a solid core of strength where Zane's welfare was concerned. A strength that maybe even Zane didn't realize.

The smile of a charming young woman replaced Trish's vexed reaction over the gold digger. She glanced at her jangling bracelet watch.

"I can't stay long. My friend, Heidi, is picking me up after she gets off work." Trish bounced up holding her glass out for examination. "Looks like I'm empty. Hang on. I'll be right back. You need a water or drink or anything?"

"I'm fine." Shoot. It wasn't bad enough that Angel was becoming attached to a man she'd never see again. Now she wanted to get to know his sister better.

Some people fantasized about winning the lottery and living a life of leisure.

She fantasized about having friends. A respectable job and a real home. Nothing elaborate, but with a man who loved her, and who would give her children.

Now that she'd met Trish, she wished she'd had a sister.

Because of the less-than-ideal household Angel had grown up in, she'd had few friends. She'd never brought guests home to be around her mother's drinking. Once news of Angel's arrest hit the papers, everyone had deserted her. She'd shunned all female relationships after the twelve months and three days she'd spent in a cell trying to survive among women who'd trade a life for a pack of cigarettes without blinking.

Now, after years of bitter disappointments, she'd met a man dreams were made of, with a sister she'd genuinely like to know better. Creating space in her life for either one was an indulgence she couldn't afford.

Her timing stank. Life continued to wave her heart's desire in front of her then snatch it away any time her fingers touched the golden ring.

Trish hummed as she passed in front of Angel's chair,

then she bumped the coffee table and lost her balance.

Angel leapt up to grab Trish's drink before it hit the glass surface, but missed. When the now-full drink hit the floor, ice and cola splattered across the carpet.

"Hang on, I'll get some towels."

With a rag from the laundry room, Angel scrubbed the soft beige carpet. She sniffed a sweet whiskey scent, but kept her thoughts to herself. With the ice picked up, the damp area was hardly noticeable. Amazingly, the drink had left no stain.

"Hey, thanks," Trish said, rubbing her eyes with the heels of her hands. "You should move here. Maybe Zane would stay home more often."

Angel smiled at her. "Well, that would be nice, but I've got a small problem I need to take care of before I can figure out where to live."

Wavy black hair bounced around Trish's flawless complexion when she checked her watch. "Heidi must be running late. I better go catch the next bus before I miss it."

Angel didn't want her to go, but neither did she want Trish to miss her bus.

"I hope you two keep seeing each other. I really like you and my brother is the best. We're a lot alike you know." Trish grinned and winked.

His sister clearly didn't want to leave yet.

Angel decided to sit back and see what else Trish would tell her about Zane. Smiling at Trish, Angel said, "I'll admit you two can't deny being brother and sister."

"Well, yeah, that too, but he's restless like me," Trish noted.

"Really? What do you mean?"

Trish warmed to the new topic. "He can't stay still for long. He's always planning something and sometimes he flies without a load, without saying where he goes. I guess just to be flying. I think he just gets bored without the adrenaline rush of flying fighter jets, but he's always off doing stuff and won't talk about his work. I call him the mystery man."

Now they were getting somewhere.

Angel leaned forward but before she could ask what Trish meant there was a knock at the door. Trish rocketed

up from her chair. She rushed to the door and swung it
wide open with no consideration for who stood on the other
side.

Angel jumped from the couch, ready to fight for herself
and for Trish if a threat came through the door, but that
didn't happen.

Two arms decorated in bangles and rings wrapped
around Trish's back, then a head of spiked blond hair
appeared over her shoulder when this new person hugged
Trish.

Turning to Angel, Trish announced, "This is my friend,
Heidi and Heidi, this is my friend, Angel."

"Nice to meet you." Angel walked over to shake hands.

"Same here. Wow, you're even taller than Trish. I'm
living in the land of giants."

An understandable observation from someone who only
reached Angel's shoulder.

Trish's uninhibited grin radiated happiness. Angel
swallowed a lump of jealousy over the noticeably close
friendship.

No brother, no sister, no girlfriends, no man in Angel's
life. Why couldn't she have *one* person in her life who cared
for her?

Was she destined to spend her life alone?

Heidi told Trish, "Ready to go home?"

"Sure thing." Trish turned to Angel. "Tell Zane I had to
go, but I'll see him later." She gave Angel a big hug and
whispered, "Thanks. I owe you."

"What for?"

"Not lecturing me about drinking and helping me clean
up the floor, which means you don't plan to tell Zane."

The unrestrained hug warmed Angel's heart. She didn't
want to lecture Trish, but she would like to help the young
woman. "I won't say a word, but take care of yourself."

Trish nodded then snatched up her purse from the
kitchen, and waved as she left in a flurry of chattering as
Heidi closed the door behind them.

Leaving Zane *and* Trish would be hard, but never seeing
either one again was going to hurt. Once she went into a
witness protection program, no way could she have contact
with either.

She smacked her head. "Stupid, stupid, stupid. I cannot believe I didn't ask her about the damn boat curtains. Next time I need to keep my nose stuck in my own business," she complained to the empty room. Shaking her head, she dropped onto the dark green leather chair, wishing she really lived here and had Trish as a friend.

Trish would probably say, "Just do it, Sug. Take care of that small problem and hang around."

Angel had stretched the truth with that adjective.

A *small* problem would be if no one showed up in a week to pay the rent on her tiny house back in Raleigh. Playing keep-away with Mason and his goons ranked up with a nightmare-level crisis.

What few worldly possessions she owned would soon be set on the street, including a used racing bike and her acceptance notice to compete in the Tamarind Triathlon.

All the hard work she'd invested to compete in the high-profile event was wiped away.

Angel glanced at the door. Should she duck out the back and head for the marina to search for the coins?

After all it took to get back here without being seen?

At least she hoped she hadn't been seen.

Patience, she reminded herself.

With no idea where Zane had gone, or when he'd return, she pondered Trish's comment about Zane being a mystery man. Trish might have said more if Heidi hadn't shown up.

Zane might be a mystery to his sister, but he'd been nothing short of a lifesaver since Angel had met him. As if it hadn't been enough to rescue her the night she'd escaped, he'd shown up in the abandoned gas station out of thin air after someone had taken a shot at her.

Questionable timing? Yes, but she'd been damned glad to see him.

The man chiseled at the barriers she'd built around her emotions. His first kiss had surprised her, but now that she'd tasted Zane Black's kisses, she wanted more. She licked her lips, savoring the memory of his taste.

Years of debilitating setbacks had hardened her soul. She knew better than to trust a man with her life, but trusting one with her heart? Now that was a real stretch.

Dreams are for other women. Her throat tightened. She didn't have a future and not a chance of one with him. Nice guys didn't want a convicted criminal for a girlfriend.

Nothing could change the past.

Angel never indulged in self-pity, but her eyes burned with tears she refused to let fall.

She was falling in love with Zane.

Stupid, stupid, *stupid!*

Must be your lot in life to want only what you can't have.

Of all the things she'd lost in her life, losing him would be the hardest.

Chapter 25

Zane dialed Ben's lab number as he whipped his truck around the marina parking lot to head for the exit.

After ten rings he hung up and dialed the cell Ben carried for work.

"This is Ben."

"Hey, buddy, it's Zane. Where are you?"

"I'm at the hospital. Kerry went into labor. I just stepped out to call her parents."

Zane was torn between being thrilled for Ben and disheartened he couldn't ask his friend to run the prints. "Don't let me keep you."

"The doctor says it's going to be a while, so I'm good."

What kind of friend didn't go to be with his buddy for the birth of his first baby? *Shit.* Ben might not want anyone there now anyhow, but Zane had to go once the baby was born. "Congrats, man. I'll pick up some bubbly so we can toast when Little Ben pops out."

"Kerry will kick your ass if you bring in champagne and she can't have any yet. So what's up, Zane? You called for a reason."

"It'll wait."

"Don't tell me you finally got prints?" Ben razzed.

"Yeah. I've got some data to run, too."

"You don't sound thrilled. Why do I get the impression something's not right?" Ben asked, no longer in teasing mode.

"You could say things have gotten ... involved," Zane said.

"I don't like the direction this is going. Why don't you

turn this over to somebody else? You've got a lot on the line, which reminds me. I have news."

"What?" Mac came by to see me on his way out of town." Mac was Dan MacPherson, the SAC or Special Agent in Charge of the DEA task force that used the information Zane uncovered. "He wants to talk to you. The stuff you've been handing us is great, and I think they're wanting to do something permanent or maybe bring you in to work more closely with a team."

"No way. I'm not flying a desk for anything. Not even part of the time." Zane hated bureaucracy. Yeah, he knew how to work the politics, had done it for years in the Air Force, but that was the one part of flying fighter jets he'd been glad to give up. Besides. The informant gig he had was too sweet to let go.

"Hold your fuckin' horses, Luke Skywalker. You don't know what they're gonna offer."

Zane's response came out as an irritated growl. He couldn't stay in one spot long enough to organize his own package tracking system. He just held everything in his brain. No way could he play their game.

Besides, he'd take a pay cut he couldn't afford.

Desk jockey was out.

Ben's heavy, weary sigh came through loud and clear on the phone. "Listen, I'm guessing you're holding back about this woman because you two are doin' the mattress dance."

"I'm – "

Ben bulldozed right over him. "If you blow your cover – *and this gig* – because of her, I'm gonna kick your butt into next year."

Zane couldn't argue that point with Ben. He was supposed to be helping *catch* criminals. If he was caught hiding one, he'd face more than watching a reputation and a business crash and burn.

Still, he couldn't stop trying until he knew for sure. That's why he trusted no one but Ben to check out the prints. Even Vance didn't need to know because it would put him in a tight spot, and that wasn't fair to their friend who played the third musketeer alongside him and Ben in his small cadre of buddies.

One thing Zane had learned from flying. He had to go

with his gut. He could no more turn his back on Angel at this point than he could his sister.

Angel needed him. She was too stubborn to accept his help willingly. Tough. She was getting it anyhow.

"It's complicated, Ben. I have to find out this woman's background."

Ben made a noisy sound of blowing out air. "I finished taking apart that chopped-up silver band you brought me. It did have a tracking device inside."

"Agency model?"

"No. Latest technology. Expensive stuff from the private sector, which does *not* make this better. What if she *is* a criminal?"

"Then I'll deal with it," Zane stated emphatically.

"You may be getting in over your head on this one, bud," Ben warned.

"It is what it is."

"Oh, man, this does not sound good, but you aren't listening so I'll shut up now. Drop off everything you've got. I'll run it through as soon as I get back to the lab, but I'm telling you I won't sugarcoat it."

"Thanks, Ben."

"And another thing. If the people who tagged her come after her, you damn well better call me, hotshot. You're not bullet proof. I'll have your back."

Zane wouldn't even answer that. No way would he bring Ben anywhere near this. "Give my love to Kerry."

Zane thumbed the button to end the call, but heard Ben mutter something profane that questioned the position of Zane's head relative to his ass.

Two more turns until he reached his apartment.

Streetlights flickered on along the highway in the dusty, early-evening glow as the sun was swallowed by the western tree line. Three hours had passed since Angel had vanished.

Sick disappointment settled in his chest.

She hadn't been at the airport or the boat. He couldn't think of anywhere else she might go.

With Ben and his wife in the delivery room, Zane wouldn't get a rundown on the fingerprints for at least another day or two.

By the time he found out who she was it could very well be a moot point.

Angel would be long gone, maybe permanently.

His stomach churned at the idea that someone was trying to kill her. He forced his thoughts away from the idea that they might succeed.

She'd been a frustrating puzzle from the minute he'd met her – a multi-layered, three-dimensional puzzle with dangerous, razor-sharp pieces missing.

Where had she been kept against her will, and why?

All he knew was she had the talent of an elite athlete and had lost a scholarship for some unknown reason. Everything came back to that one word – unknown.

He wanted to shake some sense into her, make her understand how much she needed his help. The thugs he'd met in Jacksonville had been dressed in two-thousand-dollar tailored suits.

Against an organized and financially robust lethal group, how did she expect to protect herself, much less him, too?

He couldn't recall when a woman had put him first in her life. Certainly not Sylvia, the dazzling jewel he'd fallen for in Texas. She'd been anything but what she'd presented. Truly a woman who planned for her future by covering all bases, Sylvia had still been engaged while dating him.

Just when Sylvia had convinced Zane she loved him, he'd discovered she had a clueless fiancé who couldn't wait to marry the lying bitch.

Good thing Ben had still lived in Houston then. Observing Sylvia with objective eyes had given Ben cause to run a very revealing background check.

All Sylvia'd really sought was the material wealth Zane's family name and eventual inheritance would offer. Basically a businesswoman, Sylvia had been shopping her engagement deal to see if she could improve the return on her investment. Since then, Zane had given few women more than casual interest. Others had proved to be just as materialistically driven.

Except for Angel.

For someone who desperately needed assistance just to stay alive, she'd refused his every offer until she'd been forced to take his help.

Trusting few people in his life, he understood Angel's reluctance to share her private problems, but she wouldn't survive on her own for long. Not without a lot of luck and a chunk of money. Neither of which appeared readily available to her. What would it take to convince her she could depend on him?

He might never find out.

She was gone, maybe forever. Out of sight, out of mind?

Whoever came up with that saying had never met Angel. Auburn hair and mile-long legs remained emblazoned as a header to all his thoughts.

As he made the last corner into his apartment complex, images of Angel clicked past his mind's eye in slow motion. Wide-eyed and terrified in his airplane, then sleeping curled up on his patio.

Dancing her fingers through the wind as she'd ridden beside him in the truck. Shampooed and showered, draped in a single towel next to his laundry. Zane smiled, remembering the look on her face when he'd found her.

Then there was the one vision he'd never forget – her half-covered in his shirt and sleeping in his bed.

Her hazel eyes flashed with fire when he annoyed her, but they were pure whiskey – warm and intoxicating – when he kissed her.

He shook his head at his wandering thoughts. What was he going to do? He couldn't keep walking this damned fence between right and wrong. Indecision was ripping his insides apart.

Go back to the basics. Stick with what you know.

Ben was right. If Zane did corral Angel again, he should turn her over to the authorities. They had more time to deal with an uncooperative female in trouble.

Right?

He parked the truck and sat there, watching the halogen parking lot lamps begin to brighten.

Who was he kidding? He snorted at his lack of honesty.

Even if he didn't have concerns over their ability to shield her, would he really hand her over to a bunch of strangers? No way. If he found her, he knew what he'd do – drag her into his arms and kiss her senseless. There'd never been a woman he'd been driven to have in the way he desired Angel.

Correction. If he got her in his hands again, he'd do a hell of a lot more than kiss her.

Chapter 26

CK needed to do some housecleaning. And he would when this job was finished. Joe was one of his best men, but one more mistake and he'd be demoted.

Demotion in CK's world was permanent, all the way down to the bottom of a lake.

"I don't have wings," Joe complained, his exasperation coming through. "Not much we can do when she takes off on foot through six lanes of traffic. Besides, we had company."

"Who?" Had Mason gotten nervous and hired a backup group? He'd called CK twice in the past twenty-four hours. Mason was high-maintenance but not usually a nuisance, which meant someone had his nuts clamped in a vise.

Who? Now *that* would be valuable information.

Joe said, "Don't know, but I think that's why she ran. Some guy jumped out of a dark blue Yukon not far behind her and the pilot in a turn lane. When the girl took off like a bat outta hell, the guy from the Yukon jumped back in the passenger side and the truck turned at the light. They were too far away to nail a tag number."

Joe had just added another demerit point to his next evaluation. CK couldn't believe this bitch was outmaneuvering some of his best men.

"Cover all the bases and don't lose the pilot. She thinks she's safe with him. She'll go back to him at some point."

"How long we going to do this? Be easier to grab her."

Joe echoed CK's thoughts. "My orders are to pick her up only when she's alone and without drawing any attention. If those orders change, you'll know."

CK ended the call and set the phone on the desk in his

hotel room. This didn't fit Mason's MO. What was stopping Mason from turning CK loose to grab the girl, and disappear anybody else who got in the way?

Mason wanted the girl in hand no later than Saturday and CK wasn't leaving without getting his bounty. That meant, as far as CK was concerned, that deadline would override the "don't draw attention" orders if his men couldn't corner Angel before tomorrow morning.

And if that happened, Mason would just have to live with the consequences.

Chapter 27

Zane parked the truck then trudged to his apartment, hating the emptiness that awaited him inside. He unlocked the door. When the alarm system failed to sound its warning beep, he tensed.

He'd set his alarm when he left.

Reaching down into his boot to retrieve his Keltec, Zane eased the door ajar. Through the dark shadows cast across the room he could just make out a figure in the low light filtering into his living room from the kitchen.

His throat closed.

Angel. He couldn't believe she was there.

She stood with her back to him, but he'd seen her tense when he'd opened the door.

He stepped inside, closed the door, and dropped the gun back into his boot. He moved gradually into the room, afraid she'd vanish. His lungs struggled to draw air.

She was really here.

How? The how didn't matter so much right now as his relief that threatened to take the starch out of his knees.

An arm's length away, he stopped. She knew he was here, but hadn't moved to acknowledge him. Scattered thoughts raced across his mind, but only one broke through to the surface.

She'd come back to him.

He swallowed and whispered, "Angel?"

A soft glow from the under-counter lights in the kitchen barely reached this room. With her back to it, her face was hidden in shadows until she lifted her head. The sight of the pain in her eyes broke his heart.

He opened his arms and she came into them. Zane wrapped her in a close embrace, so very glad to feel her warm body next to his.

"I thought you were gone," he said, his voice raw with emotion. "Forever."

She shook her head against his chest. Tears dampened his shirt.

"Are you okay?" he asked.

She nodded against his chest, hugging him around the waist.

"How'd you get in?"

"Trish came by. Saw me on the patio and thought I'd gotten locked out."

He stroked up and down her back, his fingers massaging along her spine. His chin rested against her silky hair. A lump of gratitude formed in his throat. She was alive.

Angel tilted her head back. Sad eyes beseeched him through wet lashes. "I had to get them away from you."

Her fervent declaration shook him. She didn't need to protect him. It was the other way around.

He breathed out a deep sigh and leaned his forehead against hers, pleading in a whisper, "Honey, I wish you'd trust me enough to tell me what's going on."

She pushed her hands up his chest then clasped each side of his face, stroking lightly until two fingers rested on his lips.

He kissed the soft pads.

"I told you, you're the one person I *do* trust, but I'm not taking you down with me if my situation goes bad. If that happens, you need to be able to distance yourself from me."

There was one problem with that advice.

He couldn't distance himself because he couldn't let her go. With or without her help, he'd get to the bottom of this and find a way to stop whoever was after her.

Her sheer breath flowed against his neck. She trailed her fingers across his face and neck, tormenting him with the wispy touch. "I'm sorry. I shouldn't have come back here, but I had nowhere else to go."

"I'm glad you came back. You can always come to me."

"My being here puts you at risk. I never meant to cause you trouble. I don't want anything to happen to you."

He hugged her close. From *what* was she trying to protect him? "Who's the guy that's after you?" he urged.

She shook her head "no" against him.

He'd have laughed at her favorite word if he weren't so damned worried. "I can't keep guessing. Help me out here," Zane said. "He's not your boyfriend or husband, is he?"

"No," she said, barely above a whisper.

"Then you either did something to make him angry as hell or you have something he wants," Zane said.

"Yes."

"Which is it?"

"Both."

What did she have? Zane had the compass, but that couldn't be it. Could it?

"If you give it back, will he leave you alone?" Zane asked.

"No."

"Why not?"

"It doesn't belong to him," she explained.

Zane drew his head back. She was killing him. None of this made sense.

All his questions fled when she blinked up at him through wet lashes.

Nothing mattered at that moment. Not her past, not his future, nothing but the luxury of her in his arms.

Zane lowered his lips, gently raking across hers. He kissed her cheek, her nose, her eyes, tasting the salty tears.

He moved his lips along her chin up to the crest of her ear and buried his face in her hair, inhaling the wonderful fresh smell. She'd showered again. Between that sweet scent and her wearing nothing but his T-shirt, relief gave way to a want so deep and hungry his hand shook when he stroked his hand along the smooth contour of her back.

Caution sirens screamed in his head.

Her scent overrode them.

Her fingers twined around the back of his neck, drawing herself up against him. His lips swept softly over her warm mouth when he wanted to do so much more.

She surged up, returning his kiss with an intensity that rocked him.

He clenched a fistful of her T-shirt. Her mouth urged him to take what she offered. He scooped her bottom and lifted her against him.

Her legs wrapped around his waist then she rubbed up and down against his arousal, sending what blood was left in his body surging into his groin.

Holy mother of...

He held her with one arm and used his other hand to reach up under her T-shirt to cup her breast. The minute his finger brushed over her nipple, she surged against him again.

One more time like that and they'd end up on the floor.

He turned and lowered her to his sofa then hovered above her on his knees. Now he could touch all of her. Pushing her shirt up, he stared at her plump breasts rising and falling with labored breaths. His gaze raked down across all that smooth skin blanketing her abdomen to a thatch of dark auburn hair.

When he lifted his gaze back to her face, eyes hot with passion stared up at him until she looked away, embarrassed. "I'm skinny."

"No, baby, you're magnificent." Then he lowered his mouth to her breast, bent on proving just how perfect she was. He licked her nipples and she squeezed her legs against him. Then he suckled one breast while teasing the other one with his finger.

She clenched harder against him. "I want..."

He lifted his head then gently tortured both nipples with his thumbs. "This?"

She made a sound that was half cry and half yes.

Not enough. He wanted more. He released one breast, sliding his fingertips lightly over her skin, watching her tremble. When his fingers tangled in the curls between her legs, she started panting. "Please don't..."

He stilled his hand. "Don't what?"

"Don't ... stop."

Damned glad to hear they both had the same idea. He caressed the soft folds that were already damp and pressed a finger inside her.

She cried out, shaking, so close ... but not quite.

He bent down and nibbled on her breast, lightly scraping his teeth over the turgid tip. At the same moment, he pulled his finger out of her and drew a wet stroke to the spot that sent her arching. He'd only flicked back and forth twice over the sensitive nub and she tensed. He quickened his pace and she shrieked while he held her there until she collapsed.

Nothing could be more beautiful than watching that.

He kissed her, sending his tongue in to enjoy the sweet taste that could only be Angel. Her arms had fallen limp, but she lifted her hands again, holding his head to her.

A chirping noise broke through his fervor.

What the hell was that?

She tugged on his hair when he tore his mouth away. He moved his lips along her shoulders. She stretched against him, a sated feline leaning in to be stroked.

The chirping grew more constant.

Damn. What was that?

Ah, hell, his damned cell phone was ringing. He pictured it sailing across the room and slamming against the wall.

With each loud chirp of the phone, consciousness hammered his aroused senses back to reality. Angel said Trish had been by today. His sister and her friend Heidi had the number for emergencies.

High Vision's dispatch could be calling.

Just once, Zane wished he was undisciplined enough to ignore his responsibilities.

Every nerve in his body stood on end. He was so hard the zipper outline had to be embossed on his erection.

Resigned to his fate, Zane pulled his hand from Angel's breast. He stroked her shoulder and kissed her face. God, he didn't want to take his hands off of her.

"Honey, I'm sorry," he whispered.

Sorry they weren't in his bed, sorry his life was not his own, sorry some jerk had invented cell phones.

Angel lifted her head. She stared at him as though he'd said there were elephants coming at them. Her swollen lips begged to be kissed.

If their lips touched again, he wasn't sure he could back away.

Quiet reigned for several seconds once the phone ceased, but then the irritating sound resumed.

"Damn." He kissed her forehead. "I've got to take this call." He eased out of her arms, off the couch and stood, pulling the phone from his hip.

"Zane," he snapped, anger, frustration and self-disgust wrapped around the short salutation.

"This is Heidi. I'm sorry to bug you, but you said to call if Trish ever needed you." As his sister's best friend from Houston, Heidi had decided to stay in Ft. Lauderdale after one visit. She was the closest Trish had ever come to having a sister. Her concern for Trish rivaled Zane's, the reason she was the only person besides his sister who had his cell number.

"What's wrong? Where is she?" Several possible situations crossed Zane's mind, all of which soured his stomach.

"She's okay," Heidi said. "But she's at the Pink Baby and some guy is giving her a hard time. I dropped her at the shop earlier and was supposed to meet her there, but when I went home to let Dazzle out in the yard my car died. I can't get it started. I know you don't want her walking to a bus at night."

Zane growled under his breath.

"She heard from one of the other girls this guy's into weird stuff. I think he scares her. Trish didn't want to bother you, so I told her I'd get a ride and come get her, but you're only fifteen minutes away. I'm close to an hour once I get the car going."

Zane looked over at Angel. She was standing a foot away now, staring out the patio doors. In the minute since he'd answered his phone she'd withdrawn. The distance between them felt as wide as the ocean crashing against the beach outside.

"Okay, Heidi. I'll get her."

He snapped the phone shut. "Angel..."

She held up a hand to stop him. "I'm torn between thanking you for that and apologizing for letting it happen. I shouldn't be doing this, but it's not your fault and I won't let it happen again."

He closed his eyes then opened them. When would his life get any easier?

"Look, Angel, there is no fault. I want you, and I'm pretty sure you feel the same way, but this probably isn't the time. Not until we solve your problem." Because she wouldn't listen to what he had to say until then. He *would* convince her that she belonged with him.

"If you say so." She looked at the phone in his hand. "Is something wrong?"

He hadn't realized he was gripping the phone so hard. "I've got to go pick up Trish. Do you want to go with me?"

"No. I'd rather stay here," she said.

Zane sighed. Trish had to be picked up now. Before she got hurt.

"Will you promise me you won't leave the apartment?" he asked. "I don't think I can take too many more surprises today. When I get back, I want you to tell me why you took off earlier."

"I won't leave," she said, then added, "I promise."

Based on her posture – arms crossed, back straight, chin high – a casual observer would think her confidence had returned. Not Zane. He'd noticed her habit of chewing on her bottom lip when she was nervous. "That's not all I asked for."

Disappointment filled her eyes. "I can't tell you the truth about why I left earlier and I'd rather not lie to you."

They'd tackle this when he returned. "After I get Trish, I'll pick up something to eat on the way home. What would you like?"

"Pizza?"

Her predilection for one food group amused him, but he had a tough time smiling with his heart in his throat.

He hated walking away from her right now, but knew better than to leave Trish for long when she was partying hard.

Angel must have misread his reluctance as concern that she'd disappear.

"Don't worry. I'll be here."

Would she?

Chapter 28

Angel dug through the basket full of clean clothes next to the dryer. A blazing red shirt with a chest pocket was perfect. It suited her blazing fury. She hadn't quite figured out who she was angrier with, herself or Zane, but red covered all bases.

Had she completely lost all sense of priority? Okay, she'd admit the truth. He'd been right. She did want him as badly as he obviously wanted her.

She should have known that once Zane Black touched a woman there would be no other man after him. Not that she wanted another man, but once she went into the WITSEC program – or ended up back in prison – they'd never see each other again.

How was that fair to Zane?

It wasn't. Not any more than it was fair for her to be the only one to benefit by his lovemaking tonight. Staying here lulled her into complacency and had her starting to think Zane was right. That she could solve her problems and stick around.

If he knew everything, he'd realize how wrong he was.

Should she tell him everything?

Why not? She trusted him.

She propped a hip against the dryer, considering the pluses and minuses of doing that. If she told him about Mason, how she ended up at the compound, and about the coins, Zane would believe her. Then he'd bring in the police who would bring in the FBI. Everyone would listen to her and maybe even believe her.

Until she failed to produce someone to corroborate her

alibi.

The FBI would also bring in Mason who would have to explain his fingerprints on the plastic coin sleeves.

What would she do in Mason's shoes?

Claim that he and Angel had been intimate right before she disappeared from work. That some sleeves from his own rare coin collection had gone missing, but he hadn't put it together until now.

No matter how ludicrous an idea, they'd buy it once he marched out all the philanthropic things he did each year and how he'd never had so much as a traffic ticket. Then he'd say how he'd wanted to give her a second chance, thought she'd changed her ways since being released from prison. Felt sorry for her when she came to him looking for a job, but couldn't resist when she stripped in front of him, then threw herself at him.

He was a guy, after all. He'd bow his head in fake shame over his one weakness.

Everyone would turn suspicious eyes on Angel at that point.

Then Zane would get involved and try to convince the FBI that Mason was lying because Zane had met her when she escaped Mason.

By the time the FBI went to the airfield to corroborate that, anyone who'd been around that night would be gone or dead. More innocent lives on her conscience.

It would continue to spiral out of control until Angel ended up in prison and Zane was accused of helping her, maybe landing in prison, too. Or dead, which was a more realistic possibility.

A possibility she could not let happen.

No, she would keep him out of this and get the heck away from him as soon as she could do it when he wouldn't be able to follow. She'd panicked and run here as the only safe place she knew, but nowhere she stayed was safe.

If she hadn't promised not to leave tonight, she'd be gone now.

Grabbing the T-shirt, she stalked into the bathroom and cranked the shower lever to one degree below lobster-boiling temperature. The scalding water charged over her screaming muscles, drawing out the tension.

Showering at any opportunity, and alone, was a luxury she never took for granted and rarely passed up.

Refreshed, she dried her hair quickly before relaxing on the leather sofa. She started to wipe everything down, but she'd been forgetting around Zane, a couple of times. And why should she continue with her habitual cleaning here at Zane's apartment?

It wasn't as though a pilot would care if she left a fingerprint, or would have reason to watch for them.

Finding the television remote, she flipped channels until local news crawled across the screen. A perky anchorwoman shared the latest stock market concerns and weather before moving to national interests.

Angel had curled up against the wide armrest of the sofa and almost drifted off to sleep when a news report broke through her slumber.

"The body found in a dumpster near Raleigh, North Carolina has been identified as Jeff Jurnowski," the news anchor announced. "Initial report on cause of death is a gunshot wound to the head. The police have several leads, but are not discussing those at this time."

She sat up, paralyzed by the words.

That was Mason's former employee, Jeff. With the bullet hole in the head Mason had put there to teach *her* a lesson.

Jeff had been nice to her, even showing her a picture of his pet Beagle. He'd worked on the wrong side of the law, but no one deserved to be murdered in cold blood.

The news report rattled her. Mason wasn't stupid. Jeff had been shot just days before her escape. His body hadn't just disappeared and shown up in a dumpster by mistake. Not when Mason could make use of it. What was Mason up to?

Her hands trembled when she lifted the remote to click up the volume.

The news anchor finished with, "The authorities are running fingerprints found on the man's possessions. His employer, Mason Lorde, has issued a statement of the company's sympathy over the loss of a respected employee. Lorde went on to say he will aid the police in any way and alluded to a female employee who went missing around the time of Jurnowski's death. Police refused to comment on whether the female is a suspect in the case, but said they are working all possible angles. They are not releasing her name at this time."

Angel's mouth fell open. *...authorities are running fingerprints found on the man's possessions.* She'd touched the photo of Jeff's dog.

Mason intended to hang Jeff's murder on her.

Chapter 29

Zane shuffled through the front door with Trish and a pizza. His sister's glum face and quiet countenance were a result of his own discontent.

He'd decided to bring her home rather than spend two hours on the road delivering her to the house she shared with Heidi. Worry about Angel slipping away had driven that decision.

Women would put him in an early grave.

"Sorry to screw up your evening," Trish whispered with a slur. The anguish in her upturned face told him he'd hit a nerve with his black mood.

The last thing he wanted to do was hurt his sister, especially in her present condition. He shouldn't take his aggravation out on her. But keeping her out of trouble and unharmed became tougher each week. Every trip he made out of town meant he might be gone when she needed him there to save her.

She had no one but him.

He owed her for all she'd been denied, and for leaving her to go into the Air Force when she'd needed him. He was convinced he could've prevented her downfall if he'd been here.

As the first born and only child his parents really wanted, he'd gotten everything. Trish had been ignored, thrown nothing more than leftovers. Growing up, he'd rarely seen his parents himself, but at least they hadn't blatantly avoided him the way they had their late-in-life daughter.

He was angry all right, with everybody, including

himself.

Angel walked tentatively into the living room from the bathroom hallway. Jazz music playing low seeped into the room from speakers hidden in the corners.

His red T-shirt hung on her like an oversize nightgown. Angel must have dug it out of the clean laundry and showered.

Her hair was damp. The smell of soap and shampoo was going to drive him crazy for the rest of his life if he lost her. Drained from dealing with Trish, his brain teetered between behaving responsibly and the desire to strip Angel bare in the shower.

Trish weaved in place. "I 'pologized to Zane, so I'll 'pologize to you, Angel. Sorry."

Angel shot him a questioning look.

He fought the urge to tape his sister's mouth shut. Zane loved his sister, but he'd like one night of peace and quiet. One night he wasn't reminded of all the bad things that had happened to Trish.

"I asked him to take me home, but noooo," Trish said. "I'll bunk somewhere ... outta the way."

Zane rubbed his neck. "You can have the fold-out. Angel's in the bedroom. I'll find another spot."

Trish gave him a strange look. She was clearly surprised that he and Angel were not sleeping together.

"Absolutely not," Angel stated. "I hardly use up a third of that king sized bed. Trish can sleep in there, too."

"You sure?" Trish said, her confused gaze flicking between the two of them.

Zane gave Trish a don't-go-there look he'd given her plenty of times in the past.

Trish shrugged. "Going to change and hit the sack then." She gave them each another look then hugged her brother and said, "Love you. So, so sorry. Promise not to be a pain again."

His throat tightened. She was good as gold and he'd crawl through broken glass for her. Trish hadn't really done anything wrong, hadn't slipped much in months, but she needed to be in a program and needed his support. Heidi had been Trish's sponsor once in the past, but Zane couldn't leave this for Heidi to handle alone. He hugged her. "Love you, too. Don't mind me."

"You need a vacation," Trish whispered. "With someone like Angel. Do a world of good for what ails you."

He squeezed her. "Goodnight."

Trish turned to Angel and tottered over to give her a hug. Zane warmed at the surprise on Angel's face that softened into a look of genuine caring. Again, he wondered about the woman who never left his thoughts. Where did she come from? Who was her family?

Who wants to kill her?

When Trish tripped down the hall and closed the bedroom door, Zane explained, "I called Heidi back and told her I'd just bring Trish here for the night."

"I'm glad you did."

That didn't sound good. Was Angel worried he'd push her to finish what they'd started?

Having Trish here *would* ensure he kept his hands off Angel. Dammit.

Zane stretched the stiff muscles of his neck. "Want something to drink?"

"Sounds good. I'm going to get my things off the bed and make sure Trish is set. I'll be back in just a minute."

Zane trudged to the kitchen and carried a cold bottle of water to the patio. A beer normally tasted good on a hot evening, but after watching Trish tonight he didn't have the taste for one.

He left the outside lights off intentionally and navigated by the glow from the lamp inside. A soft breeze dispelled some of the humidity. Weather in South Florida reminded him of visiting the coast in Galveston.

He'd loved Texas, but couldn't stay there with the memories. Besides he'd needed a new home for Trish and somewhere to work where he wasn't known by half the city. Being a third generation son of the reputed Jackson Oil dynasty had its pros and cons. Zane couldn't buy a cup of coffee without some reporter making news out of whether he drank it alone or not.

Everyone had expected him to sign on as a company man once he'd returned from the military. He'd surprised his extended relatives and the city when he turned his back on Texas for Florida. Ben had already met Kerry and settled here. At the time, moving Trish to Ft. Lauderdale, hanging with his best friend and flying charters seemed like a hell of a plan.

He'd gotten busy – and successful – fast because of his willingness to fly when others wouldn't. Then the informant gig had come along, complete with an unusually large electronic transfer from a DEA cover business into his bank account to pay off his loan on the Titan. That had been a relief for certain, but worrying about Trish and keeping up with his business were starting to wear him down.

And he still didn't know if he had the High Vision contract the DEA was after. He expected more tests like the CFO's fancy dog drop. If so, those tests would have to come this weekend, during the last few days of the performance period for the bids.

Damn. The waiting sucked up every drop of patience he possessed. Maybe that's why he couldn't keep his hands off of Angel – too much untapped energy.

Liar. The truth stared him in the face, whether he wanted to put it into words or not. Just thinking about her vanishing from his life scared him to his toes.

He was in love with her.

For the good of his own self-respect, he'd walked away from the easy ride his parents' money could have given him and joined the Air Force. For his sister, he'd turned his back on a career as an officer and a pilot. A job nobody walked away from willingly – at least not in one piece.

What did he think he was going to do now?

Chuck all his responsibilities to help a strange woman who *still* might be a criminal?

No matter which way he went, he hit walls. He couldn't risk losing the High Vision contract or the money for Trish he got from the DEA, but neither could he let Angel face a threat alone.

He didn't even know her whole name, where she came from, or how she'd spent her life until now.

He didn't know what she ate besides pizza.

What he did know was how his insides flip flopped when she walked into a room. How she could look at him as if she believed he slayed dragons and make him want to go hunt one down for her.

He had it bad. This had all the earmarks of a critical mission that was doomed from the start.

A soft shuffling brought Zane from his mental meandering. Wisps of Angel's hair floated softly about her shoulders as she settled in a chair across from him. He understood her need for distance, but ached with the desire to hold her.

"What's Trish's story?" she asked quietly.

Zane leaned forward in his chair with his hands on the patio table. For too many years to count, he'd defended Trish against his parents' criticisms and nasty comments from relatives who didn't understand when Trish acted out. Time and guilt had developed Zane's hair trigger about anything regarding Trish. But Angel hadn't accused or passed judgment. She sounded sincerely interested.

"Trish is getting a late start in life," Zane said. "My fault."

"Why is it your fault?"

"I deserted her along with everyone else when I went in the military. I could see my parents felt burdened with an unwanted child, but I was eighteen and too caught up in what I wanted to notice the damage being done to Trish." Zane clenched his hand into a fist, then forced himself to relax it, spreading his fingers across the table.

Angel leaned forward and laid her hand over his. A simple touch that said she understood while she waited for him to go on.

"When our parents were killed, they left an inheritance with stipulations." He didn't give a rat's ass about money or wills, and hated what this one had done to his sister. "Trish knows I'll take care of her and share everything I have, but that didn't change what they did to her." He hung his head, recalling the agony and the guilt for the way his parents had dealt Trish a final blow.

"What your parents did?"

Unwanted memories flooded back. Zane paused to consider the damage a piece of paper could inflict. "Yes. They died and then they gutted her with words – or more the lack of words. I'll never forget her face at the reading of the will."

"They left her *out* of the will?"

"Oh, yes. Everything went to me, the golden boy, and not until I reach forty, which won't be for a few years. Nothing to Trish, not even a fare-thee-well. She was young and didn't understand the cold logic our parents had used. They thought I'd invest the funds where Trish would only squander money." He'd read those papers over and over again, sure they'd left her something, even a token amount, that proved she was just as much their child as he was.

Angel lifted his hand in her two slender ones. Her compassionate touch drew away some of his pain.

Zane glanced up to see the sadness in his soul reflected in her face. "I tried to tell Trish that our parents would have changed the will once she was an adult, and that their intention had been for me to watch out for her. That didn't erase the hurt. It wasn't about the money. Trish just needed to hear her name mentioned, to know she counted."

"I'm sorry for both of you," Angel whispered, her voice heavy with understanding. "But you can't blame yourself," she soothed. "Your parents deserted her. You didn't. She idolizes you. And I see the strength adversity has given her. She's much tougher than you think."

He'd like to think so, but Angel hadn't seen how far Trish had fallen after the reading of the will. Hadn't seen her in the hospital half dead. She'd come so far since then, but in the past few months, he'd sensed he was losing her again. He was afraid if he blinked he'd open his eyes and she'd be too far gone to save. "I didn't realize until after the will that she'd known for a while that she was an unwanted surprise. The will just hammered it home. That's when Trish took a downturn. She started drinking. Then some scumbag got her on coke."

The vision of her in a scumbag hotel, being beaten would forever be stuck in his head. He shook it off and said, "She tried AA in Houston. Worked for a while, but she didn't stick with it. She's been doing okay here." Oh, sure. Talk about denial. "But I'm blowing it being gone on such a crazy schedule."

"You're a good brother. Trish is very lucky. I wish I'd had a sibling."

Angel hadn't given him the usual platitudes about how Trish was young and would bounce back. With reminding him he was fortunate to have a sibling, Angel had unintentionally given him a tiny piece to the puzzle of her background.

She was an only child.

He'd had enough of dissecting his screwed up life. "Where are your parents?""My mother's dead. Died when I was twelve." She said that with a finality that stopped him from asking more.

Neither spoke for a while as the ocean's surf stirred against the shore. Zane felt Angel's fingers stroke over his hand. When was the last time anyone had comforted *him*? A vague memory of being held as a small child came to mind, but nothing since then.

Her depth of caring for others, in the face of her own immense problems, humbled him.

He was a fool to want this woman so much he ached, but he longed to hold her. Just to feel her in his arms.

After a bit, she moved her hands away and stood. "Think I'll turn in. We can talk tomorrow. Don't worry about Trish. I'll watch over her tonight." She'd stepped back to the glass doors.

He was up and around the table before she reached the opening, blocking her path.

"Angel."

"What?" She lifted her head.

"This."

He threaded his fingers around her neck up into her hair, lifting her face to his. His lips touched hers in a kiss full of compassion, not carnal desire.

After a slight hesitation, she surrendered. Her hands knifed up between them, then around his neck.

Oh, man, she felt like all his best wishes come true wrapped in one gorgeous package. Desire licked at every spot she touched. He loved her lips, soft, full on the bottom, hungry.

She grazed his lips with her teeth and ran her tongue across his mouth. One delicate hand slid down his neck, sending chills up his spine. If they didn't stop soon, he'd take her right there on the patio.

Stopping was his job.

Time to be responsible whether he liked it or not.

Zane ended the kiss, slowly, touching his lips to her cheeks and forehead.

"Honey." He cleared his tight throat and tried again, careful not to mention law enforcement since that always sent her running for cover. "We'll figure this out. I know you don't understand how, but I *can* help you. We'll work through this tomorrow. Okay?"

She nodded into his chest when he hugged her tight.

Reluctantly, he let her ease away from him, watching her until she disappeared down the hallway.

Zane settled back into his chair and listened to a seagull call in the distance. Wheels in his brain churned with the new information. He'd learned Angel was only twelve when her mother had died. She didn't even mention her father. What had life thrown at her after losing her mother? He had to know. Every minute with her tied him in one more knot.

Tomorrow he'd persuade her to tell him her full name, and he'd tell her about Ben. He couldn't tell her he worked with the DEA because keeping that secret was part of the gig. Even Trish didn't know. But he *would* find a way to convince Angel that she could trust his friend.

Chapter 30

Zane was sure he'd only just fallen asleep when his cell phone woke him. He checked the digital clock on his DVD player. Four-ten in the morning. He flipped the phone open.

"Zane."

"Sammy here. Got a High Vision shipment being cleared at the docks in Jacksonville. Will you be able to pick it up and deliver to Birmingham by 1900 local time?"

If not, Sammy would call one of the other two charter groups who would jump at the chance to shut out Black Jack Charters.

Zane stretched his stiff neck. This was the shipment he hoped would seal the deal. "What time do I need to be in Jacksonville?"

"They want you there at oh-nine hundred today."

Couldn't they have informed Zane yesterday, even last night, that he had to fly this morning? This had to be the test he'd expected. He'd bet the shipment didn't have to be picked up on a holiday weekend, but High Vision wanted to see how he'd handle this. In fact, now that he thought about it, they probably had both of the other charter groups flying this weekend as well.

They'd test everyone. See who put their business ahead of personal life.

He assured Sammy, "I'll be there."

Sammy gave him the numbers he'd need to verify he had the correct shipment, then said, "Anything else?"

Yeah, dude. Fix my woman problems by the time I get back. "No. I'll check in before I fly out with the cargo." He twisted right and left trying to unkink his aching back. The sofa bed needed a new mattress, one that would hold his bulk.

Unless he figured out Angel's problem and fixed it.

They could share his bed then.

Talk about screwed up logic, but he *was* a guy. All equations involving a woman ended with sex, especially when he was going to do his damnedest to keep said woman.

By the time he'd made up the bed and dashed through a shower, the coffee had finished perking. He sipped a cup of the hot brew and glanced around the spotless kitchen. He couldn't take credit for a cleaning that well done.

An uneasy feeling settled over him at the thought of leaving Angel alone. He knew she'd take care of Trish until Heidi arrived, but would he come home to find her gone again?

He'd been absentmindedly studying the room when his eyes passed the door, then stopped. Yellow running shoes were parked to the right of the entrance.

Oh, yeah. Thanks again to Ben-the-techno-wizard teaching him stuff he probably shouldn't, Zane knew what to do and had the tools for the job.

Next to his laundry, he unlocked the utility room and snapped the light on. Hidden under piles of boxes and junk he used for camouflage was a locked toolbox. Inside was a mix of tools he had from black ops assignments he'd participated in during his Air Force days – stuff that had needed to disappear for the good of the op – along with electronic surveillance and tracking equipment he'd gotten from Ben.

Ben might not ever pick up a weapon, but he'd always had Zane's back, even as a teen.

Zane's gadget-happy friend had given him every possible toy Ben could come up with, knowing Zane might make use of them for clandestine surveillance at some point. Not always kosher for the agents to do that, but no case would hinge on whether a *nonexistent* informant like Zane followed the rules.

He pointed the agents in the right direction.

They gathered hard evidence.

Nobody was the wiser or needed to be. There was even a

gadget or two that Ben had designed and built. He'd given the units to Zane for testing.

After he found a GPS transmitter the size of a shirt button, he put everything back in place. He took the sneakers and his Swiss army knife outside.

He opened the driver's door on his truck to work under the dome light where he had enough time to hide what he was doing if someone walked up. Rumbling in the distance was a precursor of the weather he'd have to fly through. He made a mental note to swing by the marina and check on the boat.

Too much stretch in the ropes and his boat would be damaged along each side where it beat against the pilings separating the boat slips.

Pulling the laces of Angel's running shoe very loose allowed better access. He slit an opening at the base of the tongue. The tiny tracker was a prototype that Ben had been developing, and Zane had helped him try out several of the versions a while back, carrying them with him on flights and when he went on his grueling morning runs.

Zane tested the performance, beat the hell out of the equipment, and Ben worked out bugs.

Ben wanted Zane to keep this one and give it a run once in a while to see if the electronics held up over time.

If Angel took off, this gadget would get a real-world test, and the run of its life. Zane hoped not, but he was done with getting sucker punched every time she disappeared.

With tweezers he worked the transmitter inside the padded covering, deep enough that Angel would never feel it.

The next time she pulled a Houdini vanishing act, he would have a magic wand to make her reappear.

Pleased with himself, he almost whistled as he went back in the door until he met Angel on the other side.

"What are you doing with my shoes?"

Busted. "I noticed some dirt on the bottom of one, and you're so neat I knew you wouldn't want to track through the apartment."

She inspected the shoes.

He'd pulled the laces back as close to where she'd left them as he could. The bottoms were spotless when she turned them over, just the way he'd found them.

She cut her eyes up at him. "Are you sure? I could swear I cleaned them last night."

"You probably couldn't see well in the dark. Not a big deal. I didn't mind doing it."

"Well ... thanks." Her appreciation was more dubious than sincere.

"Don't worry about it. Look, I've got to make a run. I hate to ask you to do anything else after last night, but I'd like to let Trish sleep some more."

"I don't mind. Where are you going?"

"Gotta help someone with a problem."

"When will you be back?" she asked, a slight catch in her voice.

Would she miss him? "Not sure, maybe tonight, but it could be tomorrow. I'll call later and let you know. Will you be here?"

He watched her face as she juggled possible answers.

"I'll try to."

"What does that mean?" he demanded, instantly irritated. "Why would you leave? At least stay where you're safe until I get back."

"Don't worry about me, Zane. You have plenty of other things to think about." She shifted the shoes to her other hand.

He loved the way she said his name. He wanted to hear it again and again. Hear it in her early morning voice, husky with sleep. Yeah, she'd moan his name as he made love to her.

God, he was losing it. She had *better* be here when he returned.

He smiled. At least he had a backup plan.

It was time to go, but not before he did one last thing.

Zane gathered her into his arms and kissed her like he'd never get another chance, because that's exactly what worried him.

The shoes hit the floor.

She tasted like toothpaste and Angel. Her fingers drove through his hair, dragging him closer to her as if she, too, expected it to be their last.

Ecstasy and misery flowed through him. He loved her

scent, the feel of her lips, her smooth skin. But the question of her being there when he returned haunted the recesses of his mind.

Duty called. It was close to five-thirty. He had to go. If he stayed any longer there wouldn't be time to swing by the boat, check the bowlines and the bilge pump. Many a boat had sunk at the dock due to a faulty bilge pump or low battery.

Zane hugged her close and pressed his lips to her forehead. "I left my cell phone number on the counter and the code to set the motion detector bypass on the alarm so you can reset it once Trish leaves. I'll be back as soon as I can and we'll figure out your problem together."

"But, Zane..."

"Shh. We'll talk when I get back. Just promise me you won't take any chances."

She dropped her head to his chest.

"Promise me, Angel. Please." He'd figured out that she'd rather be silent than lie and believed she'd stick to a commitment.

"Okay, I promise," she whispered.

He lifted her chin, gave her a brief kiss then left.

Chapter 31

Mason's cell phone beeped twice, then beeped again while he crossed the living room of his Manhattan flat to retrieve it. Dawn wouldn't come for another two hours, but he hadn't slept all night.

"Sir, this is Richardson..." Richardson oversaw the security of all Mason's warehouses. He was privy to every shipment, legitimate and otherwise.

Mason eased down on the sofa and sat back. "Is there a problem?"

"The Feds stopped by while I was in Raleigh. They wanted to ask questions about Farentino."

The local police should be handling Jeff's death and Angelina's disappearance. "What questions?"

"They wanted to know her specific duties and if she handled any transactions."

Like Mason would have been stupid enough to let Angelina have access to records? "What did you tell them?"

"That she'd been hired as a set of hands in the warehouse and that we didn't give client file access to anyone with a prison record. I stuck to what your man Kenner said was the official statement. I told the Feds everyone was in shock. We all thought she was sweet and a hard worker, etcetera, but we obviously didn't know what she was capable of, or the kind of skills she'd learned in prison."

So far so good. "Did they want anything else?"

"Not really ... but..."

"But *what?*" Mason sat up straight, alerted to the worry in Richardson's voice.

"One of them asked if I knew of any personal relationship between you and Farentino. I told them absolutely not. That our Raleigh warehouse manager had hired her after you and I reviewed her file and approved it. I added that I took full responsibility for hiring her and that I had to talk you into giving her a chance."

"Nice touch." Mason drummed his fingers on the arm of the sofa, trying to figure out what the Feds were after. "Think that satisfied them?"

Richardson was silent for a moment. "I don't think so, sir. I can't put my finger on it, but I had a feeling they weren't just asking about Jeff's death. I think they were interested in Farentino for something else."

Angelina may not have seen the news report about Jeff's body yet, but that didn't matter. Mason had told Angelina she'd played a role in smuggling the paintings, whether she'd known it or not, and that he'd planted evidence of her participation in the coin theft.

That he could hang her and he'd walk away unscathed.

Angelina had believed him. He was certain of it.

He knew her type, and he knew people. Nobody in any agency would believe she was innocent, nor would they buy any claim she made about Mason. Not with her record.

As long as she ran, he felt certain she'd avoid the authorities.

The minute she tried to sell those coins, she'd be arrested. She should realize that, but if he were Angelina, he'd be trying to get out of the country. To do that, she'd need money and might gamble on selling one of them.

Regardless, Mason couldn't risk the FBI getting to her first and hearing something that could be used against him. He had no idea what else she might have on him that she hadn't admitted. She'd been cleverer than he'd anticipated.

Underestimating her at this point would be stupid.

Stupid was one thing he'd never been.

He dismissed Richardson and ended the call, then punched the speed dial key for his bounty hunter. "I want an update."

CK didn't launch into his usual report. "We'll get her, but looks like somebody else has an interest. You don't have another team down here do you?"

"No. What are you talking about?" Mason didn't need this shit right now. It couldn't be Czarion interfering, not after Mason had suggested Czarion go after Angelina and the coins, only to have the prick toss that back in Mason's lap.

"Another group tried to intercept her. I don't have anything on them, but if *anyone* gets in my way, I'll remove them," CK warned.

"You're the only one on my tab, but we may have interest from a federal agency." Time was not on Mason's side with Czarion breathing down his neck. That bastard would get his coins, but on Mason's terms. "Where is she?" he asked.

"At the pilot's apartment."

"Go get her. I have a meeting just before noon, then I'll fly down. I can be there tonight. Call me as soon as she's secure."

Even if Angelina had hidden the coins, Mason knew how to make her talk.

"She might not be alone when I get to her. What about your orders to not draw attention?"

Mason weighed the prospect of getting his hands on Angelina quickly against the problem of doing it in a way that might annoy Czarion. The need to find those coins before Czarion's Sunday deadline ended all debate. "Things have changed. We don't have time to waste. I need this done now. I'll put my resources at your disposal."

"What about the pilot?" CK asked.

"If you can't grab her without involving him, I don't care what you do with him. Just don't leave a trail."

"I never do."

Chapter 32

Wind lifted whitecaps over the waves where the canal to the Gulf Winds Marina met the bay. Zane hurried down the dock to secure the boat so he could get to the airfield and take off ahead of the coming storm. Just another headache he didn't need this morning.

The lines had slackened during the night. After making quick work of tightening the ropes and checking the bilge pump that removed water from the hull, he climbed down into the cabin.

Under the front bunk, he lifted the lid to access a lower compartment and reached deep inside to drag out the new side curtains he'd stored there. He'd been surprised they were ready when he'd come through Raleigh. After replacing the lid and cushion, he tore the brown paper packaging away, smiling over the smell of new canvas and plastic. It reminded him of opening the package on a rubber pool floatie.

The first upgrade to his boat.

He carried the four curtain sections onto the deck to sort them. Zane picked one up, decided it was for the starboard side then tossed it to his right.

Thunk!

Curious, he lifted the section back up. The bottom hemmed pocket bulged. He squeezed two fingers into the pocket, and felt something hard surrounded by plastic. He retrieved a pair of needle-nose pliers from the dash – one of the better gets from the junk left onboard by the previous owner. Pinching the corner of the plastic carefully with the pliers, he wiggled the clear sleeve out far enough to see a coin.

A gold coin. He carried the canvas to the captain's chair in the open cockpit and carefully pulled the rest of the snaking plastic length out.

Eight gold coins ranging in dates from 1922 through 1933 were embellished with a maiden in a long gown running with a torch on the front. The flip side had an eagle. He knew nothing about coin collecting, but it didn't take an expert to realize he held something extremely rare.

How had they gotten into his canvas curtains? Zane retraced the package's path in his mind. He'd picked them up from the custom shop on his last trip to Raleigh, and carried them around until he'd loaded them into the Titan. They were with him all the way until he unloaded them when he landed.

Raleigh. Where Angel had stowed away.

His skin chilled at his next thought. Had she stolen these? Was that why someone chased her? This must have been what she'd been searching for in the storage room *and* when he'd found her going through the cabin of the boat.

Disappointment sickened him. He'd believed he could help her out of whatever she'd gotten into, but this was not a warrant for unpaid parking tickets. If she'd stolen these coins, he'd face his greatest challenge – turning the woman he loved over to the authorities.

He couldn't harbor a fugitive.

Angel said she'd taken something from the guy chasing her, but it didn't belong to him.

But these coins belonged to someone.

If confronted with the coins, would she admit the truth? Or, refuse to share her secrets until she absolutely had to give them up?

He left all the individually wrapped twenty-dollar gold pieces on the seat and went in search of three plastic Ziploc bags from a drawer under the sink where he'd stashed a few supplies in anticipation of a first outing this weekend. Fat chance of that happening now. Using his knife he slit the side of one sleeve. With the pliers, he lifted the package over one open Ziploc bag, shaking it carefully until the coin dropped into the bag.

He held the empty plastic sleeve up to the light. She

hadn't wiped these clean. Zane dropped the sleeve into the other Ziploc, then placed the remaining coins, in their sleeves, in the last bag.

In the cabin, he pulled the cushions out of the way and rooted around for a good spot to hide the coins. A safe deposit box in the bank would be the best place, but since this was Labor Day weekend the banks were closed until Tuesday.

The least likely area to be disturbed by an intruder was under the anchor rope stored in the very front compartment deep inside the nose of the bow. He lifted several layers of rope and slipped the plastic bag containing the coins between the loops.

Zane quickly snapped the side curtains into place and closed up the boat. He had large brown envelopes in his truck under the back seat. Ben had given him the envelopes on the outside chance he ever found evidence he'd need to turn in.

He'd drop the coin and plastic sleeve, along with the cup Angel had touched, at Ben's office on his way to the airport. Ben hadn't called with news of a baby yet, so he wouldn't be in the lab today, but Zane didn't know when he'd be back home and wanted Ben to be the only one privy to this.

There was no way he'd let anyone else in on it until he knew the origin of the coins.

Angel might have a reasonable explanation.

He might believe pigs could fly.

Chapter 33

The balmy tropical weather was threatening to turn downright mean pretty soon, but CK welcomed the low depression hanging off the coast of south Florida. He stretched his shoulders, pulling on the long sleeved gray T-shirt he wore. He'd have to replace it soon with a Triple X. Staying in shape came with a cost.

Thunder rolled overhead, offering the perfect cover for what he had to do this morning.

He lifted his SkyHawk binoculars and studied the woman walking around inside the pilot's apartment. Angel carried a mug of coffee to the sofa.

He'd been in this spot all night, and knew exactly when lights had come on in the apartment and the minute the pilot had left. Talk about timing. CK's cell phone vibrated against his hip. He lifted it up to his ear. "Speak."

"We followed the pilot to the marina," Joe reported. "He messed with the ropes on the boat and put some covering around the cabin. Couldn't see much from where we were, but no female with him. He just pulled out and turned in the direction of Sunshine Airfield."

Was Angel's boyfriend called away on a Saturday morning to fly? That'd be too good to be true. The rest of CK's operation would turn into child's play with the pilot out of the way.

"If he flies out, find out where he's going. I want to know the minute he's airborne."

"Got it."

CK thumbed the end button and shoved the phone back into his pants. He lifted his field glasses.

Angel had stood up and walked to the glass doors and stared out as if she had seen something, but she couldn't see CK. No one could when he wanted to disappear into the landscape. The red nightshirt she wore clung to her plump breasts and narrow hips.

Mason had said to keep the damage to a minimum, but he hadn't dictated any specific parameters.

CK lowered the glasses, letting them lie against his chest. He leaned back into his dark cubbyhole. He lifted his phone and sent a text to his man in charge of accessing the power feed for the apartment complex. The text reply came back immediately. All set. The longer he watched her, the more he appreciated the occasional pleasure offered by his line of work.

Angel stepped to the side and drew the drapes closed.

CK grinned. That would only work in his favor.

Chapter 34

Angel had showered and dressed in her running shorts and top when Trish tottered out of the bedroom to the kitchen.

"Morning, Trish. Want some coffee?"

"Is the Pope Catholic?"

Angel smiled and poured her a mug. "Cream or sugar?"

"No, the blacker the better."

Trish swigged a drink. "Well damn, Sug, this is much better than that sludge Zane makes. Speaking of, where is he?"

"He had a job to fly or something. He didn't really tell me much."

Trish half smiled and nodded. "Mystery man. You aren't mad at me for last night are you?"

"No." The counter didn't have a dust molecule left after Angel had cleaned earlier, but she grabbed a rag to wipe anyhow. "Trish, your brother and I are, um, friends." Friends? Why did that sound so lame? "He's letting me stay here for a few days. That's all. I don't want to give you the wrong impression."

"Friends, huh? Sure. If you say so." Trish snickered quietly then lowered her gaze to study her coffee as if she could read the inky brew like tea leaves.

Angel let the quiet settle while Trish gathered her thoughts on whatever was causing the pucker between her eyebrows.

"I've got to get my act together," Trish muttered to her mug. "I'm getting in the way of Zane's life."

What do you say to that? Angel wiped the counter

harder. Zane would be able to perform surgery on this surface if she didn't stop.

"Angel, have you ever had something you wanted real bad just out of your reach?"

Angel paused her scrubbing and stared at the counter.

For five years she'd trained, studied, and competed to earn the coveted athletic scholarship to Stanford, only to have it snatched away. The first two weeks in jail she'd almost folded under the weight of her loss and what lay ahead of her, but deep inside, the drive to stick it out had burned. Once she'd been released, she'd wanted to prove she was better than the stranger described in a stack of court documents.

She'd trained to compete in the Tamarind, but more than that, all those hours of hard work had been to regain a grain of respect. To be treated just like any other human being.

All she'd wanted was to belong to this world again and stop feeling like a second-class citizen.

Mason had stolen that from her.

"Yes, Trish, I've had something *very* important I worked *very* hard for taken away. Twice, in fact." Angel understood that they were talking about two different things, but the dynamics were the same. "If you want something bad enough, you have to be willing to fight for it no matter what."

Trish stared at her with soulful eyes then nodded slowly. "Yeah. I think I know what you're saying." Her polite smile didn't reach her sad eyes. "Thanks."

Angel glanced at the clock on the microwave. Ten minutes until seven. "What're your plans for today?"

"Nothing in particular." Trish brightened. "We can hang out together while Zane's gone and get to know each other better."

No. Trish had to go. Now. "What about your shop?"

"Heidi will open up."

This was Zane's apartment. Angel couldn't very well ask his sister to leave if she didn't want to go.

She was stuck here. Unbelievable.

Chapter 35

Palm leaves slapped together as the wind whipped through the lush landscape surrounding the pilot's apartment. Still tucked away from sight, CK's phone vibrated at seven-fifteen.

"Speak."

"The pilot's airborne and on his way to Jacksonville."

CK grinned. Gotta love it when a plan falls into place.

"Go to the meet point," CK ordered. "I'll be there in a couple of hours." He ended the call and put the phone away.

Standing up straight from where he'd been leaning, he flexed his chest, loosening muscles tightened by hours at his weight bench. After a habitual check of his 9mm Glock at his hip, he lifted his phone and typed a text. He had a man waiting in position to cut the power feed to the apartment. Once CK sent that text, his man would vanish and CK would show why he got paid the big bucks.

Unlike the rest of these men, CK didn't need help with one scrawny girl.

He started moving slowly toward the only patio with drapes drawn over the glass doors.

Chapter 36

Squatted down next to the kitchen counter, Angel tied her yellow shoelaces and prayed Trish would reach her friend Heidi, who she was calling on Zane's landline.

Come on, Heidi, be home. Angel enjoyed Trish, but Angel couldn't leave until Trish did.

Patience. At least Trish had changed her mind about staying to "spend the day together" after Angel reminded her how busy holiday shopping traffic might be this weekend at Trish's store.

Trish held the house phone to her ear for thirty seconds again before she hung up, grabbed her coffee mug, and plopped onto a barstool. "Heidi probably went to breakfast with someone. She loves Saturday brunch."

Angel smiled politely and hid her frustration. None of Angel's problems were Trish's fault, but it would be nice if Zane's sister had somewhere to be.

Like at the gift shop.

Trish's lack of concern over her business grated after listening to how much Zane wanted this to work for his sister. What Angel wouldn't give to have a normal life where she ran her own business and no one wanted to kill her.

Zane had been right about one thing. His sister did not like to be alone.

Each sibling thought they had the other figured out. Although Zane's description of his sister as a social butterfly was fairly apt, she wasn't sure why Trish painted her brother as mysterious.

Finished with her shoes, Angel stood and leaned a hip

against the counter. "What did you mean when you called Zane a mystery man?"

Trish shot up a conspiratorial eyebrow, then seemed to reconsider something and picked up a pen she'd been doodling with. She started drawing shapes on a scratch pad again. "He doesn't like me to talk about his work."

"Why?"

Trish lifted a shoulder. "Beats me. He gets cranky when I ask how long he's going to be out of town or what his schedule is, but he comes and goes all hours of the day and night."

Angel frowned at Trish's roundabout answer. "That's sort of expected of a charter pilot isn't it? The nature of his particular business."

"Maybe," Trish answered evasively.

Intrigued, Angel asked, "What do you mean?"

Trish studied her mug. "When he started the charter business, it took off like crazy. He's a great pilot, you know?"

Both women jumped when thunder boomed and rain started pounding outside. Trish lifted her head. "Wow, that's really coming down."

Please, Trish, try to stay on topic. "Nasty out there. You were saying ... about Zane."

"Oh, yeah." Trish returned to her mug, turning it round and round between her hands. "He's fearless. He'll fly in any kind of weather, when other pilots won't. He's not afraid to take risks."

Angel couldn't counter that with any intelligent argument since Zane had stuck his neck out to save her more than once. But she didn't think that was what Trish alluded to and asked, "You're worried about the hours Zane's putting in?"

Abandoning her mug, Trish seemed to calculate something before she raised her head to smile wryly at Angel. "He must think something of you or you wouldn't be sleeping here. He never brings anyone here."

Oh. Angel's silly heart smiled over hearing that until she reminded herself that Zane's sister didn't know how Angel had ended up here. Rather than correct Trish, Angel stuck with her plan to find out more about Zane the mystery man.

"We've become friends and I've enjoyed flying with him. I worry about him, too."

Trish nodded as if that were the sign that she could share her deepest secrets with Angel. "A few months after he opened the charter business, he got more secretive about what he was doing and where he was flying. He won't say who he's flying for, and that's when he told me I shouldn't talk about his business." She squinted her eyes at Angel. "Usually I don't. But..." She hesitated, then seemed to waver on her decision.

"I would never share anything about Zane," Angel said, trying to tip that decision in her favor.

Trish had been sitting with her shoulders hunched forward, then all at once she relaxed as if a pressure valve in her neck had been released. "I wouldn't talk to just *anyone* about him, but I'm worried he's taking on some risky cargo, something that pays too good to refuse."

What? Angel hadn't seen that one coming. Was Trish saying that Zane would carry illegal goods? Keeping her voice neutral as possible when her heart was thumping wildly, Angel asked, "What specifically makes you think that?"

"Sometimes he takes off with hardly more than a goodbye and won't talk about what he's hauling – then he shows up anywhere from a couple of days to a week later."

Just like Zane had this morning.

If his sister knew little about her brother's activities, Angel knew even less about Zane Black. What if he *did* transport illegal shipments? That would mean he dealt with criminals.

Lowlifes like Mason.

Was that what Zane had meant when he assured her he could help with her problem? That he knew people who could make a problem go away permanently? Or was her imagination going Hollywood, imagining ridiculous possibilities?

But Zane *had* flown out of that airport in Raleigh fully aware she'd stowed away with armed men chasing her.

He hadn't been overly concerned about any of those issues. Most men – if they weren't involved in dangerous or illegal work – would have been.

What about his offer to contact law enforcement? Had that been just to convince her he was aboveboard?

What if federal agents were watching him?

They'd see her, too.

Was it her lot in life to become involved with men leading secret lives? Had she stepped right back into the fire? Her head hurt from so many conflicting thoughts.

Who was the real Zane Black?

She sifted through everything she knew about Zane and could put her finger on a couple of odd coincidences, but nothing of significance. He had an edgy, dangerous side, but that could be attributed to his protective nature mixed with a military background. He watched over his sister, worked hard at *whatever* he did, and had shown Angel an unprecedented kindness.

Her conscience took issue with the direction of her thinking.

He'd told her that he couldn't abide drugs, so he couldn't be involved with drugs. How could she fault a man who'd opened his home to a woman he knew absolutely nothing about? His elusiveness about his schedule might be little more than reluctance to trust an alcoholic sister with sensitive business information.

Angel felt she owed it to Zane to speak up on his behalf. She knew that Trish was completely loyal to Zane, but he wouldn't want his sister worrying. "From what I've seen, he's doing a great job of building Black Jack Airlines. Look at today. He's flying on a holiday weekend."

"My point exactly. Who needs something flown at the last minute on a holiday weekend that's not a medical emergency?" Trish shrugged again. Preoccupied with the squiggles and boxes she was drawing, she mumbled, "I don't know. You have to be around for a while to see it the way I do, but it doesn't matter. He's the best man to ever come out of the Jackson bloodline."

"Jackson bloodline?" Angel queried. "Who's that?"

"Us." Trish slowly lowered her mug and stared.

"Are you saying Zane's last name is *not* Black?" Angel's temple pounded. She waited to hear a simple explanation, that Black was a middle name or a nickname or Zane had changed his name.

"Ah, I see what happened." Trish visibly relaxed, then continued, "You misunderstood. The name of his company is Black Jack."

Angel hadn't misunderstood. Zane had introduced himself as Zane Black. She remained silent while Trish mused in a curious tone.

"I suppose Jack is short for Jackson or maybe he named the business Black Jack because he's always been good at cards. He never said why he named it that, but I didn't ask." She took a sip from her mug and grinned, Zane's grin. "Anyhow, now you know. Our last name is Jackson, but if you called him Zane Black in front of someone he wouldn't have corrected you. He's too nice to embarrass you."

Too nice or too sly. Which was the apt description?

Angel fought the urge to pound on the counter top.

He'd misled her from the beginning.

Why would he use an alias last name? Her heart started beating double time. She began to understand why Trish interpreted her brother's activities as mysterious.

That's because Trish would never make the leap to think of her brother as a true criminal. Not that Angel could blame her because she couldn't think of Zane that way either.

She'd heard enough. Curiosity would serve no purpose but to waste time and right now it was time to go. The minute Angel pushed Trish out the door, she was gone, too.

But she had to get Trish out of here first. Zane might have dark secrets, but he cared about his sister and had trusted Angel to make sure Trish was passed off safely to Heidi.

A whine from the laundry room announced the spin cycle on the washing machine. Trish had changed to fresh clothes from the ones stored in Zane's closet, opting to wash the smelly ones from the night before while she waited on Heidi.

Thunder rumbled, and rain didn't sound as though it would let up anytime soon.

Snagging the receiver from the wall phone, Trish switched topics as she dialed with more vigor than before. "Heidi should be home with this crummy weather. Wish she'd left the answering machine on. I'd take the bus, but I left my pass somewhere."

If Heidi showed up soon, Angel might leave with them after all. First she'd have to come up with a viable reason for wanting to be taken to the beach and dropped near the marina. No one would believe she wanted to go for a run in this downpour.

She could barely hear herself think over the noise of the rain pounding the building.

"Still can't find her," Trish complained, hanging up the phone.

Angel wished she had enough money to offer Trish bus fare, but she'd need every penny of her pitiful resources once she found the coins and left.

Thunder boomed loud enough to shake the windows this time.

Trish had walked over to the refrigerator and paused in opening the door. "Hear that wind? Sounds like the patio door is open."

"Can't be. I closed it and locked it." Angel hadn't put the metal bar in the slot that stopped the door from sliding open, but the security alarm was on and it was daytime. She'd secure everything in the apartment before she left.

The lights went out in the kitchen.

Trish closed the refrigerator. "Crap. I hate the dark."

"Not a problem," Angel said, getting up. "I saw some candles and matches in the living room. Sit tight and I'll be right back."

Angel jumped from her stool and ran into the living room just as sheets of rain started blowing sideways outside.

She'd made two steps into the darkened room, barely lit by the dim daylight from the patio, when a black-clothed figure stepped through the open glass door.

Panic iced her insides. She couldn't breathe, paralyzed by disbelief.

The intruder lifted cold, steel-gray eyes to hers. A face more evil than Mason's stared at her from less than twenty feet away for only a second.

He moved forward faster than she'd imagined possible for anyone that huge.

That triggered her fight or flight reaction. Angel streaked for the hallway, thinking she wouldn't reach the

front door and unlock it fast enough. He flew around the
sofa, hard on her heels. A concrete hand shoved into Angel's
back, knocking her to the floor. She felt the blow in her ribs
and rolled in pain, determined to keep moving.

"Sugar, that's some storm brew – "

Trish's words ended on a scream.

The attacker had snatched Angel up by the hair. White
hot pain daggered her skull when he wrenched around,
cursing. Tears spilled from Angel's eyes. She pushed up to
her knees and yelled, "*Run, Trish!*"

He let go of her hair.

Trish screamed again.

Angel shot up as the giant turned on Trish.

Face deathly white, and mouth and eyes stretched wide
open in horror, Trish backed away on shaky steps.

When her attacker took a step toward Trish, Angel
leaped up and landed on his back. She clutched at his face,
gouging his eyes with her fingers. "*Run, Trish, go, go,
gooooo!*"

The beast she rode snarled a vicious noise.

As he bent forward, huge fingers locked on Angel's
forearms with a gorilla grip and snatched her over his head.
She landed hard. Her back smashed against the floor
between him and Trish. The blow knocked the air from her
lungs. She wheezed, struggling for breath.

The front door banged open in the distance.

Vision watery, Angel watched her attacker's polished
bald head snap up at the sound.

He raised a foot to step over her.

She bent a leg and shoved her foot up into his groin with
everything she had.

He howled, "*Fuuucckkk!*" and fell to one knee. He made a
sound like a wounded beast.

She rolled over, every move demanding air she couldn't
pull in. She struggled to her feet.

The door stood open. Thank God.

She lunged forward, and almost made it.

He yanked her by the hair again. Her head snapped
back, stars flashed in her vision. Could she hold him off
long enough for Trish to get away?

He swung her around like a doll on a string and plowed a

steel fist into her jaw.

Help!

Trish?

Zane?

Pain faded away. She sank into a black void.

Chapter 37

Zane paced the waiting area inside the terminal at the regional airport he'd flown into. The stale smell of greasy fast food creeping out of the waste can in the corner irritated him, but not as much as this hold up. He should have received the High Vision shipment an hour ago.

Something had gone wrong.

A paper glitch? Probably the damn storm. Computers could be down with this weather.

He'd made it out of Ft. Lauderdale ahead of the incoming squall ripping off the ocean, only to land in a wicked thunderstorm. A low pressure system he hoped would not turn into a hurricane.

But his gut was telling him the weather and computers weren't to blame. He'd left one message for dispatch that hadn't been returned yet.

Zane phoned his apartment again while he waited on Sammy to call and explain what was going on with the shipment. His home phone rang six, seven, eight times.

He jammed the off button. It was barely after eight in the morning. Where the hell were Angel and Trish? He hoped Angel hadn't left the apartment. She'd promised to be careful.

What about those coins she was searching for? Was she at the marina, going through his boat now?

His phone lit up with a text. He thumbed the button for the display and read: High Vision will no longer need your services.

What the hell? He punched the numbers for the dispatcher. When Sammy answered, Zane demanded,

"What's going on? I flew through a tropical depression to be here on time. No one's shown with the shipment."

"You should have received a text."

"I got some *bullshit* message about not needing my services. What's with that?"

"I don't know. I only coordinate shipments."

"Oh, come on, Sammy. I've been working with you for months. I've gone above and beyond. Tell me something, dammit."

Sammy's low grumble came through the lines. "Okay, but I'm not at liberty to say much and even if I could, I don't know squat. From what I hear, local authorities and harbor patrol are all over the ship and our containers."

What. The. Hell? Wouldn't Ben and Vance know about this? Zane wasn't hanging up without clarification on not needing his services.

Just today or not anymore?

Sammy cut into his thoughts. "I hear the front blowing into Miami is picking up steam. You may want to get rolling or find somewhere to hole up overnight. From the weather report I got, I doubt anyone can fly back in this mess."

Zane didn't want a weather report and knew when he was getting blown off. "Is High Vision cutting me loose?"

The silence that answered Zane churned the nausea building in his gut.

Sammy finally said, "All I know is High Vision goes apeshit over anything like this. There'll be an internal investigation and only a few people even knew about this shipment today. Shit runs downhill and right now you're at the low end of the pipeline. Don't call the office. If they want anything, they'll call you."

In other words, yes, you are cut loose, Zane.

Shit! He pulled back his foot to kick the cheap wall paneling and stopped before he destroyed someone else's property. "Gotta go," Sammy said and the line died.

Zane pulled the phone away and stared at it. All his hard work, all the insane flying and sacrifices he'd made to get this contract just did a nosedive into the sewer.

He clutched his forehead, trying to hold back the headache wanting to explode. What the hell had happened? *Fuck it.* He was not staying here another minute.

Screw the weather.

He headed for his airplane. His cell phone rang. The ID was his home phone number. Maybe Trish was still asleep and Angel had been in the shower.

Relief took the edge off his frustration, but he still couldn't help his rough tone. "Angel?"

"No, it's Heidi. I'm at your apartment. We've got a problem." Her frantic voice made that clear.

"Why? What's wrong?" Fear hammered his chest, his mind jumping to every bad scenario possible.

"When I got here, your front door was wide open and nobody's here."

"Nobody?" he shouted. He hadn't considered *that* scenario.

"No. I forgot to leave the answering machine on. I don't know where Trish is, but she said she'd lost her bus pass last night." Heidi's normally high-pitched, calm voice reached the squeaky stage when she got upset. "Your front door and patio doors were wide open."

"Listen to me, Heidi." He started running to his Titan. "I'm on my way back from Jacksonville right now. Get out of the apartment."

"Do you want me to call the police?"

"No." He didn't want anyone there until he'd had a chance to check it out himself before anyone contaminated the scene. The police might not agree, but they would only look at it like a break-in at this point. They wouldn't go after Trish or Angel for twenty-four hours.

Heidi argued, "I don't want to leave in case Trish comes back. I'm worried about her."

"I am, too, but until I get there and figure out what happened, I don't want you in the apartment. It might not be safe. If you want to wait, stay in your car. Leave immediately if anyone strange shows up. Got it?"

"Okay. I'll wait outside until you get here."

His worst nightmare had come to life.

Chapter 38

Air. Angel needed air. Her chest wouldn't expand for a simple breath. She was going to suffocate.

She could hear a deep rumbling noise. Thunder. Her clothes hung heavy on her body, soaked. She opened one eye.

Black pavement shined under a veil of water. She faced down, but she was moving. Raindrops beat across her back. Water ran around her neck, across her throbbing face and into her eyes. Hair hung around her face, slapping her outstretched arms as she bounced.

Someone had an arm hooked around her legs, carrying her fireman style across his shoulder. She pushed against the rock-hard back, desperate to give her chest room for air.

"Be still." The rough order left no room for argument.

"I ... can't ... breath." She squeezed the words past her sore jaw.

He shoved her higher on his shoulder as if she were nothing more than a child. She pulled in a deep breath. Her head throbbed, nausea threatened.

Everything started coming back to her. The black-clothed figure standing inside Zane's patio doors. The intruder attacked her ... in the apartment.

With Trish. Did Zane's sister get away?

Please, God, don't let Trish be hurt. That would kill Zane.

The thought of Zane brought tears to her eyes. She was beyond miserable physically, but now the emotional torture of never seeing him again set in. That's what she got for letting her guard down, getting comfortable.

Opening her heart to a man.

The bouncing stopped. Keys jingled. Then a car door opened. He slid her down in front of him, picked her up, and pitched her onto the backseat of a huge sport utility. What was it about thugs and big, dark SUVs?

Guess a white minivan just didn't get the job done when it came to the fear factor.

She tried to push herself up on her elbows.

Either he moved with amazing speed or she was sluggish from the battering. Frigid gray eyes hovered over her. His noxious cologne and sweaty masculine odor accosted her.

A black gun handle protruded from the waistband of his pants.

With his left hand, he reached over the seat into the rear cargo area.

She breathed in shallow pants, anxious at what he'd do next.

Fighting him would only get her injured worse, but he'd think he had a crazed animal in this car if he tried to rape her.

He glanced at the rear area, his arm moving as though he had opened something. When his gaze sliced to her again, a nasty smile spread across his face.

Goose bumps pebbled along her arms.

Shifting his body support to his knees, he slid his right hand across the front of her shirt.

She sank backwards deep into the seat, moving away from his touch. He squeezed one breast as if to gauge her cup size then moved his hand under her neck.

Waiting to see if he would do worse than grope her, she shivered in revulsion.

He misunderstood her reaction.

"That's better. I like my women more agreeable than you were earlier."

His coarse voice drove terror through her. Her mind shifted from fear of Mason to a new threat. Maybe this man had no connection to Mason. There were hundreds of mega-sized sport utility vehicles in the country. Maybe he was just a sexual predator.

Just a sexual predator?

She'd spent too much time around Mason to downgrade a deviant like this one.

Her fear climbed higher every second he hovered over her. The giant had her pinned to the seat. Fighting a bulldozer would be easier. Muscles bulged in his left arm as he raised his hand from the cargo area behind the seat.

Waves of panic shot through her. All the survival training in the world wouldn't save her from this creep.

Angel sucked in a breath and opened her mouth to scream for help.

He slapped a damp cloth over her face, forcing her to breathe deeply of the acrid smell.

She flinched, then everything went black again.

Chapter 39

Zane slammed on brakes in front of his apartment. He'd battled weather all the way back, but he couldn't attribute sweaty palms to the vicious weather he'd confronted. Flying into a tropical depression didn't compare with the sick fear something had happened to both Angel and his sister.

Heidi's ancient, lime-green Volkswagen bug sat in the lot. Empty.

Damn. Couldn't at least one woman he knew follow directions?

Rain soaked his shirt by the time he'd raced around the corner and flung open his unlocked front door.

Heidi jumped up from the sofa, her spiked hair wilder than normal. "Am I ever glad to see you," she declared.

"You shouldn't have waited in here, Heidi. It wasn't safe."

"But, Zane – "

"I don't even know what happened to them. You could have been hurt," he blazed on.

"But, Zane, you don't understand – "

"Yes, I do."

"No you don't, Sugar."

Zane spun to his left. A pale Trish emerged from the bathroom, tears streaming down her face.

She ran to him. Zane clutched her shaking frame. Thank God *she* was safe.

Trish sobbed against his chest, oblivious to his wet clothes.

"Are you okay, honey? Are you hurt?" he asked, his voice strained.

"I'm okay." She hiccupped between sobs. "It's Angel."

"What happened?" He hadn't meant to snap, but worry for Angel now took front and center.

"I'm so sorry," Trish wailed. "I couldn't help her. I tried, but I didn't know what to do. I just stood there until she told me to run." Another sob escaped.

He clenched his teeth to keep from shouting. The more anxious Trish became the less coherent she'd be, and he needed all the information he could get right now.

Zane coaxed her, "It's okay. Just calm down and tell me what happened."

She sniffled and cleared her throat. "We were in the kitchen and the power went out so Angel went into the living room to get candles, but she didn't come back. So I went out there and some guy was in the apartment. Could have wrestled on TV. He'd knocked her down. I screamed ... he turned around and I froze." Her eyes welled up with tears again. "I'm so sorry."

Zane's nerves were being dragged through a field of razor blades each second he waited on Trish to tell him everything. Did Angel lie hurt in a hospital somewhere? He took a deep breath to keep from shouting and pushed his sister for more.

"Okay, take it easy, but tell me what happened to her."

Trish raised pained eyes to him. "He came after me, but Angel jumped on his back and screamed at me to run." Her voice dropped to a whisper. "So I did. I ran way down to the end of the complex, scared out of my mind. I hid behind some bushes by one of the buildings. I was crying, trying to figure out what to do."

"What else?" Zane silently pleaded for Trish to get it all out.

She sniffled. "I wanted to come back here and check on Angel and I thought maybe I could get his tag number."

Patience was paying off, but at the cost of his sanity. Chinese water torture would be easier than waiting for Trish to tell him where the hell Angel had gone. "So you got a tag number?"

Trish shook her head. "I came back to help Angel and found Heidi." Tears poured out of her swollen eyes. "Angel's gone and I can't tell you where."

He wanted to say it was okay, that he would get her back because he had a tracking device in Angel's sneaker.

But finding the chip didn't mean Angel would be alive when he got to it.

Chapter 40

Pain drove nails through Angel's head. That jerked her from a dark fog. Her first tick of consciousness brought with it a chill that shook the length of her body.

Where was she?

She blinked to clear the cobwebs from her brain. A dank, oily odor overpowered her. With another blink, her vision began to clear.

Way up, maybe twenty feet from where she was lying on her back, flashes of light backlit a row of dingy windows near the top of a rusting metal wall. Cold seeped through her bones. Wet clothes clung to her clammy skin.

When she slid her elbows to push her head and shoulders up, the room spun. A sharp pain stabbed her side. She swallowed hard to settle her roiling stomach. Barefoot pygmies had tromped through her mouth leaving a nasty taste and a dusty trail.

Very slowly, to control the dizziness, Angel shifted her head around, surveying the room. A tall overhead garage door stood on one end of the fifty-foot-long room. Wires hung loose from a panel next to the door as if someone had ripped the control box from the wall. Her eyes trailed down to a silver padlock the size of her palm that had been threaded through a shiny new hasp at the bottom of the door.

No exit there.

She scanned the next wall, opposite the windows. This one was a short interior wall, but still close to fifteen feet. It must separate the room she was in from another area. A pigeon landed on the top ledge of the wall and cooed.

Several holes large enough to drop a chair through yawned across the ragged metal roof. Water pooled on the floor from past rain showers. At least it wasn't raining now.

Dreading the dizziness, Angel forced herself to turn further to check out the last barrier of her prison.

An oil-stained floor spanned the distance between her and a standard office door. The building appeared to have been a commercial truck garage long ago.

Other than a five-gallon plastic bucket next to an office-type door, the room was void of any furnishings.

She should go check the door, but common sense, fickle animal that it was, came to her aid. Sometimes common sense told her to do something she'd really rather not. Other times, like now, it convinced her to sit still since she felt sick as the devil and that door was very likely locked. And, even if it wasn't, there was a good chance someone guarded the other side.

Sliding back down to a horizontal position, she tried to use mind over matter to will her body to stop hurting, but a full night's sleep and an ice pack would do more good.

She massaged her forehead and worked to recall what had happened. Blurry images of running through the apartment and being knocked to her knees were the first things she remembered. Most details were vague, but not the chilling gray eyes belonging to a behemoth of a man.

What had he done? She took a quick mental inventory of her body. Of all the pain coursing through her, none indicated she'd been sexually attacked.

Yet.

An attacker with restraint? Morals? Her mind rambled back to the apartment and Trish stepping into the room. She'd yelled at Trish to run.

The fact that Trish was not here with her should indicate she'd gotten away. Or, had the man left Angel alone because he'd attacked Trish?

Her stomach flopped again. Had Zane's sister been hurt or worse? Guilt pushed through her physical misery. She'd brought this danger into Zane's home. What a way to repay his generosity.

If he returned to find Trish hurt he'd never regret anything more in his life than the night Angel had stowed away on his airplane.

She sucked in a breath, rolled over, and eased into a sitting position, then slapped a hand over her mouth in a feeble attempt to stop the coffee she'd drunk that morning from showing up again.

Her head pounded in complaint over the thirty-inch change in altitude. Little by little, stars chasing around in front of her eyes disappeared. Her watch was missing, along with one of her shoes. How long had she been there?

Prepared for the ache in her side, she struggled to a standing position. The room listed to one side, then righted.

Careful not to make a noise, she tiptoed across the room. She pressed her ear against the scarred door, but her gaze traveled down to the five-gallon bucket half-filled with sand. A roll of paper towels sat beside it.

Her litter box?

Muffled voices came through.

She recognized the first one as belonging to the man who'd caught her.

" – me back a double burger, two fries and a big Coke. Make that two double burgers. I worked up an appetite dragging that bitch here."

"How long we staying, CK?" came from a second nasally voice.

"Until ML gets here. Says he'll deal with her himself."

So her attacker was called CK. What could that stand for?

"What about the storm? How's ML going to get here if the airport shuts down?" the whiny one asked.

"He'll get here. It may take a little longer, but he's coming. Don't doubt it. The man wants her bad," CK said.

Angel couldn't come up with anyone she'd met whose initials were CK, but ML had to be Mason Lorde.

Through the door, she heard high-pitched laughter fade with footsteps. CK must have stayed to guard her.

She knew exactly what Mason meant by *dealing with her himself*. He'd physically punish her until she gave him the location of the coins.

Then he'd finish her off.

How could she tell Mason where the coins were if she didn't know? The only person who knew was Zane, but she refused to inflict any more pain on him or Trish. She would not sacrifice Zane for her own safety.

Angel steeled herself for what was to come.

Chapter 41

Zane closed the door behind Heidi and Trish, feeling bad over rushing them out, but he had to go after Angel. Once more, he was thankful for Heidi's friendship with his sister. Trish had been so distraught over Angel she almost wouldn't leave.

His sister had always appeared unconcerned about the world around her, at least to him, but she'd been ready to ride shotgun with him to get Angel back. In that instant, Zane realized he'd severely underestimated Trish's resilience.

Angel had tried to point out Trish's strength to him.

He'd assured Trish that Angel meant a lot to him, too, and he wasn't coming back without her.

Now that he had the coins, he knew what someone wanted from her. The coins had to be stolen. Coins like that didn't float around without security.

Who was the thief and who was the rightful owner?

Worry about that once you get Angel back. He'd noticed her jeans and white shirt folded on top of the dryer. She should be easy to spot in her yellow running clothes.

Zane carried Ben's electronic tablet out to the truck. He'd booted it up inside and by the time he'd backed out of the parking space, the device had located a signal for the GPS tracking chip hidden in Angel's shoe.

Ben claimed there were still a few bugs in the software that translated the chip's signal. Zane just hoped the little prototype in Angel's shoe didn't die on him.

He zoomed the screen on the tablet, bringing up the map of an industrial area in an old section south of Miami. A thirty-minute drive, depending on traffic. He'd never wanted to be a helicopter pilot, until now.

How had Angel gotten so deep inside his world in such a short time?

Didn't know. Didn't care. Just wanted her back.

Chapter 42

Mason carried a single bag across the tarmac to the flight he'd chartered. Blue skies wouldn't last past north Florida based upon the weather report his pilot had shared, but Mason had gotten another call from Czarion. The prick asked if Mason intended to let a little storm prevent him from saving his operation from obliteration and reminded him not to try to move his *private* inventory until he delivered the coins.

Right behind CK's report that he had Angelina but no coins, Czarion had called. Mason had used his backup cell phone to communicate with CK.

Czarion had called on *that* phone.

A number *nobody* should have who hadn't received it personally from Mason. The prick just kept on needling him.

Sweeping every room in the compound had not turned up a bug. As soon as Mason got this handled, he *would* find out who Czarion was and who within his operation was snitching to the guy. If Angelina told Mason where the coins were right away, she'd be in shape to make the trip home to Raleigh in a day or so. If not, well, he might give her to CK once he'd taken what he wanted.

His cell phone rang just as he reached the Lear jet. "Lorde."

"CK here. You still flying in to Miami today with this weather?"

"With enough money, there's always someone who will fly. I'll be there tonight. Don't let her out of your sight," Mason warned.

"She can't get out. You want her fed?"

"No. She'll be more pliable if she's hungry. I should arrive by ten o'clock. Have someone waiting for me," Mason ordered, then gave CK his flight time and where he wanted a man to meet him in the main terminal.

"Got it. She's awake. Think she'd like a little activity to keep from getting bored?"

Mason started to bark an order at CK to keep his hands off of Angelina, but changed his mind. Her fault he had to go through all this trouble to get the coins back only to give them up. He warned CK, "You know what I expect to find when I arrive."

"Yes, I do." The chuckle that followed had a feral edge. Then the line disconnected.

Chapter 43

Zane zigzagged his way south on I-95 from Ft. Lauderdale to the target point indicated by the tracking program. He'd assumed Angel was in a fixed location until the transmitter began to move. Too fast to be Angel on foot, even with *her* running ability. She was being transported in a vehicle.

Constant glances at the tablet confirmed the vehicle was headed for the interstate.

When the directional blip reached I-95, it turned north.

Cutting through traffic and flooring his accelerator every chance he got, Zane tried to close the twelve-mile gap without pricking the attention of the highway patrol. A screaming red truck made an easy target for ticket writers, and he didn't have the time to show his identification and answer questions. When the vehicle he tracked turned off of I-95 to I-195 east, he had a good idea where she was headed and wished he was wrong.

Miami International Airport.

Chapter 44

Angel sat at the farthest point from the office door. She'd been over every inch of the room. Unless she grew wings, she had no way out.

If it didn't stop raining soon, her skin would wrinkle worse than a prune. The storm bellowed outside. Water poured through the gaping holes in the ceiling. The floor thankfully sloped to a center drain or she'd have been without the one dry corner she'd found in her cave-like room.

Mason was coming.

To deal with her.

Her hands trembled. She prayed for strength not to give up Zane's name – no matter what Mason did. She had to convince them that she'd tricked Zane into letting her stay at his apartment. That he knew nothing.

Light glowed from under the office door.

No one had been in this leaking room since she'd awakened to see if she was still there. They might have a peephole, but it wouldn't make any difference. They knew, as well as she did, there was no way out that didn't involve her guards.

As if someone had heard her wandering thoughts, the office door opened.

CK loomed in the opening.

"You're up." He started forward. "'Bout time. Thought you were gonna sleep all day. Where's the fun in that?" His sinister voice reverberated through the vacant room.

"Cat got your tongue?" he taunted, ambling towards her, a black silhouette against the bright room behind him.

She hunched down in the corner, considered trying to run past him, but experience had taught her better. He'd been amazingly fast for his massive bulk. She'd just hurt herself worse. Better to save all her strength to endure Mason.

CK squatted down in front of her and said softly, "Been trying to think of how to repay you for the kick in the nuts."

She flinched at the memory. No man took that move well. What would he do in retaliation?

With a flick of his hand, he ripped her pale yellow shirt down the front, leaving her dressed in the jog bra and shorts. She braced for his next move, but instead of tearing more clothes he wrapped his hand around the back of her neck, wrenched her forward.

Bile rose in her throat when she realized he wanted to kiss her. She forced her hands not to claw at him, yet. Not until he wanted more. It would take every ounce of strength she had to fight him off if he tried to rape her and she didn't honestly believe she'd win.

He closed his mouth over hers.

Her stomach revolted at the combined odor of hamburger and sour breath. When he ended the kiss, he rocked back on his heels letting his rough palm trail over her damp hair.

Her sharp breaths echoed the fear riding up her throat. His touch moved down her chest to the jog bra.

She trembled in terror. He wrapped thick fingers around her right breast and squeezed. She jerked in disgust and pain, tears burning her eyes, but refused to make a sound.

He released her breast. "I know ML better than most. When he's finished, you'll get a chance to make it up to me. If you give him whatever you took, I'll make sure he doesn't kill you."

Agile as a gymnast, he rose to his feet and turned. The glow from the office rimmed him in backlight and illuminated half of his face.

Like a glowing Satan.

Angel let out a pent up breath as a fate worse than Mason walked out of the room.

Chapter 45

Early evening settled over the city under a blanket of ominous clouds. Zane wheeled his truck into the covered parking garage at Miami International Airport minutes behind the vehicle he'd been tracking. He pulled into the first open space, ready to track the transmitter on foot now that it appeared to be stationary.

Carrying the tablet with the tracking receiver concealed in a magazine, he followed the signal until it indicated he'd reached the target. In the far, outer region of the crowded garage sat a black Land Rover still dripping from the rain.

Zane waited until he was reasonably sure no one remained in the vehicle, then strolled forward casually, scouting the area each step. With a building sense of dread, he sidled around the far side of the SUV and glanced inside.

No bodies were visible.

That was a plus. A soft drink can was lodged in the drink holder between the front seats, but other than that the interior appeared spotless. When he moved toward the rear to check the cargo area, a flash of yellow in the back seat caused him to do a double take.

Angel's running shoe sat on the floor.

He'd been tracking her shoe, not her. His heart sank.

So where was she? After a quick perusal of the empty rear cargo, he made a mental note of the tag number and the gold triangle logo on the side. What was Lorde Industries?

Zane returned to his truck where he punched the screen on the tablet to take the tracking program back to the last fixed position before the blip had started moving toward the airport.

When he reached that location, Angel had better be there.

If not, what then?

After the fiasco with High Vision, could he still call Ben for help? His best friend would be there for him for sure, but maybe not the agency.

Ben was a last resort option.

Zane wouldn't take any chance of putting Ben's job at risk or pull him away from his wife right now.

He threw the truck into gear and jockeyed his way out of the thick airport traffic. Playing "what if" wasted energy and time. He had to find her. Period.

And he *would.*

The minute Ben called, Zane would have his friend search Lorde Industries.

Dodging in and out of showers through congested roadways transformed the drive back to I-95 from arduous to excruciating. At the exit for an industrial district, he turned south to Kendall, an older area just below Miami. Four miles west of the interstate, he entered a commercial zone and slowed to cruise through industrial parks inundated with mammoth buildings.

Tractor-trailer rigs were backed up to loading docks on several properties, but little activity stirred at eight-thirty on a holiday weekend night. He circled and crossed over railroad tracks, then hung an immediate left down an access road. Dilapidated buildings with real estate signs offering the properties for sale or lease were scattered from one street to the next.

His truck crawled along the dark corridor.

The original tracking signal had come from here, but when he enlarged the map to pinpoint the exact spot, the signal blinked and jumped. Maybe one of the bugs Ben had talked about. Zane squinted to see through sheets of rain, on the verge of deciding to cover the area on foot if he had to, when a cat ran across the street in front of him. He slammed on his brakes.

His gaze followed the feline's path as the tabby scampered off to his right.

At the end of a vacant alley, a bright glow flickered from a tall street lamp and reflected off of something shiny. He flipped open his console and dug out a set of infrared night-vision binoculars.

A vehicle came into focus. Not a vacant alley after all.

He pulled forward a foot or two for a better angle. It was a Land Rover. Just like the one in the airport garage.

Coincidence? His gut said no.

He just hoped Angel was there, and alive.

First he had to hide his flashy truck, and was suddenly not as thrilled about the color as the day he'd picked it out. No time to get another vehicle now. And he needed to locate a second access to the building other than the alley. He wove his way through the bleak commercial area. An offshoot railroad track from the main line ran through a clearing in the trees. The track appeared to run alongside the building.

He backed the truck off of the shoulder, positioning it behind a clump of grown-up scrub alongside the track. Not great, but not in easy view of the road unless you were looking. If Angel was in that building, the chances of going through a door were slim. He'd seen some high windows. He'd take what he needed to recon the area and gain access if he could find a way in.

Zane set his phone on vibrate, shoved his Sig into a holster that clipped inside the waistband of his jeans, and fit it against his hip. He threw a poncho on and shoved his hands into a pair of leather work gloves.

Now would be a good time to have the thermal imaging system he'd used in his fighter plane. Even a small night vision monocular would be a great substitute, but he didn't have that either. The binoculars would work, but would be in the way if he had to climb. He'd do without.

He was just thankful he'd had Ben's tracking device.

Lightning ripped across the black skies and rain continued in a steady downpour. He reached in the back seat for the roll of anchor rope and wound about fifty feet into a loop, hanging the pile over his shoulder.

Using the tight beam of his LED flashlight, he jogged down the track, then flipped the beam off as he neared the sport utility.

On close inspection, the Land Rover was branded with a gold triangle logo identical to the one from the airport. He picked his way around the tall metal structure, stumbling through a minefield of piled buckets, weeds, and scattered boards. Rain drummed against every hard object in its way, camouflaging any unintentional noise.

Most tall warehouses had a ladder for accessing the roof, but as he rounded the last side, checking out the building, this one proved him wrong.

He felt his way around toward the front.

When his hand plowed through a web of thick vines and caught on a metal rung, he expelled a sigh of relief. Vines wrapped the ladder and covered the wall as high as he could reach. With no idea if the metal was rusted to pieces or still strong, he tentatively placed his weight on each step. Once he stood on the roof, shafts of light shone upward through small holes in the ceiling.

The only illuminated room was near the front quarter of the structure.

Lightning flashed and exposed gaping holes in the roof where water funneled into the building.

He switched on his small flashlight to hunt the center beam at the pitch of the roof rather than risk crashing through a weak area. Once there, he navigated to the light source.

He knelt down and crawled close enough to peer into a bright opening.

One of the largest men Zane had ever seen sat reclined in a chair with his tree-trunk legs propped on a crate. His meaty fingers tapped a rhythm to hard rock music vibrating out of a boom box. What had Trish said? *Angel's attacker could be a professional wrestler.*

If Angel was here, Zane would have to get her without tangling with this brute, or he'd be forced to use his weapon. He had to squint into the opening and move around without stopping the roof leak while he searched the room's layout.

There were two doorways in the small room. One exited the building and the other accessed another room. Zane shined his light over the roof to what should be the next room. Water streamed into the pitch-black hole through two ragged openings in the tin.

He crawled to the edge of a hole as wide as his overstuffed chair. He couldn't see a thing inside until lightning fingered across the sky, turning the dark night to daylight for several seconds.

During the momentary brilliance, a dash of yellow brightened one corner.

He'd found Angel.

Chapter 46

CK's phone vibrated against his hip. He turned down the music, but still had to click up the receiver volume to hear over the downpour pounding the metal roof.

"Speak."

"This is Joe. The plane just landed. I'll let you know when I have ML and we're on the way. Shouldn't be more than thirty minutes."

"I'll be here." CK thumbed the phone off and cranked up the music.

His leggy captive should be primed for Mason after today. Mason wanted her pliable. Last time he'd seen her, she was close to being putty. Wouldn't take much more to have her begging.

Chapter 47

Angel shivered hard. She tucked herself into a tighter ball on the damp floor. Rain clattered down on the building. The racket echoed through the room, sounding as though a thousand nails showered against the metallic surface. Something furry bumped her hand.

She went from exhausted to terrified in less than three seconds. A rat? She wobbled to her feet, ready to flee if the animal jumped on her.

Lightning exploded outside, sending a flash of light charging through the wide hole in the ceiling.

A figure appeared in the center of the room. Was the giant sneaking up on her? Mason would be next.

She couldn't take any more. Fear snapped her control.

Angel ran in the direction of the door, praying he'd left it unlocked when he came into the room. Halfway across the room, she was snatched off of her feet.

"Noo..." died in her throat when a hand clamped over her mouth. Strain and fear had taken a toll. She made one puny attempt to struggle against the rock hard body and knew she couldn't defeat his strength.

She crumbled emotionally. Tears gushed down the sides of her face. Her knees gave way.

Before she could fall to the ground, the hand covering her mouth slid away and two strong arms wrapped around her chest to support her. She heard, "Shhh. It's me, Zane."

That was the last straw. Her mind had snapped if she actually thought Zane would materialize out of thin air.

Unable to stop, she cried in broken sobs smothered by the deafening rain. She felt herself shifted around until she cried against a broad chest. Long fingers on one hand supported her around the waist as another began stroking up and down her back.

Her phantom kissed her forehead and whispered next to her ear. "Shhh, baby, it's okay. I'm going to get you out of here."

Zane was so very warm, even if he were a hallucination. She wanted to climb inside his heat. A shudder racked her body and he tucked her closer.

"Honey, don't cry. I swear I'll get you out of here."

A hand cupped her chin, lifting it. Warm lips she recognized kissed her gently. He was no hallucination.

Nothing had ever felt as real as Zane.

Finally, she quieted and ran a hand over Zane's face. "It is you," she said, her voice full of awe.

"Are you hurt, honey?"

The concern in his voice soothed her.

"I'm okay n-now that you're here." She remembered the giant nearby and whispered, "We have to get out. How'd you get in here?"

His hot breath flowed over her ear when he spoke. "We're going out through the roof. You ready?"

The roof?

If he said so, she would do it. She nodded then realized he couldn't see her and said, "I'm ready."

Zane's arms fell away. Her body mourned the loss. He whispered, "I'm pulling a poncho over your head. Don't panic." When he had the poncho on her, he took her hand and led her to the wall with the windows.

"Do you know how to climb a rope and walk your feet up the wall?" he asked quietly.

She'd done that plenty of times in her training classes. "Yes."

"You go first, I'll be right behind you. When you get on the roof, don't move until I'm up there."

"Okay," she whispered and grabbed the rope to start up. At the sharp pain in her side, she sucked in air and hesitated.

"What's wrong?" he asked.

Angel gritted her teeth. She could do this. Adrenaline kicked in. "Nothing. Let's go."

Hand over hand, her moves painfully slow, she made it to the roof while rain pelted her face. She struggled over the edge until she was on her hands and knees, waiting.

Zane popped up right behind her.

Water ran over the top of her shoeless foot from the flood rushing across the corrugated roof. He handed her the flashlight then pulled the rope up in loops and slung it over his shoulder. With his hands on her shoulders, he bent down close to her ear.

"Hold my belt and walk in my tracks as close as you can." Before letting go he brushed her lips with his. "Hang in there just a little longer and we'll be out of here."

Reaching zombie state, she nodded, but he must have caught her movement. He gave her a little squeeze then hooked her hand through his belt and took the flashlight. She slipped twice on the slick metal as they scooted across the roof and down the ladder.

~*~

Zane could feel Angel's fear and heard her soft whimper more than once, enough to know she was in pain, but they couldn't stop yet. He towed her through the thick weeds. When he neared the entrance to the building, headlights from the alley shot crossways in front of them. He hauled her up between him and the building.

That way he could see who arrived without being spotted.

Another sport utility swung around the first one to park.

The driver stepped from the vehicle and raced around to open the passenger door. When a statuesque blond male stepped out of the new vehicle, Angel stiffened against Zane. Was that the bastard who'd hurt her?

Zane spoke very low. "Do you know him?"

She hesitated then nodded under his chin.

The two men moved out of view then a door banged shut.

"Let's go." Zane dragged her quickly through the thicket. At the Land Rover, he made her squat down next to one of the vehicles, telling her not to move. With a knife from his boot, he slashed the tires, moved to the second vehicle and did the same, then shoved the knife back in place and grabbed her hand, taking off again.

They rushed along the tracks in a jog, slower than they'd

go if she weren't minus one shoe. Zane needed two or three more minutes to get Angel to the truck. They'd made it a third of the way there when shouts erupted behind them.

High-powered searchlights beamed frantically, scouring the ground outside the building.

Zane jerked Angel to a stop. "Take the flashlight and keep it pointed the way we were running. Go to where the tracks meet the street. My truck is there. Stay out of sight when you get there. I'll be right behind you."

"No. I – "

"Arguing will get us both killed. Do as I say," Zane ordered, whipping out his weapon.

A beam of light shined down the tracks, picking them up.

"Now!" Zane shoved the light into her hands.

She stumbled away.

A zing sounded on the tracks just short of where he stood. He fired two shots, then sprinted down the tracks behind Angel and the bobbing flashlight.

Shots rang out, landing all around him. He tripped once, caught his balance and fired back, this time lower.

One high beam disappeared.

At the truck, he threw the rope in the back. Angel dove in on the passenger side. He cranked the engine and spun the wheels over the loose, muddy ground, tearing onto the dark road with his headlights off. A shot pinged off the body of the truck. He shoved Angel's head to her knees.

"Stay down." He wove through turns and side streets until he felt sure nobody could have followed on foot, then headed for the I-95 and turned north to Ft. Lauderdale.

Then where? This group knew his apartment. They probably had his Titan under surveillance.

While keeping his eyes on the road and rearview mirror, he removed his hand from Angel's back then used his arm to lift her up to a sitting position.

One look at Angel worried him.

She hadn't taken the poncho off and still shivered violently, even with the heater blowing. He reached over and ran the back of his hand across her cheek. She turned a deathly white face to him, her eyes glazed with shock.

Zane had to find a secure location soon. No one appeared to be following them, but he couldn't be sure. They might have planted a tracking unit on his truck at some point.

He didn't have the time it would take to go over the truck thoroughly to find it.

Chapter 48

Mason walked out of the warehouse as two more sport utilities rolled up. He stepped past the two incapacitated vehicles sporting flat tires.

At the door to his ride, he stopped to give CK his parameters. "You have twelve hours to find her if you want your money."

Weapon still in hand, CK said, "I'll find her. I always have a backup plan."

Mason did, too, and doubted CK would like his. But the bounty hunter had a reputation of never failing to produce. CK did not walk away from this much money. "I don't care what it takes, just do it."

"Now you're talking my language." CK grinned.

Chapter 49

Traffic thinned along Sunrise Boulevard after ten at night. Zane crossed over the bridge and peeled off north on Bayview Drive to a small upscale community east of downtown Ft. Lauderdale. The rain had slacked to a drizzle. He zipped into an expansive parking lot for a high-rise apartment complex.

"There's a hotel a block from here. We're going to check in for the night. I know you're tired, honey, but we're close," Zane said.

Angel nodded mutely, giving him reason to believe she'd hit her physical and emotional limit.

His overnight bag was still in the truck, forgotten when he'd returned from Jacksonville. After tossing his cell phone into the bag, he left his weapon on his hip and pulled his shirttail loose to cover it.

Zane circled the truck to Angel's side and helped her down. Her icy hand barely clung to his as she shuffled along beside him.

They stepped into the lobby of La Shasta, Ft. Lauderdale's newest five-star hotel, and dripped puddles on the marble floor fit for a palace.

As he approached the front desk, Zane kept his arm around Angel, who still wore the black poncho.

An impeccably dressed middle-aged man, wearing a charcoal gray suit and crisp white linen shirt, stared at them in momentary shock. After a moment, he closed his severe mouth, affecting the perfect hotel manager demeanor.

"Can I help you?" the manager asked with a hint of

doubt in his voice.

As the son of a powerful man who'd amassed a fortune in the oil business, Zane knew exactly how to handle this guy. He read "Robert Sommers" on the man's name badge.

"I certainly hope someone can, Robert," Zane said, biting out each word in an annoyed tone. "First the damn flight lands three hours late, then they manage to lose our Louis Vuitton luggage. Next the rental car leaves us stranded two blocks away. So much for a vacation."

Robert's face shifted into his concerned manager expression from Hospitality 101. "I'm so sorry, sir. What can I do for you?"

"Just don't tell me our reservation has been lost. If that happens, I'm calling my sister, so she can warn the world against this disaster zone. She writes a syndicated travel column and does an occasional stint for the *Travel Channel*."

That got Robert's full attention.

La Shasta hadn't been open long. Zane recalled that a simple problem with a recent high-profile guest had been blown out of proportion in the local news. Everyone had talked about the embarrassing event for days.

Robert punched up his computer screen. "Can I have your last name, sir?"

"Mr. and Mrs. Black."

At his words, Angel cocked her head towards him.

He winked at her shocked expression. In addition to a wad of cash he kept on hand to pay for information, he'd been supplied a credit card under the name Zane Black. Even better was the Tallahassee, Florida payment address. Far from his true home in Ft. Lauderdale, which wouldn't support Zane's "vacation" story.

The Tallahassee address was just another layer of protection Zane had wanted in place in case he ever had to use the card.

Robert clicked keys furiously, frowned, squinted, clicked more keys, narrowed his eyes at the computer and glanced up. "Is that spelled B-l-a-c-k?"

"Yes."

More clicking and deep sighs followed. Robert relented and offered a professional, but completely artificial, smile when he said, "I have your room, Mr. Black."

Several elderly couples strolled through the grand lobby, casting appalled looks toward the desk as Zane handed over the card, instructing Robert that there had better not be a charge made until he determined the room and hotel were satisfactory.

Robert paused at that, which was going to be a deal breaker for Zane. He didn't want to risk any chance that someone chasing Angel might have a way to track his credit card before they left. But Mr. Helpful at the registration desk made quick work of processing the paperwork before handing over two room key cards.

Zane took them and said, "Please call when the luggage arrives. In the meantime, we'll need some toiletries. I have mine in a carry on, but my wife's things were in the other suitcases."

Stepping into an office behind the desk, Robert returned with a bag full of items. "Please take these, compliments of La Shasta. We'd like to do whatever we can to make this a pleasurable stay for you."

Zane nodded his appreciation, thanked him, then guided Angel to the elevator. If Robert had any concerns about her single bare foot, he didn't voice them.

She continued to tremble while they rode silently on the elevator, her shivers worrying Zane as much as her near-catatonic state. He had an endless list of questions, but those could wait until she'd gotten a hot shower, food, and he'd assessed her injuries. Plus she could probably use some sleep.

He opened the door to a luxurious room with a single king-size bed. The dainty sofa in the corner didn't appear to hold a foldout or be long enough for his frame. Returning to the lobby to request a room change was out of the question. He'd sleep on the floor before he put Angel under any more strain. He had no idea what she'd endured, but her clothes had been ripped down the front, and she had bruises on the skin he could see.

Someone was going to bleed, from multiple wounds, the next time they tried to hurt her.

Zane slipped the poncho over her head. He tossed it in the corner and flipped on the light in the bathroom that was thankfully subdued since the place had been decorated in white marble and gold hardware. He clenched his fists when he saw her bruised, swollen jaw and the red welts on her ribs.

Tomorrow she'd tell him who had done this and why. Tonight he had to take care of Angel.

Tap, tap, Tap.

Squinting into the door peephole, Zane saw Robert, their accommodating manager, standing on the other side.

Zane eased Angel into the bathroom then answered the door.

"Mr. Black, I'm sorry to bother you," Robert began. "I noticed your wife had the misfortune of losing a shoe and thought we could be of assistance. If she doesn't care for these, tell her to feel free to exchange them for another pair in our gift shop on the mezzanine level, our compliments."

Robert held a beautiful basket with fruit, chocolates, and a pair of dazzling jeweled sneakers fitting for a New Year's Eve party. The whole bizarre situation would have been hilarious if it weren't so serious.

"Thank you, Robert. I appreciate your concern." Zane took the shoes and the basket, and offered Robert a tip, which he graciously refused.

Zane bolted the door.

Angel emerged from the bathroom and stared at the basket. Strange probably didn't begin to describe her thoughts.

Tipping her chin up with two fingers, Zane asked softly, "How does a hot shower sound? There's two robes in the bathroom." He brushed his hand across her forehead, pushing a long wet strand of hair away from her vacant eyes.

She nodded, but without a word, she took the bag of complimentary toiletries and shuffled back into the bathroom, shutting the door. He placed the basket on the dresser, called Ben's voice mail and left the tag number to the Land Rover. Ben had a buddy in motor vehicles who would trace it for him, but Zane hadn't heard a word from Ben in hours. He hoped there weren't complications with the birth.

Next he called Trish to tell her to stay with Heidi, and

stay far away from his apartment.

The sound of rushing water ended as the shower cut off and a few minutes later the door breezed open. There was his Angel, showered and wearing a white terry cloth robe that hit her at the knees, showing only the bottom half of those awesome legs.

His Angel. Warmth spread through him.

Regardless of everything he knew he still wanted her to be his. Had never felt this way about a woman and he didn't even know Angel's last name.

He took slow steps toward her.

The scent of her shampooed hair sparked a riot of lust. He'd missed her from the moment he'd left the apartment this morning. Missed her touch, her voice, the feel of her lips.

Swallowing to help his dry mouth, he couldn't stop envisioning her in his arms, her long legs wrapped around him. He imagined the robe sliding off her shoulders to pool at her feet ... until he lifted his eyes to her ashen face.

She'd never appeared vulnerable before. The spark was gone from her amber eyes. Her slender body trembled under the bulky robe.

Zane closed the distance between them. He gently cupped her shoulders and whispered, "Go lie down. I'll get a quick shower and be right out. Are you hungry? Do you want anything?"

Her eyes never strayed from his when she shook her head.

Drawing a deep breath as if just moving took all she had to give, she walked away and climbed into the sprawling bed. He drew the covers over her and she curled into a ball.

Grabbing his shaving kit and a pair of shorts, he headed to the bathroom, pausing to look back before he closed the door. He always worried about her being a flight risk, but right now he didn't think she had it in her to walk to the elevator.

Chapter 50

Cold spread through Angel from head to toe no matter how tightly she tucked her body under the down coverlet. She peeked through her lashes, watching as Zane disappeared into the bathroom.

Squirming to get warm, she groaned every time she moved her battered body.

Dear God, how was she going to keep Mason's men away from Zane now? Would Zane tell her where the package with the coins had gone if she explained?

Or would he call in the police?

And what was his real name anyway? Zane Jackson? Or Zane Black? If it was Jackson, why did he have an alias?

The situation was way out of hand. What was she going to do? Her spent brain had nothing to offer and threatened to shut down on her if she kept pushing. Tomorrow she'd think everything through, not tonight.

Zane had come for her. She didn't care what his last name was right now, only that he was alive and here with her.

She quivered and her teeth chattered. The hot shower had helped, but right now she thought she'd never be warm again.

She must have dosed off, but not deeply. The shuffle of clothing brought her back awake. A single lamp glowed on the nightstand next to the bed. Just enough light for her to see Zane step out of the dark bathroom. Her mysterious savior's hair glistened from the shower. Dressed only in a pair of black shorts, sculpted muscles rippled along his back and shoulders as he toweled his hair.

He tossed the towel in the corner and walked to the closet. His washboard abdomen flexed when he stretched up to pull a pillow and blanket down then dropped them on the floor between the bed and the door.

After all he'd been through, Zane was going to sleep on the floor.

She didn't want him on the floor or the couch or anywhere that didn't include her. She wanted him close to her, forever.

Angel squeezed her eyes to stem the tears.

She couldn't have forever, because forever only happened in fairy tales. But she could have tonight. And one night with the man she loved would have to last her a lifetime, because no other man would ever replace him.

Zane wouldn't want to hear a vow of love from her, not after what she'd put him through. She'd hold those feelings deep inside, close to her heart.

He switched off the lamp. Soft light outside the open drapes threw hazy shadows across the room. He stepped over to the bed. She knew he only meant to check on her, but she grabbed his hand before he could turn away.

"Zane, stay with me."

He stood still, as if he were unsure, then said, "Honey, I'm right here. I'm not going anywhere." He gave her fingers a squeeze and tried to let go.

She pulled the covers back and tugged on his hand. "Please. I don't want to sleep alone."

Had she not shivered at that moment, she thought he might have refused. When her hand twitched from the movement of her shaking he slid down next to her. The bed gave with his weight.

Not sure what to do next, she lay perfectly still on her side facing him. Not that she could hide her nervousness, but she was breathing as if she'd just run a sprint.

He stared at her, desire burning through his gaze. He did want her. What was holding him back?

She shook with another chill.

He reached for her, pulling her into his arms. She melted into his heat and teased his neck with her lips. She kissed his skin, tasting him, and inched her hand up the curved muscles covering his chest.

When she wiggled closer, he shuddered against her. But still he wasn't taking what she offered.

She had no question that he was interested when the thick bulge in his shorts hardened and prodded her stomach. Any left over exhaustion evaporated as her body went on full alert.

He muttered, "If you don't go to sleep soon this isn't going to work. I'm not a saint."

His fingers kneaded gently along her shoulders. He kissed the top of her head and breathed out a ragged sigh.

She moved her hand down his chest, sliding her nails lightly up and down across the contour of his abs. He sucked in a sharp breath. His hand stopped massaging her shoulders.

"Angel." Her name sounded forced through clenched teeth. "Go. To. Sleep," he said, each word a clear warning.

She'd never felt so safe in her life. Being alone with Zane brought out a side of her she'd been afraid to expose to any man before.

She wanted this man, all of him, tonight.

One more touch should convince him she wasn't the least bit sleepy. Her hand drifted lower to the rim of his shorts. She slid a finger under the elastic waistband and ran a sensuous trail south.

She was flipped over on her back and covered with his body before she could blink. He had her arms pinned above her head, but his weight rested on his elbows.

"Look," Zane warned again, but this time in a tight voice. "I'm *not* made of stone."

She looked down between them. "Liar."

Growling, he said, "You're about ten seconds from pushing me past the point of no return."

"Then take me with you. I want you, Zane."

~*~

Zane stared at Angel, not believing his ears. What blood hadn't squeezed into his aching arousal found its way there now. He was harder than the foundation under their hotel.

He couldn't take advantage of Angel. This wasn't like last night in his apartment. She'd been in shock for hours. She'd regret the decision tomorrow and he'd feel lower than pond scum.

But, dammit, he wanted her.

Digging deep, he edged past his raging libido and uttered the words that would surely qualify him for sainthood.

"Honey, you don't know what you're saying. It's the stress you've been through. We can't do this."

"I *do* know what I'm saying. I may not live through this."

"Don't say that," he ordered. Nothing was going to happen to her. He wouldn't allow it.

More than wanting her right now, he needed her.

"Whether we want to face it or not," she whispered. "I may not survive. I've only been with one person, a boy in high school and that wasn't very special. I want a special night with you. Don't you want me?"

His head drooped.

Hell, he'd never wanted to be a saint.

"Baby," he whispered, "I've wanted you so bad, I can't think." He released her hands, rubbing her palms with his thumbs.

"Then love me tonight," she pleaded.

Neither moved for a long second, then he lowered his head to gently kiss her brow and cheeks.

He paused and released an exasperated deep breath. "We can't." His voice was loaded with regret. "I don't have any condoms here. I won't put you at risk of getting pregnant. You may not think you're going to live, but I intend to make damn sure you do."

Zane wanted to assure her everything would be okay, but he wouldn't lie to her. He *could* tell her she wouldn't face the world alone no matter how determined she was to keep him away from her problem. She'd just have to get used to seeing him, because he wasn't leaving her side.

"The pill is just as safe," Angel offered. She moved her hands away from his loosened grasp, ran her fingers over his ribs, then up to lightly caress his chest. With her index finger, she teased each of his pebbled nipples.

"Just touch me," she breathed against his neck.

That broke the thin hold he had on his control. With a swipe, he raised both of her hands above her head again to end her erotic torture before she set off a physical chain reaction that he couldn't stop.

He lowered his lips to hers. The tender kiss held

everything he wanted to promise her, all the words he didn't know how to say. His tongue probed inside her mouth in search of the taste he loved. His sweet and saucy Angel. Her lips molded to his, her hunger every bit as strong as his.

With one hand he untied her robe. His heart beat a rhythm in time with the pulsing in his groin. The robe fell away from shoulder to thigh.

Oh yeah, he never wanted to be a saint if it meant missing out on something this fantastic. He kissed along her neck and shoulders, nuzzling against what terry cloth remained in his way.

He gently cupped her breast and used one finger to draw lazy circles around the nipple. She twisted up against him, her smooth abdomen rubbing his erection.

A throaty whimper escaped her.

Lingering on one breast with his finger, he lowered his head to the other luscious mound and mimicked the movement with his tongue, then barely grazed the tense nipple with his teeth.

Angel lifted off the bed, the whimper stretching into pained plea.

She'd said special.

He wanted to give her the moon.

Her passion drove waves of heat spiraling through him. It would take everything he had to keep from erupting the minute he entered her. Blood pounded in his ears from the need to be inside her.

Angel's fingers raked through his hair, raising the nerves across his scalp. The feather touch danced along his neck to his shoulders, changing to an anguished grip when he removed both finger and tongue from her breast.

His lips covered hers, his tongue probing past her swollen lips. Her velvet tongue stroked over his, driving him wild.

No matter how much she gave, he wanted more. He kissed her again and again, hot, hungry, needy.

With one free hand, he caressed her breast, palming the erect nipple. A purred "mmm" escaped her. She wasn't large, just a perfect handful. But then, he had big hands.

He stroked a path down through the curls shielding the

heat between her thighs. With a finger, he entered the sensitive furnace and lit a fire.

She arched up, drew in a labored breath, and uttered a long moan.

With his thumb, he teased the pressure point, moving across the sensitive nub back and forth.

"Oh, Zane ... uhmmm."

He needed to slow down, find his control.

She wouldn't let him.

Her teeth scraped his neck. She wrapped her fingers around his head, pulled him down to kiss him. When they broke apart, her warm breath poured across his cheek.

"You feel so good, baby," he murmured. Nothing beyond this minute was real.

Every move, each response from her was a gift he wanted to take his time unwrapping.

For once, fantasy couldn't compare with reality.

He kept moving his thumb and finger, pushing her closer to exploding.

She arched forward, pressing against his arousal. "Oh, Zane...oh, I...yes..." She cried unintelligible pleas, each more passion-filled than the next.

Every time she trembled and whimpered she threatened to snap the thin tether he held on his control. All he could think about was driving into her with mindless abandon, but he wouldn't go further until he was sure she was ready.

It'd better be soon.

"Baby, just tell me what you want." The strained words croaked out of his dry throat.

She panted twice. "You have ... to ask?"

He'd have smiled at the frustration in her husky voice if he hadn't been equally desperate. Changing up the pace of his fingers, he gave her a gentle push over the edge.

She held her breath for a second then cried out, shaking with the intensity of her climax.

He held her there, savoring the joy of watching her until she fell back to the bed, winded.

Within seconds, his shorts were gone and he settled between her thighs. He cupped her soft bottom, lifting her up, and slowly entered her.

He heard a soft moan of, "Yesss," before she clenched

around him.

She fit him like a second skin, surrounded him, hot and tight. Nothing he'd ever experienced before came close to being inside Angel.

Slow and gentle. He had to take it easy with her.

But she wrapped the endless legs of his dreams around his back and shoved up, driving him deep into her.

He'd live outside the realm of sainthood forever to feel this ecstasy for the rest of his life.

The harder he pushed, the tighter she dug into his shoulders, urging him on. He'd been barely hanging on to his control, but one more clench from her would destroy it. Zane reached between them to stroke her fire, to drive her to the point of combusting.

Her body strained under him, rocking in perfect sync with him.

She cried out, her muscles clenching as she climaxed. Frantic fingers locked on his shoulders as wave after wave coursed through her.

Right damned behind her, his world splintered. His body separated from his mind. He'd never felt an orgasm so deeply.

He'd never been in love before either.

He was never giving her up.

Chapter 51

Angel awoke with her face against Zane's warm chest, wrapped in his arms, smelling the musky scent of their lovemaking. After years of accepting every miserable injustice life had dished out as status quo, she'd altered her future.

Might have only been for one night, but that was more than she'd come to expect.

Whether she lived or died, she'd carry last night in her heart as she faced her fate.

Over Zane's shoulder, puffy purple clouds dusted with tangerine tufts floated past the separation in the drapes. Maybe the tropical depression had moved away.

Thinking he was still asleep, she tried to ease away. His arm locked around her waist, holding her in place.

"Where do you think you're going?"

She smiled at the humor in his rough morning voice and said, "I was going to look out the window to see if the storm was passing."

"I'm not letting you that far away. Every time you get further than an arm's length from me, you disappear," he teased.

"Not fair," she answered, indignant over the remark. "I didn't leave your apartment by choice."

When his hold almost cut her breath off, she figured that hadn't been a good choice of topics to bring up. She smoothed her hand across the patch of dark hair centering his chest to soothe him and felt his embrace loosen.

"I'm getting a shower," she announced.

He made a move with his left hand, stroking along the

inside of her thigh in an obvious attempt to deter her from moving. When his finger teased the fragile folds between her legs, Angel clutched his shoulders and conceded immediate defeat.

As if that weren't enough capitulation, he smoothed a hand up to cup her breast and tease one nipple mercilessly.

Zane had a sure way to keep her within arm's reach. Or at least fingertip reach. One of his incredibly talented fingers dipped inside her, in and out, then he drew the wet finger over her folds and started the dance all over of driving her insane.

She gripped his shoulders, shaking with need. She pleaded, "Don't stop."

He lifted up and suckled her other breast then scraped the beaded nipple with his teeth. Then his lips closed over the nipple and his tongue drove her mad.

She forgot about everything but the finger teasing her folds, taking her closer and closer to release. Almost there.

Then his fingers slid down inside her. He said, "I want you ready."

"I am."

"Not yet." He pushed two fingers inside.

She ground her hips down to help him, desperately fighting to reach that point her body begged for, but he'd change the rhythm at the last second as if he could see inside her. He lifted his head and kissed her, loving her with his mouth. Then he teased her damp folds once more.

She trembled from the heat pooling in her loins faster and faster. Time to shift the control.

In a quick move, Angel lifted away from his hands, shifted forward. When she felt the tip of his arousal, she impaled herself on him. Air sucked from her lungs in a gasp of pleasure.

Zane's eyes flew open, dark and hungry.

She grinned down at him. "Maybe I'll just hold you here and see how long it takes before..."

He grasped her hips, lifting her almost off of his member then pulling her down as he drove up inside her. Two times, three times, the rhythm fast and gripping.

Then he reached between them and went right to her go button.

Heat and energy balled in her womb and shattered. She made a sound of pleasure she'd never heard before. Heat zinged all the way to her nipples.

Zane pumped several more powerful strokes and she stayed with him, loving the feel of him inside her. He exploded, growling out his pleasure as he filled her. She collapsed on him, laboring for air.

He hugged her tight, his heart pounding beneath her.

"You're unbelievable," he murmured.

She glowed under the compliment and smiled. "I like it, too." Her breathing had steadied when his hand swept down her spine then smoothed across her bottom.

"What are you doing?" she asked suspiciously.

"What do you want me to do?" He grazed each cheek with his fingers.

"Answering that would be dangerous."

His hand slid further down and under to toy with her, again. Got to love a man with long arms and great hands.

She was close to giving in when his cell phone interrupted.

"You better get that. It could be Trish." Angel rolled off of his chest.

Zane's grumble ended in a vicious curse by the time he reached over to the nightstand for the phone. "One day this thing is going out the window."

He hit the on button and snapped, "Zane."

Angel slipped away to the bathroom when she heard him say, "She had it? Mom and baby healthy?" Pause. "Congratulations, Ben."

~*~

Zane grinned, relieved to hear Ben's good news. Angel's shower roared on as Ben told him he was on his way to the lab.

"I left you something else to check out when you get there," Zane said.

"What? Toe prints?" Ben joked.

"Very funny. There's a gold coin in your drop box, in a brown evidence envelope marked Personal. I took a chance leaving it, but getting into your office is almost as tough as penetrating Ft. Knox. Run a check to see if anything fitting that description has come up missing."

"Oh, man," Ben moaned. "Don't tell me this has to do with your vanishing girl."

"Okay, I won't. Just let me know when you find out anything. I really appreciate this, Ben."

"I know, but this doesn't sound like you. I hope you've got a good handle on her."

Ben had no idea how good a handle he'd just had, but that wasn't something he'd share even with his best friend.

The sound of a car door slamming came through the line. Ben said, "What the hell happened in Jacksonville? Got your voice mail."

"You know what I know. Everything was rocking along just fine until yesterday morning. Every shipment has been dead on the money. They oughta be begging me to take their contract, but now the damn thing's a bust."

"Don't write it off yet, Zane. Mac's pissed. He sent Vance up to Jacksonville this morning to sort through the mess. If anyone can do damage control, Vance can."

That was one giant *if.* "Sorting out who has jurisdiction on this between the DEA and local authorities isn't going to help my chances at this gig."

"Mac doesn't give two shits about everyone playing nice. He wants bigger fish at High Vision. His resources say local authorities jumped too soon. Didn't get what they expected. Somebody's head will go on the block for busting a federal investigation. You talked to Mac yet?"

"No." Zane wasn't in a hurry to do that.

"If he doesn't call you in before Tuesday morning, you need to just show up. In the meantime, give Vance a chance to do his thing before you write the High Vision gig off completely. And whatever you do, don't screw up your future because of this girl."

"I'm being careful." *Yeah, right.*

"You may hear back from me pretty soon. I just walked into my office."

"Thanks."

Zane dropped the phone on the stand and propped another pillow behind his head. He was still reeling. Last night had gone beyond his fantasies, but that wasn't the problem.

He reached over and ordered room service with enough

selection to cover any taste.

Angel had to be the one who'd stashed those coins in his boat curtains. She'd worked fervently to keep her identity hidden. If she had good intentions, why was she hiding the coins?

Much as he tried to avoid the obvious, Angel had disaster stamped across her future in bold print. Everything he'd discovered pointed to criminal activities.

So, what was his problem?

For the first time in his life something wasn't clearly right or wrong. And he couldn't depend on cold objectivity. He cared too much.

And he couldn't imagine life without her. Maybe she had a tainted past, but in his heart he wouldn't accept that she was a criminal. That didn't change the fact that he had to have answers. Now.

Angel stepped out of the bathroom smiling, dressed in her jog bra and shorts. "I washed them out last night so I'd have clean clothes."

He grinned back at her until he saw the purple and black bruise on her ribcage. "If someone puts another bruise on you I'm going to make sure they don't see their next birthday."

Lowering her eyes, she covered the bruise with her hand. "It's not so bad."

"That's not your fault so stop looking embarrassed."

The dainty shrug she gave him said she didn't want to talk about the abuse she'd been through.

He'd given her all the time he could. Zane crossed his arms over his chest. "It's time we talked about what's going on."

"Don't you want to get a shower first? Can't we talk over breakfast?"

No. He wanted answers, but she'd probably eaten little in the last twenty-four hours and he did need a shower. "I ordered room service." Zane climbed out of bed and walked over to her. "Don't go anywhere. Promise me."

"I promise," she said. "Go shower. I'll be here when you come out."

Zane cupped the back of her head and kissed her deeply then touched a kiss to her forehead. "Last night was terrific. We have something very special and it's not just for one night. Understand?"

Tears pooled in her eyes. She turned her face up to him. "*You're* terrific and last night *was* wonderful, but I have to take it one day at a time."

His stomach twisted. She still didn't believe she would survive her ordeal. He planned to make a believer out of her. "We'll talk. I'll be quick so don't answer the door to anyone. I want whoever comes in here to see me first."

She nodded.

He hated to push her when her world teetered on its edge, but they weren't leaving this room until he knew who she was, why she had the coins, and who was trying to kill her.

Chapter 52

CK hit the speed dial number on his cell phone, noting the time. Eight o'clock. He had two more hours. When ML answered, CK started reporting. "We found the pilot's truck. They didn't go back to his apartment or out to his airplane."

"Do you know where they are?" ML asked calmly, but only a fool would believe that Mason Lorde was not seething right now.

"Not yet. I tagged the truck with a transmitter. We tracked it to an apartment complex, but they were gone by the time my men arrived. Could be anywhere. Hard to pry in this tight little area, but soon, very soon," CK promised.

"And she never said a word about the coins while you had her?"

"No, but I didn't use my skills since you indicated the condition you wanted to find her in." CK could have gotten all the information ML needed if ML wasn't such a control freak. "Got two men following the truck and his apartment is covered."

"Don't take out the pilot until we have her in hand. He may either know where the coins are or we can use him to make her talk. Once I have the coins, I have plans for that pilot."

"I understand." If CK was capable of sympathy, which he wasn't, he'd feel sorry for the pilot. ML was a twisted mother with sick ideas. CK would just pop the pilot between the eyes and be done, but that wouldn't satisfy someone like ML.

Chapter 53

Angel slipped her feet into the garish sneakers the night manager had given her, surprised when they fit. She snagged another apple from the basket and munched on it then strolled over and opened the sliding glass door. Balmy morning air met her on the balcony. The clouds were dissipating, leaving a happy blue sky in their place.

Fresh air carrying a salty flavor breezed by.

Even with all the water around Manhattan, it never smelled like this. She didn't want to leave.

She didn't want to see Zane hurt either.

What was she going to tell him?

He deserved the truth after everything he'd done for her. She thought back on last night's events. The fact that he'd located her in that warehouse was amazing. Then he'd rescued her.

No simple task there either. He handled a gun proficiently. A lot of guys could handle a weapon, but he'd been in his element.

She finished her second apple, feeling much improved with the simple nourishment.

From the bathroom door, Zane called her name sharply.

"I'm right here. Don't panic," she joked, then spun around and stopped short at the sight of him. He was naked from the khaki pants up. She ran her tongue over her dry lips.

His gaze darkened.

Her breathing hiccupped. How could she want him again so soon? They'd made love three times during the night. If she let him touch her now, they'd never get out of here.

"Where are we?" she asked, hoping to divert his attention. She dropped the apple core into a wastebasket on her way back in.

A smile kicked up on one side of his mouth. "Changing the subject?"

"There was no subject," she clarified.

"Yes, there was. It just wasn't being spoken."

She suppressed a smile, refusing to concede that her mind had traveled along the same path as his. "In that case, yes, I'm changing the subject. Where are we?"

He strolled over to her as he spoke. "This is part of greater Ft. Lauderdale. It's a small upscale community chosen by large yacht owners because of the canal. You could say this is home to the local rich and shameless."

"What makes this canal so good for big boats?" Angel asked, wanting to confirm her guess.

"The smaller canals are shallower. The channel in this one is fifty feet deep so even when the tide is low you can run a hundred-foot yacht through here."

She followed him over to the thick rail on the balcony. They were three floors up and overhung a green chain-link fence that sprouted from the seawall. That must be to deter anyone from walking along the top of the seawall since only about two feet of landscape separated it from the hotel.

Zane's tone changed to a more somber one. "Before we have breakfast, I want you to tell me what's going on."

She shifted around and leaned back against the concrete rail. A balmy wind lifted tendrils of hair across her face for the heartbeat it took to form her answer. "I got involved with the wrong group of people, but it wasn't my fault."

"I need a few more details than that. What do you have that they want?"

His tone didn't change. She couldn't read him. His face had blanked into an inscrutable mask. How much could she say without going too far?

She said, "I have some ... items that someone *else* stole."

"So you stole it from him?" His eyebrow lifted slightly.

"No. I don't consider taking these items from him as stealing," she stated.

"Why?"

"Because I intend to return them to the rightful owners."

She was encouraged to see his face relax but still had to add, "Eventually."

His mouth compressed into a stern line. "What do you mean by *eventually*, Angel?"

"I need them for just a little while. Considering no one knew who had them and I'm going to return them, the owners should be considerate enough to let me borrow them," she reasoned.

He opened his mouth, shut it, then asked incredulously, "Just what do you have in mind?"

"I can't tell you everything."

"Oh, yes, you can. Someone is trying to kill you. Starting right now, I want the whole truth," he demanded.

"No."

Anger banked across his dark gaze. "I *hate* that word. Say anything you want, but don't use that damn word again," he ordered.

"Fine!" she snapped, arms crossed. "I'm not telling you anything else. How's that?" She slapped a hand on each hip and leaned forward. "And, by the way, how did you find me last night?"

"Don't change the subject. We're talking about what you have that belongs to someone else."

"It's no big deal," she dismissed.

"No big deal?" he shouted. "Stolen gold coins are no big deal?"

They both stared at each other in silence.

"You have them," she accused. "They're on that boat, aren't they?"

A muscle in his clenched jaw twitched. He obviously hadn't intended to share that little tidbit of information.

"They're safe," he said.

"I need those coins," she stressed.

"For what? If you're innocent, why don't you just turn them over to the police?"

Her shoulders fell. Hearing Zane say *if* she was innocent hurt more than she'd ever let him know.

She stomped her foot. "Okay, here's the deal. Once I can confirm my alibi for when they were taken, I plan to use them to prove my employer stole the coins."

~*~

Zane's cell phone rang and he stood in indecision. He wanted to shake some sense into Angel, but the last thing he'd ever do was touch her in anger. The cell phone rang again. Ignore it and finish this conversation or miss talking to Ben, who had to be calling him back?

He and Angel stared at each other for a nanosecond before he stepped into the room and around the bed to the other nightstand. He snatched up his phone. "Zane, here."

"Hey, bud, this is Ben. Man, have you got a hot one."

Zane didn't think he was going to like the news from the level of Ben's excitement. "What have you got?"

The sound of papers rustling came across the line and then Ben's voice. "Her name is Angelina Farentino. She's got a record."

A lead ball landed in the pit of Zane's stomach.

"Go on."

"She works for Mason Lorde, or she did work for him. Left under questionable circumstances is all I could find out without saying too much. He's listed as one of the top twenty wealthiest men in the country." More papers shuffled and Ben mumbled to himself before he continued.

"Lorde Industries is one of the largest import-export businesses on the east coast, but he also deals in rare art and collectibles."

Oh, yeah, the hits just keep on coming. Zane never took his eyes off of Angel. Watching her and listening to the rundown was tearing his insides apart.

"What's on her record?" Zane knew by the way Angel straightened away from the railing that she'd heard him.

"She did a year in a New York prison at eighteen for transporting drugs. Her father went down for the charge of dealing and she was busted as the mule."

Drugs. Of all the things she could have done, drugs fell way down on Zane's forgive list after what he'd watched Trish go through.

He was sure it couldn't get any worse until Ben remembered one more thing.

"Zane, buddy, you listening?"

"I'm here."

"If you can't turn her in, you need to get the hell away from her. She's hot. The Feds are in serious pursuit of her, too. Hang on." Ben's phone rattled against something solid like he'd laid it down.

Zane stared at Angel. Her face had lost color on that one question about her record.

Ben was back on the line. "Her fingerprint turned up on a photograph in the pocket of the guy they found in the dumpster in Raleigh. The one that's been on the news. Turns out he was one of Mason Lorde's employees. Worked for him for the last ten years."

Zane didn't think he could take any more, but Ben hadn't mentioned the coin.

"Did you run the coin?"

"Yeah. That's a *Saint-Gauden's Double Eagle* gold coin. Those aren't easy to come by so I'm betting it came from that heist in Boston last month. I'm not sure yet, because a set of eight were stolen. One coin was a 1933 Double Eagle valued at over seven million. You don't just find a buyer for these coins, because it's not legal to even own that one coin. Takes a while to move them."

The other seven coins hidden on his boat confirmed Angel had been transporting stolen property. Had that been why she was hiding them? To buy time to find someone who could move them?

"I'll get back with you, Ben." Zane dropped his phone on the nightstand at his right. He was at a loss for words. Did he start with "Why did you do it?" or go straight to "I have to call the police."

Like he could just make that decision on the spot?

He'd made thousands of quick decisions, but his black and white world had turned gray with Angel. He'd rather take a bullet to the gut than see her arrested.

Angel moved inside the glass doors. "Who are *you*, Zane *Jackson?*"

He must have looked surprised, because she said, "I just learned that yesterday while you were gone."

Hell and damnation. Trish must have said something. He'd never considered the danger of leaving Trish and Angel alone.

There was no point in continuing the pretense. He'd have to blow his cover to take her in to the authorities.

"You're right. My real name is Zane Jackson. I work with

a special task force under the DEA."

She nodded slowly. "And that man, your friend Ben, he does, too?"

Zane nodded, his throat getting thicker by the moment.

Tears pooled at the corners of Angel's eyes, killing him. The muscles in her throat moved when she swallowed. Her voice came out raspy with emotion. "So you know who I am and what my background is, or at least you think you know."

"I don't know anything anymore," he said, despair wrapping his words. "So, maybe the question is, just *who* are you?"

Her chin lifted. "I'm not a thief and I never dealt drugs. No matter what that person just told you, I'm not lying to you. I got screwed by my father and the legal system when I was eighteen. The gold coins you found were stolen from a gallery in Boston by someone working for Mason Lorde."

But *she* was an employee of Mason Lorde, he reasoned. Or she had been until she stole the coins from the head of Lorde Industries, a prominent businessman probably seen on the covers of a half-dozen business magazines in any given month.

She continued, "I worked for Mason, in his warehouse as a *legitimate* employee, and found some stolen paintings, small ones hidden inside the lining of a shipping crate. They had been all over the news the week before. I recognized one of them and thought someone in the company was the thief, so I brought the paintings to Mason's attention."

"Why didn't you go to the police?" Zane asked. Now his throat sounded as if he'd swallowed rusty nails.

She held up her finger for him to wait. "He'd given me a position in his organization in spite of my record. At least that's what I thought. What I didn't know was he'd hired me *because* I had a record. One I didn't deserve. Silly me, I thought I'd gotten a break, no more cleaning toilets or shoveling crap at the dump. Decent companies don't hire people with a record, but you probably know that. I was so excited. I finally had a real job." One tear leaked down her cheek.

Zane started to move around the bed. He wanted to hold

her and make all the pain go away.

She halted him again with a raised finger and continued.

"So, when Mason realized I wasn't going to cooperate he locked me away in his private compound in Raleigh near the airport where I met you. Mason had a second ... more personal interest in me. The night I stowed away on your airplane was my second attempt at escape. The first – " Her voice broke, but she swallowed and kept talking.

"The first time I tried to run, I only made it to the house garage. The man who guarded me, Jeff, took too long on his smoke break. That allowed me the couple of minutes I needed to get through the house undetected."

She sniffled and whispered, "Mason made me watch when he shot Jeff for his lapse in duty. I have to live with that." Fire flashed in her eyes when she glared at him. "But I didn't commit any of the other sins. I've had to live with the ones that have been forced on me."

Muscles tightened across Zane's chest like a vise.

Did he go with the evidence that Ben gave him or what his gut was telling him? Had an obscenely wealthy man stolen art?

And rare coins?

Had she been forced to mule drugs? Had her *father* forced her? She'd been eighteen.

Some teens were hardened adults at that age and others were still naïve. Which had Angel been?

His heart screamed at him that she'd been naïve and that she was telling the truth. But he'd been taught to never let emotion overrule logic and evidence.

There was only one way he could find out. One way to solve this. Only one way to really help Angel, and he'd be there for her every step of the way.

His throat constricted, but he managed to get the words out. "Turn yourself in and I'll help you any way I can. I'll do this with you." If it cost him the deal with the DEA, so be it.

The disappointment in her face rocked him to the core.

"You don't believe me," she whispered. She clutched her throat and laughed, a pained sound full of hurt and anger.

"Baby, you have to understand – "

"Oh, God, how could I have been such a *fool?*" she raged.

"I can see it written on your face. *You*, the one person I trusted to know the real me, believes I'm guilty of everything."

He took that one to the midsection. Six feet of bed stood between them, but she might as well be on the other side of an ocean.

Zane made another step.

"Stop. Don't touch me. Don't come near me," she warned. Her voice vibrated with unrestrained anger.

"Angel, please. I'm trying to help you."

His damned cell phone rang again.

Neither moved.

The insistent chirping pierced the chasm between them.

Zane finally twisted to his right for the phone, but Angel's movement in his peripheral vision spun him back around.

She'd climbed up on the railing, facing out to nothing.

"*Angel, nooooo...*" he yelled, leaping on the bed and over it to reach the balcony.

She dove off the edge before he got to the glass doors.

He slammed into the rail and stared in horror as she fell to the canal. Blood rushed through his head, he couldn't hear past the roaring in his ears, couldn't think.

Her slender frame disappeared into the water.

A lifetime dragged by until she popped up, yards out from where she'd entered the canal clean as a knife.

Zane clutched his chest. His heart pounded against his breastbone like it wanted out. His breathing slowed as he watched her stroke across the canal.

Angel climbed out on the other side, kneeled on the grass, her body heaving.

She stared up at him and shook her head "no."

He understood. She still contended he was wrong. As she stood up and jogged away, Zane wondered if he might be.

All the bones in his body had turned to rubber. He staggered back into the room trying to absorb what had happened.

Then it dawned on him where she was headed.

The boat.

He snatched up his bag and phone, running to the door.

Mason was out there. The beast who had kidnapped her

was out there. And the Feds had a bead on her.

He had to get to her first.

Chapter 54

Zane ran down the block like he was on fire and hopped into his truck, gunned the engine, and slid a corner leaving the apartment complex where he'd parked the night before. An old couple, literally on a Sunday drive, in a powder blue mid-1980's land yacht got in his way.

Unable to pass against the steady traffic coming toward him, he ground his teeth.

He made the turn onto Sunrise Boulevard and drove toward the bridge he had to cross to reach the beach highway. Heedless of getting pulled over this time, he whipped through traffic.

Any law enforcement would just have to chase him to the marina.

Cars slowed to a stop just as he started up the bridge incline. Sirens screamed in the distance.

Ah, hell, a wreck.

"Dammit," he swore in disbelief.

This would take forever.

On the seat beside his leg, the cell phone began chirping. He cast a furious glance at the evil messenger then snapped it open and roared, *"What?"*

"Whoa, bud. Just thought I'd give you, as an old radio announcer used to say, *the rest of the story*," Ben answered.

"You've told me enough to hang her. What else is there?"

"I've actually got something good to tell you."

"Oh?" Good news would be a welcome change.

"Here's the rundown. She was a high school champion track star and long distance runner, Olympic material. Fifteen or twenty top universities offered her a scholarship, but Stanford won out, then reneged after she was arrested."

"I'd figured something along those lines," Zane interjected.

"She spent her summers working as a bicycle courier in New York," Ben continued. "Her mother died of alcoholism. Doesn't look like she knew her father dealt drugs. Her arrest was the only instance when she'd ever been involved in anything illegal. There's speculation that she got railroaded by the DA and the detective, some questionable circumstances. Something about the whole case was predicated on one fingerprint."

No wonder she meticulously wipes her prints away.

Red taillights glared at Zane all the way up to the span of the bridge. Throwing himself from the pinnacle of the steel structure was a consideration, but too kind for what he deserved. He'd never really listened to Angel's side once he'd gotten Ben's first report, just assumed the worst.

She must hate him.

Join the club. He hated himself.

"One more thing." Ben interrupted Zane's self-abasement.

Zane cut him off. "I don't know which is irritating me more right now, your voice or this damn phone that brings it to me."

"Hey, bud, you've got to hear this. That *1933 Saint-Gauden's Double Eagle* gold piece *is* from the Boston heist."

"She claims she wasn't involved in the heist." But he hadn't believed her. Not hands down the way she'd expected. She'd still believed in him even though she'd known since yesterday that he hadn't given her his real name. The belief humbled him to his toes.

He hadn't deserved it. Still didn't.

"She might be telling the truth," Ben said, moving on with his damned report. "She doesn't sound sophisticated enough to be the original thief, because we're talking only a handful of people in the world who could have gotten past that security. Whoever she took it from is probably very unhappy. Add that to the FBI and she has some major players gunning for her."

Sweat broke out on Zane's forehead. Everything was so convoluted at this point. He needed backup, but that would mean bringing Vance in on this, which put Ben on the spot because of doing these favors for Zane off the record. There was protocol for everything. The last thing he wanted to do was tarnish Ben's reputation. And he sure as hell wasn't asking Ben to back him up in the field when Ben hadn't even taken his wife and baby home from the hospital yet.

The best he could do right now was call in a tip to local authorities or the FBI. And with Mason Lorde's resources, that could well get Angel killed.

Shit.

Zane had no one to call.

Traffic turned into a parking lot on the bridge.

That left Angel running solo until he found her.

Chapter 55

The tropical depression had definitely disintegrated by mid-morning, turning Ft. Lauderdale into a sauna. Angel climbed out of the parts delivery truck in which she'd hitched a ride and thanked the young guy for the lift. He'd been kind enough to drop her close to the marina.

She watched her back, jogging toward the far end. To enter through the front gates didn't seem at all prudent with everybody and their brother after her. At the property line, she skirted the outside of the fence until she located an opening in the ragged box-wire.

Not much of a deterrent.

A few boats traveled from the direction of the bay down the wide canal toward the marina. More cars and trucks filled the lot than had the day she'd stopped by with Zane. People were still out celebrating the holiday.

Easing over to the closest dock, she slipped into the bathtub temperature saltwater and found it refreshing compared to the humidity she'd endured since diving off the balcony.

Training for triathlons meant swimming miles of rough currents, but little diving practice. Zane's frantic scream had trailed behind her until she'd hit the water, jarring her teeth.

She'd made a few dives over the years and would like to say she'd calculated the jump, but the truth was that luck had smiled on her.

She just as easily could have broken her neck. The dive had been her last resort. From the look on Zane's face after he'd heard her record, she'd known he was going to turn her over to the police. His suggestion that she turn *herself* in had pushed her onto the rail and over the balcony edge.

Turning herself in would have been suicidal with Mason still loose.

Her choices seemed destined to go from bad to unbelievably worse. Zane hated drugs. Worked for the blasted DEA. He had to be sickened once he heard she'd been convicted of transporting drugs, especially after spending the night making love.

She'd been prepared for the hurt of walking away from him.

That he immediately assumed the worst of her was a crushing blow, worse than anything she'd faced before. She tried not to fault him, but it broke her heart to find out, too late, that he was no different than any of the other people who'd turned their backs on her and believed what was easy.

When would *one* person give her a break?

She should be upset with him for deceiving her, for sneaking around behind her back to dig into her business. However, she hadn't told him anything about her situation. In Zane's shoes, would she have reacted the same way?

Maybe, maybe not. She'd never been in love until now, but cared enough for Zane to give *him* the benefit of the doubt. And she'd prove her innocence to him before she left.

First, she had to drive Mason away.

A few marina inhabitants reclined lazily on the rear decks of their boats backed up to the dock walkway. They were clueless that a woman stroked silently through the water beyond their bows.

Angel made the turn at the end of the dock so she could swim past each row until reaching the one for Zane's boat. She dove under water, paddling hard, and surfaced at the next dock, then continued the same process.

When she reached Zane's boat, she floated to the rear and climbed up a short metal ladder. The first thing she noticed were the boat curtains, which meant he'd put the coins somewhere else, and finding them would be even more difficult.

If they were even on the boat.

With a fast check of the parking lot and dock, she

scurried down into the cabin to search for the coins.

She dug through cabinets and felt along cubbyholes, then stuck her head out carefully to see if anyone approached. Mason had men everywhere. If they'd found her at Zane's apartment, wouldn't they know about the boat? If so, why hadn't they searched it?

Nothing had been disturbed. The only alteration was the elusive canvas curtain now surrounding the cockpit.

Where would Zane hide the coins if he'd left them here?

She didn't think he'd found them until yesterday morning when he came by to check on the boat without her. They could be here or in his truck. Or in his airplane.

But when she'd nailed him about the boat, he hadn't denied it.

She was wasting time wondering. She'd search the boat and pray for a miracle.

Shoving aside the cushions covering the bed in the cabin, she began methodically going through compartments that stored life jackets and stopped again to scan outside for anyone within close proximity. She went back to hunting through watertight bags and tackle boxes she found, almost forgetting to keep watch.

The next time Angel stuck her head out of the cabin, a black Land Rover swung inside the marina and parked across the lot near the entrance. She squinted to see if they were just going to observe or come to the boat.

CK climbed out of the sport utility. Oh God, the monster who'd abducted her.

She ducked into the cabin and yanked drawers open until she found the ignition keys, then jumped up on deck. Her heart climbed into her throat when another Land Rover drove up to the first one and Mason emerged.

Her hand shook violently. She stabbed the first key at the ignition, hitting all around the hole until it went in. She got the second one in place and realized she had to untie ropes then flip on the battery and pump the do-ma-hickey down in the deck to prime something.

Mason was talking to CK who pointed toward the boat a couple of times, then CK started striding toward her dock.

She tucked down close to the deck, crab-walking across the weathered teak. At each cleat above her head, she reached up and unwound the ropes, jerking them loose and letting them fall to the water. Thank goodness they were all looped in simple S formations.

Down on the boat deck, she twisted a pitted chrome catch to open a section of the floor covering the engines. When the latch flipped up, she pushed the covering aside, shoved her hand in until she found the rubber balls and squeezed hard several times.

She stayed hunched over and scuttled through the curtains to the cockpit, jumped up and pulled the control handles to the middle like Zane had. When she glanced over her shoulder to check on CK, he was nearing the beginning of the dock to Zane's boat.

Angel twisted both keys at once. The motors turned over and over, but neither cranked. She glanced back up the dock.

The demon of her future nightmares hesitated then stuck his head forward and started running like he'd just realized she was on the boat.

Somewhere behind him another man shouted something she couldn't make out.

Twisting the keys again, she begged the churning motors to start. One caught. She kept turning the other one. It caught. She pulled hard on the gears, throwing the boat in reverse, ramming the dock.

Bad idea, bad idea.

She reached over and shoved the gears ahead.

The boat lurched to one side, slamming into the walkway next to her, bouncing hard enough to toss her sideways. Motors whined in protest when the boat hung up on the right side of the slip.

She clawed her way up and watched in horror as the monster closed in to fifteen feet away.

Chapter 56

Zane spun into the marina parking lot past two black sport utilities with gold triangle logos. A man with blonde hair was climbing into one, but Zane couldn't spend the time to investigate. He'd skidded to a stop near his dock just as he caught sight of the giant who had kidnapped Angel stepping onto the wooden planks.

Jumping from his truck, Zane raced after the kidnapper.

The hulking beast hesitated briefly then started running.

Angel had to be on his boat.

"*Hey!*" Zane bellowed as he charged ahead with his weapon drawn, glad to see most of the slips empty with boats out for the holiday after the front had passed.

The giant didn't slow his pace.

Zane's gaze shot past him to the stern of his boat that hit the dock, rattling the pilings. "Stop or I'll shoot," he yelled.

A man came out of the cabin of a boat way down the dock, shouted something then disappeared into his boat.

Never missing a step, the big man threw his arm behind him and fired wildly at Zane. A shot ricocheted off a boat and splintered a wooden rafter.

Chapter 57

Angel ducked when she heard gunshots then lunged for the boat controls.

She wrenched hard on the wheel. The boat bounced left, knocking her sideways, but she held on. She threw a look over her shoulder.

Ten feet out from the boat, CK dove forward, angled for the rear corner.

Released from being hung up, the heavy cabin cruiser lunged forward under full power. The boat wheel slipped from her grip. She turned to fight for control, to spin the boat away from two boats in the next dock over.

Another gunshot and gargled shouts carried over the motor rumble, but she couldn't let go of the wheel to look. She fought to get the boat to open water. Zane's ark plowed around the small waterway between the two rows of docks like an out-of-control, wind-up toy. Every turn she made was over-steered, curving the boat around in a hard left, then a hard right.

She missed a sleek yacht sticking out from the next dock over, but bounced a piling on a slip at the end. Comprehension struck as she exited the marina and her panic level lowered. Angel tugged the controls back halfway to neutral. The bow lowered in the water when the motors chugged down to an idle.

With the boat under control, she jerked around to see what had happened to her pursuer, but by now other boats blocked her view.

More gunfire popped.

Chapter 58

"Hey, you!" Zane shouted again, pounding down the dock to where his boat was fighting its way out of the slip.

Heavy soles pounded the wooden boards behind him. A squeeze play was coming with him in the middle.

Another shot blasted at him from up ahead. The bullet skipped against the piling next to his foot. The crazy bastard dove towards his boat.

Zane leveled his Sig and fired at the bulky target stretched out in mid-air. When he reached the slip, his boat was gyrating its way out of the marina and blood spread across the water in the slip.

He was a crack shot and he'd aimed for center of body mass. Anything it took to stop the threat to Angel.

The man's bald head bobbed along, face down on the surface. He thrashed a hand against the water.

Zane shoved his weapon into the holster he'd tucked into the waistband at the small of his back, and picked up a rope to throw. "Hold on!" he shouted, intending to keep the enormous mass from drowning.

The giant's shiny head rolled back, baring a heinous smile. He raised his good arm from under water to point a Glock 45 at Zane.

With both hands full of rope and no time to react, Zane flinched and turned sideways to present a smaller target.

A shot fired from close by centered the kidnapper's forehead. He disappeared beneath the surface, sinking like a lead ball.

Who the hell had...

A baritone yelled, "Drop your weapon and show your hands."

Ah, shit. Zane's weapon hit the wooden dock with a clatter. He lifted his hands as he jerked around to see who had killed the kidnapper.

Two African American men in dark gray suits jogged up, both with guns drawn. The taller of the two kept coming and kicked Zane's gun away.

"Who the hell are you?" Zane demanded, but he could make a pretty good guess.

"FBI. Are you Zane Jackson?"

Well, hell. Just as he thought. *This won't go well.* "Yes."

"Was that Angelina Farentino in the boat?"

Angel. Zane spun away, all concern for his safety gone. His hands shook as he ran to the end of the dock.

Mason had almost gotten her.

One of the two FBI agents close behind Zane yelled, "She can't go anywhere. We've got the entrance to the bay blocked. In another fifteen minutes, we'll have her."

Zane's mind raced. How was he going to protect Angel from the FBI? He couldn't let them take her. She'd trusted him and he'd turned his back on her. She'd pleaded her innocence. He had to get to her first and tell her he believed her. Then he'd find a way to get her out of this mess.

He reached the end of the dock, barely able to see his boat motoring slowly down the far side of the empty canal.

Drawing in a breath to yell her name, he hoped against the odds of being heard.

The cabin cruiser exploded into a fireball.

Zane's screams echoed across the calm water.

Chapter 59

Information flew around Zane's head like angry, fluttering birds, some of it finding a way into his mind.

Some of it passed by unnoticed with the end of the day. Twilight was overtaking the water. The FBI and local police had cordoned off the marina, but people who'd been on their boats when the shooting started couldn't leave, and were milling around.

Everyone was talking about the explosion.

No one had been near Zane's boat when it blew. Angel had been running the boat down the undeveloped side of the canal so the casualties were low.

Just one dead Angel and an emotionally destroyed pilot.

Zane had been numb as he'd gone through the motions of crime scene wrap up as if caught in the world of the walking dead. He'd answered questions over and over.

Yes, he had a permit to carry his weapon.

No, he shouldn't have been firing it in a public area.

Yes, he knew who had been on his boat. No, he didn't know the actual identity of the man the FBI had shot.

And all the time he kept waiting for somebody to slap handcuffs on *him* for taking the first shot at the hulking kidnapper. Carrying a weapon with a permit was fine in Florida.

Using it to shoot another person?

That got a lot more complicated.

Turns out Ben and the DEA had let the FBI know that Zane was *one of them*. Zane had no clue how they'd pulled that off, or whether that would end his gig as an informant.

Finally Ben had arrived at the scene with Dan

MacPherson, the boss they called Mac, and he'd pulled some strings with the local police, not-so-subtly hinting that they, too, should back the hell off. Ben swore they'd done it all without blowing whatever was left of Zane's informant cover, but Zane had his doubts.

Then Mac did the oddest thing. He hung around and talked to Zane about nothing in particular. As though Mac wanted to console him. Maybe because at that point, FBI agents and emergency personnel had pulled back from him, as though he were a rabid wolf to be avoided.

Understandable. They'd watched him howl like a wounded animal at the end of the dock, after all.

He didn't care.

His cell phone had chirped one time too many. It had sunk faster than CK. He now knew the street name of the bastard who'd taken Angel from Zane's apartment.

Useful information. He supposed.

Mac talked quietly. He'd heard about the High Vision shipment and how the bust had fallen apart. Zane needed to come in for a debrief, but that could wait for a couple days.

Zane nodded every so often. He wasn't processing much, but he owed Mac for pulling the strings to keep him out of one hell of a red tape snarl. Ordinarily he'd have to go in for questioning.

Still, nodding was the best he could do when he teetered so close to losing his mind.

Speaking softly, Mac shared what he knew on Angel that he'd put together between Ben's information and talking to the FBI. Once Ben had told Zane that Angel was probably innocent, he'd made a judgment call and gone straight to Mac for help. That had paid off, but Ben had clearly been worried that his best friend would take it as betrayal.

No way in hell. Zane had told him so, but Zane sucked at putting words together right now. He'd explain better later.

"The FBI didn't want Angel caught in the crossfire," Mac explained.

Zane surfaced from his semi-catatonic state at hearing her name.

Mac continued in that same even cadence. "FBI knew she wasn't involved with Mason. They'd had her under surveillance for a while, planning to approach her as a possible way into Mason's illegal activities. They assumed when she disappeared from her job at the warehouse that Mason was likely the reason. They'd had agents watching for her all over the southeast. One of their local men reported seeing her the night she was at De Nikki's with you." *So that's why she ran – that time.* Zane nodded at Mac. "She spotted the agent even when I didn't," he said, drawing on his ingrained discipline to function or they'd drag him off in a straightjacket. "She took off out the bathroom window."

And Zane had assumed she was being irrational. *Oh how the mighty had fallen.*

Mac nodded. "Sounds like she was running scared from everybody, including Mason."

Somehow, that bastard Mason had slipped away from the marina when all the action started, but the FBI believed they could still nail him.

It would have made their lives easier if Angel had lived.

Mine, too.

The FBI had uncovered enough about her one conviction to prove she hadn't intentionally delivered drugs, Mac had told him. She'd been set up.

Hmm, that was also good to know, Zane mused, not giving a flying damn about any of it.

Someone walked up to ask him if he wanted the paramedics to check him out before they packed up and left. "No," he answered. He wasn't injured – physically.

Mac finally realized he was talking to an empty shell and asked Zane to come see him next week then walked away.

Someone else tried to talk to Zane about the coins again. Zane had lost interest and wandered away. He didn't care about coins.

He wanted Angel.

He had no idea how much time had passed when he noticed dark had settled over the marina, but the divers had gone home, exhausted, without finding a second body.

Only CK's.

Eventually everyone else had dispersed. The FBI agent who returned Zane's weapon – yet another string Mac had pulled – mentioned he'd be in touch in a day or two, when

Zane was feeling better.

A day or two? Was that all it would take to stop the gut-wrenching pain?

Fog drifted in off the water. Tears trickled down each side of his nose as he strolled along the deserted seawall away from the marina, away from the world.

He didn't want to leave here.

He wanted Angel.

As if he'd conjured her ghost, Angel floated along the seawall toward him, surrounded by a heavy mist. She wore the jog bra and shorts from earlier. He'd always wondered if ghosts really looked the same as when they'd lived.

Her dark copper hair glowed. She looked every bit an angel.

His angel was talking. *Cool.* If he were going completely mad, then he wanted to hear her voice, too.

"I'm sorry," Angel said. She floated closer and closer. "I had to get Mason to leave. I didn't mean to hurt you."

His throat constricted. He hoped Angel could hear him, from wherever she was now. Wherever angels went when they left this realm. He forced the words out. "It was my fault. I should have believed you. I'm the one who's sorry." Seeing her was killing him. He wanted to touch her, but you couldn't touch a vision. Could you?

She kept coming nearer.

He could see her legs and feet moving.

"Zane, I'm sorry about your boat."

"I don't care. I wish you'd come back to me." Strips of his heart peeled away, one raw section at a time.

"I did come back to you," she said fervently, almost close enough for him to grab. The mist swirled between them and he blinked quickly so he wouldn't lose her.

"But I want you alive!" he cried out. "I love you and I should have protected you."

"I am alive," she whispered right in front of him. "You did protect me." She reached up and touched his face.

Dear God. Was she really here? Had he gone off the deep end?

Zane hovered between reality and fantasy for a split second then forced himself to accept the truth. "You're not real."

"Yes I am, Zane. Touch me."

He reached out, hand quivering with the desire to believe she still lived. His fingers touched her face that was solid ... and warm. She *was* real?

He pulled her into his arms. Joy like he'd never felt in his life filled him. He had Angel back in his arms. He kissed her everywhere. He couldn't stop touching her.

"You're alive," he croaked in a raspy voice. "I don't understand, but I don't care."

"I'm so sorry," she cried against his throat.

He was afraid she'd disappear, afraid this wasn't real, but none of that mattered.

Angel was back.

Their lips met. His kiss begged her forgiveness, promised her the world and thanked God for a miracle called Angel.

She pushed back a tiny bit, but Zane wouldn't relinquish his hold. He'd never let go.

"How can you be here?" he asked in wonder.

"I had to make Mason go away. He wouldn't as long as I was alive," she explained. "While the boat was going slow, I dug out some rags and tied them together. Then I stuffed them down the gas tank and found matches in the drawers."

She kissed him, a gentle wisp across his chin. "You said gas fumes were combustible, worse than fuel. So I lit the end of the rags and slipped overboard on the far side of the boat and swam for all I was worth. I'm sorry I blew up your boat."

"Honey, I'll let you blow up a thousand boats if you promise to stay with me forever."

She smiled, her eyes full of hope. "I will now that I know I can prove my innocence. Just give me some time."

He hadn't thought he'd ever laugh again, but a chuckle bubbled up. "You aren't guilty of anything, just like you said. Nobody wants to arrest you."

"I don't understand."

"The FBI had you under surveillance. They knew you weren't part of Mason's operation and were hunting you to use as a witness against Mason. They also have information to clear your name from the drug transporting conviction when you were a teen."

"Really?" That one breathless word conveyed just how much she'd been hurt by the wrongful conviction.

Zane caressed her soft cheek. "I'm so sorry about not accepting what you told me, and for what your father did to you. No one can give you that back, but I'm willing to spend the rest of my life making you happy. I'll tell the FBI *I* hid the coins on the boat and they're gone. They'll just have to deal with it."

She graced him with a blazing smile. "The coins aren't gone."

"Yes they are, baby. I stuck them under the anchor rope."

"I know. When I pulled the anchor rope out to tie the wheel, I found them. The bag of coins is lying about fifty feet behind me on the seawall."

Chapter 60

Chatton finished washing her hands in the bathroom onboard the private jet traveling from London to Paris. The airplane offered a safe meeting location for three passengers who trusted no one, especially each other.

Being seen together would be unwise considering their individual positions within three different governments.

As an MI6 agent, she worked alone, but she'd wormed her way into the Czarion alliance to find out who had been systematically killing off everyone in her Macintosh family line for over three decades.

She should be dead, too. The assassin who'd killed her mother must have been bloody pissed when he couldn't find Chatton, a two-year-old at the time.

She'd had a habit of climbing into cabinets and falling asleep. That's where her father, an MI6 agent at the time, had discovered her.

He'd made sure she was never vulnerable again. Before he'd died, he'd passed on files detailing deaths in her Macintosh family, both accidental and intentional. He'd taught her many valuable lessons, but one to be remembered above all.

Those with the money manipulate power in the civilized world, but the one who knows their secrets owns the money movers.

Possessing a powerful secret trumped bank accounts any day and provided the best resource for tracking prey.

Her father's research went back many generations and had uncovered a surprise – an ancient group known as the Orion Hunters. People who searched for five artifacts believed to unlock the mystery behind Orion's Legacy that prophesized the Final Conflict, a war to end all others.

Chatton's eye muscles should be stretched out from rolling them every time she read another warning about the "Final Conflict" of the world. She was a skeptic of the nth degree on this Orion Legacy crap, but no believer had ever studied the Orion Hunters as thoroughly as she had.

She'd used that knowledge to locate Wayan, an advisor to China's Party Chief, and the General, a powerful player in the US Pentagon. Both were her traveling companions on this private flight.

Time for the Czarion meeting. Only the second one since she'd joined ten months ago. She did a final touch on the pretty thirty-two-year-old face she still didn't recognize sometimes, any more than she recognized the golden-brown hair that fell to her shoulders.

Giving one last brush of her hand down the front of her flawless black Christian Dior suit, she exited the bathroom at the rear of the aircraft, feeling naked without a weapon.

She glided past two of Wayan's guards who eyed everyone as if constantly assessing the quickest way to kill them. She and the General had security personnel onboard as well and all six guards had swept the cabin for bugs.

Her personal guard stepped forward as soon as she entered the cabin. She said, "Yes?"

"Your purse was searched."

She'd intentionally left her Hermis Birkin purse in the meeting area when she'd excused herself. "As I expected."

Having made his report, her man nodded and returned to his position behind where she'd sit across from the other two men who lounged in identical cushy leather armchairs. "Gentlemen."

Wayan nodded in his formal way with elbows on the chair, arms and hands steepled. His round face, chopped black hair, and thin black mustache reminded her of a little boy playing grown-up due to the youthful face and slender build for a man of forty-four years.

The General's buzz cut kept his odd red hair to a minimum distraction since he was African American. An attractive forty-nine-year-old who wasn't really a general.

That made her the baby of the group, if they were foolish

enough to discount her as such.

Lifting her purse, she stuffed the small cosmetic bag inside. She wanted to smile, because neither of the two men had opened the tampon package that concealed her listening device.

Men. So predictable when it came to feminine products. As if their testosterone levels would drop by touching one.

She opened the meeting by addressing the General. "Did you acquire the St. Gaulden's coins needed for the exchange?"

"No."

Wayan immediately frowned, hands tensing slightly then easing quickly to hide the reaction. "You lost the coins?"

"That's not what I said," the General replied in a gravelly voice full of curt censure. "Mason Lorde had an employee who stole the coins. I gave Lorde a five-day deadline to produce them or lose his operation."

"So he missed the deadline?" Chatton asked, considering what it would take to coordinate an operation in the States right now. The beauty of having partners was that someone else could perform an op in your home country and insulate you from suspicion.

"Not exactly. The FBI found the coins first and are moving them to a protected location to keep as evidence."

Wayan inquired in his polite way that hid the sociopath inside, "Will the coins be vulnerable during this transport?"

The General shook his head. "No, but the personnel involved in the transport and security of the coins include *my* resources."

"But *that* will not gain us the panel from the Amber Room," Wayan argued, impatiently patting his fingers against each other.

The Amber Room panel was one of the world's greatest treasures and had once belonged to King Wilhelm I then Tsar Peter the Great. Many believed that all of the room was lost when Königsberg Castle burned during World War II.

But four panels were saved – or so the legend said – one of which held a part of the Orion Legacy.

She didn't care about ancient mysteries. She wanted to

find the person or persons behind the mass murder of her family. And to know what these two would do on the off chance they actually *found* all five artifacts of the legacy.

Whether the prophecy was real or not, Wayan and the General were both in positions to influence the leaders of the US and China, and they could orchestrate a crisis that would trigger a world war.

She played along and offered a smidgeon of support to Wayan. "I agree with Wayan *if* we can confirm which one of the four Amber panels is on the market – "

Wayan cut in. "We must acquire *all* the panels no matter what."

"But the one we're looking for has an identifying mark."

"This is not negotiable." Wayan threw a sharp look at the General. "We must have those coins."

She hated dealing with fanatics.

When the General sighed, he sounded like a grizzly, put out at having to kill a critter that wasn't worth the effort to leave his cave. "*Once* we confirm the Amber Room panel is definitely available, I *will* get to the coins." Dismissing Wayan by swinging his attention to Chatton, the General asked, "What have you found out?"

She did enjoy seeing those two eyeing each other like reptiles on the attack. "Mason Lorde thought he was going to trade the coins to Mendelson, but the German does not have the panel." Mendelson had been tough to investigate and would be even harder to find, but she was not easily deterred. "I haven't discovered Mendelson's true interest since he's basically an intel broker. The best I can determine, he picked up rumors that another party has one of the panels, and he understood that this person would trade for eight St. Gaulden Double Eagle coins *if* one of them was a 1933."

"A fortune hunter," Wayan interjected with disgust. As though he thought being a fortune hunter was a perversion. Then Wayan lifted one of his thin black eyebrows. "Is there any chance this Mendelson could be an Orion Hunter, perhaps one of the Teutonic Knights?"

Chatton had considered that possibility and executed thorough research. She felt reasonably certain Mendelson was *not* a descendant of the German family believed to possess one of the five artifacts.

"I don't think so," she answered Wayan. "Mendelson deals in illegal arms and classified information. He's known for capturing assets and either negotiating a profitable trade immediately or..." She paused when the repugnant pictures of Mendelson's interrogations clicked past her mind's eye. "...*extracting* information, which he then sells. I believe his interest is purely monetary, but that does not keep him from being a useful tool."

"The coins were recovered in Florida?" Wayan asked.

The General shifted in his chair, a sign his back was bothering him again. "Yes. Just north of Miami, which reminds me. I have news on High Vision. I orchestrated a bust on one of their shipments going into Jacksonville."

He did *what*? Chatton rounded on him. "High Vision doesn't ship anything *illegal* into Jacksonville. As I understood it, they needed a gateway into Miami for their black market drugs, and you were going to arrange that."

"They do and I did," the General confirmed. "But for the past month High Vision wouldn't come to the table no matter what I offered them. They didn't want to be in our debt. I had to show them that they could either work with us or face constant scrutiny from authorities of all their operations in the United States. Once I had their attention with the Jacksonville shipment, they changed their tune and asked to meet. I've assured them easy access to south Florida."

Wayan didn't actually smile, but his eyes brightened with enthusiasm. "And they understand what we expect in trade?"

In trade? More like an international shakedown plan. Chatton had to give these two credit some days. She might not always agree with their methods, but they did get results.

The General shifted again and grunted at an ache. "When the time comes for them to repay this favor, they will use their people to transport our shipment."

"Excellent." Wayan said. It was the closest he came to a fist pump celebration.

Chatton had heard nothing of this. "What are they transporting?"

Waving a hand in dismissal, the General said, "Something Wayan and I agreed upon before you came along."

Did he really think she would allow them to keep her out of the loop on anything? She let it go for now and turned the conversation back to getting the rest of the General's report on the coins. "What of Mason Lorde, General? Is he contained?"

The General rarely smiled, but the tiny lift at the corner of his mouth counted as one. "Oh, yes, he is contained." The corner of his mouth lifted higher. "Yes, indeed."

Chapter 61

Four months later...

Zane placed the Titan on autopilot and leaned back, content in a way he'd never expected. More so now that he was back with Angel after a fourteen-hour stint for the DEA. Being gone for days had never been a problem before, but now he counted minutes every time he left home until he could get back to Angel.

That's what happened when you found the woman you couldn't live without.

"How dressy is this party?" Angel wondered aloud as she poured Zane a cup of coffee. "I don't know how anyone can get excited about Christmas in Florida."

"The longer you live here, the more normal it seems. You'll see all kind of styles tomorrow night." He took a sip and said, "Everything you wear looks terrific on ... or off."

She rolled her eyes at him and switched topics. "I can't wait for Trish to get back from her buying trip."

"She probably misses you and Heidi just as much. I'm amazed at the change in her in only four months. I never realized she had the makings of a business dynamo."

"Her new shop is going to go gangbusters," Angel said then grimaced. "I hope she takes some time off after she gets back. She's been on the road a lot."

Talk about reasons to be happy. Trish had shifted into high gear after she'd gone through rehab. Those days had been tough, but Angel's presence had made the difference for him and Trish. His sister had blossomed into the strong woman Angel had seen even when he couldn't.

Zane chuckled. "I don't think you're going to slow her down anytime soon and she's fine. Heidi would let us know if anything changed." He leaned across to run his hand over Angel's cheek. "Don't get chilled. I can push the heat up if you're cold."

"I'm fine, so stop fussing over me." She smiled then sighed. "I'll be *really* fine when the trial is done."

"Honey, get used to being doted on." He grinned back at her, thinking he'd never get tired of having her near to pamper. "And the trial is going to be a cakewalk. The FBI only needs you to corroborate their information and timelines."

"Lorde's organization imploded once his people realized he was gone. Everyone's rolling over and cutting deals." Reaching over again, he brushed a strand of hair behind her ear, another excuse to touch her. Seeing her mother's heirloom ring dangling from the chain around her neck had him wishing she'd have hocked a dozen rings.

You'd think he'd brought her the Hope diamond the night he walked in with that. Damn, he got hard just thinking about the way she'd thanked him that night.

She asked, "Didn't you think it was suspicious that he committed suicide?"

Yes, but he didn't want her worrying over it. "Not really. He had to know the FBI was close on his trail. Took the coward's way out, which fit."

She scrunched her shoulders. "I just couldn't see Mason Lorde eating a bullet out of fear. Not someone with his international contacts and financial resources. I would have expected him to run for a while, at least. But I'm glad I don't have to face him in court."

Zane was, too.

She asked, "How's the High Vision thing coming along?"

Angel could change mental gears faster than he flipped switches in the cockpit.

"Everything with that group is strange. They get busted in Jacksonville and end up the victims. Not one thing illegal ever turned up in that shipment. The DEA knows they're smuggling contraband into the country through Florida because they follow the trail in reverse when they find it on the street. But High Vision keeps getting tipped to their raids. Has to be a leak in the operation somewhere." He did a quick check of the instruments and the open skies around the plane and added, "But Mac's got a plan."

"Is it something you can tell me?"

He appreciated that she understood when he couldn't talk about some things. Mac had brought Zane in to work more closely with his group, and that meant Zane had more sensitive information. "He's bringing in some new blood. Individuals from different agencies to work on the task force. Especially one guy who we hope can find the mole."

"A field operative?"

"Probably."

Angel tapped her fingers nervously on her thigh. "Will you have to work much with this new guy?" she asked in a pensive voice.

"Nah, from what I hear, it's mostly just keeping an eye on him. He's something of a loner."

She still drummed her fingers, worrying.

He couldn't have that.

Mac didn't want anyone talking about changes taking place, but the part involving Zane wasn't classified and his wife's peace of mind was his priority at the moment. "Speaking of my work, Mac is making some changes in their charter service needs."

Her finger tapping picked up speed. "Like what?"

"He wants to add more planes to the operation."

She swung around, mouth open. "He's going to split up your business with others?"

"No, honey. He's giving me three more airplanes, paid for, that will operate like I've been doing. They'll be part of Black Jack Charters. They'll work for me."

Her eyes lit up. "That's great news."

It was. Much as he loved flying, he was looking forward to being home more. He had reason.

He made a minor adjustment to the controls then returned the airplane to autopilot and switched topics on her this time. "What are you going to do with the reward money for finding the coins?"

He'd never forget the surprise on her face when Angel heard about the six-figure reward offered for the return of the coins. In an effort to make up for the wrongs she'd suffered, the FBI made sure Angel received every penny.

"I'd like to go back to school," she began. "But I also want to help other women. I don't have an exact plan, but Trish and I have kicked around some ideas."

Reference to school made him reflect on her scholarship and lost running opportunities. "Are you disappointed you couldn't compete in this year's Tamarind Triathlon?"

"No, but *you* should feel guilty. It's all your fault," she declared, a teasing sparkle in her eyes.

"Nay, nay." He shook his finger tauntingly at her. "I'll take fifty percent of the responsibility, Mrs. Jackson. Good thing I made an honest woman of you when I did." He cocked an eyebrow at her.

"I did *not* lie. I just suggested that the pill was an effective birth control. I never said I was *taking* the pill. I had no idea being pregnant took so much energy. I've run marathons that didn't kick my butt the way my first three months did." Angel patted her middle that had the beginnings of a baby bump, and smiled wryly at him. "And *you* said you married me right after the explosion so you could keep me legally locked away."

Zane rolled his eyes and laughed. "You'll be able to compete next year. Junior and I will be at the finish line to cheer you on as you win."

"Junior? You better prepare yourself for the possibility of a girl."

Zane envisioned holding a little girl in another five months. She'd have pale coppery hair and border on perfection if at least half of her genes came from her mother.

"Honey, nothing would make me happier. I'm partial to angels."

The End

A WORD FROM THE AUTHOR:

"Thank you for reading my books. I hope you enjoy the Slye Temp series. Visit http://www.AuthorDiannaLove.com to find all my books. If you have a moment to leave a review at the online bookstore, GoodReads, BookLikes, Shelfari or anywhere else I'd really appreciate it. And please visit me on Facebook at Dianna Love Fan Page and on Dianna Love Street Team where I hope you'll join the team!" To collect free "signed" cover cards, visit www.KeeperKase.com

Dianna

Slye Temp romantic thrillers reading order:

Last Chance To Run
Nowhere Safe
Honeymoon To Die For
Kiss The Enemy (Fall 2013)

***

Visit www.KeeperKase.com to find out how to get FREE "signed" glossy cover cards of Dianna's books.

***

Please enjoy the following
Sneak Peek from
Nowhere Safe

Joshua Carrington and Trish Jackson's story
*He has nothing to lose
until she gives him a reason to live.*

Nowhere Safe

Slye Temp Series

CHAPTER ONE

Chelsea was late.

Twelve seconds late.

The kind of late that could cost a life.

Josh forced his grip to relax before he crushed the crystal glass of thirty-year-old scotch. It wasn't as though she'd hit traffic making the fifteen-kilometer drive from Farmlingham. Maybe dodge a sheep or two in the road, just part of the country ambience this far north of London.

He expected Chelsea to strut across the polished oak floor of this eighteenth century mansion any minute, chin cocked up as if she owned the place. She could do it, too. Pull off pretending she was one step from British royalty and not a bastard child who made her living as a liaison for touchy deals between dangerous people.

A bastard just like him. One of those little things they'd had in common from day one. Another was an obsessive penchant for being on time.

Always. And she demanded it as a nonnegotiable term for anyone wanting her liaison services.

The second hand on his watch marched on with no regard for his sanity. Something had gone wrong.

Service staff in crisp black tuxedos moved through the elegant party carrying silver platters. One of the staff paused next to Josh. "Would you care for something, sir?"

Yeah. I'd kill for a cellular signal for about ten seconds. Just long enough to check his phone for text messages.

Without a magic wand, even the best staff couldn't make that happen.

"No, thanks." He strolled past floral decorations a foot taller than he was. At six feet, two inches, Josh could see over most of the crowd. He visually swept the partygoers peppered around the enormous ballroom, searching for Chelsea and Mendelson, the German guy Josh was here to meet.

Still no vivacious beauty with a head of black hair and eyes green as spring leaves.

Ninety-nine seconds.

Frustration burrowed into the center of his skull. He hated stuffy parties, but Mendelson had dictated the location and arranged for the gilded invitation. If Josh closed his eyes, he could be back in the states at the charity ball his parents hosted for five hundred guests every spring. Same mind-numbing conversations. Same put-me-in-a-catatonic-state Baroque music played by a string ensemble much like the ones his mother hired.

She claimed the peaceful music kept people calm.

Not doing a damn thing for him right now. His heart hammered like Charlie Watts cutting loose on a drum solo at a Rolling Stones concert.

Come on, Chelsea.

She'd never missed a meeting. Not even their occasional casual rendezvous to scratch an itch.

Hell, there'd never been anything casual about the hot sex they shared. They'd burn hard and fast, like a flash fire. Then go their separate ways afterwards. No drama.

The perfect relationship to keep loneliness at bay.

Not a relationship in the true sense of the word, but he did care for her. Needed to know she was safe. He'd never had a more dependable informant or go-between. So where was she?

Had Mendelson changed the plans?

Had Chelsea backed out?

No. Not with a man's life on the line.

And she had just as much investment in extracting a captured CIA agent tonight as Josh did. The CIA asset had information on a terrorist cell planning to detonate bombs in Los Angeles and Dublin.

In two days.

Chelsea's grandmother lived in Dublin in a nursing home, too ill to be moved without risking her health.

Josh's gut snarled at him to get out of this place, disappear before he ended up in the same fix as Chelsea, who might be imprisoned with the CIA agent right now.

Good advice. That he couldn't follow.

His gut didn't get a say this time.

Josh lifted his drink slowly, his eyes trained on the second hand of his watch.

She'd blister his ears for staying. He'd let her if she'd just walk through those beveled-glass doors at the entrance.

If the muscles across his shoulders got any tighter he'd split the seams on this tux the next time he stretched. *Relax a little. Think.* She could handle herself just as proficiently with a weapon—or in hand-to-hand combat – as he could.

Another commonality between them even if she wasn't trained as an operative. She'd gained survival skills on the streets in Liverpool where failure meant a short life.

His hard-times training had been back in New York as a street rat, but it was nothing like the professional training he'd received.

He and Chelsea had one major difference.

His team of hired mercs was loyal to the US.

Chelsea pledged her allegiance to the almighty dollar and the highest offer. Strictly business with her.

Or it had been until this op, when she discovered her grandmother was at risk.

Had cool-as-ice Chelsea allowed emotions to rule her actions this once and made a mistake?

If she had and couldn't contact him, there was no way for him to know what kind of trouble she was in or for him to help her. He should follow SOP at this point and disappear.

Especially after the cryptic warning in her last text. She'd typed that damned XOXO at the end of the text.

When they first slept together, she'd told him two things to never forget. She didn't do late, so if she ever failed to show on time, he should not wait for her. And if she sent XOXO in a message it meant she might have to vanish.

Might.

A word that would haunt him forever if he left now.

The sound of a familiar footstep tapping across polished oak floors reached his ears. He honed in on it, listening as he turned to scan the crowd. There it was, moving toward him. A confident click, click, click that lifted just above polite conversation.

Black hair flashed into view. Halle-damn-lujah. Chelsea headed toward him with her signature smooth gait on a pair of five-inch black heels.

He caught himself before his face revealed a reaction to the punch of relief slamming his solar plexus. *Showtime.* He shoved cold disregard into his eyes.

What had been the delay?

Shiny black hair fell past her shoulders, a long strand dipping to touch the enticing hint of breasts he'd spent hours appreciating on their stolen encounters. She'd showcased them nicely tonight, in a strapless black sequined dress that sparkled under
the crystal chandeliers. Sexy-as-hell body, but that hadn't been what he'd noticed when they'd first met. It was the sparkle of Irish in her husky voice that had turned his head.

She wasn't the love of his life. He couldn't have one. Neither could she, with their career choices. But even though they sometimes went months without a word from each other, he'd realized tonight that she'd carved a spot in his world he didn't want vacated.

She played her role, too, chilly expression in eyes he'd seen laughing only a day ago. She ignored the admiring gazes snapping in her direction as servers opened a path for her.

Ludwig Mendelson followed a half step behind Chelsea, his shoulders back, body square and thick like a wrestler. His hair was short and too silver for a man only in his forties. Pale skin stretched across a pudgy face punctuated by two unforgiving, ice-chip blue eyes. An inch or so shy of six feet tall, he strode as if the world should drop at his feet and pay homage.

If that were true he wouldn't need the two bodyguards following close behind, both stuffed into tuxedos tailored for the Hulk.

Mendelson had a reputation for being unpredictable.

He'd chosen this party, but could've just as easily demanded a meeting at a location that required mountain climbing gear. Josh had the German's file memorized and had come to England prepared to do pretty much anything required to finalize this exchange on Mendelson's terms.

He knew more than he wanted to know about a man with a preference for over-the-top, perverted styles of interrogation.

Just seeing Mendelson walk so close to Chelsea twisted a fist inside Josh's gut, but she'd built one hell of a reputation in the international crime community for arranging meetings like this one, and for punishing anyone who tried to harm her.

Still, something was amiss or she'd have been on time.

When she reached Josh, she waited until Mendelson stepped up next to her before speaking first to Josh. "Mr. Taylor, meet my associate, Herr Mendelson."

Offering neither his hand nor any verbal acknowledgment, Josh announced, "You're late."

Mendelson moved his chunky shoulders in a slight shrug then glanced over at Chelsea who didn't bat an eyelash. His German accent came out as blunt as his face. "Beauty is not a rushed process. Men have always waited on women."

Had she really been the reason for the delay? Or not?

If so, had she done so on purpose?

Cognizant of Mendelson's close scrutiny, Josh swirled his scotch and took a sip. He tinged his words with just enough irritation to hide the concern that brewed in his gut over Chelsea. "I came here to retrieve my client's asset and deliver your payment." He targeted Chelsea with his next verbal shot. "You were chosen as liaison because of your reliability *and* your reputation for being punctual." *Tell me what's going on. Any sign.*

"You could have gone on your way if waitin' was a burden," Chelsea warned with just enough venom in her Irish lilt to sell the deadly glint in her eyes.

What the hell was that supposed to mean? Had she *wanted* him to leave?

She pressed on. "We've all an investment in tonight's meeting. The sooner we stop natterin' on, the sooner we'll each be enjoyin' the spoils."

Josh leveled Mendelson with a let's-get-to-the-bottom-line look. "Satisfied that I'm here alone?"

"If I were not, you would no longer be standing here."

Meaning Josh would be dead already. Mendelson believed Josh had a transport of weapons waiting nearby to exchange for the CIA agent, so he pointed out, "I can't keep someone mobile in this area for long without drawing attention."

Mendelson smiled, his eyes eager. "Then I suggest we get moving and complete our transaction."

"Lead on." Josh lifted his glass in a subtle gesture that said *get on with it, you're wasting my time.* He knew the exchange wouldn't go down here.

Mendelson didn't disappoint. "My car is waiting."

Sucked to be right sometimes.

Following the Mendelson entourage, Josh held his blank mask in place, but unease clawed at the back of his neck. In spite of the XOXO message, Chelsea hadn't vanished but neither could they discuss anything now that the game was on.

He was just glad to know she'd be close enough for him to snatch along with the CIA captive tonight, because he wasn't leaving this country without both of them.

If she needed to disappear, he could make that happen and keep her safe at the same time. His body might take a beating if she didn't see it his way, but he didn't think she'd purposely kill him, so he'd heal and she'd be alive.

All other details could be worked out after that.

Outside the lavish home, attendants rushed through the crisp fall air, opening car doors for late arrivals and retrieving vehicles for early departures. Josh had driven here in a rented Mercedes, but Chelsea wouldn't be riding with him. That meant there wasn't a chance of talking before they reached the location where Mendelson held the CIA agent, Len Rikker.

It had taken five days of intense negotiations to convince Mendelson that Josh represented black market weapons dealer Puno de Hierro, known as Iron Fist, who operated out of Nicaragua.

And that Len Rikker was no international spook but one of Puno de Hierro's assets.

Among Mendelson's multi-faceted enterprises, he brokered resources for terrorist operations. Josh's team had tracked the German for twelve days and finally gotten a break when the weapons shipment Mendelson needed as currency for another deal had gone missing.

Thanks to Josh's team who'd stolen it.

That team now waited to move in.

No government would admit to employing mercenary soldiers like Josh's team, but most countries tapped similar off-the-record elite operatives for missions that couldn't be run through the usual channels, or couldn't be acknowledged under any circumstances. The CIA would normally turn to one of its own elite military units to extract a captured agent, but they wanted this sterile.

A hands-off operation with none of their assets involved.

Sabrina Slye, who headed up Josh's team, had questioned the "why" behind the agency's decision to send in her team, but the powers-that-be weren't in the habit of answering to anyone.

Much less a merc. She'd turned down the mission until someone way up the CIA food chain – a man she wouldn't name – had asked her personally to bring home their agent.

And to do it soon, before Mendelson disappeared again.

He often moved his high-value assets daily.

Sabrina had freedom to execute her operations with full autonomy since her people were considered expendable resources that no government agency would admit hiring and sure as hell wouldn't lift a finger to save.

A young man rushed up to Josh and pointed as a Mercedes rental rolled up to the curb. "Your car, sir."

Right behind Mendelson's sleek black limousine.

Josh continued toward the end of the walkway lit by landscape beacons. The bodyguards took position on each side of the limo's open passenger door where Chelsea paused.

Mendelson's lips tilted with amusement. A pit viper's smile. "I have arranged a driver for you."

A driver who matched Mendelson's bodyguards in size – and grim expression – sat behind the wheel of Josh's Mercedes.

As expected.

If he refused the driver, the deal would fall apart. Everyone involved knew that. But this was all about power plays so Josh spun the tables with one of his own. He made a show of looking at his watch. "Your window of time to complete our meeting is running out."

In other words, the weapons shipment Josh was supposed to be handing Mendelson in trade would not remain in the area indefinitely.

Mendelson's gaze turned black as his soul. He ignored Josh and waved Chelsea into the car.

Chelsea glanced back with what Josh could only describe as regret in her gaze and gave a tiny shake of her head that no one could have seen but Josh.

She was definitely leaving, and saying goodbye.

Didn't she know by now that he could help her with whatever was wrong? He had until he closed the deal with Mendelson to stop her from leaving. She wouldn't go without her money after coming this far. Now that Josh had been given an unwanted driver, calling his team on the satellite phone hidden in the driver's door panel of his car was out.

Always have a backup plan.

With a subtle movement, he twisted the platinum cufflink at his right wrist, which functioned as a tracking device. That single twist sent a signal that he was mobile but not alone.

Activating his left cufflink in a similar way alerted the team to move in.

Their five-member team had been together for six years, but Josh, Sabrina and Dingo Paddock went back to Josh's days as a kid in a New York City group home, another name for an orphanage.

Once the limo with Mendelson and Chelsea moved off, Josh's Mercedes pulled up next.

His driver said not a word during the forty-five minute ride, with the Mercedes boxed in between the limo and a silver Hummer. A moonless night wrapped the windows, blacking out any view of the rolling countryside he'd seen earlier, covered in autumn's golden wash. Colors just as vibrant as a year ago when Josh and Chelsea had spent a weekend in a stone cottage an hour from here. They'd made love under a beech tree where coppery leaves floated down around them.

Sabrina had warned him and Dingo to never get attached, and Josh hadn't before now. Too many years spent alone, watching for death around every corner, had left him numb inside. Or so he'd believed until the first time Chelsea had laughed.

Then she'd made *him* laugh, a genuine from-the-chest laugh he hadn't experienced since he was a kid.

And now she intended to disappear.

Then he'd spend every day wondering if she'd survived. That was classic Chelsea. She'd never ask for help if it meant putting someone else at risk.

Too bad. Josh refused to let her face a threat, whatever it was, alone.

His driver slowed as the Mercedes passed guards at the entrance to a property. The stone entryway suggested a house was hiding beyond where the headlights pierced the night.

Mendelson's limo, Josh's Mercedes and the Hummer continued along a curved drive until a two-story stone structure took shape. Temporary lights had been set up, illuminating the yard. Ivy climbed the attractive farmhouse, probably built in the 1700s.

As soon as Josh exited the Mercedes, one of Mendelson's bodyguards from the Hummer met him at his car door. "Lift your arms."

Of course. The pat down.

Josh lifted his hands. When the guard finished, Josh emptied his pockets, showing he had no phone or anything that could be used for communicating or killing.

The guard ordered, "Follow me."

Josh's neck twitched with more unease. Chelsea hadn't gotten out of the limo yet.

He fell into step, taking stock of the few security he could locate outside the lighted area. Smoke trickled from a fireplace at one end of the house, the smell of burning hardwood riding on a light breeze. Two men with rifles posted on the rooftop. More were positioned around the perimeter, some barely visible in the shadows.

Ten, so far, counting the limo driver, who had to be armed.

But another five to ten could be hidden.

And not just hired muscle, but deadly operatives.

Josh recognized at least two from the Russian mafia. Mendelson had spared no expense, but was it to insure the safety of his prisoner, or that this weapons shipment did not get waylaid?

Sabrina and her three-person team could handle inserting past fifteen, maybe twenty guards, depending on how the security was spread around the farmhouse.

At the entrance to the house, another guard—visible guard number eleven – opened a heavy wooden door that swung on black, wrought-iron hinges. The glass lamp on a hall table supplied enough light to see the quaint foyer and a stairway against one wall.

Dried flowers and other potpourri piled in a glass bowl might have freshened the air, but it couldn't combat the stale odor of recently fried fish. Probably cooked by Mendelson's men.

Were the owners away from the property?

Or dead?

The guard at the door nodded and the bodyguard led Josh up the stairs to a narrow room with tall ceilings and an old-world feel. Dark bookcases were laden with rows of leather-bound books. Two mahogany chairs with tufted green upholstery sat sedately on a Turkish rug, and the scent of pipe tobacco lingered.

A homey picture, which did nothing to loosen the tight muscles in Josh's neck. "Tell Mendelson he has five minutes."

Heavy footsteps approached then Mendelson said, "I am here, Mr. Taylor," on his way into the room.

Without Chelsea. Shit.

Josh's shoulders constricted further, but he'd stay on task until he had reason to change course. "I'm here. You're here. But my client's asset is not. We doing this tonight or not?" *Tell me you're waiting on Chelsea again.*

"The asset is being brought up for validation." With that partial answer to Josh's question, Mendelson went to a small marble-top table. A flask of liquor and two short-stemmed glasses had been placed on a tray of inlaid wood as though in anticipation of this meeting in a gentleman's study.

There should be a reality show on the eccentric behaviors of wealthy international criminals.

Mendelson poured two glasses of the amber liquid. "I prefer a good cognac, but when in Rome..." He shrugged and offered the second glass to Josh. "Brandy?"

Josh would rather drink the devil's piss than share anything with this bastard. "Sure."

Moving to one of the chairs that faced the doorway, Mendelson took a seat. "Sit."

"I'm not interested in games, Mendelson."

Mendelson snapped his fingers and one of the bodyguards entered, sans tuxedo jacket and sporting an HK MP7 submachine gun, held loosely on a sling over one shoulder, but ready to use.

Josh got the message. He rolled his eyes as though the whole thing merely annoyed him, but sat in the other chair.

Where was Chelsea? She wouldn't have disappeared yet when she hadn't been paid his half of the fee.

He clicked through possibilities. Maybe Mendelson had paid his fee and Josh's, and sent Chelsea away?

The sound of multiple footsteps pounding up the stairs reached the library, along with something being dragged. Two guards entered, turning sideways to carry the CIA agent, Len Rikker, between them, each gripping an arm. Gaunt from five weeks in Mendelson's not-so-tender care, and bloody in too many places to count, Rikker's head hung forward.

Josh stood and took a step toward the prisoner who had a scar at the hairline. One confirmation of the CIA agent's ID. "Lift his head."

A guard grabbed Rikker's mop of scraggly brown hair and jerked his head back, raising Rikker's swollen face into view. Josh studied the eyes and jaw line long enough to give the impression he would walk away if they tried to pawn off the wrong man on him.

Mendelson said, "Satisfied?"

"Yes."

While Mendelson ordered the prisoner returned to his locked room in the basement, Josh used the distraction to twist his left cufflink twice, sending a message to move in and that the prisoner was underground.

With the prisoner out of the room, Mendelson put his glass down. "You may have your man as soon as you deliver my missiles. You have thirty minutes."

Sabrina and the team required twelve minutes to get inside the secured area undetected and in position to infiltrate the building to find Rikker. "I'll need GPS coordinates and a sat phone to call in my transport truck." His nonexistent truck.

"Give the phone number to my man – " Mendelson angled his head at his guard. "He will call with coordinates."

The guard unclipped a satellite phone from his belt and eyed Josh who rattled off the number. Sabrina had someone sitting at a predetermined location two hours away with a disposable phone, and ready to leave the minute he finished the call.

When the guard ended the call, he told his boss, "Done."

A grin spread across Mendelson's face, one that sent worry skidding along Josh's spine. He knew with that extra sense operatives develop that something had changed, even if everything seemed to be on schedule. He lifted his drink, killed the balance and set the glass back down, determined to find Chelsea. "Let's get this done. Where's Chelsea?"

"She will be along soon." Mendelson took a sip of his drink. "She is quite unusual. I could find a place in my organization for her. Maybe a personal assistant who could attend to more than negotiations for me." There was the sinister smile again when Mendelson slid a taunting look at Josh.

What was Mendelson up to with this bullshit?

Did he suspect a relationship between Chelsea and Josh? Or was he just testing with age-old bait to provoke a jealous reaction? But that would mean Mendelson knew Josh and Chelsea had been acquainted for much longer than this negotiation had taken.

No way. Josh tested right back. "What are you waiting for?"

Mendelson's gaze turned curious, as if he weighed Josh's reaction. "Then you would not mind?"

That hit too close to be fishing. Josh could count on two fingers the number of people who knew about him and

Chelsea. Only the two of them. "Me? Why would I give a shit?"

"Perhaps I was wrong to believe you placed a high value on her. Either way, I will miss her perhaps almost as much as you will, but for different reasons."

Noises in the hallway, like someone banging into the walls, turned Josh around.

The second bodyguard stepped into the room with Chelsea in his grasp. Blood ran down her arm and she struggled against a man who outweighed her by a hundred pounds.

She'd gotten in her fair share of licks, too, based on the guard's broken nose, bleeding temple and torn clothes.

Josh didn't know how it had happened, but they'd both been made.

CHAPTER 2

Josh lunged for the bodyguard with a stranglehold around Chelsea's neck.

Mendelson's other guard standing by swung the butt of his weapon and cracked the side of Josh's head with the sharp metal stock.

Stars spun through his vision. Stumbling sideways, Josh swung around and kicked the guard's chin, crushing jawbone with a satisfying crunch, and knocking him out cold. He snatched the MP7 away before the bodyguard hit the floor, dragging the sling off of the man's limp arm.

As Josh gained control of the weapon, Mendelson sighed loudly. "Put the weapon down, Mr. Taylor, or I'll order her death."

Chelsea shouted at Josh. *"Kill them!"*

The brute shoved the muzzle of a Ruger P90 semi-auto pistol against her throat. "Shut up."

Chelsea's gaze met Josh's, holding his long enough for him to see the doubt that they'd walk out of here alive. But she didn't know he had a team coming. She only knew what he'd told her to make this exchange happen.

"Go ahead and shoot or put the weapon down," Mendelson suggested. "Either way, we have a bit of a wait."

Lunging against the guard's tight hold, Chelsea shook her head at Josh to not give up the weapon, but he dropped it on the rug and turned to Mendelson. He warned in a cold voice, "You don't want to double cross me."

"Under different circumstances, I might agree, but I feel it necessary to inform you that a cellular jammer has been activated for this area."

The change in topic cut through the haze of fury threatening to steal the last of Josh's control. "And why would that matter?"

"I just thought you should know that you will not be able to reach your team even if you could get your hands on a phone."

Mendelson knew about the team?

Not possible. Only a select group of individuals were aware that Sabrina's team even existed and those were the ones she did contract work for. National security for the United States and similar departments in countries aligned with the US.

International alphabet spook groups.

Chelsea couldn't have burned him and wouldn't have, even if nothing existed between them. She had no motive, and knew Josh would use his resources to protect her grandmother. He'd already sent someone to watch over the elderly woman, but hadn't had a chance to tell Chelsea.

Had Sabrina and the team been burned, too?

How much did Mendelson know?

None of those answers will get us out of here right now.

His number one priority? How was Josh going to warn Sabrina that the mission was an ambush?

"Might as well make yourself comfortable, Mr. *Taylor*," Mendelson said in a congenial tone. He told his guard, "Give me your radio." Mendelson used the radio to call someone else in, as if this little room would hold more of the big brutes he employed. By the time Mendelson handed the radio back to his man, another guard ducked his head and stepped inside the already-crowded space.

Huge didn't begin to describe this behemoth.

Nothing about his dark eyes, black unkempt beard and oily brown hair appeared German. Maybe South African, and the MP7 he carried looked like a toy in his hands. Clearly, Mendelson supplied his expensive help with equally expensive weaponry.

Josh shoved everything aside while he focused on first sending a message to his team before they inserted and to get Chelsea out of here. But his mind seemed determine to plague him with more questions. Why hadn't Mendelson killed both of them yet? Why hadn't Mendelson waited on the weapons to show his hand? Josh needed more information. "You trade humans for commodities. How can I be of more value than making a trade for your captive?"

"Oh, but I did trade for Mr. Rikker."

He knows Rikker's real name. Not good. How could Josh use that to his advantage? He feigned surprise. "Rikker? That's not the name I was given. I think we've both been played. If that's the case, I'll make a deal for the weapons between the two of us, but the transport won't arrive until I call a second time."

Mendelson's eyes creased with humor. "Let's end this charade, Mr. Joshua *Carrington*. There is no transport and no weapons. You and your Slye team are what I received in trade for Rikker. He is being delivered to the higher bidder as we speak." Mendelson smiled with genuine pleasure.

The last trace of Josh's hope sucked away faster than water down a bottomless hole. Terror ripped through him at the level of betrayal it took for this to be happening. Something about Mendelson's calm demeanor poked its way into his thoughts. "Why aren't you upset about losing the weapons?"

"Because I don't need them. I allowed my first shipment of weapons to be taken and they're being replaced. I made a more advantageous deal for the CIA agent."

What the fuck?

Mendelson continued, "As for a truly valuable trade, Sabrina Slye is wanted by many people."

Who had screwed Sabrina? Josh forced himself to sound detached. "Well, hell, as long as I'm dead, at least tell me who sold me out."

"You're of no use to me dead. I will get much information from you and your team before I put each of you on the auction block. As to the person who set this up – I will only share that it was CIA."

Mendelson was wrong on one point.

Josh would likely die and very soon, because he would not stand by and let this unfold without a fight. He chuckled with dark humor, as if he'd always expected to be betrayed by someone, and muttered, "Should have expected that out of those bastards."

That drew a gloating smile from Mendelson so Josh asked, "Mind if I get comfortable while we wait?"

"By all means."

Taking off his jacket, Josh kept an eye on Chelsea in his

peripheral vision. She'd stopped struggling, her eyes tracking every move he made, and listening intently to how they'd both been screwed by his people. *Not my people anymore.* He jerked his bowtie loose and unfastened the first two buttons of his shirt. When he removed the cufflinks that only his team knew about, he put both metal clips in one hand and rolled them around together as if playing with a pair of dice.

Doing that for longer than ten seconds caused a signal to activate that would screech in Dingo's receiver and deactivate Josh's tracking unit.

Breaking the connection was code for FUBAR, or get the hell out of here now.

He walked over to the tall bookshelf and leaned against it, ticking off seconds in his mind, hoping ten minutes would pass with no sound.

But eight minutes later the first explosion rocked the house, not surprising him in the least that his team was here.

Josh, Sabrina and Dingo had never left each other as kids and wouldn't now, but he'd tried his best to warn them off. Mendelson shoved to his feet. Surprise burst across his face.

Gunfire rattled outside the house. Glass windows shattered downstairs.

One of the guards snatched up his radio and spoke in rapid German, but Josh easily translated the demand to know what was happening.

And the terse reply that they were under attack.

Mendelson roared, "How did four people get past twenty-seven armed guards?"

Josh knew the answer to that, but not how Sabrina and company was going to exit past that many now that every armed guard knew his target was inside the perimeter.

While Mendelson shouted orders at his people, Josh looked at Chelsea whose gaze shifted into the quiet calm he'd seen whenever she was about to kick someone's butt.

He gave her an imperceptible nod.

Her guard's attention was locked on Mendelson.

Chelsea sagged, forcing the guard to move his weapon to hold onto her dead weight.

Josh lunged at Mendelson, shoving him into the behemoth guard holding the MP7.

Mendelson shouted. His guard stumbled back but recovered quickly, knocking Mendelson aside to free his weapon hand. The giant shoved a little too hard. Mendelson's head hit the doorframe and he tumbled to the floor.

The guard got off a shot that ripped through Josh's side, but Josh grabbed the submachine gun and shoved it to the left. He held onto the foregrip with one hand while he battered steel punches to the guard's head, trying for a kill punch to the throat.

Not hurting the mountain of muscle one bit.

Chelsea head butted her captor, who lost his grip on her. She reached between his legs and twisted a fistful of his gonads. He screamed.

She grabbed for the Ruger, but missed it as the weapon fell from his hands and skidded behind him.

The guard Josh fought still held onto the MP7 with one hand. Josh battled to keep the muzzle pointed toward the ceiling – away from Chelsea. A bear-sized fist slammed Josh hard in the ribs. At least one cracked, but he hoped the flood of adrenaline would mask the pain for a while.

The guard had four more inches of reach and used it to grab Josh by the throat. He squeezed, cutting off Josh's air. Pinpricks of light shot through his gaze.

He bashed the guard's elbow joint with his free hand. Nothing gave in the hard-muscled arm.

Mendelson was sprawled on his side, still unconscious, with blood running down his face from his head wound. His body impeded any fancy maneuvering in the close quarters.

Josh finally got both hands on the tug-of-war gun. Before he gave it his all he had to break the giant's hold. Lifting his boot, he slammed the guard's kneecap.

Bone snapped. The guard screamed and Josh yanked the gun free.

Finally, a vulnerable body part on the hulking bastard.

The guard's grip on Josh's throat loosened. He sucked air through his raw throat and swung the metal rail of the MP7's fore-end into the guard's head, busting open a bleeding geyser.

Out of his peripheral vision, he saw Chelsea break free from her guard, the one she'd tried to neuter. She kicked him backward. He hit the floor hard.

She spun around and drove one of her spiked heels through his throat.

Just as effective as a double tap.

The guard Josh fought yelled and reached for him again in a haze of pain and rage.

Fighting this bastard was like trying to take down a Mac truck using his fists.

Coughing from a bruised windpipe, Josh swung the MP7 around and released a fast burst into the guard's chest. "Game over." Then he drew a hard breath, ears ringing from the gunfire in the small space. Choking, unable to speak, he turned to wave Chelsea out of the room so they could get going.

She took one look at Josh and started toward him.

That's when a movement on the floor caught his eye.

Mendelson had been playing possum, lying on his side, his upper body out of Chelsea's line of sight.

The world slowed to seconds that stretched from one loud heartbeat to the next.

Mendelson lifted the Ruger from beside him.

Josh swung up his own weapon, yelling at the same moment, but only a croaked sound came out.

Chelsea stared, confused for a split-second too long before she realized what was happening and tried to move.

Both shots exploded at the same moment.

Josh's was a hair too late.

He caught her as she folded to her knees. The bullet had passed through her chest. Had it hit her heart? Not if she was still moving. Blood spilled out the gaping hole. She covered it with her hands, eyes glassy with shock.

He scooped her into his arms, ignoring the screaming pain in his ribs and side. "Hold on," he ground out of his raw throat.

Frightened green eyes stared up at him. "Tried...to...tell you...not to come."

"I know, baby," he rasped. "Couldn't leave you."

He made it to the stairs and looked down to find two armed guards on the main floor with their weapons pointed out broken windows.

He started to lower Chelsea to the ground to free his hands.

The front window and door exploded into the house.

Both guards flew backwards, knocked off their feet. The sharp smell of burned electronics, smoke and charred wood flooded the air from the plastique his team had used to blow the door. Josh's back hit the wall, but he remained upright with Chelsea gripped tightly in his arms.

Sabrina Slye burst through the smoke-filled opening like an avenging angel, and took out both of the inside guards with quick double taps from her weapon. Black hair was pulled back in a tight ponytail. Her dark molle vest was covered in pouches holding enough ammo to take down a small city. Short blonde hair so out-of-context with his olive skin color, Dingo rushed in right behind her and looked up to where Josh stood "We got burned, mate."

Josh had never been so happy to hear that Aussie accent in his life. He raced down the stairs to the main floor, gritting against the pain cutting through his adrenaline rush. "I know. There's no package downstairs. Tell you everything later. Where's Singleton? Chelsea needs a medic."

From the way his side ached and the lightheaded feeling threatening to knock his feet out from under him, he did, too.

Dingo produced a second monocular from the vest he wore and slipped the headband over Josh's head. He pulled the single night vision lens down into place then he slipped a small headset with a boom mic over Josh's ears. No time to deal with the high-tech commo gear the rest of the team wore.

As Dingo did all that he explained, his words coming through in Josh's headset now. "Changed the plan when we lost contact with your tracker. Singleton's waiting to cover our exit through the woods."

Josh snarled a curse. The team had walked into an ambush and now medical care was out of reach, but he wouldn't put his teammates at more risk. He told Sabrina, "You four stick with the plan."

Sabrina took one look at Chelsea's wound and realized what he was saying, that he wasn't going with them. "She won't make it to a doctor."

Chelsea coughed and blood trickled from her lips. Her voice was reed thin. "She's right."

"No, she's *not*." He gripped Chelsea closer as if he could will her to live by force alone and growled at Sabrina. "Get the team out of here and I'll meet you later."

"How in the hell do you plan to do that dragging *her* around?" Sabrina said in a low voice tight with anger.

"I'm taking the Hummer."

Sabrina clenched her weapon with white knuckles and snapped out, "I told you *never* to do this."

Josh had no comeback. She was right and he'd sworn he wouldn't get involved, but he couldn't change what was and he wouldn't abandon Chelsea to make a run through the woods. "Just go and let me handle this."

Another explosion somewhere nearby shook the building.

Had to be Tanner Bodine's handiwork, the only team member Josh couldn't account for at the moment.

Fury rolled off Sabrina's bunched shoulders. She started issuing orders, no different than back when she'd run their half-pint gang. Glaring at Josh, she snapped, "Are you hurt or can you run?"

With so much of Chelsea's blood covering his shirt Sabrina's question was routine and not because she had any idea he'd taken a bullet.

"I can run." If he didn't pass out from blood loss, but any other answer or admitting he'd been wounded would start a new wave of conflict.

She turned to Dingo. "We need a path out the front gate. I'll call the other two with the change of plans."

Josh shook his head. "No, Sabrina."

"Shut up and get ready to make a dash to the Hummer or I'll shoot you myself. Stop at the limo then wait for my cover fire."

Dingo had already vanished into the night like the shadow he could be when he wanted.

Josh knew better than to waste breath he didn't have arguing with Sabrina when she had her mind made up. "Thanks."

She ground out a derogatory sound in her throat that he translated as why did men have to get stupid over women?

Casting another look at Chelsea, Sabrina muttered, "Save your thanks. You're not out of here alive and she's still bleeding like a stuck pig."

Blood poured through the fingers Chelsea had clamped over the wound. "Don't be stupid...leave me..." Her eyelashes fluttered closed.

Josh shook her gently. "Wake up, baby. Stay with me."

When her eyes blinked again, he stepped over to the side of the door opening that had been widened with that blast. Gunfire chattered back and forth outside. Bullets pinged everywhere.

Sabrina moved to the opposite side of the opening and took up the position she needed to lay down cover fire to the vehicles. Raising her HK 416 to her shoulder, she yelled, "Move," and raked the area outside with rapid bursts of fire.

Josh yelled, "Moving," and raced out into the pitch black where every light had been shot out. Now the world came to him in shades of grayish-green through the night vision monocular. He hoped he was moving fast. His legs felt like lead. Zigzagging the best he could, he reached the limo and ducked behind it, catching his breath.

His vision swirled. He shook off the dizziness.

A spray of bullets peppered the car, and Josh ducked lower, clutching Chelsea to his chest as he waited for Sabrina to reload.

He twisted, watching the window for her muzzle flash. The minute she released another burst, he took off for the Hummer. He passed the Mercedes that had been turned into Swiss cheese.

Stars sparked through his vision. Sound withdrew and a black fog rushed at him. He thrashed at it mentally and pushed harder to reach the Hummer. He couldn't lose consciousness now.

Sabrina rushed up beside him, still laying cover fire as she moved. She yelled, "Get in the damned Hummer," and the volume through his headset rattled his brains.

He growled and drove his legs harder.

She opened the rear door just as he reached the truck. Josh hit the seat with Chelsea still draped over his arms. The door slammed shut.

Sabrina jumped in the driver's seat, all the time talking to her team through her commo. "We're in the Hummer. Load up!"

Starting the engine, she threw the truck into gear and made a rock-slinging sweep around the yard. Shots battered the windows and exterior of the truck, not getting through.

Bulletproof truck. *Thanks, Mendelson, you rat bastard.*

Josh pressed his hand over Chelsea's, putting more pressure on her wound. She moved a finger to touch his hand. "My grandmother...please..."

"She's safe right now. I swear it. You'll see her again."

Her pale lips curved. "Thank you...for...us."

He kissed her forehead. "Shh. Save your energy."

Tanner Bodine yanked the front passenger door open, running with the truck then throwing his super-sized cowboy body inside.

Sabrina wheeled around hard, heading out of the property. She took one look at Tanner. "How bad?"

"Bullshit bullet in the thigh. You?"

"I'll live."

Josh heard them as if they were far away. He lifted his head. Everything spun again. Had Sabrina been hurt? "Where're you hit, Sabrina?"

"Not hit. Knife wound. Arm. I'm good."

Where was Singleton?

Sabrina slowed the truck just long enough for the rear passenger door across from Josh to open and Singleton to jump in. He scrambled to right himself and tug the door shut at the same time. Right before bullets splattered his side of the Hummer.

Josh said, "Need an IV and gotta stop the bleeding in this one."

Singleton shrugged out of his Medic's pack and lowered his monocular to look at Chelsea in the dark then raised his gaze to Josh. If not for Josh's night vision monocular, he wouldn't have been able to see the grim concern on Singleton's coffee-brown face. The soft-spoken doctor wielded a knife with unmatched skill whether he wanted to save a life or take one. "I can't, Josh."

"Why not?"

Tanner asked, "Where's Dingo?"

Explosions erupted on each side of the road ahead. Sabrina shouted, "Clearing the way."

A loud thump landed on top of the Hummer then a fist pounded twice.

Sabrina floored the Hummer. "Dingo's onboard." She punched the button to open the sunroof, and Dingo's arm appeared, snaking inside for a handhold.

Josh swallowed, so damned glad that the whole team had made it so far, but especially the two people he considered a sister and brother. Now if he could just patch up Chelsea. He ordered Singleton, "Do something, now!"

The Hummer slid right and left as Sabrina muscled the truck out onto the road. She yelled at Singleton, "Get an IV into her and Tanner. We'll be at the helo in nine minutes."

That got through Josh's muddled brain. "No. Helo's not safe. CIA burned us."

Stunned silence blanketed the truck. Sabrina found her voice first. "You're sure?"

"Mendelson said CIA traded us...for Len Rikker. He knew your name. Knew it was your team. Knew *my* name. We were the currency."

Curses blistered the air.

Pain stabbed Josh's side and he shouted, unsure if it was the wound or the broken rib. He swung around to find Singleton poking at him. "Leave it, dammit."

Someone stood in front of the truck, firing straight at the windshield. Sabrina plowed into the idiot. He hit with a hard thump. His body flew up in the air and out of the way. The man obviously hadn't realized the windshield was bulletproof.

Sabrina demanded, "What's wrong, Josh?"

"Nothing."

Singleton answered, "Two things. Josh took a bullet in his abdomen and we don't have IVs."

"Why not?"

"My pack took a hit. Pack saved my ass, but IV kits were shredded."

"Do what you can for Josh," Sabrina ordered. Her fierce gaze lit up the rearview mirror, accusing Josh of lying to her by omission. "You'll need more than an IV soon. Just hold on for me."

That last part came out weary.

Josh looked over at their medic and saw multiple faces.

Singleton pulled a wad of gauze out of his pack and shoved it up against Josh who gritted his teeth and ground out, "Told you I'm fine. Chelsea needs help."

"You're not fine," Sabrina said quietly. "I *won't* lose you."

Josh had never pleaded for anything, but he was the only one who believed Chelsea could survive. "Shingleton." His chin drooped. He shook his head and worked his lips, trying to stop the slurring. "You got some...give her...jush buy time?"

No one spoke for a moment then Sabrina said, "Tanner."

Tanner shifted around in his seat and looked back at Chelsea. "Ah, hell."

"Tell him, Singleton."

Josh struggled to pull his thoughts together and fight off the fog sucking him into a vortex. "Tell me what?"

Singleton had latched his fingers around Josh's wrist at some point, checking his pulse. He should be checking Chelsea's. "Dammit...do somesing."

Singleton spoke in his calm doctor voice, the one he used to talk patients through a disaster. He pulled off Josh's monocular and tossed it away then lifted a small LED light and shined it down on Chelsea's abdomen. "Josh, she...uh."

Josh's chin hit his chest. His eyes followed the light that moved from his blood-covered hand on Chelsea's chest to her pretty neck.

To beautiful green eyes locked open. No, no, *no...*

Pain reached into his chest and clutched his heart with steel fingers, squeezing and twisting.

Voices shouted. They ran together in a blur.

Josh lost the battle to keep his eyes open. He still saw Chelsea's dead gaze staring at him. She'd never laugh again or spend another night with him, saving him from a lonely existence. His mind wandered. Sounds dulled and faded away.

Someone had betrayed them. Had killed Chelsea. Josh would find the bastard who had done this and...he'd...

Singleton shouted, "*We're losing Josh!*"

An explosion blasted against the truck, throwing it up onto two wheels.

Josh hugged Chelsea. He was flung against the truck door and the world crashed in on him.

~*~

Nowhere Safe – February 2013
www.AuthorDiannaLove.com

~*~

HONEYMOON TO DIE FOR
Ryder Van Dyke and Bianca Brady's story

Former Slye agent RYDER VAN DYKE is facing conviction for a murder he didn't commit. When his last hope for freedom disintegrates, the FBI steps forward with a deal - a commuted sentence if Ryder helps the FBI nail a deadly criminal ... his father.

FBI analyst BIANCA BRADY wants justice for the death of her closest friend since grade school. Now all she needs is the proof that the Van Dyke patriarch is guilty of funding terrorist operations. She's willing to do whatever it takes to make Van Dyke criminals pay, or so she thinks.

A deal's a deal, but there's a catch. The only way to get an FBI agent inside the family compound and Van Dyke Enterprises is as Ryder's legal wife. Ryder has his own plan – to prove his innocence or use his Special Forces skills to escape, but deadly secrets, an international security threat and a killer with a vendetta forces Ryder to make a choice – give up his freedom or risk the life of the woman who's stolen his heart?

Available July 2013

About The Author

New York Times bestseller Dianna Love once dangled over a hundred feet in the air to create unusual marketing projects for Fortune 500 companies. The first book she wrote won a RITA® Award and sold out in six weeks. She writes the high-octane Slye Temp romantic thriller series, releasing the first four novels in 2013. Dianna also co-authors the bestselling Belador urban fantasy series with #1 NYT bestseller Sherrilyn Kenyon. To collect "signed" cover cards for free, visit www.KeeperKase.com

When not in the writing cave, Dianna is touring the country on her BMW motorcycle. She lives in the Atlanta, GA area with her husband, who is a motorcycle instructor, and a tank full of unruly saltwater critters.

http://www.AuthorDiannaLove.com

For Young Adult Fans – check out the explosive new sci-fi/fantasy series by Micah Caida (aka Dianna Love and Mary Buckham), starting with *Time Trap* (February 2013) and *Time Return* (November 2013) in ebook and print. To read an excerpt of *Time Trap*, go to http://www.MicahCaida.com

"Thanks again for taking a moment to post a review – your support is deeply appreciated!"
New York Times bestseller Dianna Love

CPSIA information can be obtained at www.ICGtesting.com
Printed in the USA
LVOW05s1851221213

366431LV00014B/430/P